She saw where his attention had gone and she licked her lips, wetting them invitingly. She opened her mouth to say "Kiss me," but he was already there. He pulled her forward onto his mouth, but savored the moment just before he really engaged her. It was a tease, a breathless pause before he covered her mouth in earnest. The taste of her spread over him like a balm. He engaged her tongue almost instantly, wanting her flavor. Her mouth was everything plush and decadent, sweet and heady . . . like strong drink, warming and dizzying. For just those few seconds he no longer felt like a cursed man.

It was a gift she gave without realizing it, and he was humbly grateful for it.

BY JACQUELYN FRANK

The Immortal Brothers
Cursed by Fire
Cursed by Ice
Bound by Sin
Bound in Darkness

The World of Nightwalkers
Forbidden
Forever
Forsaken
Forged
Nightwalker (eBook)

Three Worlds
Seduce Me in Dreams
Seduce Me in Flames

BOUND

in

DARKNESS

The
IMMORTAL
BROTHERS

JACQUELYN FRANK

BALLANTINE BOOKS • NEW YORK

Bound in Darkness is a work of fiction. Names, characters, places, and incidents are the products of the author's imagination or are used fictitiously. Any resemblance to actual events, locales, or persons, living or dead, is entirely coincidental.

A Ballantine Books Mass Market Original

Copyright © 2015 by Jacquelyn Frank

Published in the United States by Ballantine Books, an imprint of Random House, a division of Penguin Random House LLC, New York.

BALLANTINE and the HOUSE colophon are registered trademarks of Penguin Random House LLC.

ISBN 978-0-553-39345-3
eBook ISBN 978-0-553-39346-0

Cover design: Caroline Teagle
Cover photograph: © Regina Wamba/Ninestock

Printed in the United States of America

randomhousebooks.com

9 8 7 6 5 4 3 2 1

Ballantine Books mass market edition: December 2015

For my Dad

I love you, and that's all that needs to be said.

GLOSSARY
AND
PRONUNCIATION TABLE

AIRIANNE: (Ā-rē-ahn); Airi: (Ā-rē)
CAPTAIN ARUD: (Captain Ar-ŪD)
DETHAN: (DEE-thun)
DOISY: (DOY-sē)
DRU: (DROO)
GARRETH: (GAH-reth)
JAYKUN: (JAY-kun)
KILON: (KĒ-lohn)
KYNO: (KĪ-nō)
LUJO: (LOO-hō)
MAXUM: (MAK-sum)
XZONXZU: (ZAHN-zoo)

The Gods
DIATHUS: (Die-AH-thus) Goddess of the land and oceans. Married to Lothas
FRAMUN: (FRAH-moon) God of peace and tranquility.
GRIMU: (Grim-OO) God of the eight heavens.
HELLA: (HEL-uh) Goddess of fate, fortune, and wisdom. Married to Mordu.
JIKARO: (Ji-KAR-oh) God of anger and deception.
KITARI: (Ki-TAR-ee) Queen of the gods. Goddess of life and death.
LOTHAS: (LOH-thas) God of day and night. Married to Diathus

MERU: (mer-ROO) Goddess of hearth, home, and harvest.

MORDU: (mor-DOO) God of hope, love, and dreams. Married to Hella.

SABO: (SAH-boh) God of pain and suffering.

WEYSA: (WAY-suh) Goddess of conflict and war.

XAXIS: (ZAK-sis) God of the eight hells.

PROLOGUE

Maxum clawed himself up out of the soil, spitting dirt, coughing it from his lungs with a roar of fury and frustration. He would think he would be used to it by now, used to the pain that came from the sheer weight of the rock and soil that pressed against him from all sides. Suffocated him from all directions. Filled every orifice, every crack, every crevice of his body as it fought to get inside of him—crushing him didn't seem to be enough to satisfy it.

He finally pulled himself fully free of the dirt and lay on the ground, panting and coughing. He spit. Spit again. It was a lost cause. Dirt caught between his teeth, stuck to his tongue.

And so it would be. It would always be. He was cursed. Cursed to be swallowed by soil and stone every night from dusk to juquil's hour.

He supposed he should be grateful. Until several full turnings ago he had been trapped permanently in the ground, held deep in the soil of the bottom of the ocean, with no reprieve. He had since been rescued from his permanent fate and been given this one instead, thanks to his brother Jaykun, who had won the grace of a god, just as easily as the four brothers, Dethan, Jaykun, Garreth, and Maxum, had won the fury of the gods with a single act of hubris over two centuries ago.

He and his brothers had climbed the highest mountain in the world that day, finding there a fountain of immortality blessed and protected by the gods—and they had dared to drink from its waters without permission from the gods. The backlash for their gall had been instantaneous and severe. Each brother had been sent to suffer, each in his own way, each at the hands of a different god, as payment for that hubris. Dethan had been cast into the eight hells by Weysa, the goddess of conflict and war. Garreth had been chained to that very same mountain, within sight of the fountain that had been the cause of his curse, doomed to freeze time and again thanks to the bitter ironic nature of the goddess Hella. Then the god Grimu had taken Jaykun and chained him to a star, dooming him to burn endlessly again and again. None of the brothers had been given quarter, none a reprieve . . . until Weysa had fetched Dethan out of hell and set him on a path that had resulted in all three of his brothers being released from their curses. But while his brothers were now completely free of their curses, Maxum enjoyed no such reprieve. In order to be freed from his curse the god who had given it to him must lift it. But the god in question was Sabo, the god of pain and suffering, who thrived on the agony of others. It was safe to say he would never have cause to free Maxum from his curse.

And so he had lived through four winters now with his "reprieve" hours, each day living free of the curse until dusk settled over him and the ground opened to swallow him whole all over again. He didn't know which was worse. To be trapped with no reprieve from the crushing soil or to be given a taste of freedom and release only to have it snatched away each night by a devouring maw of dark, suffocating loam.

After a few minutes Maxum righted himself, feeling the pain of every bone that had been broken by the pressure of all that rock and soil pressing in on him. Cracked ribs, snapped thighbones, crushed arms. The agony of it was brutal.

But he was immortal and so he would heal from all of those injuries until he was as good as new . . . or as close to it as he could be. His head hurt, his ears ringing from what was no doubt a cracked skull. He couldn't get up and walk yet, so he dragged himself across the ground toward his campsite not too far away. Once there he rolled onto his bedroll and lay panting for breath, each one of those breaths torture thanks to his damaged ribs.

It had to stop. One way or another, he would put an end to this. The easiest solution required a god-made weapon removing Maxum's head from his shoulders. But then he would very likely be sent to the eight hells upon his death and that would only mean trading one torment for another—one far more permanent.

The other solution was much more impossible on the surface of it. Convince Sabo to free him from his curse. The idea of the god doing that was laughable. His brothers might have been lucky enough to get their curses lifted by their various gods, but there was no hope for it in Maxum's case. They all knew it. It was apparent in every pitying look his brothers had cast him. That was one of the reasons why he had left their company. That and the fact that his brothers had proven to be enviably happy and in love with their wives and it had just about made him sick to watch them.

But he didn't begrudge them their happiness or their curse-free existences. He was glad they were free. Glad they had found happiness. He was an uncle several times over now as his brothers wallowed in their joy and made babies with their wives. The most recent had been Jaykun and Jileana's son, newborn when last he had seen them. He would be two now and no doubt getting into all manner of trouble.

Part of him had wanted to stay, to enjoy what time with his family he could muster. But just as adamant was his need to do something about his situation. The plan had come to him shortly after Jaykun's son had been born. Sabo would never willingly release him from this curse, so that left him only one option.

Maxum had to kill the god.

He didn't even know if such a thing was possible, but he saw no alternative. Sabo's death was the only way he could end his own suffering. He had heard tales . . . tales of magical items that could be very powerful, possibly powerful enough to kill a god.

So he had left his brothers to go on a quest. Several quests really. He wasn't going to face a god with nothing but a single talisman that may or may not do the trick. He was going to hedge his bets and gather as many such talismans as he could. He was going to face down Sabo and he was going to do it fully prepared with anything and everything he could think of. Including, perhaps, the help of some of the gods.

For the gods were at war. There were two factions, each with six gods. Well, seven to five if you take into consideration that Kitari, the queen of the gods, was being held captive by Xaxis's faction, Xaxis being the god of the eight hells. His faction also included Grimu the god of the eight heavens; Diathus the goddess of the lands and oceans; Jikaro the god of anger and deception; and, lo and behold, Sabo, the god of pain and suffering.

The faction that warred against Xaxis's faction was Weysa's, the goddess of conflict. On her side was Hella, the goddess of fate and fortune, her husband, Mordu, the god of hope, love, and dreams. Meru, the goddess of hearth, home, and harvest, Framun, the god of peace and tranquility, and Lothas, the god of day and night.

With the help of Weysa's faction and his gathered talismans he had high hopes that it would indeed be possible to kill a god.

Now all he had to do was gather his talismans.

And win over an entire faction of gods.

Impossible?

Well, that remained to be seen.

CHAPTER
ONE

Maxum slammed the hand of the large, stinking man who had challenged him down on the table. The rowdy gathering of men cheered and jeered, some thumping Maxum hard on the back in congratulations for winning the arm wrestle. Someone slapped a mug of ale into his winning hand and the reveling men began to sing a victory song in his honor.

Maxum moved away from the boisterous group and found a reasonably quiet corner of the inn, preparing to slowly enjoy the ale in his hand. He wasn't as drunk as the other men in the room, but he was going to catch up with them. They had been celebrating since sunset but Maxum had only joined them an hour ago—two hours past juquil's hour when he had finally clawed his way out of the ground. Once he had healed enough to walk he had come to the inn to join his men.

They were a motley crew; five in all including himself. Each with their own special talents and each necessary for him to obtain his next talisman.

He reached into the pocket of his pants and fondled the amulet they had retrieved just that afternoon—along with enough treasure to keep the men satisfied for quite some time.

This talisman was said to have great power; it made the wearer invulnerable to attack. He had not tested that yet so he didn't know if it was the truth. But a talisman like that would come in quite handy in a war with a god. For, as much as he was immortal, he was not invulnerable. He could be hurt and hurt badly. And there was that little bit about a god-made weapon taking off his head and ending it all right then and there. If there was one thing he could count on, it was that a god would have a god-made weapon in his hands.

He didn't take the amulet out, he didn't put it on. He would test it tomorrow, and he didn't want to flash it in front of the other patrons in the bar. He didn't want to invite a thief to take it from him. To try anyway. A thief was more likely to lose his hand than succeed.

Maxum took a swig of his drink and looked around the room. There were two women there. One was the barmaid and she was being kept quite occupied by the graspy hands of his men. There was Kyno, the big lumbering orc halfbreed with his shining bald head and large meaty hands that swung a spiked club like nobody's business. There was Dru, a slightly shy, slim figured, fiery haired spirit mage who barely had twenty-five full turnings under his belt. There was Kilon, a slightly rotund archer whose arrows always hit their mark. And last but not least there was Doisy, a cleric, far more handsome than a religious man should be and with about just as much charm as could be fit into one person. He did not grab for the barmaid, instead preferring to tempt her with smiles and charm and wait for her to come to him. Smiles that were gaining him the fastest refills when it came to the ale in his cup.

What Maxum found interesting, however, was that his men weren't paying any attention to the other woman in the room at all. True, she was clearly a patron and should go about unaccosted, but for all she was wearing men's leggings and a shirt and vest to hide her womanly curves, Maxum could see them all the same. She was a shapely thing, her close-fitting breeches leaving little mystery to the slender shape of her thighs and the cozy roundness of her ass. The vest hid her breasts for the most part so he couldn't get a good feel for their size, but he suspected they were enough to fill a man's hands.

She was toying with a bowl of the hot stew the innkeeper was serving for dinner, nibbling at a piece of the questionable meat within it. She noticed Maxum's regard of her and she returned it in kind, looking him up and down. He let her look and smiled at the interest he saw flickering in her eyes. And she had pretty eyes. A beautiful jade green to complement her silvery blond hair, which she had plaited into two braids on either side of her head, covering her ears. He was disappointed by the style. He expected it was quite pretty when let loose. It would be straight, he surmised, like a silver-gold waterfall, reaching somewhere around her breasts. Those mysteriously hidden breasts.

She sat back a little, picking up her mug and taking a thoughtful sip. Then she stood up, skirted the boisterous goings-on in the center of the room, and came to stand before Maxum.

She was nearly a strap shorter than he was, slightly built—almost like a boy if not for those hips and . . . damn it, he wanted to see those breasts! But she had the face of a fairy, all fine bones and delicate points, right down to her small upturned nose with its gentle tip. She looked too genteel to be caught out in this kind of crowd in those kinds of clothes. She should be in a dress—with a corset that pushed up and showed off those breasts . . . wherever they were.

"A quiet corner," he said with a nod to the other side of the table. "Come and sit."

She regarded him for just a moment longer, but not

because she was debating the wisdom of sitting with him. She had pretty much made up her mind to do that before she'd even gotten out of her seat. Still he didn't know exactly what was going on behind those jade eyes. It was one of the reasons he was glad she had come over.

"I didn't take you for the quiet corner type," she said as she slid into her seat and put her mug down on the table.

"I prefer quiet corners. My men have other ideas."

"You're celebrating?"

"Is it that obvious?" he said with a grin he knew was charming. His brothers had always said the gods had gifted him with charm, good looks, and a good singing voice—all great ways to woo the ladies. And they were right. He'd caught more than his fair share with that smile.

She smiled back and relaxed in her chair. "A little bit. They're throwing coin around like they could make it for themselves. They should be careful. It might attract the wrong element."

Maxum chuckled richly. "We *are* the wrong element," he said.

She laughed. It was a light, pretty sound but not a delicate little titter like the highborn ladies used. It was a laugh. A good, feminine laugh that made you smile to hear it. Maxum liked her more the more he discovered about her.

"What's your name?"

"Airianne," she said. "But you can call me Airi."

"A light, breezy sort of name," he noted.

She grimaced. "Oh, now you're being unoriginal. I may have to rethink this whole situation."

"Ah. Well, forgive me. I'll try to be more unique from here on out."

Maxum found that ironic actually. He was as unique as they came. It was simply a matter of not wanting everyone to know about what set him apart from everyone else on the Black Continent.

She made a show of thinking about it, but then she shrugged. "I'll give you another chance if you tell me your name."

"Wouldn't that ruin the mystery of it all?"

"I rather doubt there would be much mystery if I have to call you 'You there!' the entire length of our short acquaintance."

"Our acquaintance will be short?" he asked with an arched brow.

"Oh yes. If all it is based on is the mystery of your name then it will have to be short indeed. The moment I learn it, all would be over."

"Hey, Maxum! Come roll at dice!" Doisy shouted at him from across the room.

Airi laughed. "There you see? No more mystery, nothing to compel me to stay."

"I'm sure I have other mysteries about me," he coaxed her with a lopsided grin.

"Do you? Do you think I would find them interesting?"

"I know you would. I promise I won't tell you a thing about me. You can discover the answers to all your questions on your own, thereby entertaining yourself for quite a long while."

"But I already know so much about you," she said.

"Such as?"

"I know your name." She winked at him. "And I know you do not like to be called Max."

"How do you know that?"

"Your man is so drunk he would have called you by the most familiar name he uses to address you. Since he called you Maxum and not Max I can assume he has been trained very, very well not to do it . . . so well he remembers even when in his cups."

"What else do you know?" he asked, leaning back and relaxing as he let his eyes roam over her again and again.

"Let's see . . . you are a mercenary."

"How can you be so sure?" he asked, surprise tightening him up.

"You are well outfitted. You have spent a good amount of coin on your armor and that sword you carry. That blade was not made in any ordinary forge, I'll bet my life on it."

She was right. The sword was his brother's. A god-made weapon and a gift from Weysa. Dethan had gifted him with it when he had told them he was leaving to "seek out his own life." He hadn't told them his plans or his ultimate goal. But having a god-made weapon would be crucial when fighting a god. It was a fair bet that no ordinary weapon could inflict injury otherwise.

"But being well outfitted does not a mercenary make," he pointed out.

"Ah . . . but here your friends give you away. A mage, an orc, an archer, and a religious man make for a pretty well-rounded group of skills. All quite marketable if someone is looking for a hired hand to help with this little or that problem." She tilted her head thoughtfully. "But you do not make all of your coin by being a sell-sword, and I think selling your sword is just a means to an end. You have different goals in mind."

"Now you can't possibly know that from sitting across the room," he said, shifting uncomfortably in his chair. Her insights were uncanny. A little too uncanny. He was beginning to suspect she was some kind of mage like Dru. A spirit mage could tell a lot about a person if the right powers were used.

"I know that from speaking with you. You are clearly an intelligent man. You don't throw yourself into revelry with abandon like your men do, you keep yourself separate from their behavior. That tells me a great deal about what kind of man you are."

"It is an off night. Tomorrow I will get just as drunk as they are."

"I think not. No sense trying to mislead me," she said with a smile. "Just because I can see you doesn't mean you must try to hide."

"But how do you know I have other goals in mind?"

"As I said, you are an intelligent man. An intelligent man knows he cannot sell his sword forever. Eventually he will get old and his body will not work quite the way it should. What will you do then? An intelligent man would have some other plan, something to take him into his golden years with relative ease."

Maxum smiled. "I do have other goals, but not for the reasons you surmise. So you see, there are still many mysteries about me to keep you interested."

"Perhaps," she said, pausing to take a sip of her ale. "What about me? Can you not divine anything about me?"

Maxum narrowed his eyes on her thoughtfully. "You do not like to wear dresses."

She burst out in a laugh. "How do you know that? How do you know these are not just my traveling clothes?"

"They are too well-worn to be used just for traveling. You've even mended your breeches at the knee, telling me this is likely your only set of clothing. Or perhaps one of two sets."

"Very good," she said, seeming impressed. "But that does not mean I don't like to wear dresses."

"If I were a woman used to running about in the freedom of breeches and cotton, I would not want to stuff myself into the confines of a dress and corset where certain behaviors would then be expected of me. Like this, you have all the freedom in the world. Why would you want to give that up?"

"Well, it so happens you are right, but I still say it's a lucky guess."

"No more or less lucky than your guesses."

"What else?" she asked.

"Hmm . . . I'll bet you're a scrapper. You avoid fighting where possible, because you are clearly intelligent, but get you in the mix and you'll hold your own in spite of your size."

"Oh ho! Now we're insulting?"

"Not at all. You're just being sensitive. I was merely stating an observation. It was a compliment actually . . . that I can see you holding your own in a fight even against a larger opponent."

"And what makes you think this?"

"You've got two daggers on you, one on each thigh. That tells me you're proficient with them left- and right-handed . . . a marketable skill if ever there was one. They are short daggers so that means you're used to fighting up close and personal. You travel alone which means you're pretty confident you can take care of yourself. You're too clever to mislead yourself on that count so . . . that makes you a scrapper."

"Very good." She gave him a light round of applause. He nodded his head in gracious acceptance.

"There's one other thing," he said.

"And that is?"

"You're seriously thinking about having sex with me."

She laughed, a bright short burst of sound. "Am I now? What makes you say that?"

"You got up and came over to me."

"I could just be looking for a diverting conversation. How does sex come into the picture? If I wanted sex I could choose any of your men."

"As I said, you came over to me instead of joining my

men. That shows you have taste and are discerning. You didn't want to be alone tonight, so you thought I might provide you with a little companionable distraction."

"Distraction equals sex?"

He ran his eyes down over her, letting her see his appetite, which had grown considerably in the time they had been talking.

"It does in my book. And you haven't thrown your drink in my face and stormed off. That's also telling."

She smiled, stood up, and crossed over to him. She sat in his lap and wound her arms around his neck. "And does the idea have any appeal to you at all?"

"What do your deductive powers tell you?"

"That it does indeed have merit. A great deal of merit," she said, shifting her bottom a little on top of a steadily growing erection. He hadn't planned on getting friendly with anyone tonight, didn't really engage in it at all these days, his goals consuming his time and energies. But for some reason she appealed to him a great deal and now that he had started thinking about having sex with her, he found he couldn't stop thinking of it. The idea of running his hands all over that fair, delicate skin—all the while knowing she was just as tough as she was soft—that was more than alluring to him.

His gaze dropped to the pretty bow of her lips; her top lip was sculpted perfectly and her bottom lip plump and inviting. She was close enough that he could smell the cleanness of her. She must have had a bath recently. He could say the same. Every night after he dragged himself out of the dirt the first thing he did was find somewhere to wash the grime off him, to wash away any traces of his curse. It was a small little rebellion. An empty one. But he wanted nothing to remind him of what would come again all too soon.

She saw where his attention had gone and she licked her lips, wetting them invitingly. She opened her mouth to say "Kiss me," but he was already there. He pulled her forward onto his mouth, but savored the moment just before he really engaged her. It was a tease, a breathless pause before he covered her mouth in earnest. The taste of her spread over him like a balm. He engaged her tongue almost instantly, wanting her flavor. Her mouth was everything plush and decadent, sweet and heady . . . like strong drink, warming and dizzying. For just those few seconds he no longer felt like a cursed man.

It was a gift she gave without realizing it, and he was humbly grateful for it.

His hand went to the back of her head and he found himself frustrated by the two tight braids her hair was bound into. Her hair should be free and flowing, easier to bury his hands into, easier to feel the silkiness of it. And from what he could feel, he knew it would be very smooth and soft indeed.

One kiss ended and another began. Then another. His breath came hard as her hands dove into his hair. He was keeping it long these days, so she got a good handful of his loose curls and didn't let go.

She finally broke from his mouth, but only long enough to throw her leg over him, straddling his lap and tucking the seat of her bottom tightly to his erection. He was confined by the suddenly tight material of his pants— and the fact they were in a crowded room, but that didn't keep him from sliding his free hand up over her ribs beneath her vest and then . . . oh, there it was. The elusive breast.

She wore a simple linen shirt, but he could tell she had bound herself up with a snug wrapping beneath it, in an effort to look less like a woman no doubt. Still he could feel her just the same. He was pleasantly surprised to find she was quite well endowed for such a slight figured woman. He would have thought she'd run more to being built like a boy. But it was perhaps her mode of dress that had misled him. That and the damnable vest that had hid the true wealth of her feminine features.

With breasts like these it wasn't any wonder.

Her hands grew busy, drifting out of his hair and down his neck. She was running her hands in broad strokes over his chest a moment later and he growled from the fiery sensations the caresses sent through him. Their kisses grew more and more intense the lower her hands traveled, until she caressed his hips, pausing . . . teasing him. She lifted her mouth from his and said in a throaty, purring voice, "I have a room upstairs. Normally I would camp out in the open, but I decided to splurge tonight. I'm glad I did."

"I'm glad you did too," he said, his voice rough with passion and need.

"It's at the top of the stairs. I'll meet you there in a minute. I have to . . . take care of something." She blushed a little and he realized she needed to relieve herself. He chuckled.

"All right."

He patted her bottom and she dismounted his lap and headed for the front door of the inn. She shot him a shy little teasing smile and then slipped outside.

Maxum sat back a minute, grinning to himself. His fortunes really seemed to be changing for the better these days. First he had acquired the talisman—no mean feat that—then he had found something sweet to savor for the night. Yes, indeed, things were looking up for him. If the trend continued, he might actually one day succeed in what he was attempting to do.

It wasn't as though there weren't a precedent. There had once been other gods, but the current reigning gods had usurped their positions, killing off their competition. If a god could do it, then by the gods, so could he.

Feeling happy and magnanimous he got to his feet and said, "Boys! Next round's on me!"

He tossed a gold coin to the barmaid who caught it expertly. Her eyes went wide when he said, "Keep the rest for yourself, honey." It was no wonder. She was doubtless more used to seeing copper and silver than gold. It was possible she had never seen a gold coin in her life.

"Have a good time," Kyno said. Clearly, despite their revelry, his men had been attentive enough to see what he'd been doing and they had figured out where he was going to be spending his night.

"Sleep fair, Maxum!" Dru said.

"Oy, there's not much sleeping going to be happening there, what?" Doisy said with a loud belch.

Maxum made his way up to the room at the top of the stairs with a grin on his face. He entered and found the standard for most inns. A bed just big enough to sleep two—although not two of Maxum's size, that's to be certain. It would barely suit one with its short mattress that would no doubt leave his feet dangling off at the ankles. Maxum didn't waste any time stripping off his shirt. He debated whether or not to rid himself of his pants as well, but she hadn't struck him as too much of the shy sort so he went for it and shucked them off. He was folding them when he fished into his pocket for the talisman. He wanted to make sure it was safely secured.

That was when he realized it was no longer in his pocket. He immediately searched the floor, thinking it had fallen out. Coming up empty he quickly pulled his pants back on and hurried, bare-chested, back out into the inn.

"Oy, that was quick!" Kyno belted out, making the other men laugh uproariously. Maxum ignored them and went to search the seat he had been sitting in . . . and that's when it hit him.

"Fuck me!" he cried out as he bolted for the door. He ran into the stable where he'd seen a fine stallion of dappled coloring tied up earlier. Something told him it was hers and sure enough it was missing.

He ran out into the darkness, but there was no hope for it.

The little thief had made off with his hard-earned talisman.

CHAPTER
TWO

Airianne walked around the bazaar at the west end of Gryna, the city she'd arrived at just before dawn. The first thing she had done was find an inn and gotten herself something to eat to make up for the stew she'd left behind after choosing her mark last night.

She had to admit, it had been one of her more ballsy moves, but she had been desperate. Now she had to sell the talisman in her pocket and get herself some kind of gold. The thing was encrusted with gems so it should fetch a pretty price. If no one could afford to pay the price she wanted, she could easily begin prying gems off it and selling them one by one instead.

When she had chosen her mark she hadn't known exactly what was in his pocket, only that it was valuable enough that he kept checking for the feel of it every five minutes or so. When she had finally stopped in her headlong gallop away from the inn— after she had been sure he hadn't been following her—she had paused in the moonlight and looked at the thing she had stolen. But the full brilliance of it had not struck her until that morning when she'd been able to see it in the bright light of day.

She didn't know what the talisman was for—nor did

she care. All she wanted was a good price for it. The jewels worked into it assured her of that much at least. Then she really would get a good room for the night and sleep in a real bed.

Maybe.

She wasn't prone to spending coin unwisely. She worked too hard for her money. And anyone who said thievery wasn't hard work was a liar. Sneaking in and out of places, getting the right mark and following them, waiting in the dark, tensed to react to the slightest bit of trouble—it was all very hard work indeed.

Not to mention what could happen if she got caught in the act. The price people paid for being caught as thieves varied from city to city, but you could bet it wasn't going to be any fun. Some places hanged thieves, some cut off their hands. So far she'd managed to keep from getting caught . . . well, there had been that one time, but she'd picked the lock to the cage they'd held her in and said her hasty goodbyes.

She began to ask around the marketplace for the name of someone who would move a big piece of jewelry with no questions asked and everyone told her the same thing: a woman named Fro was ready to spend money and didn't care at all where things came from. So she hastily made her way to Fro's shop and had the door in sight when someone bumped into her hard.

"Hey! Watch—"

That was all she got out because the man clamped an iron hand around her arm and jerked her in tight to his body. She looked up into a pair of familiar and furious green eyes. She knew those eyes—she had sat across from them the night before and had found them nearly entrancing. If she hadn't been desperate to steal from him, she might have thought about sleeping with him for real.

Might have.

"Let go of me!" she cried, kicking and squirming for all she was worth.

"Settle down or I'll shout 'thief!' in the middle of this crowd. When the city guard comes I'll tell them what you stole and once they search you and find my talisman on you . . . Well, do you know what they do to thieves in this city?"

She paled. *Good*, Maxum thought. She should be scared. He was so damn angry right then he could break her arm and not think twice about it. But, contradictorily, he did think twice. Her arm was so slight in his grasp and she was so gods damned small. Small and ballsy. An intriguing combination. And that pissed him off more than anything. She was still getting under his skin, even after she'd duped him and made him look like a fool in front of his men. If he had the time he'd make her pay for that. But as it stood, he didn't have the time. He had another quest to go on; another line on an artifact that would come in handy in a god fight. This one purportedly made the wearer invisible to his enemy's eye. Yes, that would be very handy indeed.

"Fine! Fine! Here's your stupid talisman!" She reached with her free hand to burrow into her shirt between her bound breasts. The action left her shirt gaping as she slapped the talisman against his chest and waited for him to take it. To stop staring at her chest and take it. "Do you want it or not?"

Maxum shook himself and grabbed for the talisman, then he let her go with a shove. She spilled back onto the street, landing hard on her ass. She grunted with anger and picked herself up.

"Listen," she said quickly as he turned and walked away from her. She kept to his heels, her legs working fast to keep up with his long, powerful stride. "Wherever you're going, you'll need me! I . . . I can cook! And mend. I can work leather. I noticed your tack was looking a little worn last night. You should really get it fixed before you snap a strap and get your neck broken falling to the ground."

"I'll take my chances," he said harshly. He continued to walk and she followed him, shoving past the people who crowded the market street in order to do so. He didn't have to shove; he was big enough and intimidating enough that people gave him a wide berth.

"Look, I wouldn't have stolen from you if I wasn't desperate," she said, panting now. It was a combination of trying to keep up with him and sheer panic rising up inside of her. She had boarded her horse without paying, coin due when she picked him up. She had thought she would be coming back with enough to pay the tab and then some so she hadn't worried. If she couldn't pay they wouldn't let her have Hero back and she needed her horse. Maybe she could get some kind of job and work the debt off, but the debt would only increase with every day the horse remained boarded until the innkeeper would have the right to sell Hero and all her tack and possessions along with it. "That and you made it so obvious you had something worth stealing in your pants pocket. You were practically asking for it."

He came to such an abrupt halt that she slammed face-first into his hard body, banging her nose.

"Ow," she said, rubbing it.

"You are unbelievable!" he roared, turning on her. "First you steal from me, then you have the gall to ask me for some kind of job, all the while blaming me for you stealing from me in the first place!"

"Well, it's true! You kept fiddling with the thing. I figured it was either a good luck charm or something worth stealing. You didn't strike me as the sentimental sort so . . ." She shrugged.

"You made me look like a fool," he ground out as he went nose to nose with her. "You seduced me and stole something I risked my life and the lives of my men for! You are lucky I don't wring your little neck!"

"But you haven't wrung my neck—"

"Yet!"

"And I don't think you will because you need me!"

"Ha! What do I need a woman for? I can cook my own meals and mend my own clothes. Women are nothing but trouble and they slow a man down—you proved that to me last night."

"You don't need a woman, you need a *thief*!" He was on the move again so she was back to following at his heels. "I've seen your men. Not one of them, including you, could sneak into a situation if you tried. I'm small and light, I can fit into hundreds of places none of you can. The smallest man on your team is the mage, and he isn't all that small with those long limbs and broad shoulders. Plus, I can detect traps and no one, I mean no one, can pick a lock like I can. Admit it, you can use me."

He had slowed and come to a stop again, but his back was to her and his fists were clenching and unclenching. When he turned suddenly to face her she ducked to avoid a blow. She was surprised when it didn't come. Something in his eyes softened when he realized she had expected him to get violent with her. She sprang at the vulnerability.

"I promise I won't get in the way. And I'll make it worth your while. All I ask is a place to sleep, food in my belly and . . . and ten percent of whatever treasure we find."

"Ten percent!" He laughed incredulously. "You really are a piece of work."

"Hey, that's a deal! I'm not even asking for an equal share. Just enough so I can get some coin and then I'll get out of your hair."

"And what makes you think there's even going to be any coin?"

"Isn't there? Isn't that what you guys do? Seek out hidden treasures?"

"What makes you say that?"

"That talisman for one. It's rare and very old, even I can see that. Probably even magical. Not the kind of thing you come across in the everyday world. That's something you go looking for. And the way your men were partying last night, I'd say whatever you were celebrating had paid off. In a huge way."

"You know what, you're too keen for your own good," he grumbled.

"So what do you say?" she asked—no begged. "Please . . . I'm good with my daggers and a one-handed crossbow. I've even got some really tricky bolts to load it with. I came across a trader who had silverwright bolts in his possession. He, uh . . . let me have some."

He snorted out an astounded laugh. "You mean you stole them."

"Maybe but he deserved it. The creep had a little girl and it was clear he—"

"You know what, I don't care why he deserved it. He probably deserved it no more or less than I deserved it. You stole from him because you wanted to, because you ruthlessly wanted whatever he had for yourself."

"I wouldn't say ruthlessly," she muttered.

"Shut up!" he snapped. She immediately pressed her lips together. Why couldn't she just keep quiet? Why did she have to keep pushing all the time? Joey Nuts, a fellow thief, had once told her that her mouth was going to land her in hot water one day and he'd been right several times over so far.

Once she was silent he ran a darkly assessing gaze over her from head to toe.

"You're too skinny. Too light. One good hit and you'll be done for."

She took offense. "I—"

"I said shut up!" he hissed in sharp warning.

She fought with herself, but she eventually shut her teeth together with a snap.

"Well, at least you can listen to commands . . . sometimes," he said wearily. "And you'd have to, you know. Listen to commands. There's only one person in charge of my group. It isn't a democracy. What I say goes. End of story."

She nodded vigorously. It was the first sign that he was actually going to accept her offer. She couldn't believe it! She hadn't thought she could convince him, but apparently she was better than she thought she was.

"Besides, my men could use some womanly entertainment," he said, crushing her hopes entirely.

"Oh no!" she ground out. "No way. I am no one's entertainment."

"Then there's no deal," he said, turning back away from her.

Damn it all she was desperate but not that desperate.

But maybe she could agree with him just long enough to get Hero out of the inn stable and then take off before she found herself in a position to entertain anybody.

"Okay fine!" she snapped. "Fine. I'll do whatever you want. Just let me come with you."

Maxum turned back to her, working for all he was worth to hide his incredulousness. He couldn't believe what she had just agreed to. It made him realize just how desperate she was and he felt a pang of guilt and regret. Of course, he had no intention of letting her service all of his men, he'd simply been trying to find a way to get rid of her. But now he found himself entertaining the idea of acquiring a thief—one who had just agreed to be the sexual slave of a group of rowdy men.

Hmm. He eyed her lithe body from head to toe. Screw the rest of his men, but the idea of her being his sexual slave had definite merits. He was still craving her, he discovered, even in spite of what she had done to him. More the fool he. But he would make her sweat a bit before he let the little wench off the hook. He might want her, but he'd be damned if he let himself have her in that way.

Oh, this is a bad idea, Maxum, he told himself with a groan. *You have a goal and it's something like this that can make you lose sight of it.*

For all he knew one of the gods had put her in his path for expressly that purpose. The thought made him frown. Now he was being paranoid. But the fact of the matter was that one day the gods would figure out what he was up to and then there would be a hefty price to pay. He simply had to make sure he was more than ready for it by the time they caught on.

Besides, what price could he pay that would be steeper than the one he was already paying? He had made the leap for immortality and had paid the price for it. Many times over. And the only other choice was to continue to pay that price for the rest of eternity.

He regarded her once again.

Come to think of it, she had a point. A thief could come in very handy. Provided she wasn't overselling her skills, he might be able to use her in their next little adventure.

"Cooking, mending, thievery, and . . . sex," he said, grinning on the last lasciviously—at least to her eye he was. "And five percent of the take."

"Ten or you can forget it!" she snapped.

"Fine. Forget it then."

She had no choice but to blink first. "Oh, all right. Five percent! But with the option to bump it up to ten after I have proved my worth."

"You must be quite good in bed," he mused, scratching his chin, "to merit ten percent."

"I meant proving myself as a thief!"

"Oh," he said, clearly being purposely obtuse. "Well, I guess that'd be fair. But I decide when you've proven yourself."

"Of course," she muttered.

"Now let's go. I've already wasted enough time chasing after you."

"Um . . ." They were moving again and she hurried to keep up with him. "There's one other thing. I stabled my horse and I . . . um . . . don't have the money to pay to get him back."

He shot her a glare. "That was stupid," he said.

"Well, I was planning on having cash and plenty of it," she pointed out. "The gems on that thing would have fed me and my horse for a couple of months at least."

He sighed, sounding very put upon. "Where is he?"

"The Ox and Lamb."

"Lead the way," he said, sweeping a hand in front of himself. She hurried to get in front of him, which left him with a rather nice view of her bottom in the skin-tight breeches she wore. They were practically obscene, he thought grouchily as he forced his gaze to the crowd, making sure to keep an eye out for trouble in case there was any. Cities were known for being wild cards. There was always the potential for trouble. Of course some were maintained better than others. When his brothers ruled a city there was very little in the way of crime and discontented behaviors. People didn't starve in his brothers' cities.

But none of that mattered. What mattered now was getting to the Ox and Lamb and then gathering up his men. Upon reaching the city he had immediately sought out the five most likely places a thief might go to sell a pricey item. Fro's had come up first and foremost, so he had taken to watching for her there. He had sent his men to the four other likely places on the off chance she would go there but he had suspected she would take the easiest and quickest route first and he had been right. She was damn smart, but desperation had made her drop her guard. He had no doubt that she would have preferred to skip the nearest city and ride to the next one just to avoid the possibility of getting caught, but clearly she'd had no other choice.

And now, looking at her more critically, she did look a little thin. Like she hadn't been eating regularly. He wondered how she had let it get so bad.

"So if you're such a good thief, why are you starving?"

Her step faltered a little and she stole a glance at him over her shoulder. "A string of bad luck," she said. "Besides if I can avoid thieving I do. Getting caught is always a possibility no matter how good you are and some things just aren't worth the risk."

"And yet you risked thieving from someone like me," he said, his tone low and dangerous, almost angry. Was he still peeved about her swiping the talisman? That was over and done with, he should learn to move on, she thought.

What she didn't know was that he wasn't angry because she had stolen from him but that she had risked her little neck stealing from someone like him. Had he been a different man he might have sought a fierce retribution. He could have easily been the type to kill a thief for something like that, woman or no.

"I didn't have much of a choice. As you've noted, I am in a bad way."

"Maybe you should give up thieving, find a good man, and settle down."

She scoffed and shot him an acidic glare. "You're just saying that because I'm a woman."

"You're damn right I am! Traveling the open country is no place for a woman alone. You could find yourself in all kinds of trouble."

"You mean like now?" she muttered. Louder she said, "Are you going to lecture me the entire time we're together? If so, I'm going to have to rethink this situation. I could easily go back to the market and pick a few pockets for the cost of my horse."

It would be a risk . . . a great risk. Each pocket picked was one pocket closer to getting caught. But risk was a thief's forte. She was just afraid desperation would make her sloppy. As it already had. Otherwise he'd have never caught her.

"Consider it a perk of being with my group," he said with a smug grin.

She grumbled some more and continued to lead the way.

CHAPTER
THREE

They reached the Ox and Lamb a few minutes later and fetched Hero. Then they made their way back to the market where they gathered up his men one by one. If his men thought anything of a woman joining their ranks, they didn't say much about it. Clearly Maxum was in charge and what he said was what happened and there were no arguments about it. Well, that might work for them, but she wasn't exactly the docile following type.

"So where are we going?" she asked once they had retrieved their horses and left the city behind them.

"East," Maxum said shortly.

"East *where*?" she asked.

"We're going east. That's all you need to know."

"That is not all I need to know. Where east? Why east? How far east? What will we do when we get east?"

He released a put-upon sigh. "We are going east to Docking Bay."

"There, now was that so bad?" she asked smugly. "Why are we going to Docking Bay?"

"Why does anyone go to Docking Bay?" he countered wearily.

"To catch a boat?" she asked.

He glanced at her with a raised brow.

"So we're catching a boat. To where? How far is it? Why?"

"Enough! Enough questions!" he barked. "Keep quiet or I'll bind and gag you and you'll ride the rest of the way fanny up across my lap!"

"You wouldn't dare!"

"Wouldn't I?" he asked, the gleam in his eyes dangerous.

She swallowed noisily. "Fine. I'll stop asking questions. For now. But if you think I'm going to just blindly follow you you're sorely mistaken. I haven't kept my neck safe on my shoulders this long only to have you get me in trouble."

"You're already in trouble," he said. "Or have you forgotten how you got here and the agreement you made to stay?"

She blanched.

He really should let her off the hook, but he was enjoying putting her in her place too much to do so quite yet. Besides, he wasn't sure if he was going to let her out of her predicament completely. He rather liked the idea of having that sweet little backside all to himself.

He sighed.

No, he wouldn't do that. But still, it was fun to imagine. Especially when she was irritating him with a thousand questions.

Airi found herself fidgeting in her saddle frequently as they traveled the rest of the day. She knew they would eventually make camp and when that happened she would be forced to keep her end of the bargain. She was working her mind incessantly to try and think of what her next step should be. There was no way Hero could outrun the powerful stallion he was riding, and anyway there were no opportunities to escape along the way.

She had finally settled on a course of action by the time they had made camp. She could only hope it was enough to keep her out of trouble until they reached Docking Bay and she could make her escape.

"Make yourself useful," he said. A pit of dread sank into her stomach. Useful how? She decided to build a fire.

She made up the fire from dead wood she found along the path of the forest they were riding through. She could wait until everyone was asleep and sneak away then, but there was only one way in and one way out on horseback and that was via the road. There was a good chance they'd catch up to her so that was not an option.

Kilon disappeared into the woods as she built the fire and returned a short time later with three xixi pheasants hanging from his belt. He dropped them unceremoniously in front of Airi and it was clear they wanted her to pluck and cook the birds while they kicked back and relaxed. As the sun set, Maxum disappeared from sight, having walked off into the deep woods for some unexplained reason.

She began the task without complaint. She had signed on for this, offering her skills. And more, she thought with a gulp. Maybe if she performed her other duties satisfactorily she could weasel her way out of her other expected services.

She plucked the birds, then went into the forest in search of wild herbs and vegetables. She asked for and received a tin pot and prepared the potatoes and mushrooms she'd found within it. The mem, the religious woman at the orphanage where she'd grown up, had taught her how to cook. It was a key skill for any woman, she had said. Of course, the mem had thought she was going to use the skill when she married and settled down. Airi snorted to herself. Like that would ever happen. She wasn't ever going to tie herself down to one place, never mind one man. Far too many men looked at women as their possessions. Someone to care for them and fuck them when needed and to keep quiet and out of sight the rest of the time.

Well, no thanks. She couldn't keep quiet if she tried. As was obvious all through dinner as she made nervous conversation with Maxum's men.

"So how long have you all been together?"

"A year or less," Dru said. "I've known Maxum the longest. We set out on the road together from the moment we landed on the Black Continent. I was with Jaykun's army until then."

"Who's Jaykun?"

"Maxum's brother. Anyway, we were on the road about a month when we came across Doisy. Then a few weeks later we met up with Kyno. A month after that Kilon. We've been together ever since."

"And I gather from last night's celebrations that you've had a good deal of success together?"

"That's right," Doisy said. "Some good treasure to be had in Maxum's company!"

The men agreed with a round of grunts. During the conversation she found out they'd had a great deal of success; if she could bear staying, five percent would net her a great deal indeed. By the time Maxum returned, sometime after juquil's hour, she was heavily weighing her options.

Maxum went to the fire and reached for what remained of the game birds. He sat across from her and watched her steadily as he ate. His regard felt lecherous to Airi. She shivered in the cool night air. Winter was coming soon. She needed to secure a warm place before the snow fell. Maybe she could barter passage on a boat heading south . . . or maybe she could find a job at an inn in Docking Bay. Something just to get her through the winter.

If only she could stay with Maxum's men without this idea of servicing their sexual needs hanging over her head. She could probably gain a small amount of prosperity if she stuck with them. It could be the turn in her fortunes she had been needing. Perhaps she could renegotiate the terms of their agreement, she thought.

But one look at the hungry way he was devouring her from across the way quickly dissolved that notion. As she narrowed her eyes on him she thought he looked freshly bruised along his cheekbones. As if he'd been punched in the face and broken his nose. There appeared to be dark circles under his eyes.

No. That had to be a trick of the firelight and darkness. How could he possibly have gotten into a fight all the way out here? Wouldn't he have said something about it?

He was still staring at her and she looked away, terribly discomforted.

Maxum was toying with her. It was cruel, he knew, but he couldn't seem to help himself. Of course, it wasn't all that hard for him to imagine himself taking advantage of that supple young body. He had come close to it the night before only to be denied in a cruel twist of fate. The fact that she had conned him hadn't seemed to put a damper on the way his body had wanted hers. Neither did hours of being crushed beneath the rock and soil. He had found himself a stream to wash up in after the dirt had spit him out, but he still felt the grime of it under his skin and he still was healing broken bones.

Still he wanted her. He had to admit that. His appetite for her had not waned. In fact, it seemed to be growing. Damn her for teasing him . . . for kissing him. He couldn't seem to forget the sweetness of her flavor, couldn't keep himself from wanting more.

But he wouldn't take her until they were on equal footing. He didn't want her to give herself to him because she felt she had no other choices. He would wait until she had some fortune in her pockets . . . until she no longer needed to be with them . . . until she only wanted to be with them. Then he might take her.

Might. He wasn't going to give it too much thought. He had other goals. Bedding a little thief should not be one of them. Bedding her would not get him what he needed.

Still, that didn't mean he couldn't entertain himself in the interim.

He made a show of stretching out and yawning.

"All right, boys. It's time for bed. Come on, little thief. You'll be sharing my bedroll tonight."

He watched her pale in the firelight. She stood up and he could see her hands were shaking. But she took a deep breath and followed him to where he'd laid out his bedroll. He dropped down onto it and pulled off his boots. Other than that, he didn't disrobe. He never did when they were on the road. He wanted to be able to move at a moment's notice if needed. Sometimes he didn't even take his boots off. But he wanted to give her the impression he was undressing so he pulled his shirt free of his breeches.

The panicked look that entered her eyes almost made him laugh and give himself away. But he wanted to enjoy this to the last possible second. Payback for her stealing from him.

"I have my monthly woman's blood!" she blurted out suddenly.

He froze for a minute, absorbing the missile. Then he smiled and said, "So? I do not care. I am not squeamish about such things."

He reached out for her and she yelped and jumped back. He grinned, enjoying himself a great deal.

"Come now, a bargain is a bargain. It's me or . . . if you'd prefer the rest of the men . . ." He trailed off meaningfully.

She looked from him to the other men. Doisy chose

that moment to give in to a bout of flatulence. Kyno was picking at his nose. Kilon was scratching his ass. Maxum couldn't have orchestrated the moment any better. She deflated. "No," she said glumly. "You'll do."

He ought to have been insulted. And he was. But that didn't keep him from ringing an arm around her waist and jerking her forward, her small body thumping against his. Just the feel of her up against him was stimulating to him. He should tell her she was free of the promise to service him and his men, but he wasn't quite ready yet. He jerked her mouth beneath his and kissed her until she melted bonelessly in his arms. All the tension simply bled out of her and she went lax and sweet against him. Her mouth fell open and he readily took the invitation, slipping a searching tongue into her mouth.

Ah, damn she was sweet. There was just something about the way she tasted, so smooth and sultry and beckoning. He found himself wishing she hadn't stolen from him the night before, wishing they were on equal terms and he'd been able to bed her like he'd wanted to in that inn room.

Then she bit down on his tongue, kneed him in the crotch, and ran.

She reached Hero in a flash, throwing herself up onto his bare back. She heard a bellowing roar of pain and fury, but she didn't stop to look. She kicked Hero's sides and sent the horse bolting forward. So what if Hero's saddle, her saddlebags, and provisions were all on the ground by the bedroll she had laid out? She didn't care. She was getting out of there as fast as she could.

She was riding like the eight hells were yawning open to get her. She didn't look back once, which was why she wasn't expecting a hand to grab her at the back of her neck, seizing a fistful of her shirt and plucking her right off Hero's back.

She screamed and kicked and fought against him. She

went for a dagger but only got it out of the sheath before he was wrenching her wrist and forcing her to drop it to the ground.

"Enough, you little hellcat! Enough!" he bellowed.

He dragged her across his lap, her fanny up in the air as he kneed the horse to a halt. He smacked a hand down hard on her buttocks and she yelped with pain and indignation.

"Let me go!" she cried, as she tried to wriggle away.

"If you'd shut up and sit still for two seconds we can put an end to this!" he roared.

With that terrible tone it sank in that she was done for. There was nothing she could do. She might as well stop fighting. If he was this determined to have her, she would just shut her eyes and be done with it. She would find a way to escape him come the morning . . . or whenever they got to Docking Bay.

She deflated in his lap, hanging there over the sides of his horse dejectedly. She rode like that as he walked the horses back to the campsite in total silence. Maxum's men were all still sitting around the fire, watching their leader with an unconcerned air. When they approached his bedroll he dropped her unceremoniously to the ground, sending her onto her butt in the dirt, and dismounted. Then he reached for her, causing her to back away on hands and heels. But, of course, he caught her and yanked her up off the ground and into his body.

"Take off your pants," he barked at her.

"No!" she shouted back, unable to keep from fighting him even though it was a lost cause.

"Do it!"

Defeated and with shaking hands she moved to obey, untying the laces of her breeches. She then hooked her thumbs into the waistband and shucked them down her legs.

She stood there shivering in her underwear as she

handed him the pants. She tried to hide herself from the interested gazes of his men but there was little she could do other than to put Maxum between their eyes and her body. He folded her pants neatly, dropped down onto his bedroll and tucked them under his head like a pillow as he settled in. She stood there in puzzlement as he closed his eyes and made as though he were going to sleep. She stood indecisively for a full minute.

"Go lie down and go to sleep," he barked at her. "Cover up. It's chilly tonight."

Not knowing what else to do, she dropped down onto his bedroll and snuggled up under the blanket. He was right—it was cold and he had her pants.

Maxum had meant for her to go to her own bedroll, but she had misunderstood. True, he'd made no effort to explain, but he had thought it would be obvious he wasn't interested in her. Not anymore. His tongue and balls still hurt from her last attack on him.

"I lost my dagger," she said softly.

He opened his eyes and looked at her. "We'll get it in the morning."

"I only have the two."

"Go to sleep," he commanded.

Recognizing that it was too cold for him to lie outside of the blanket, he lifted it up and joined her beneath it. Her warmth immediately seeped into him from head to toe even though she went rigid and held herself as far away from him as she could and yet still remain under the blanket. Growling with frustration and annoyance he ringed an arm around her waist and jerked her back into the bend of his body, seating her bottom into the lee of his hips and her back to his chest. They would keep each other warm at least.

She lay there stiffly for a good ten minutes, until she was sure he wasn't going to do anything else. Puzzled and exhausted, she finally drifted off to sleep.

CHAPTER
FOUR

The next morning she awoke to the feel of an erection prodding against her bottom. With a squeak she went to pull away, but there was a powerful arm banded around her waist keeping her right where she was. She slowly inched around until she could see his face.

He was asleep. Or most of him was—there was still that stellar erection to consider. She finally took the time to really look at him. He was blond—a dark gold blond—a perfect foil for those green eyes. His hair was shoulder length and fell in fat, lazy curls. Sleeping as he was, his hair fell haphazardly over his face and gave him an almost innocent appearance.

Almost.

There was too much ruggedness and hard living on his features. Not that he looked aged and worn, but just . . . hard. She got the feeling that life had not been very kind to him. She felt a little guilty for her attack on him the night before, but what had he expected? That she would just roll over and service his needs?

Well, at least she had figured out a way to avoid that. But that was one night. What was she going to do all the other nights if she stayed with them? No. She had to get to Docking Bay and find some other way to make her way in the world. She simply could not live up to this agreement.

"I didn't plan on making you, you know," he said suddenly, startling her. Her gaze shot to his.

"Making me?"

"I was just giving you a hard time. I wasn't really going to make you service me and my men. I wouldn't do that."

"You wouldn't?" she asked suspiciously.

"No," he said.

She instantly flared with temper. "Then why did you take my pants? Why didn't you tell me this last night?"

"I didn't want you trying to run away in the middle of the night. And last night I was angry. I tend to get that way after someone bites off my tongue and knees me in my balls."

"Ooo!" she ground out. She leapt to her feet and held out her hand with a snap. "Give me my pants!"

With an unrepentant grin he let his eyes roam down her body, taking his time as he coasted down her bare legs. She shivered . . . and not entirely from the fact that she was standing in her drawers in the cold of the damp morning. Slowly, without any sign of regret, he removed her pants from beneath his head and held them out to her.

"Besides, it's better to sleep together when it's cold like this."

"Then sleep with Doisy next time!" she spat as she shoved one leg into her pants dancing around as she struggled to get her other leg into the tight breeches. Eventually she was forced to sit back down on his bedroll and squirm into them on the ground. She laced them up tightly, yanking at the laces in a temper. "That had to be the most despicable thing I've ever been a victim to!"

"And that's just what burns you," he said with a lazy

stretch. "That you feel you were a victim. I'm thinking you don't like thinking that way about yourself."

"Does anyone like thinking themselves a victim?" she snapped.

"Some do. Don't be so defensive. It's one of the things I like about you. One of the reasons I'm letting you stay on with us."

Her temper cooled a little bit and she looked at him from the corner of her eye. "You're going to let me stay on?"

"For a little while. Provided you make yourself useful and not a hindrance to our goals. But the minute you become too much trouble I'll drop you like a hot rock."

She still regarded him with suspicion. "No other conditions?"

"You cook, you clean up, you mend. Just like we agreed. But other than that, no other conditions."

"And I want ten percent."

"Five," he said mildly. But before she could get her back up he said, "Prove yourself once and I'll seriously consider bumping you up to ten."

She snorted. "'Seriously consider'? That's man-speak for 'it'll never happen.'"

"Not true. My, what a jaded view of men you have."

"Is there any reason why I shouldn't?" she groused.

"True. Men aren't the least bit trustworthy."

"Some more than others," she said meaningfully.

He laughed. "Put your boots on and go into my saddlebags. You'll find dried pork and hard bread for breaking our fast."

"And what are you going to do?"

"Watch you," he said, lying back and tucking his hands behind his head with a grin.

"You . . . you . . ." But she forced herself to bite her tongue. She should be grateful that she was going to be able to stay with them. That there were no longer any untenable conditions to her staying. As she marched over to his bags, which were only two feet away, she began to understand that her luck might be changing. The understanding made it hard for her to stay angry with him.

She fetched the bread and the pork and returned to his side. Sitting cross-legged, she pulled the bread apart and gave him half and handed him several pieces of the pork jerky. The meat was very salty, so she got up and fetched some water from an animal skin that also hung from his saddle. They traded the skin back and forth in silence for several long minutes.

"So where are we going?" she asked. He laughed out loud.

"I knew it was too good to last."

"What?"

"The silence from you. Why is it so important for you to know where we are going? We're going to Docking Bay, like I said."

"But then where?" she asked. She winced at his dirty look. "Why can't you just tell me?"

"Because it doesn't really matter where we're going now, does it? You're going to follow us no matter what. You don't really have any other choice now, do you?"

"I could leave. I could go somewhere . . . steal something . . . make my way. I've done it before."

"Except you owe me and you have to repay your debt first."

"Debt! What debt?" she demanded.

"I got your horse out of the inn for you."

"Oh please. What was that, a silver? One silver and a few coppers? It's not like you can't afford it. I saw the way you all were throwing your money around at the inn."

"It's the principle of the thing," he said.

"Oh, like you have so many principles." She belched a scoffing laugh.

"I do. You don't know me well enough to say otherwise."

"I know enough. I know you tricked me into thinking I was going to have to service every man in this group."

"I didn't trick you into anything. You agreed to it, remember? You're the one reneging on an agreement, not me."

Damn it, he had a point. But she was going to be the last to admit that. "Well, it was very wrong of you to make me think . . . it was very wrong."

"Mayhap it was. But I suppose it's all a matter of perspective now, isn't it?"

He sat up and stretched again before snatching up one of his boots and putting it on. "Come on, let's find that dagger of yours."

She had forgotten all about it. Eager to find it she pulled on her boots and followed him to his saddle. When he picked it up she went over to hers and made her way to Hero. She saddled him with practiced ease then swung up into the saddle.

Maxum wouldn't admit it to her, but he was impressed with her strength and determination. She hoisted her saddle with ease, didn't ask for a lick of help. Clearly didn't need to. She was unlike so many of the women he knew. Oh, he knew a few female warriors, but not many. Certainly none her size. Most of the women he came across were pretty much helpless. He supposed they could keep a house or some such thing, but overall, pretty useless. Women were meant to look pretty and make babies in his opinion. But every so often one would surprise him—like Airianne. Although he had never met anyone quite like her. He wondered what she'd be like in pitched battle. Not very useful, he surmised. She was just too small really. He wondered if he was going to regret bringing her with them. He already knew some of the men questioned the wisdom of the thing. They didn't question *him*, they didn't dare, but he knew they were questioning it just the same.

He rode beside her down the forest path, his eyes scanning over the ground. It had been dark last night and he didn't really know how far they'd made it before turning back, so he really didn't know what the chances were of them finding the missing dagger.

After half an hour of looking, he opened his mouth to tell her it was lost and they should head back.

"Don't say it!" she said.

"It's just a dagger. I'll get you a new one."

"I don't want a new one. I want that one. It's my lucky dagger."

"What's so lucky about it?"

"You wouldn't understand," she said with a frown, her eyes still tracking over the ground.

"Try and explain," he said.

She shot him a wary glance.

"An old friend gave it to me. He said it would never fail me and so far it hasn't."

"It failed you last night," he pointed out.

"It didn't fail me," she said. "I just wasn't meant to use it on you."

He laughed condescendingly. "You weren't *meant* to?"

"Well, look at the big picture. Do you believe in fate? In the way of Hella?"

"You're *religious*?" he asked incredulously.

"No. I just believe in fate. Fate led me to you, didn't she? And fate knew that you were just being an ass and you didn't deserve to get a dagger in the ribs for it. A kick in the head maybe, but not a dagger in the ribs."

"So in that line of thinking, does this mean fate isn't letting you find your lucky—"

"There it is!"

She swung down out of her saddle and scooped up the dagger, holding it up triumphantly. "See! Fate!"

"Luck is more like it," he mumbled.

"I heard that. Fate and luck are sometimes the same thing. Come on, let's go back."

"You know, the gods aren't responsible for every little thing that happens to us. And even if they were, it wouldn't be a good thing."

She glanced over at him. "That's a very jaded view of the gods. What'd they ever do to you?"

He grimaced but remained silent. She shrugged and followed him back to camp. By the time they returned the other men were up and about, clearing up the campsite.

"Where've you been?" Kilon asked, spitting on the ground as he slung his longbow across his body at an angle, his crossbow hitched onto his back with a quick release knot. He could pull the deadly weapon in a moment's notice and Airi believed he wouldn't think twice about using it—on a man as much as on an animal. Still, the archer would keep them fed as long as there was game to be found, and just because he was something of a jerk she couldn't begrudge that fact. "Or do I need to ask," he added with a lecherous leer of contempt. "I hope you plan on sharing the goods, slink." He used the derogatory word for whore. "There's more than one man here in need of servicing."

"Kilon!" Maxum barked in warning.

Kilon let a moment of surprise flit across his features at Maxum's tone, then he grew even darker and angrier, glaring at Airi.

"It's not like she's going to be good for anything else!"

"You'd be surprised at what I'm good for," she said breezily, refusing to let him get to her.

"No, I wouldn't. Women are only good for two

things . . . and holding up a headstone's the other one."
Kilon turned his back on her before she could get over
her shock enough to reply. She shouldn't be shocked
really. She was used to men's attitudes when it came to
her capabilities. But like she had said to Kilon, it was
surprising what she could do when her back was to a
wall.

The group got under way shortly after that. She noticed that Doisy had a staff strapped to his saddle—the
same staff she'd seen him with the day before. Since he
didn't walk with a limp, she didn't think he used it for
support. She suspected he could use it in very nonclerical
ways. He was a handsome man overall, blond haired
and blue eyed, always a smile toying with his lips. He
came up and rode beside her when Maxum rode on
ahead of them to scout.

"So, my lady, how fare you this fine day?"

She laughed. It had been raining at a drizzle for most
of the morning.

"I am well, and I'm not 'my lady.' "

"Ah, but all women are 'my lady' to me. I mean no
offense by it, only that my sainted mother would never
forgive me if I forgot my manners."

"His mother was a whore," Kilon barked.

"All women are whores to you, my friend," Doisy said
with a good-natured grin. He clearly didn't pay any attention to Kilon's surly temper and she decided that
she wouldn't either. Still, she wouldn't turn her back on
him. "So you are something of an accomplished thief, I
take it."

"Not so accomplished if I got caught."

"Ah well, you just had the bad fortune to steal from
the one man who could outthink the most learned
scholar or the most devious thief in these lands and all
the others."

She preened. "Thank you. I do consider myself to be quite devious. Clever anyway."

"I have no doubt." He reached to take her free hand from the pommel of her saddle and leaned over to bring it to his lips. "No doubt on a better day you would even outthink Maxum."

She laughed when Kilon made a disgusted sound. "No doubt," she agreed, taking her hand back.

"Oh, for Hella's left tit, you're making me sick already," Kilon said before springing his horse ahead and putting his back to them. Kyno came up on his mighty looking destrier and took the surly man's place so they were riding three abreast again.

"So where you from, little one?" the giant man asked her.

"Here and there," she answered vaguely. She didn't much care to talk about herself when they were the more interesting ones. "What about you?"

"Same place," Kyno said with a chuckle. The sound was deep and rolling, as if it were coming from a very low place in his belly.

"What about you, Doisy? Where are you from?"

"Koysis, a small town of no fame on the Red Continent. But we are known for making the most delicious breadcakes in the many kingdoms."

"I love breadcakes! Can you make them?"

"Indeed I can, my lady. When next we avail ourselves of an inn I will buy supplies and ask the innkeeper to use his oven. I suspect if I offer to make enough to go 'round he won't mind."

"You would do that for me?" she asked, surprised.

"But of course. It is good for a man's soul to please a lady."

"Good for a lady's soul too!" she quipped. They all laughed and she decided right then that she liked these two men very much. They were certainly better company than Kilon.

She looked over her shoulder to where Dru was pulling up the rear. The road became narrow a short while later and she took the opportunity to fall back and ride abreast of Dru.

"Hello," she greeted him. Dru had been the only one to really converse with her the night before and she wondered at his silence today. "Are you well?"

"Very, I thank you."

"You seem quiet."

"I like to be sometimes. You hear more interesting things that way."

"Very true," she agreed with a smile. He returned the smile and she relaxed. "Do you know where we're headed after Docking Bay?"

"I only know that we are going to the Isle of Thiss in the middle of the bay."

"Thiss! Isn't that . . . I heard there were weredragons on Thiss."

"Mayhap there are. I've never been."

"Why would he want to go to such a place?"

"I don't question why as long as we come out of it with gold and our skins intact."

"So you just blindly follow him? Why?"

"I don't do it blindly, just with faith. His brother Garreth is one of the best men I know, and his brother Jaykun, who leads Weysa's army, is one of the finest warriors around. With such a pedigree, can you blame me for trusting him?"

"Weysa's army? I've heard of this army! It is supposed to be massive and is rolling through the lands defeating cities in Weysa's name."

"That would be the one," Dru said with a nod.

"His *brother* leads that army?"

"He does indeed. And Garreth and Dethan, his youngest and eldest brothers respectively, also join the army in the summer turning. When the cold comes they return to the arms of their loving wives."

"So Maxum has sisters by marriage?"

"Three in all. Each brother has found his love. Each is a most romantic tale—there is bardsong about them. In the army and elsewhere."

"Oh, how nice," she said. Then she gave a chuckle. "I wonder if Maxum is in any bardsong. Isn't it true of all the great adventurers? And with such a famous brother surely—"

"I wouldn't make jokes or tease about that if I were you," he said hastily and almost harshly. "Maxum would not be amused."

"But I was just—"

"Please. Do not . . . I don't know why, but he doesn't like bardsong. There was a bard at one of the inns we last went to and he was singing and something about it rubbed Maxum the wrong way. The bard ended up with a harp being cracked over his head. Needless to say . . ."

"Why do you suppose that is?"

"I wouldn't hazard a guess. But perhaps there was some love lost to him. The song the bard was singing was one of the Songs of the Gods, but it was about a tragic love story between a mortal woman and Sabo, the god of pain and suffering. 'Solange's Secret.'"

"'Solange's Secret'?" she asked.

"The song is the story of a beautiful maiden named Solange who was sleeping in a meadow one day when Sabo came upon her and instantly fell in love with her. But when Solange awoke she was terrified to see the god in all his magnificence staring down at her. Sabo knew that she would never accept the cruel god of pain and suffering so he told her he was Mordu, the god of hope, love, and dreams. He told her that he was in love with her but she must keep their relationship a secret because his wife, Hella, the goddess of fate, would kill her instantly if she were to discover their love.

"So Solange kept her secret and met with her god lover every night from summer's turntide to fall's turntide. Then, one day, Solange could not keep her secret to herself any longer for she was with child. She begged Sabo to put his wife aside and take her to wife instead, to raise her up as a demigod so she could protect herself against Hella and so they might live their love in the open. He flatly refused of course.

"So Solange threw all caution to the wind and went to Kitari's temple and prayed to the queen of the gods for her help. If anyone could keep Hella from harming her or her child it would be the queen of the gods. Solange prayed so long and so hard that at last she gained Kitari's attention. That was when Kitari revealed to Solange that the god she was in love with was not Mordu but was in fact Sabo.

"Solange was so horrified by this that she went to the nearest cliff and threw herself down onto the rocky waters below. It was a tragic love story to be sure."

"But what makes you think that was somehow related to Maxum having lost a love?"

"What other reason could there be?"

Honestly, she couldn't think of one. And it wouldn't surprise her to find out he had been in love and hurt by that love. He was a very beautiful man; handsome and rugged, with beautiful green eyes worthy of love sonnets and bardsongs. But it was hard to believe a woman not loving him in return or throwing him over for another man. True, she knew very little about him and he had acted like something of a bastard with her, but she could easily imagine him being worthy of some woman somewhere.

Perhaps she was being too kind. That really wasn't like her to give someone the benefit of the doubt. She usually expected the worst of people until they proved otherwise. So far all he'd proved to her was that he could be an ass.

Although he was an ass with scruples. He hadn't just handed her over to his men like a piece of clothing they all borrowed from one another.

Honestly she didn't know what to make of him. She didn't know what to make of any of them yet. The only one she was sure about was Kilon. Kilon was a mean bastard, end of story.

Maxum seemed to be more of a loner sort, the sort who would be happier with only his own company. So why so many men? Unless it was all about the money. That had to be it. Which told her just how lucrative Maxum's ventures had been so far. Maybe five percent wouldn't be so bad . . . but ten percent would certainly be better. She was going to have to make sure that she was indispensible. In some way that didn't require her to take off her clothes and jump from bedroll to bedroll every night.

They reached Docking Bay just before sunset. Maxum led them to the nearest inn inside the city gate then immediately left them there. She didn't see him again until some time later that night. She had eaten her fill of mutton chops and little potatoes and, thanks to Doisy, breadcakes that were out of this world. The men had all chosen to share a large room with two beds to sleep in, but there wasn't a bed for her that didn't require her to cozy up to Kilon. Doisy was sharing some woman's bed and Dru was sleeping with Kyno. That left her downstairs in the common room waiting for Maxum to return.

She was dozing off in her seat in the corner of the room when he came in at last. This time when she saw the bruises on his face there was no denying it. They were livid and purple and she sat up straight and looked at him with shock written clearly in her eyes.

"Got into a fight," he slurred.

"I can see that. Where?"

"At an inn."

"You went to another inn and got drunk and got into a fight? What was wrong with this inn where your friends are to back you up?"

"Don't need any backup." He stumbled toward her and she leapt up and levered herself under his arm, holding up a little more of his weight than she could comfortably bear.

"All right, let's get you to bed," she said, hauling him toward the innkeeper. "I need a couple of rooms."

"Only got one," the innkeeper said.

Airi rolled her eyes and sighed. "We'll take it."

"Coin," the keep said gruffly.

The men had brought all their belongings in, including Maxum's saddlebags. Any coin he might have in them was up in the room with them. With a grumble she began to pat down Maxum's pockets until she felt one with a hard circle within it. Triumphantly she pulled out a gold sovereign.

"What am I supposed to do with this? It only costs two silver for the room. I ain' got change like this!"

"Keep it until the morning then we'll give you your two silver and you can give us the sovereign back. This way you know you'll get paid and if we don't give you your silver you can keep the rest."

The innkeeper fondled the coin. "All right. But it's two silver for the room and another for the meal you ate."

"A whole silver for that? We made the breadcakes!"

"With my flour!"

"Very well then! You'll get your silver. Now which room?"

"Up the stairs, end of the row."

It was a fairly nice inn overall, and the room didn't really disappoint. The bed linens were clean anyway and the bed was almost long enough to accommodate a man of Maxum's height and build. She led him to it and dropped him onto it. She rolled the drunken sot onto his back and pulled one boot off. When she did the same to the other he growled as if he were in pain. He must have gotten beaten pretty bad, she thought. As she undressed him she saw he was covered in ugly, vivid bruises of every deep color of the rainbow. It looked painful and by the sounds he made as she stripped him of his shirt and pants, it was. Finally he was left in only his drawers, which were briefly cut unlike most which went to the knee. It was funny because she wore hers the same way, had made them special herself. Oh, she had long woolen drawers she wore in winter, but for every other time . . . it just seemed to make it more comfortable, easier to move. Clearly he felt the same way. It also meant there was very little left to the imagination. She was seeing him as good as naked—and what a fine sight it was. The man was big—not gigantic like Kyno, not even bulky really. But tall and oh so very muscular. It was obvious he swung a sword for a living. There wasn't a single stone of fat on him. He had to weigh in at about 175 rocks, maybe 190. She wasn't good at guessing. But it was all muscle. From the thickness of his thighs to the bulging of his upper arms, he was an incredible example of a man in his prime . . . except for all the fresh bruises. Damn it, what kind of idiot goes out spoiling for a fight? Between this and the story about the bard she wondered if he made a habit of beating up on people. Was he a bully? Or just a drunken idiot?

She opted for the latter. Kilon was the bullying sort; she didn't get that sense from Maxum. Of course it wouldn't be the first time she'd read a man all wrong. For instance, she hadn't thought he would engage in this kind of stupidity. He had struck her as a man who wanted to be in control of himself and his surroundings at all times. This simply didn't fit her picture of him.

Clearly she was reading him wrong.

Left with no other choice, she kicked off her boots and stripped off her vest. She hesitated, but then heard a soft, rumbly snore. Shrugging, she stripped off her pants and shirt. She unbound her breasts for the first time since the night before last when she'd had a bath in an obliging stream and sighed with relief. Then she quickly put her shirt back on, letting the tails cover her to the tops of her thighs. Hesitating only slightly she then climbed into bed beside him. She would wake up early tomorrow and be out of bed and dressed before he woke from his drunken slumber. She judiciously kept to the far side of the bed.

It wasn't long before she fell asleep.

Maxum, however, was very much awake when she did. He rolled over onto his side, bringing himself closer to her. He could feel the sheer heat radiating off her and he found it to be all too compelling.

When he had walked into the inn and seen her sitting there wide awake and waiting for him he'd quickly acted as though he were drunk and had been in a fight to explain his physical state. He hadn't expected her to be there and he cursed his companions for being the idiots they were and not providing her with a place to sleep in his absence. He would have at least thought Doisy would have been thoughtful enough to see to it, but knowing Doisy, he was no doubt sleeping comfortably in a woman's bed with his head nestled on her soft breasts.

And here he was, with a lovely pair of soft breasts nearby as well, and yet his head was a far, far cry from resting upon them.

He let his eyes travel over her in the darkness and wished she had not blown out the lantern before getting

in bed so that he could see her better. And yet he had
seen her well enough as he had feigned his sleeping state
and watched through slitted eyes as she had unbound
her beautiful breasts.

He hated that she restricted herself in such a way. To
what purpose? It was easy to tell she was a woman.
What did it matter if she showed her breasts in their
natural state? While they were in town he was determined to find her something else to wear, something
that enhanced her figure and yet protected her. What he
needed was to find an armorer who specialized in wom-
en's armor. Not an easy task to be sure, but being a port
of trade, Docking Bay was sure to have someone somewhere who could suit his needs.

He had the oddest craving to reach out and caress her,
but he was afraid of waking her. He suspected she had
learned to sleep with one eye open, being a woman alone
in the world.

He took in a slow breath, breathing in the warm scent
of her. She smelled of the outdoors and of the smoky inn
common room. The air had been heavy with the scent of
hot food and strong ale and she had carried it up with
her. He found he liked it. It was earthy and real—not
false and perfumed to cover the odors around her like
so-called refined women used.

He would have to be more careful in the future. She
was too observant and too sharp not to begin to question the state he would return in every night. He would
have to stay in a separate inn from the rest of the group.
His men had never questioned why he showed up bruised
and freshly washed every night; nor did they question it
when those bruises disappeared come the morning. They
knew something was different about him, but as long as
he continued to line their pockets with gold, they didn't
care.

The only one who potentially knew the truth of the

matter was Dru. He had been by each brother's side as they had worked through and survived their curses. He hadn't known the actual details, but anyone with enough skills of observation who worked that closely with his brothers was bound to figure things out. He suspected that was part of the reason the mage had asked to come with him when he had taken his leave of his brothers.

With a sigh Maxum closed his eyes.

He had a long and arduous journey ahead with many dangers in his path. The other men knew what they were getting into but did she? Was he wrong to risk her in such ways? And why should he be feeling so protective of her all of a sudden?

No. She was a tough little thief who had seen her share of hard things. She was making her own choices, and well . . . if she didn't know what she was getting herself into, she would very quickly find out.

Because very shortly he would be putting all of their lives on the line.

CHAPTER FIVE

The next morning Airi woke up pinned against a heated male body with an erection nudging into her backside . . . again.

She had to stop doing this. He was going to get the wrong idea and one of these mornings the arousal he felt in his sleep might very well carry into his waking state of mind.

Working slowly and gingerly, she extricated herself from his hold. When she was finally able to stand up, she quickly pulled her pants on. She took off her shirt and, standing bare-breasted, she reached for her binding cloth and began to wrap it around her body.

"Don't do that."

She yelped and covered her breasts with the cloth. She met his warm green-eyed regard.

"You were supposed to be asleep!" she said, as if she were accusing him of a crime.

"You woke me with all your wiggling and squirming."

"I was trying to get out of the bearish hug of your body. Don't you know how to keep to your side of the bed?"

"If it bothers you so much don't get into bed with me."

"I didn't have a choice!"

Maxum stood up and stretched and she could see his erection standing out proudly beneath his drawers. He didn't even try to conceal it. He reached for his pants and she wondered how he was going to stuff all of himself into the snug fabric of his breeches in that particular state.

She quickly forced herself to look away when she realized she was staring—and that he realized she was staring. She heard him chuckle and her face bloomed with heated color.

Oh, for the sake of the gods! She had been around men before, coarser men than he was. What was she being so missish for all of a sudden?

She hastily focused on binding her breasts.

"I said don't do that."

He grabbed the end of the cloth and with a snap yanked it out of her hands. She squeaked in dismay and immediately leapt for her shirt to cover herself . . . although he had certainly gotten a good look at her by now.

"Give that back!"

"No," he said mildly. "You're a woman. Everyone knows it. So why hide your breasts?"

"Because the bigger the breasts the less seriously a man takes you. I find the more boyish I look the more likely I am to be treated like an equal."

"But you aren't an equal. Every man knows that, whether they can see your breasts or not. Don't make yourself uncomfortable just to suit their comfort. Be what you are and be proud of it. That will be what gains you respect."

"We'll disagree on that. Now give it back."

"No."

With a single motion he tore the binding in two.

"Hey!" she cried in dismay.

"Put your shirt on. Your vest will hide what you're so

eager to conceal from everyone . . . for the time being. Today we'll shop for an alternative."

"I don't want an alternative. And I don't have the money to shop."

"I'll do the buying, you'll do the wearing. Consider it a gift."

"I'd much rather you gift me with a new pair of boots. That would be more useful."

"You'll be able to buy your own new boots soon enough. I'll gift you the way I want to gift you. Now shut up for a change and put on your shirt. Or I can stand here and stare at your bare breasts if you like. Perhaps I can open the door and the whole of the inn can stare." He moved toward the door and she yelped in alarm. She hastily donned her shirt, tucking it into her breeches, and then pulled on her vest. She tugged it tight and close, feeling naked without her bindings.

Maxum finished dressing in silence, then, just as he was reaching for the door, he turned to her and said, "Thank you for last night. For helping me." Mischief twinkled in his jade green eyes for an instant. "And for keeping me warm."

"Believe me, that was not intentional!" she said as she pushed past him out of the door.

"Come on. Admit it. You liked being naked with me."

"I wasn't naked with you. And don't you dare say that in front of anyone."

"Who am I going to say it in front of?" he asked innocently. "Oh, you mean Doisy? Good morning, Doisy."

Airi spun around and found herself nose to chest with Doisy, who was standing on the walkway. That was when she realized that the walkway leading to all the rooms was a balcony on one side that looked down on the inn common room. She could see people looking up at her with interest and she blushed with temper.

"You're an ass!" she declared before pushing past Doisy and making her way downstairs.

Doisy looked askance at Maxum. "I think she meant you. I haven't done anything to warrant that."

"Haven't you? You left her last night without a room. You all know she has no money."

Doisy looked chagrined. "Ah. I forgot. So sorry. I'll apologize to her later when she's not in such a fit. What'd you do to her?"

"Not a thing. And I wasn't naked with her. Or so she says."

Doisy chuckled. "Well, I won't hold it against her. Though I thought she had better taste."

"She does. It's not like that," he made certain to point out. "I'm just teasing her a little bit. Gets the juices flowing. Now come on. Let's eat a good meal. We have a ship to find. But I promised someone we'd go shopping first."

He rubbed his hands together in eager anticipation.

"I am *not* wearing this!" Airianne cried.

Maxum was holding the steel boned and leather corset in his hands and examining it with a discerning eye.

"Why not? It's perfect for you. The steel will protect you and it will bind you just the way you like."

"Partly. The whole top part of me will be spilling out of this thing!"

"You won't be spilling out. Just try it on. Wear this shirt underneath it." He handed her a soft, nearly sheer cotton shirt in black with a gathered ruffle along the neckline. "Do it or we'll be parting ways here and now."

Airi snatched up the shirt and corset with a grumble and disappeared behind a makeshift curtained area to change into the contraption. She put on the shirt first and then, wriggling her way into it, put on the corset, which tied in the front between her breasts.

Once she had it on she had to admit it did bind her breasts pretty snugly, but as predicted she swelled up over the top of it, though not as much as she had feared. The ruffles of the shirt covered her cleavage well enough, she supposed. She slowly came out from behind the curtain, tugging here and pulling there along the way self-consciously. But the minute she saw his eyes light up with what could only be described as genuine male appreciation, she instantly felt more comfortable. Which was funny because she usually tried to avoid garnering male appreciation. But from Maxum . . . she wasn't so bothered by it.

He took hold of her arm and guided her to a looking glass in the armory. Airi sucked in her breath, surprised at the image she saw there. Both the shirt and the corset leather was black so they set off the warmth of her skin. She looked exposed and confined all at the same time—and she looked tough. Like she was prepared for anything. The tooling of the hard leather was beautiful and graceful, but the corset was also practical. The leather and steel would protect her in a fight, slow down or glance off a blade that may come at her. She could see the usefulness of the garment.

"You see? It's perfect. You can look like you demand respect and like a woman at the same time," he said.

"Well . . ." She eyed herself a minute longer. "I'm not so sure people will take me seriously."

"I know I would," he said.

"You're just saying that."

"No. I'm not. I've taken you seriously from the start, even though you sat in my lap only minutes after meeting me."

She gaped at him. "I was distracting my mark!"

"So you say. Now come on. We need to get down to the docks."

"To catch a boat to Thiss?" she asked, hurrying to

scoop up her shirt as he tossed several coins to the armorer carelessly. The armorer scrambled to catch them, but when he saw the surplus, he broke out in a grin. Especially when Maxum left without asking for change. Appalled at the lavish way he spent money when she didn't even have two coppers to rub together, she hesitated, thinking of asking for the change and keeping it for herself.

But Maxum had breezed out of the shop and she had to scramble to catch up with him. He was a man on a mission it seemed and he wasn't in the mood to wait for her or anyone.

They were almost to the docks before she could say the corset was comfortable on her. It took some getting used to. It did restrict her breathing a little bit at first, but that took a simple loosening of the laces and then it was fine. She could say this much, she certainly was walking straighter!

She watched with no small amount of awe as Maxum confidently navigated the noisy, smelly docks. He occasionally drew someone aside and asked them a question, until at last he seemed to hone in on what he wanted. The fact was, no one at that dock was going to the Isle of Thiss. Everyone knew it was loaded with weredragons and that it was wisest to steer clear. But Maxum already seemed to know this and was looking for someone else. A certain kind of captain.

"There's Cap'n Arud's ship," a scrawny little lad said, his docksy accent heavy and his clothing worn lightly on his bony body. "Ee's goin' to Calandria and ee might stop alon' the way."

"Good lad," Maxum said, handing the boy a silver coin and cuffing him playfully. The boy's eyes went wide, no doubt because that silver piece could feed him and his family for a full week or more. Airi just shook her head. He had to be out of his mind. That was all she could think. She didn't care how lucrative their adventures were, spending money so frivolously was insane.

Before she knew it they were heading up the gangway of a mighty wooden ship. The deck was loud with shouting and full of thunderous activity as cargo was hoisted and carried aboard. The ship was readying to set sail and soon by the look of it. Maxum went up to the deckhand nearest him and asked for Captain Arud. The hand nodded to the foredeck where a man stood shouting orders and watching the goings-on on deck with an eagle eye. He was of middling height—about three and a half straps, maybe closer to four, unlike Maxum who was a little ways under four and a half straps and towered over just about everyone. The captain was made of coarse muscle and had weather-beaten skin on his hands and face, a ruddy sort of cracked condition that simply screamed toughness. Adding to that image was a weapons belt slung beneath a slight paunch that held a hefty stryker sword with its curved blade and not one but two sheathed stilettos. There was also some kind of pouch attached at the back and who knew what was kept inside of it. Another weapon perhaps?

"Captain Arud?" Maxum called over the din.

"That I am. Who're you?"

"A paying passenger is my hope. I need passage for a party of six."

"I don't take living cargo," the captain barked. "Be on your way."

"Surely you can be convinced to change your mind. For say, a gold sovereign per head?"

The captain did a double take and then eyed Maxum with a look that crossed between curiosity and suspicion.

"What's the catch?" he asked.

"You're headed to Calandria?"

"Aye, I am."

"Then just drop us off at the isle on the way."

"Thiss? You want me to take you to Thiss? Are you stark? No one of sound mind goes near that place, never mind docking up."

"Rumor has it you go to Thiss. That you have quite a lucrative trade going with the weredragons."

"Rumor is wrong," the captain snapped. "No one in their right mind goes to Thiss."

"No one said you were in your right mind," he countered. "There's several colonies on Thiss. They have to get their supplies from somewhere. No doubt there's a pretty penny in it for any captain willing to make the route. There'll be gold in it for you to do this as well. As I said, one sovereign per head just to take us where we both know you're going anyway."

"One way?" the captain asked.

"There'll be the same price per head if you wait a day and take us off the isle as well. One day and another gold per head. Surely you can manage that. It'll take you the better part of a day to offload your goods on Thiss anyway."

"I don't usually spend the night. Much rather sail in the dark than lurk around dragon waters for long."

"Two gold per head if you wait the full day. That includes horses. And we set sail an hour past juquil's hour tonight."

"What?" Airi cried incredulously. "*Two* gold?"

"Hush," Maxum said softly to her, never once taking his eyes off the captain. "Do we have a deal?"

The captain hesitated, seeming to think on it very seriously. "I'm not coming back to Docking Bay after Thiss. I'm heading on to Calandria."

"That's just fine," Maxum said.

"Very well." He eyed Airi. "Keep this one under control. I don't like women on board. Makes the men restless and stupid."

"I'll keep an eye on her," Maxum promised, hustling her away before she could work herself up into getting offended. "Come on," he said. "We have to fetch the men."

"I can't believe you negotiated a price like that! How am I ever supposed to pay you back three gold?"

"Don't worry about it."

"I am worried about it! Why are we even going to Thiss?"

"Someone there has something I need."

"Are you always going to be this evasive? Will I ever get a full answer out of you about anything?" she demanded.

"Probably not," he said honestly.

"Wonderful." She sighed and let him lead her back through the city to the inn where they had left the men and their horses.

All of the men except Kilon were there waiting. Maxum frowned when he saw Kilon was missing.

"Where is he?"

"He said he had some business to take care of," Doisy said with a grimace. He knew what was coming next.

"I told him to wait here!" Maxum snapped. "This is my party and we follow my instructions!"

"Tried to tell him that," Dru said. "Wouldn't listen."

"I've booked us passage to Thiss. Pack up and ready the horses. If he isn't here by the time we're ready he gets left behind."

"You heard the man, boys," Doisy said, jumping to his feet. "Let's be on our way!"

Suddenly unsure about her choices, Airi went to the stable and saddled up Hero, checking all of her bags and putting her shirt in one of them. She had already grown used to the way the corset felt, but she wasn't used to the way people were looking at her. Doisy raised a brow at her and Dru flushed when presented with the new view of her cleavage. But Kyno thought nothing of it, probably hadn't even noticed. She turned to Doisy, who was as well kempt as he was handsome.

"Do I look all right?" she asked.

"You look wonderful," he assured her.

"All right," she said, believing his enthusiasm. "But do you think it's smart to be so . . . so . . ."

"Bold?"

"Yes." She exhaled with relief. He understood her perfectly. "Bold."

"I think it's great. The trick to it though, is you have to believe in it. If you act like you're not to be trifled with, then no one will trifle with you. Got it?"

She nodded. She agreed with that much at least. And that's what she would do. She would own this new look and to the eight hells with anyone who tried to tell her different.

"So what do you think about this whole Isle of Thiss thing?" she asked him.

"I think that Maxum has made me very well-off so far and I think I would probably follow him anywhere, knowing it meant great rewards were in the offing."

"What exactly do you do in this group . . . besides bring a level of charm and companionability?" She grinned at him.

He grinned back. "As a cleric I am the male version of a mem. Some mems, as you know, have the gift of healing. I am actually a very powerful healer. I can help anyone who is injured, both in and out of battle."

"And the staff?"

"Even a man of the gods has to be able to defend himself."

"I suspect you can do more than just defend."

"Perhaps," he said with a sly smile. "But only to a point. We all have our limitations. I am not meant to be a great fighter. I am meant to look good and seduce women."

She laughed at him when he winked at her. "And seducing women is not contrary to your duties as a cleric?" she asked.

"Not at all. It is merely another form of healing. I make the woman I am with feel good—sometimes that is a form of healing in itself. All women need to feel beautiful and worthy. I try to bring that to them, even if it's only for a little while."

"I see," Airi said, still smiling at the roguish man.

"You know, you could always stay here in Docking Bay," he said suddenly. "Where we are going is very dangerous."

"I know it is. But you keep telling me that the rewards are worth putting my trust in Maxum's hands."

"Not your trust. Never your trust," Doisy said seriously. "Maxum has an agenda. Something is driving him. It isn't just power and glory for him. I think that, given a choice, Maxum would sacrifice anyone who got in the way of his goals. We're just along for the ride, plain and simple."

Doisy turned back to his horse, cinching his saddle, leaving Airianne to absorb that perspective for a minute.

She had to stop equivocating, she decided sternly. She had to make a choice and stick to her choice for all she was worth. Doubt wouldn't do her any good. But did she trust Maxum to know what he was doing?

She was pretty sure she did. Maxum was determined to get to Thiss. There was something there that he wanted, something he thought would only take him a day to retrieve. And she was pretty certain he would go after whatever it was alone if he had to. If anything, he needed his men to help protect him from himself. She could be a part of that. The question was, did she want to?

Well . . . yes. She had nowhere else to go, no obligations to anyone but herself. She had been alone in the world since she was eleven. She could and did take care of herself. And she didn't know why, but she was up for the idea of taking care of someone else for a while. Someone needed to look out for Maxum, and for some reason she felt it should be her.

Strange.

Maybe it was just because he'd been sort of nice to her, buying her something new to wear, putting a roof over her head.

Sure, he'd also been an ass, but it hadn't been anything she couldn't handle. No, this was the right thing to do, the right place for her to be. She was going to put herself into this venture with both feet and keep her eyes wide open.

Besides, everyone was kind of growing on her . . .

"Finally you are dressing the part."

There was no mistaking that nasty sneer of contempt. But Kilon's attempt to insult her had the opposite effect than he desired. She put back her shoulders and said, "Yes. Yes, I am."

"I meant the part of a whore," he said coldly. "Proud of that are you, slink?"

"I could be the cheapest whore in town . . . the hungriest . . . the neediest . . . and I still wouldn't fuck you if it meant saving my life or starving in the streets."

"Oh ho!" Doisy chortled.

She heard Dru chuckling back behind his horse somewhere. Kilon's face went hard, his eyes cold with anger as he went toe to toe with her, his unpleasant breath flowing with sour warmth over her face.

"When we get in trouble out there—and I can assure you that there's going to be trouble and plenty of it—when that happens and something is coming after you and the only thing between you and certain death is one of my arrows . . . I *am* going to fuck you. Be sure of it."

"Enough, Kilon," came the barking command from over Kilon's shoulder. "Where have you been?"

"Out," he said shortly.

"I said to wait here. So we wouldn't be held up waiting for you."

"I'm here now. No sense complaining about it when no one was inconvenienced."

"This time," Maxum said. "I won't let there be a next time. I'll leave your surly ass behind."

Kilon didn't say anything else. He just turned and walked over to his horse and began to saddle it. Maxum walked up to her and laid a hand on her shoulder.

"Everything all right?"

"It's fine," she said breezily. "Let's get going. I have a feeling I'm going to get to see my first weredragon."

"The idea is to avoid seeing one at all costs," he said. "One thing you don't want to do is to get in the way of a weredragon."

"I kind of figured that part out."

"All right, men. Let's go," Maxum said. "We push off just after juquil's hour, but I want us all packed aboard as soon as possible. Just in case the captain thinks about changing his mind."

They traveled back to the docks in relative silence and boarded the boat without any problems. It was a huge ship really, with two cabins set aside for their needs. One had two bunks in it and the other had only one. Airi sighed. It looked like she was going to be sharing a bunk with someone again tonight. She had a sneaking suspicion who that someone would be. If she were a paranoid person, she'd begin to think he was planning things like this.

Still she could always bed down with Doisy or Dru. Maybe if she worked it out early enough . . .

"So who's sleeping with whom?"

"Usually Kyno and Kilon bunk in together, leaving me

and Dru. But Dru will gladly sleep in Maxum's bed if it means gracing me with your lovely self," Doisy said, suddenly seeming far too interested. More interested than he had been previously.

It must be the corset, she thought with a sigh.

"I could always bed with Dru and you could sleep with Maxum," she said hopefully.

"Poor Dru wouldn't get a wink of sleep if you did that to him," Doisy said with a laugh.

"You're sleeping with me," Maxum said in a no-nonsense bark that put an end to the topic instantly. Doisy gave her an amused look that said he knew that was going to happen all along.

She sighed and threw her saddle bags under the single bunk.

She'd never been on a ship before. Had never been out in the open water. She had traveled all over the Black Continent, but she'd never crossed the bays or oceans.

She'd always wanted to. She'd dreamed of going to the Green Continent, with all its lush green lands and beautiful beaches at its southern tip . . . or at least that's what she'd heard it was like. That's the way it was described in bardsong. But she had always figured she would probably never make it there. It was a vast ocean away. The Red Continent was very close to the Black Continent, so it was far more likely she would travel there . . . if ever she was of a mind to go. But she had never been to Calandria either or Thiss and this was more than enough adventure for now.

She was nervous about going to Thiss. An island populated by weredragons. What was a place like that even like? All she knew was that it promised to be very dangerous. The idea of that kind of danger made her nervous . . . and excited. She felt amazingly alive all of a sudden. She couldn't explain it. All she knew was that fortune waited for her and she was on her way to greet it. Maybe, if this was really as lucrative as Doisy was anticipating, maybe she could retire somewhere, give up thieving. For her thieving was only a means to an end. It was all about survival. She took only from those who could afford to lose and she took only enough to keep herself and Hero alive and moderately comfortable—if you could call camping out under the stars living in comfort. Which she did. She liked living out in the open. Except when the cold came. And when it came on the Black Continent, it came hard.

Maxum was out on deck, looking toward the blue sun as it crept lower in the sky. She watched him for a while, wondering why he had chosen to set sail an hour past juquil's hour. It seemed a strange time. But she imagined he wouldn't take to being questioned about that any more than he took to being questioned about anything else. She just had to resign herself to being kept half in the dark.

Or at least she had to *try* to resign herself to it. She wasn't sure how much success she was going to have with it.

They all went ashore for something to eat, but then Maxum sent them back to the ship without him. The sun set while they waited for him . . . and waited . . . and waited. The men seemed completely unconcerned, leading her to believe they didn't find his behavior strange at all. Apparently he was prone to disappearing for hours at a time without any explanation. All she could do was hope he would be in better shape when he showed up this time.

One odd thing she had taken note of outside of his behavior was his bruising. The marks had been there that morning, although not as vivid as she had expected, but he had healed remarkably from them by the mid afternoon. To the point where she could hardly see a sign of them.

Doisy. Doisy must have healed him, she realized. That impressed her. She didn't know clerics could heal so completely. The mems she had known who were healers had always been able to aid in the more rapid healing of an injury, keeping it from getting infected and the like, but not healing to the point of near perfection. It made her realize what a powerful asset the cleric was to a group of men bent on danger.

She could only hope she would not be needing to avail herself of his services any time soon.

But she was glad he was there all the same.

CHAPTER SIX

Maxum rode Killu, his russet stallion, to a secluded place well outside the city walls as the sun set in earnest. He walked a safe distance away from his horse and quickly stripped down to his skin. He had picked this spot the night before because there was a stream running not too far away from it, allowing him a place to wash up when it was all said and done.

But tonight would be different, he thought firmly. He looked down at the talisman in his hand. He'd had a chain attached to it just a little while ago and now he dropped it over his head. Had he had the opportunity to attach the chain sooner, he would have tried this the night before. But as it stood . . .

He didn't know what was going to happen. The talisman was supposed to make the wearer invulnerable. Was it true? Would it work? And if it did work, would it negate any of the curse he suffered?

He was about to find out.

It started as a rumble, then became a quaking of the ground beneath him. The ground beneath his feet rocked and began to churn and froth up until it covered his ankles. Then, the ground split open, yawning beneath him until there was no way he could remain on his feet. Every night he tried to resign himself to the inevitable, tried to tell himself that fighting was useless. And yet, like every night before, he struggled to maintain a grasp on solid ground. But that solid ground gave way and then he was falling into the gaping maw of soil and rock.

Almost immediately the ground closed around him, crushing him from all sides, pushing into his nose and gritting up his eyes.

But tonight something was different. Oh, he was suffocating just as he did every night, the pressure nearly unbearable, but tonight his bones did not crack under the force of it, his skeleton was not pulverized and his skin was not bruised.

The talisman was working! It didn't change the meat of the curse, but at least now he could not be physically damaged by it. It made his heart soar with hope in spite of the driving pain and crushing suffocation he still suffered. This told him that not only did the talisman protect him from harm, but it had the power to alter the will of a god. And if this were possible with one item, then there had to be others—things that could thwart the power of a god.

It meant that gods were not the all-powerful beings men mistook them for. It meant they were vulnerable.

He had suspected this already because on the day he and his brothers had gained their immortality the gods had said they did not have the power to take their immortality away from them, but they could make them rue ever having wanted it in the first place. They had been true to their word. However, if they were gods then why couldn't they take the immortality away just as easily as it was given? It told him they were not all-powerful, that not everything was within their reach and ability.

This was the hope that held him through the endless suffering and suffocation that was his curse. This was what led him to believe his goal was not an unattainable one. For if a god could be vulnerable, then a god could be killed by a man. His years as a mercenary had taught him this. All enemies could be defeated; it was a matter of finding their weakest point and applying pressure to it.

This was a beginning. The beginning that he needed.

The beginning of the end of Sabo.

The captain was readying to set sail and Maxum was not yet on board.

"You have to wait!" Airi implored him.

"He said an hour past juquil's hour and it's that and more. I'll not tarry another minute. There are people waiting for this cargo and I've delayed long enough for your boss."

"If you want to get paid you'll wait," Doisy said mildly.

"I've already been paid for the first leg. If you don't want to find yourselves stranded on Thiss you'll pay me then for the second leg. Don't make no difference to me if your boss is here or not."

"It's two gold per head to take us off Thiss. You'll be out two gold," Airi pointed out.

This made the captain hesitate.

"He's got ten minutes more. No longer."

"No need. There he is, Airi!" Doisy said pointing down to the dock.

Sure enough there was Maxum, swinging down out of his saddle and leading his horse to the gangplank. He walked the animal aboard and, without a word to anyone, led the horse down belowdecks into the cargo hold. He came up shortly after.

"Ready to go, Captain?"

"We was just waiting on you," the captain said a bit churlishly. Then he began shouting orders down to his men on the docks, pulling up lines and preparing the sails to get under way.

Airi turned to Maxum with an inquisitive brow.

"You almost found yourself left behind," she pointed out.

"Almost," he said. "But not quite. Would you have missed me?"

"Of course! I didn't relish the idea of finding myself stranded on Thiss since you have all the gold!"

"Doisy has plenty enough gold. He wouldn't have let you get stranded."

"That's not the point!"

"Then what is the point?"

"Where were you?"

"I don't have to answer that. I do not answer to any man . . . or woman. If I wanted to answer to a woman I'd get myself a wife."

Frustration boiled up inside of her. "Would it kill you to answer a question?"

"It might," he said mildly. "So best not to answer just in case."

"You're a real bastard, you know that?" she said with a huff. Then she turned and walked away from him, her back burning because she knew—just *knew*—he was staring at her backside as she walked away.

Fine. Let him be a jerk. But she wouldn't stop questioning him just because he thought she should just shut up and obey. She'd been taking care of herself too long to let a man like Maxum walk all over her.

She spent the next hour on the top deck, her face in the wind, the smell of the ocean in her nose. The ship rolled softly beneath her feet, making her roll with it. She was tired and should really go down below and get some sleep, but she wasn't looking forward to getting into bed with Maxum again. It was far too risky a proposition. She knew very well that there was a sexual undertone in their dealings with one another. There had been from the very instant she had laid eyes on him and sat in his lap. He had kissed her then with a great deal of heat and need and it had been honest and stark. And her response, while she'd liked to think it had been an act to get him to drop his guard so she could pick his pocket, had been just as stark. The man knew how to kiss, there was no denying that. It was a dangerous set of circumstances. It would be better if she felt no attraction toward him.

She could control this, she told herself sternly. She wasn't the sort to let her desires rule her head. There was too much danger of ramifications. She could barely take care of herself and Hero ... she didn't need to add a potential baby to the mix. For that reason she'd only had one lover in her life. It had been when she'd been young and foolish and she'd been damn lucky nothing had come of it. Well, she was neither young nor foolish any longer.

She could control this situation. She could.

She turned her back on the darkness of the ocean and made her way belowdecks. She staggered down the gangway, her legs not used to functioning aboard a ship. She reached the door to their cabin and opened it just as the ship rolled hard. She was flung off her feet and into the bunk with a slam, her body hitting a wall of solid muscle, an answering grunt in her ear.

"No need to throw yourself at me," a rich voice rumbled in her ear, "I'm more than happy to oblige you at any time."

She squirmed around in his hold, meeting his eyes in the near complete darkness, the only light a small candle melting on the ledge nearby.

"I'd rather drown," she oozed out acidly.

"Really?" He regarded her for a long moment, his hands coming to rest on her back, their fronts still mashed together. She tried to leverage some space between them but the bunk was small and he wasn't budging on his own. In fact it was quite the opposite. He was holding her very tightly. So tightly she could feel the presence of something solid beneath his shirt, hanging around his neck. Unless she missed her guess by the shape and size of it, it was the talisman she had stolen. He'd had a chain made for it? What was so damn special about that talisman? It was actually quite ugly for all its gems. And he hadn't struck her as the sort to wear jewelry anyway.

"I seem to recall waking up with you in my bed not once but twice in as many days."

"You stole my pants the first night! And you were drunk the second! Anyway in both cases I had nowhere else to go." She frowned. "Will you let me go?"

"I like you right here," he said, his tone dropping a notch. A shiver skipped its way down her spine. "Cold?" he asked.

She couldn't say no. He'd know he was getting to her and that absolutely could not happen.

"Freezing," she lied.

"Then it's a good thing we're bunking together. I'll keep you warm." His palm drifted down the length of her side until it was perched on her hip. Heat blossomed under her skin wherever he touched her and she shivered again.

Feeling her small body tremble just about did Maxum in. He knew she wasn't cold. Knew she was responding to his touch . . . though she'd rather die than admit it. Well, he would just have to make her admit it. Make her realize they could provide more than a little comfort to each other while they had nothing better to do. And the truth was, he'd been hard for her ever since she'd sat in his lap back at that tavern. He was hard for her now, feeling her compact, lithe little body tucked against him. He could feel the steel stays of the corset and the rigid line of it against his chest. Her breasts, swelling above the top of it, glowed pale in the wan candlelight.

"Come and be comfortable. It's a long night of voyaging before we reach Thiss." He reached to trace a lone finger along the top edge of her corset, through the ruffle of the shirt beneath it. "It may be practical, but it isn't comfortable to sleep in."

"I am not getting undressed with you. Now let me go!"

"You're being stubborn," he said, reaching to twirl a finger around the bow of the laces that keep the corset tightly in place. "Just take the corset off. Leave the shirt on."

She was still for a long moment then with a sigh she pushed herself out of his arms and sat up on the edge of the bunk. She pulled the laces and slowly put slack into them, finally making it possible to pull the corset off over her head. She dropped it to the floor and he heard her exhale with relief.

"That's tighter than I realized," she said.

"No different than binding."

"A little different. Bindings are softer."

"True."

"But I wouldn't trade back," she said almost shyly.

"Good. I'm glad you like my gift."

"It's not a gift," she said sternly. "I'm going to pay you back for it as soon as I am able."

"It's a gift," he said firmly. "It wasn't anything you thought you needed and you wouldn't have chosen to spend your money that way. So a gift. One I was very happy to give."

"Well . . . then I guess I should thank you."

"I guess you should," he said with a low chuckle.

"Well . . . thank you."

"You are welcome. Now come into bed."

"Just so we are clear," she said, her tone going stern

again, "this is just for sleeping. I am not going to make love with you."

"Oh, it would be far too hot and dirty to be called making love," he said wickedly. She stiffened and he laughed at her. "Come and lay down. Nothing will happen that you don't want to happen."

She eyed him warily for a good long minute, then she turned her back to him and stiffly lay down in the bed beside him. He chuckled.

"You need to relax," he said, his hand drifting whispery fingers down her neck and the yoke of her shoulder.

"Stop touching me," she said, shooing him away with a flutter of her hand.

"It's a small bunk. We're going to have to touch."

He wrapped an arm around her waist and jerked her body back against his. His chest was to her back and her bottom was pressed against his erection. She squeaked when she felt it and realized what it was. He was unapologetic about it too, pressing his hips against her in a slow roll of movement.

"Stop! I'm going to sleep on deck!" She tried to leave the bed but he jerked her right back down.

"You heard the captain. I'm to keep an eye on you. And a woman alone on a ship full of coarse men is a recipe for disaster. You're safer with me."

"Somehow I doubt that," she said, squirming around until they were facing each other, her backside no longer intimately settled.

There. That was better, she thought.

Until she looked up into his shadowy green eyes and saw the blatant hunger there. His eyes roamed her face and form slowly, almost to the point that it felt like an actual physical caress. It was dangerous, the heat she saw there.

"Maybe I could sleep on the floor," she whispered.

"You could. But why do that when the bed is right here?"

"Because it would be safer."

"Safer?"

"The way you're looking at me isn't safe. Not for me, anyway."

"How am I looking at you?"

"Like you want to eat me alive," she said softly.

"Oh, I do. I want to dine on every single inch of you," he said huskily a second before he caught up her mouth with his.

She meant to resist him. She really did. She meant to reject him and push him away and sleep on the floor in safety.

But the moment his mouth touched hers she melted into a puddle of compliancy. She let him draw her back up against his body, her breasts pillowing against his hard, broad chest, her fingers curling into the fabric of his shirt at his back. When had she put her arm around him? She didn't know and, for a moment, she didn't care. All she could feel was the muscular warmth of him connecting with her from head to toe . . . and the strong voyage of his lips against hers as he explored her suddenly willing mouth.

He tasted incredibly good . . . like anise, a darkly sinister sweetness. His tongue delved and dipped into her mouth and she helplessly dueled with it, loving the decadent feel of it filling her taste buds and senses with masculine confidence. He knew how to kiss a woman until she shimmered like jelly in his hands, turning sweet and sticky and easily devoured. She should be wary of the practiced ease he used, but she couldn't seem to remember why.

His hand crept up her rib cage, leaving a trail of heat in its wake, and then suddenly closed over the weight of her breast. He shaped her lovingly, his thumb coasting ever so lightly across her nipple until it hardened and poked out eagerly for his next caress. She burned for his next caress. Yearned to feel his lips on her. Her back arched up in invitation as she broke from his mouth and gasped for breath. Keenly understanding her need, his fingers curled into the ruffled edge of her shirt and pulled it down until the whole of her left breast was exposed to the cool air. She felt the abrasion of his whiskery face as he nuzzled her. He had shaved that morning, but already his whiskers were growing in enough to be felt.

Then his mouth opened against her and he sucked her nipple strongly into it. He groaned low in his chest and she gasped aloud. She arched against him, pressing herself into the biting caresses he offered. He sucked and nibbled, drew and toyed, all the while sending heat plummeting down through her body again and again until she was soft and wet and wanting.

Her right hand found its way into his hair, holding him to herself even as her left hung on to his shirt for dear life . . . as if she would let go and suddenly lose anchor on the whole of the world.

Maxum growled low in his throat as he tasted her, as the hardness of her nipple rolled against the play of his tongue. She was beyond sweet. A sultry combination of sweet and erotic and he was burning with the need for more. More than just a taste of her. He wanted it all. Wanted every flavor she had to offer him. He filled his hands with her, stroking her everywhere he could reach, feeling the wantonness of her surrender to him and feeling the sudden weight of the responsibility to her. He had to make her feel pleasure. Whatever he did, he had to see to that most of all. He would not cheat her with a hurried, cheap coupling. She was worth far more than that. She was worth more than a tumble in the cramped bunk of a cramped cabin.

He lifted his mouth from her skin, groaning at the loss of her flavor on his tongue.

What are you doing? he asked himself a moment before words left his mouth.

"Not here. Not like this," he said hoarsely.

"Wh-what?" Her voice trembled.

"When I have you—and I *will* have you—I want it to be in a bed big enough to move in. Big enough to roll you this way and that way and any way I want to have you." He paused to give her nipple a longing lick. "And I want you to come to me willingly and knowingly. Fully aware and not just lost in the moment. Do you understand?"

"N-no," she said with clear confusion.

"You will," he said, pulling up her shirt and covering her breast. "Now turn over and go to sleep."

He helped her to do just that, knowing her movements were automatic, that it hadn't quite sunk in what he was saying and doing. He knew the moment that it did because she went suddenly stiff in his arms.

"I won't," she said.

"You will," he countered. "And you will enjoy every minute of it."

She didn't have a reply so he closed his eyes and tried to calm his overheated body enough to go to sleep. It was a very long time coming, and she fell asleep long before he did. But at last he relaxed and let the dreams take him. Dreams of earth swallowing him and suffocating him were abandoned and in their stead were dreams of a soft, willing woman.

CHAPTER
SEVEN

By midmorning the Isle of Thiss was looming off the side of the ship. In the air they could see mist-shrouded buttes and the occasional large body flying through that mist.

Dragons.

Airi felt anxiety, a cross of fear and excitement, clenching in her belly. It was strong enough to quell her confused feelings about what had happened the night before in the cabin bunk.

She was grateful, of course, that it hadn't gone any further than it had. She would have regretted it come the morning.

Or at least she thought she would have. She should have. She should be regretting what had happened, but every time she tried she remembered the fiery feel of his mouth on her skin and she flushed with heat anew. She feared that now all he had to do was ask and she would willingly give herself to him in the way he had said he wanted her. At his leisure. At her free will.

She put aside those thoughts and concentrated on the ship as it came up to the dock. The dock was abandoned it seemed, but there was what appeared to be a small village nearby.

As soon as the plank was lowered to the dock, the group was leading their horses off the ship.

"We leave at dawn," the captain warned them.

"You'll leave an hour past juquil's hour tomorrow night," Maxum said.

"You said one day," the captain reminded him.

"Very well . . . an hour past juquil's hour tonight and then straight on to Calandria as fast as your sails can take us. We'll need to land there by sunset tomorrow."

"We should make that easy, provided you are on time."

"We will be. You had better be here and ready to go."

"I'm a man of my word," the captain said, looking affronted.

"So you weren't about to leave me behind last night?" Maxum countered.

The captain just grunted in response. "Be sure you're here!" he barked.

Maxum simply nodded and kneed his horse down the dock. The group followed him and as soon as they were on land he headed for the village.

Once there, Maxum pulled up to a young boy. Airi wondered if these people were weredragons. They looked normal enough to her. Did weredragons live in villages like this?

"I am looking for Lujo," Maxum said. "Do you know where his lair is?"

"Everyone knows that. He's the king of the weres. His lair is up there." The boy pointed to the nearest butte. "It's the only lair on the butte. But he doesn't like visitors."

"He'll like us," Maxum said assuredly. The boy just shrugged and went on his way. Maxum went straight for the road that appeared to lead to the butte he wanted. They all followed him. The going was easy and fast, the butte not very steep nor very high. The road ended, however, at the base of it, leaving them to pick their way up the rocky shale, which slowed them down considerably.

But Maxum pushed them hard.

"Daylight's wasting and we have to be down off this butte by sunset."

"Why sunset? I thought we had until juquil's hour at least," Airi said.

"Those are my orders," he said shortly.

It had taken the better part of an hour just to get to the foot of the butte. He would need that time after his curse was over to make it back to the ship at least. That left no time for bathing and he didn't care. Let them see him covered in dirt. All he cared about was getting what he needed to defeat Sabo. If it meant revealing his curse he would do so but not unless it was absolutely necessary.

They reached an impasse about an hour later. The angle was too steep for horses and they would need to climb the rest of the way up on foot. It was slow going and the blue sun burned in the sky, beating down on them, heating the rock beneath their hands. They were almost to the top when she took a moment to look around herself. The view was dizzying and breathtaking. Airianne could see the whole of the island. It was a contrast between the white beach, the forest treetops that skirted it to the base of the buttes and then the red and gray stone of the buttes themselves. From her perch she could see those large bodies circling the buttes better.

Dragons! Enormous dragons! She had never seen anything like it. They were still a good distance away, but she could tell just how large they were. And unless her eyes were deceiving her, they were glittering in the afternoon sunlight.

She suddenly felt very exposed on that cliff face. What if one of them should see them and decide to investigate? Didn't dragons eat people?

No. If that were true then there wouldn't be a colony of people on the island. Would there? Then again, it was a beautiful island, full of trees lush with fruits—it would make for a perfect paradise and easy living. But was it worth having dragons in your backyard?

"We should hurry," she said nervously. She didn't want to find out the answer to her question the hard way. "What's the plan once we find this Lujo?"

"Actually, the idea is not to find him," Maxum said as he hoisted himself up onto a ledge. He reached down a hand to her and pulled her up beside himself. "Trust me, you don't want to meet a dragon face-to-face. And were-dragons are the worst. They live in the world of men part of the time so they know just how untrustworthy we are."

"Not all men are untrustworthy," she said.

"So says the thief," he quipped.

She flushed. He had a point.

"If you don't want to see this dragon, why are we heading right into his lair?"

"Because in his lair is something I want very badly and I'm going to get it."

"You're going to *steal* from a *dragon*?"

"Not me. *Us.*" He turned to the other men once they had reached the ledge as well. Doisy dusted off his hands and Kilon looked out of breath. So it seemed the only thing he exercised regularly was his bow arm and his bad temper. Airi chuckled to herself at her own wit. But her amusement didn't last long because the import of Maxum's plan was settling in cold and hard.

The man was absolutely insane.

"And what are we supposed to do if he's there?" she asked heatedly.

"We wait and hope he leaves with enough time to get us to the foot of this mountain by sunset."

"You're out of your mind," she whispered harshly, afraid to raise her voice.

"Come on. We'll skirt around to the mouth of his lair from this side," Maxum said to the men who looked very ready to follow him anywhere.

"Doesn't this bother any of you?" she asked.

"There's no reward without great risk," Doisy said philosophically.

"Just shut your hole and get with the fucking game. Or go back to the ship and do your whining there," Kilon snapped.

She bristled and would have set him down, but it was neither the time nor place. So, unfortunately, she had to do as he said. Shut up and go with them. Leaving wasn't an option for her. She needed to get some money so she could support herself again, and she wasn't going to get it by playing it safe. And remaining dependent on Maxum just wasn't an option. He'd already given her far too much, far more than she deserved. She needed the means to leave as soon as possible. Last night had been too close. Much too close. If she stayed with him too much longer she might find herself doing something really foolish. Even now, as she watched him pick his way along the ledge, she found it hard to take her eyes off his tall and powerful body. He moved with a certain amount of grace, surprising for a man of his size. And confidence. He was walking into the danger of the situation as if he wasn't afraid at all. She had to admit, there was something very stimulating about that.

And stimulating was bad. Very bad. She needed to keep her head on straight and her pants on if she was going to make her way safely through the world.

Maxum suddenly stopped, flattened himself to the cliff side, and waved to the others to do the same. Then he looked around the corner of stone he was pressed up against. He pulled back then gestured for Airi to come forward. The ledge was a bit narrow, so it was a balancing act to get past Kilon and Doisy. Rubbing up against Kilon and getting a full-fledged breath of his poor bathing habits was something she could have done without.

When she reached Maxum, he took her hand and stepped forward around the corner, signaling the others to stay behind. As they rounded the corner they stepped into the mouth of a huge cave. It was enormous, towering above and around her like a great citadel. Only the cave wasn't open as she might expect. It was closed off by a wooden wall. The wall nearly ran the entire mouth of the cave from all corners, and the cave's mouth had been clawed out to fit the square of it perfectly. The only gap was at the very top of the wall . . . it didn't quite meet the top of the opening. She could see a series of pulleys and metal tracks. Her keen eyes took in every detail and she began to understand what she was seeing.

The door was weighted so that someone could pull on the bottom of it and it would lift easily and glide back into the roof of the cave beyond. It was a clever series of mechanisms that allowed for the mouth of the cave to be fully open when the dragon was in residence or closed and locked when he was away. And that was exactly what it was . . . closed and locked. And the lock was an iron inset lock with what promised to be a tricky set of tumblers and probably a surprise or two along the way. Oh, this dragon was smart—and very intent on keeping others out of his cave.

Though . . . how that lock sang to her. She checked the sky for only the briefest moment before moving forward to get a good look at it. The keyhole opening was about the size of a man and she peered inside of it. All around the keyhole were smaller holes peppering the metal, giving it a pockmarked appearance.

"Can you do it?" Maxum asked.

Maxum watched impatiently as she didn't answer him

and instead studied the lock carefully. He didn't want to rush her, but there was no telling when the dragon would return, and he didn't want to be there when it did.

"Can you?" he asked again as she mumbled to herself under her breath and touched the outer edges of the lock.

"I'll need your sword," she said finally, holding out her hand to him.

Maxum hesitated. But only for a second. It wasn't likely she could damage it, but it was going to be key in his fight against Sabo.

He drew the sword and handed it to her. Whatever she was planning to do, it had to be worth the risk for the reward.

She slowly, gingerly, slid the sword into the keyhole. As she worked, he watched her face. She bit her lip, no doubt without realizing it, and a strand of hair had escaped her braid and hung in a crooked wisp over her forehead. She pursed her lips and blew air upward, moving the strand out of her eyes. After about ten minutes of working at the lock, she began to perspire, little drops of salty water beading on her lip and forehead. He didn't know if it was because of the heat beating down on them or because she was anxious about her struggle with the lock. He imagined it was a combination of both.

There was a click and she exhaled in relief, but she didn't withdraw from the lock.

"Trap," she said in explanation.

She had disarmed a device that had been set into the lock. He hadn't even thought about traps. He dreaded to know the kind of a trap a dragon would use against human interlopers. No doubt it was something very extreme.

After another minute of her working the sword around in the lock there was a much louder click and the whole door seemed to loosen up.

"Done!" she cried triumphantly.

"Amazing!" Maxum laughed, scooping her up against his body and hugging her tight. She hugged him back enthusiastically . . . then they both lingered a moment too long. He drew back to look at her and was overwhelmed with the urge to kiss her. But now was not the time or the place. They were exposed and in danger and he wouldn't risk her any more than he already had.

She stepped out of his embrace, smoothing her straggling hair back unsuccessfully. Two rose-colored stains appeared on her cheeks.

"How do you plan to open the door? It's huge! You'll never be able to manage that much weight. Not even with all of us combined. It's weighted to glide open of course, but only after it is raised to a certain point."

"I don't have to open it all the way. Just enough for us to get in and get out." He turned and gestured to the men who still waited around the corner. Then, once they were all grouped together, they grabbed the handle of the door and pulled as hard as they could. The door budged just a little bit, but it was enough to create a gap between the floor of the cave and the door. Big enough for a man to wriggle in through.

One at a time they did just that, working their way into the torchlit cavern.

"Uh oh," Airi said.

"What?" Dru asked nervously. "Don't say uh oh when we're standing in the middle of a dragon's lair."

"The dragon left torches burning," she pointed out. "That could mean he wasn't planning on being gone for very long. It certainly means he hasn't been gone for more than a few hours."

"Oh," Dru said sheepishly. "Sorry."

"No. You're nervous. So am I," she said with understanding.

They took in the surroundings slowly . . . and with awe.

The center of the cave was piled high with a nest of shining, glittering objects. Everything from precious gems and golden coins to suits of armor and decorative shields. It was beautiful and priceless, but all Airi kept wondering was whether or not those suits of armor were empty—or if they had been emptied like a clam being shucked of its shell only to have the insides slurped down in one gulp.

She slowly walked up to the edge of the mass of coins and picked one up. It was gold, but she had never seen its make or stamping before. That told her it came from a land she had never been to; somewhere far away but easily reached by dragon wings. In that moment she envied the weredragon. Being so big meant he had few enemies to fear and with such massive wings the world was no doubt a much smaller place for them. They need not use horses or ships, they could just fly wherever they wished. Whenever they wished. At a moment's desire they could fly to the Red Continent from here and be there in time for supper.

Thinking of the dragon dining snapped her out of her longings and she became aware of the men shoveling gold and gems into their pouches and pockets. Well, Kyno and Doisy and Kilon were. Dru was being more discerning, peering at each gemstone in the torchlight before stuffing it into a small leather pouch tied to his belt. She realized he had limited space for treasure, so he was going to make the most of it.

She caught sight of Maxum hurrying around the bulk of the hoard and she hesitated, torn between getting treasure for herself and following him. Where was he going? They had all they could carry right here. There was no need to go farther in.

She hastily grabbed up a fistful of coins and gems and

stuffed it into her pocket before she took off after Maxum. She wasn't going to go through all of this with nothing to show for it, but Maxum was up to something and she was going to find out what.

It didn't take her long to catch up with him because he had come to a stop somewhere on the opposite side of the hoard at the back of the cave. He was staring at something, and she followed his gaze. There, suspended in midair, lit by torchlight, was a small shiny object spinning around and around. It was a ring, she realized. About the shape of a coin, clearly meant to be worn by a man. It would have fallen right off even her thickest finger.

Maxum reached out, but she grabbed his arm and stopped him.

"Maxum! It's suspended there by magic! You can bet it's protected by magic as well!"

"Then you better step back," he said firmly.

"Are you insane? Maxum, you can't—"

"Step. Back." His tone was low and measured and very dangerous. He wouldn't tolerate her interference. There was clearly nothing more she could do.

She stepped back several feet. Then she watched in horror as he reached out for the ring.

The minute he breeched the outer bubble of the magic holding the ring a sudden storm of lightning exploded around Maxum. She screamed as he was picked up by it, lashed hard by it, turned and twisted about by it. But all the while she could see him fighting it, saw him reaching and reaching . . . until his hand closed around the ring. The minute he had hold of it the lightning stopped and he fell to the floor hard. Heedlessly Airianne rushed up to him, kneeling at his head and driving her hands into his hair to force his face around to hers.

He opened his eyes and smiled.

"Got it," he said.

"Oh!" He wasn't hurt at all! There were burn and scorch marks all over his clothes and the hard leather of his armor, but he barely had a smudge of dirt on him after that tortuous attack. "Damn you, Maxum! You aged me a year and a day!"

"Sorry," he said with an unrepentant grin. Then he leaned in and gave her a quick kiss before leaping to his feet and saying, "Let's get out of here."

She had no choice but to follow him as he hurried around the mound of sparkling coin. She realized then that the ring had been his sole purpose for coming there. Why he had chosen to raid this particular dragon's lair. The others might think he was leading them to reward and riches, but Airi saw someone who was reckless and dangerous, who was willing to risk everything to get what he wanted . . . including the lives of his men.

"Let's go, boys!" he called out as he came around to the front of the hoard.

"But my pouch isn't full," Dru complained.

"Dally here much longer and that pouch will be cut away with the top half of your body when the dragon comes calling. I have a feeling we've rung an alarm bell. Let's go!"

Dru grabbed a wild handful of coins and stuffed them into his pouch, then all of the men hurried back toward the door, the sound of coins falling from overstuffed pockets tinkling as they hit the ground.

They had just wriggled out from under the door when they heard the first roar. It was a cross between the roar of an enormous kika bear and the thunderous screech of a giant jollo jola bird.

It was the roar of a dragon. A very angry dragon.

They ran toward the ledge but suddenly Maxum stopped.

"We'll be exposed on the cliff side. He'll pick us off

like cherries on a tree. We have to face him here on strong ground."

"Face him? Face a dragon?" Dru cried. "Are you mad?"

"He's coming. Kyno, you, me, and Kilon take the front. Doisy, you and Dru fall back with Airi. Don't engage unless you have to."

"You plan to take on a dragon? Just the three of you? That's insane!" Airi cried.

"No more or less so than coming up here in the first place," Maxum said with a shrug.

"There has to be a better way!"

"I'm open to suggestions," he said as he drew his sword.

Airi cast about for a solution.

"Dru! You're a spirit mage! You can make people see things that aren't there!"

"Yes, but—"

"Can you make someone not see something that is there?"

"You mean make us invisible? I-I-I don't think I can do that."

"Have you ever tried? It's not really making us invisible, it's making the dragon not perceive our true location."

"I don't know. I could try."

"Get ready to fight. Dru . . . do your best!" Maxum said.

Dru, shaking so hard she could hear his teeth rattling, closed his eyes and tried to focus. Airi came up to him and reached a calming hand out to touch him on the back of the neck, petting him softly . . . soothingly.

Then suddenly there was a mighty roar right on top of them and they all shrank back against the ledge wall. The dragon, a huge iridescent scaled beast that appeared mostly blue in color, landed on the ledge of the butte. It was an enormous beast, overshadowing the small people just off to its right. It had massive golden scales that reached all the way up its legs to the underside of its belly. The dragon glittered and gleamed and she realized it was because there were gems and coins caught between its scales from the lining of its hoarded nest. As it slept on its bed the gems must've worked their way beneath the scales and there they stayed.

The dragon's wings splayed out in the sun, the sunlight backlighting the membranes of the wings and showing the blood vessels within. Each wing had three sections to it and each section was tipped with a claw.

The dragon roared, its heavy head swinging back and forth, its large eye, a russet color, scanning back and forth. Looking for the intruders that had invaded its nest.

It looked right at the small group and everyone tensed in readiness.

Then it looked away, moving forward, each heavy footstep sending a tremor through the rock beneath their feet. It went to its door and with a clawed foot it swung open the massive door, sending the weights dropping and the door gliding back into the roof of the cave. It lumbered into the cave, a heavy but graceful creature and every movement seemed to ripple along its outer skin.

"It worked!" Airi said. "Good for you, Dru!"

"Shh. I can trick its sight but maybe not its hearing," he whispered fiercely. "And I don't know how much longer I can do this so we better go!"

Everyone agreed and with haste they began to pick their way down the face of the butte. They reached the horses about an hour before sunset and then hastened to make it to the tree line. They felt a massive shadow run over them and knew the dragon was flying overhead in search of the thieves that had stolen from him. They had just reached the tree line only minutes before sunset.

"Go on without me!" Maxum called to them. "There's something I need to do!"

"What could you possibly—?"

"Don't argue with me, Airi. Just go back to the ship. I'll be there at the appointed hour. Do not follow me. Understood?"

Airi burned with temper, but what choice did she have? They had to get out of sight before the dragon came looking for them again. Who knew how much longer Dru's magic would work? But if Maxum went off on his own without Dru, he would not be protected by his magic.

"But what if the dragon finds you?" she demanded of him.

"He won't."

With that he took the ring he had stolen and slipped it onto his finger. In an instant he disappeared from sight. Airi gasped and Doisy said, "Fuck me!"

"Maybe later," came Maxum's disembodied voice. "Now go. I'll be there on time."

They had no choice but to go. Maxum's empty-saddled horse was kicked into a gallop and hastened away into the woods.

Shortly after there was a mighty rumble that trembled through the ground, as though the dragon were walking by them once again. Only the dragon was nowhere in sight.

Airi and the men went back to the ship and climbed aboard. The men were chortling over their treasure, although quietly so no one knew they had it. Airi went to the bunk she'd shared with Maxum and emptied her pocket. She had not made off with as much as the others, but she had done well in spite of it. She had twelve gold coins, one star ruby, two glass emeralds, and an intricate necklace full of pearls and gay stones. There were seven silvers and ten coppers. All in all a very nice haul. She hadn't had this much money at one time since . . . well, since ever.

She had a thieves' belt—or so it was called. It was a belt that lined the inside waistband of her breeches. It held coins and wealth securely so no one could pick her pocket, and no one could steal it off her unless they stripped her of her pants.

So she tucked her new wealth away. She had to repay Maxum for the corset and for the cost of the voyage and everything he'd had to spend on her up until then. That should leave her with about eight gold and all the gems, silver, and copper.

She wondered at Maxum, now that she was alone and had the chance to do so. Clearly he had not been interested in the dragon's wealth at all. He had gone there for one thing and one thing only. That ring. A ring that made the wearer invisible. She had heard of such magics, but she had never seen it before.

As a thief she could see the intrinsic value in having such a ring. A thief could sneak in and out of anywhere completely undetected. It was worth a dragon's weight in gold.

But Maxum wasn't a thief, so why had the ring been so important to him? Important enough to risk being struck down by such a violent trap? And what about that? How was it he had not been hurt by the lightning? He should have been nearly incinerated.

That was when she thought of the talisman. He had put it on a chain and wore it around his neck and suddenly he couldn't be hurt? Is that why the talisman had been so important to him? Because the wearer became . . . indestructible?

That meant Maxum now had the ability to become invisible and to be indestructible.

A man with that kind of strength and magic would be nearly unstoppable.

No wonder he had been willing to risk his life. There had been no real risk at all.

Not for him.

But for everyone else . . .

CHAPTER
EIGHT

"What's this?"

Airianne opened her eyes sleepily. She had fallen asleep waiting for him to return. He held four gold coins in his fingers. The gold coins she had left on his pillow.

"It's what I owe you. For the cost of passage, the corset, food, and such."

He frowned.

"You don't owe me anything," he said, holding the coins out to her. "You're part of the group now. I pay for the group's expenses and they pay me back by risking their lives."

"Is that how it works?" she asked, narrowing her eyes on him. "They risk their lives but you don't risk yours?"

He didn't say anything, just set his jaw. Then he said, "They are well compensated. As you saw."

"For now. But what happens when you leave them?"

"Who says I'm going to leave them?"

"You are indestructible and can be invisible. You don't need them anymore. You're not even really close to any of them. They're just a means to an end. And you've gotten what you wanted."

"Not all of what I wanted. I need more."

"We always need more. Your men have just become ridiculously wealthy, but they'll continue to follow you because they want more. We were lucky today."

"Thanks to you."

"Thanks to Dru. He pulled off a miracle."

"He never would have been able to come up with the idea if not for you."

Airi sat up in the bed, drawing her knees up to her chest. She had taken the corset off and was in the ruffled shirt. The neck of the shirt teased at the crests of both her shoulders, showing off a lot of the tanned landscape in between. The ruffled neckline hinted at her breasts, making her seem busty even without the aid of the corset. Then again, she was busty—when she wasn't trying to hide it. She had beautiful breasts . . . breasts that had taunted him mercilessly from the moment he had set eyes on her. And last night he had tasted them. She had been incredibly sweet, her nipple a hard, excited little point, her surrounding flesh as soft as could be. He wanted more . . . and now that they were on more equal footing, he would take more. As soon as he could get her to an inn and a decent bed.

"Keep your money. You earned it today," he said, burrowing for her palm and placing the coins within. "So what kind was it?"

"What kind was what?"

"The trap on the lock. What was it?"

"A spike. Remember those little holes all around the keyhole? They were full of spikes that would have shot out at the person in front of the lock. Unless you had the right key."

"Or the right thief."

She smiled a little. "Yeah."

"You handled it well. You've proven yourself to be an invaluable member of the team. That means you get your ten percent."

"But I thought . . . I thought we all just got what we took."

"No. We pool our treasure and exchange it for pure coin then divide it among us fairly. We all have a part in the escapade so we all get our share. I get the lion's share, of course."

"Of course."

"But the rest we divide in four parts, five now."

"So fifty percent gets divided among us and fifty percent goes to you?"

"And that's why I pay for passage, food, and other costs." He reached out and smacked her hip, indicating she should move over in the bed. She did so and he lay down with a groan. "Wow. What a day. I'm exhausted."

"Me too. Are we under way?"

"Yes. The captain says we'll reach Calandria tomorrow late afternoon if the weather holds. And believe me when I say you should pray that it holds."

"To which god?"

"I didn't mean it like that. I don't pray to the gods."

There was a hard bitterness in his voice and she let it roll over her. He had made it clear how he felt about the gods. Personally, she found it risky to denounce them. She didn't know whether she believed in the gods per se, but she was hedging her bets just in case. And after what she had seen today, she had to believe there were powerful things out there that she had no clue of.

"So what will we do now?" she asked.

"There you go again, asking questions."

"I can't help it. I feel a desperate need to know exactly what you have planned. Especially after what you led us into today."

He regarded her a minute. "Actually, I don't have a plan after this. I'm going to go where the next adventure leads me."

"What does that mean?" she asked with a frown.

"It means . . . you'll see what's next tomorrow."

He closed his eyes and sighed. She watched in silence as he slowly drifted off to sleep. She opened her hand and regarded the coins within. She realized the other men had stuffed their pouches with treasure and if she had a share of that, it meant she was suddenly a wealthy woman. She could take her earnings and get a nice little cottage for the winter months. She could live a quiet life of comfort for a while. It sounded like such a nice idea.

She looked down at his face.

If she stayed with him she would most likely get herself killed. He might be invulnerable, but she wasn't.

She reached out gingerly and pulled aside the gaping neckline of his shirt until she could see the talisman. She wondered what it would feel like . . . to not be hurt by anything. But then that only protected the physical body. There wasn't a talisman to protect the heart. If there were she would steal it and wear it to keep herself from getting hurt.

But since that kind of talisman didn't exist, she was just going to have to protect herself the way she had always done. Very carefully.

That should be easy, she thought. There was little likelihood that her heart would become involved with any of these men. The nicest one there was Doisy. With his charm and easygoing personality it was hard not to like him. But when she left—and she would leave eventually—she wouldn't be heartbroken about it.

Then there was shy Dru. He was really sweet and she could already see that she would miss him. But she wouldn't feel any differently than she had for all the others she had left behind in her transient life.

Kilon . . . well, that went without saying. She would be glad to be quit of the surly, mean-tempered man.

As for Kyno, she didn't know all that much about the lumbering half-orc. And it was best she kept it that way.

Luckily his social skills left much to be desired and she wasn't in any danger of becoming overly attached.

That left Maxum. Maxum was a whole other issue.

No. Wait. He was no different than any of the others. He had no real place of importance other than the fact that he had her life in his hands as he took them on these little journeys of his. She didn't know him well enough otherwise. Although she had to admit she found something compelling about him. And, forcing herself to be honest, she found him very attractive. Not just because of the physical chemistry, though he certainly had that, but because of his dynamic personality and general presence. He was a force you couldn't help but feel . . . whether he wanted to be or not. She suspected that, given a choice in the matter, he wouldn't want any focus directed on him. He was far too busy with his own plans. He didn't have time to play hero for anyone else.

But what were those plans? It was clear he was gathering power but to what purpose?

She might never know. She might leave without ever finding out the answer. She was fairly certain he wasn't going to share the information willingly. But what should that matter to her? She should live her life and let everyone else live theirs, just as she'd always done.

Only right now her life was tied up with his and he seemed to have no compunctions about putting her neck on the line. All of their necks.

But who was worse? Him for doing it or them for going along with it? There was blame to be had all around, she supposed.

But right now this was where the money was. Being with Maxum had proven far more profitable than any one thing she'd ever taken part in before—and she'd lent her services to other groups in the past. Never with this much success. If Maxum could keep them raking in rewards like this, she could soon retire for the rest of her life, if she wanted to. A quiet life sounded nice in the winter months, but she was a nomad at heart, feeling best when she wandered about from place to place. Or maybe she just thought that way because it was what she'd always had to do to keep ahead of those she had stolen from.

She didn't really know. And she would worry about it when the time came to worry about it. Right now she had to dedicate all of her focus onto her present situation. She had two things she absolutely had to do at all costs.

One, she had to keep herself from getting killed.

And two, she absolutely, positively had to keep out of Maxum's bed. Not an easy trick so far. She'd been in his bed every night since they'd met. But she didn't mean sleeping in his bed, she meant the part where she was in danger of having sex with him. His sexual magnetism was undeniable and she had an inching fear that he had the goods to back it up. She suspected he would be a damn good lover given the chance to prove himself. A thoughtful one to be sure.

But he had said he wanted her to come willingly to his bed and she was certain she wouldn't be doing that. There was far too much on the line to risk it all for a few moments of passion with someone who wouldn't be there the next time she turned around. And if she wanted to stay in the group without any conflicts it was best she kept her distance.

She lay back in the bed, staring up at the wooden planks of the ceiling for several minutes. As sleepiness overcame her she couldn't help but think about how hard it was going to be to maintain a cool distance.

Because nothing about Maxum engendered keeping a level head and a safe distance.

* * *

When Maxum awoke the next morning the bunk was empty and the ship was rolling and bucking fiercely. He staggered to his feet, banging his head against the wall as he lurched to the side. Luckily, thanks to the talisman it didn't hurt. But he doubted the others could say the same if they were being tossed about in the same manner.

The first thing he did was make it up on deck. There the decks were being lashed hard with rain and lightning was dancing along the edges of low black clouds all around them. The blue sun was so completely blocked out by the storm that it looked almost as if it were dusk. That thought disturbed him and he went in search of the captain. He found him in his quarters.

"What can I do for you, sir?" the captain asked, not sounding at all accommodating in spite of the pleasant address.

"When will we make Calandria?"

"No telling with this squall kicked up. Not until well past dark that's for sure."

Maxum swore violently in his head. "Is there anywhere closer we can put in?"

"I'm going to Calandria. The storm's not bad enough to warrant changing my plans. It'll blow over soon enough."

"You don't understand, I need to be on land by sunset."

"No, *you* don't understand, Calandria's the nearest port I'm willing to go to. You'll just have to delay whatever plans you have until after sunset."

"Not going to happen," Maxum muttered under his breath.

"What's that?"

"Nothing . . ." He would have to deal with the problem when it came up. There was still a chance they could make it in time. If not . . . he had no idea what would happen if he was in the water. He knew one thing for certain . . . being over water wasn't going to stop the curse from happening. In fact, until he had been freed he had been buried under the dirt and silt of the ocean floor—Sabo's way of adding insult to injury. Not only was he buried underground, but he had been forced to bear the pressure of all of the ocean bearing down on him.

"Do your best, Captain," he said shortly.

"Don't need you to tell me that," the captain grumbled.

Maxum ignored him and went in search of his men. He found most of them in the galley. Lanterns were swinging and swaying on their hooks, casting strange shadows on the faces before him. Of all of them, Kyno looked the worst. Apparently the rolling seas weren't agreeing with his insides. Maxum had barely gotten two words out of him before he'd turned and vomited in a bucket.

"Been doing that all morning," Kilon said. "You'd think the ass would have enough sense to stop eating."

"I was hungry!"

Kyno erupted again.

"Where's Airi?"

"I don't keep tabs on her," Kilon said. "She's your piece. That's your job."

"She's not my 'piece.' She's an equal member of this crew due an equal share."

"Equal share!" Kilon ejaculated. "Over my dead body."

"Very well, where would you like my dagger, the neck or the chest?" Maxum asked coldly.

"Look, just because you're fucking her doesn't mean she's got a right to an equal share of my profits!"

"I'm not fucking her. And even if I was, you wouldn't have any of those profits if not for her."

"She didn't even have sense to pack a sack. She didn't even fill her pockets!"

"She picked that lock and she gave Dru the idea of making us invisible to the dragon. If not for her you would likely be dead by now. She gets equal share and I'm done arguing about it."

Kilon set his jaw, clearly wanting to take it further, but for all his foul temperament, he knew better than to cross Maxum. For now anyway. There might come a time when that would change.

Maxum would have to be vigilant to make sure the group didn't lose its cohesiveness. He would be happier if he didn't need Kilon, but as it stood he did need him. He was a great source of firepower and his skill with the bow was crucial when it came to fighting. If they'd been forced to fight that dragon yesterday, the only way they would have had a hope was if Kyno, Kilon, and he had somehow struck the right places at the right time.

It had definitely come too close for comfort.

He went in search of Airi. He had promised the captain he would keep her out of trouble, and he had a suspicion that trouble followed her everywhere she went. But a search of the crew decks came up empty and he was fairly certain she wasn't up on the main deck. It took braver souls than she to bear up on a deck that was rolling and churning the way the top deck was. Not that she wasn't brave; she had far more courage than she should for someone of her size and of her sex. But she wasn't foolhardy either, and the men on deck had been bred to it.

He made his way down into the belly of the ship, coming into the fore cargo hold. When he opened the door it was to a sudden raucous shout. The shout of a crowd of men cheering and jeering all at the same time.

"Okay watch her now, boys . . . she's going to scream this time!"

"Give it to her, Harry!"

"Oh!" the crowd cried in unison.

Maxum knew there was only one woman on board so he knew who the "her" was. With a worked up crowd like that, he could only anticipate the worst. He came around the barrels and crates in the hold ready for anything, ready to have to beat a crowd of men off her and rescue her from whatever hell she'd gotten into while he had slept peacefully by.

He stumbled onto the group just as the crowd groaned in unison once more. Then he saw a familiar platinum head pop up. There she was, crowded around a couple of lanterns, rolling dice between her hands as a group of eight men watched her. She rolled the dice and shouted with glee as she won the point.

"Ha! That'll teach you to bet against a woman, Harry!" she cried. Harry chuckled good-naturedly.

"That'll teach me to bet against you! Most women are bad luck . . . but you . . . I've never seen that kind of luck!"

"What can I say? It's just my lucky day."

"All right, boys, let me take her away before she robs you blind," Maxum said, anxious to get her away from the room of rowdy sailors. She was lucky they were in a good mood. They could just as easily have turned against her. She was simply out of her mind for having engaged them in the first place. He wanted to wring her little neck for being so reckless.

He grabbed her arm and hauled her back to the entrance of the hold.

"Hey! I was having fun!" she cried as he dragged her through the entrance. He noted she still had the dice in her hand. He shut the hold door.

"Are those your dice?"

"Of course they are!"

"Are they loaded?"

"What?" She bit her lip. "Of course not."

"You're lying to me."

"Will you keep your voice down!" she hissed at him.

He dragged her up to the crew deck and into their cabin, his teeth gritted in anger. He slammed the door shut and shoved her onto the bed.

"You are on a ship with rowdy, unmannered, coarse men and you have the gall to *cheat them* at dice? What in the eight hells is wrong with you?"

"I was just having fun!"

"Would it have been fun when they figured it out and hung you from the yardarm? That is, after they raped you. I'm amazed they weren't all over you already!"

"Just because you can't keep your hands to yourself where I'm concerned doesn't mean everyone else can't control themselves. Besides, I'm not the kind of woman people go crazy for. I'm too small."

"For men like this *any* kind of woman is worth going crazy for!" He frowned. "And there's nothing wrong with you, believe me. You have all the right things to drive a man to do . . . well . . . whatever a man wants to do."

She gave him a once-over. "Am I supposed to be flattered by that?" she asked him. She tucked her dice away into a pocket of her pants.

"No. Yes. I don't know. I'm just stating facts."

"If I'm so desirable, why hasn't Doisy gone after me? He goes after anything in a skirt. Maybe that's it. Maybe I need to put on a dress."

"You will not be putting on a dress!" That was the last thing he needed. To see her in traditional women's clothing. That would really screw up his head about her.

"Why not? I bet I'd look good in a dress."

She was purposely baiting him and it was written all over her face. Still he couldn't help but mutter, "I have no doubt."

"I wouldn't be able to move, but I'd look good."

"Just do me a favor. Don't leave the cabin until we get to Calandria."

"What? I'm supposed to stay locked away in here like some kind of prized virgin? No, thank you!"

She got up and went to push past him, but he planted his feet and refused to move. No mean feat in rolling seas. He grabbed hold of her and pushed her back down on the bed.

"What is it with you wanting me in your bed?"

"Just stay there!"

"You're going to have to keep guard the whole time because that's the only way you're keeping me in here."

He narrowed his eyes on her and slowly let his eyes travel the length of her compact but gorgeous body.

"It's not the only way," he said silkily.

That shut her up instantly.

"Okay fine. I'll stay!"

"Good." He watched her lie back with a sullen expression on her face and heard himself asking, "Would it really be so bad? Staying . . . with me?"

She knew what he was asking but played obtuse.

"I am staying with you. I have no choice. Besides, I haven't gotten my share yet. I figure if I'm going to risk getting munched on by a dragon, I better get paid for it."

He was disappointed by her dodge and he couldn't figure out why. Couldn't figure out why he was expecting her to act like anything other than what she was . . . a thief. And a very good one by the look of it. She'd conned a whole boatload of hardened sailors into thinking she was winning because of luck. Well the truth was she was lucky. Very lucky. Lucky they hadn't caught on mostly. Lucky that he'd let her join them even after she stole his talisman. And what about that? Why had he taken on the trouble of a thieving little woman? It was clear Kilon hated her very presence. Despite what she thought, Doisy *had* noticed her. And he suspected Dru was well on his way to having a little crush on her. Especially after she had pushed him into that magic he'd never tried before. He had to say he was pretty surprised. It wasn't the first time Dru had performed under the gun, but that had been really asking a lot of him.

Well, in any event, overall she was good for the group . . . so far. And she had proved her worth and then some. Actually he was pretty pleased with himself for being smart enough to see her potential. Sure she came with a few problems, but didn't they all? Kilon was a prime example of a member of the group who could easily turn out to be more trouble than he was worth.

"Just stay here. I'll be right back."

"Sure. When you come back we'll play some dice."

She snorted with laughter when he shot her a look. He turned and ducked out of the door.

Then he shut the door and waited.

And waited.

And just when he was going to give up, the door creaked open and she peeked out. When she saw him standing there she growled in frustration, letting the door hang open as she kicked the wall.

"Are you going to stand out here the whole time?"

"I was thinking about it."

"Fine! Do whatever your little heart desires. I am going to the captain to see if he has anything to read."

"You can read?" he asked with surprise.

"And write and cipher. Don't look so surprised."

"You're the only one besides me in the group who can. Well . . . Kilon, Dru, and Doisy can cipher."

"Why doesn't that surprise me? But what does surprise me is that Doisy can't read. He seemed a little more . . . literate."

"He has a good memory. Can remember the words to

any song he's heard once. Can recite poetry. But that's just to get the women."

"Of course."

"Dru is young. I've been trying to teach him a little, but he gets frustrated easily."

"Well, so would I if I was failing at something in front of someone I admired. I should try to teach him a little. See if that works."

"You would do that?"

"Sure. Why not?"

"It seems so . . . not you."

"You mean unselfish."

"I didn't say that," he said quickly.

"It doesn't matter," she said, poking at a splinter in the doorframe. "I am a selfish person. Aren't we all? We're all trying to take care of ourselves the best way we know how. How about you go find Dru and send him in here? I've got some paper in my saddlebags. We can work on the basics since I'm going to be stuck here and there's not much else to do."

"All right. But no more dice. I don't need you cheating one of my men. That'll cause far more of a headache than you'll be worth. Besides, I plan on telling them all about your dice."

"That is not fair!"

"Be happy I'm not telling the boat crew."

She tightened her lips and turned back into the room, slamming the door shut hard.

CHAPTER NINE

The group was dining in the galley—save for Kyno—shortly before sunset. Kyno wasn't even in the room, claiming the smell and sight of the food was enough to make him sick. The storm had stopped several hours earlier, but the seas remained rough and rolling. It had slowed their progress toward Calandria significantly. Before they had come down to eat they had been able to make out the dot that was the coastal city on the horizon.

Now the sun was about to set and they were finishing their supper. Maxum, who looked incredibly on edge, rapped the table for attention.

"Listen, I have to leave the ship," he said.

"We all have to leave the ship. We'll be at Calandria in a few—"

"No. I have to leave the ship *now*."

"*Now?*" Airi was aghast. "What are you going to do, just jump in the water?"

"Yes."

"But . . . why would you do that? That's crazy!" she ejected. She looked around at the mildly interested faces of the rest of the group. "Am I the only one having problems with this?"

Kilon shrugged. "I don't ask questions unless it concerns me. If he dies I'll just take my share and go. Makes no difference to me."

"It should make a difference to you! He's your source of revenue at the very least! Without him you don't make good money."

"Like I said, I'll just take my share and go find another way of making coin."

Airi growled in frustration. "What about you?" she demanded of Doisy.

"I've learned that very little can harm our great leader. It's not really my concern what he chooses to do with his time at sunset every evening."

"It is every evening, isn't it," she said, understanding dawning. "Sunset to . . . to juquil's hour or shortly after. Why? Where do you go? Why do you do it?"

"I'm only going to say this once, so make certain you are listening very closely," Maxum said softly. She leaned in, ready for an explanation. "It is no business of yours what I choose to do with my time."

"That isn't good enough. You're just going to jump overboard and . . . do what? Swim to shore? That's ridiculous! We'd go much faster *on* the ship. Those seas are outrageous. You'd never surv—"

She cut herself off. Maybe he would survive. After all, he had that talisman. But nothing was certain. The talisman could be lost in those wild seas. Why would he take such a risk?

Whatever the reason, he wasn't willing to share. He got up and walked out of the galley. Airi was hot on his heels.

"This is insane!" she shouted as she followed him above deck. He didn't hesitate as he walked to the rear of the vessel. "Stop it!" He reached the railing and threw his leg over. She grabbed his arm with all of her strength and shouted, "If you do this I'm coming with you!"

That made him hesitate, a dark storm of anger sweeping over his face. He reached out and grabbed her by the ruffles on her shirt and jerked her close so they were nose to nose.

"That has to be the stupidest thing I've heard come out of your mouth, and you are not a woman prone to stupidity. What does it matter to you where I go and why? You'll get your cut. Doisy will see to that."

"You think that's what concerns me? My *cut*?"

He glanced up, looking toward the setting sun. "What else is it?" he wanted to know.

Airi bit her lip. What else indeed? Why did it matter so much to her what happened to him? She barely knew the man.

"Doisy can't take on Kyno and Kilon. Dru would play fair, but the other two I'm not so sure. Yeah, this is about my cut."

A brief glimmer of disappointment flickered in his eyes.

"I've told the others. We'll meet in the Calandria town square at noontide tomorrow. I'll be there and so will your cut. Doisy will be trading in the gems and such for gold so it can be split. You'll have your cut tomorrow as long as you show up."

She bit her lip. "Just make sure *you* show up," she said.

He gave her a smile, a brief charming expression. "I always turn up, one way or another. You'll not be rid of me this easily."

And with that, he threw himself over the back of the boat. With a cry she leaned over the rail and searched for him in the churning ocean waves . . . but he never surfaced as far as she could see. For some reason tears stung in her eyes and she angrily rubbed them away.

What did she care if he chose to gamble with his life? It was his life. He could do whatever he wanted with it.

This was about her getting her cut. That was all that should matter.

But somehow . . . it wasn't.

Airi was pacing the Calandria town square anxiously. She had been there since midmorning, searching the crowded square constantly, looking for a man who stood head and shoulders above the rest. She had tried to think of other things. Had tried to take it in stride the way the others were, but she'd had very little success. She found it impossible that he would have made it there, and yet she kept hoping for the impossible.

She saw Doisy first. He came up to her hefting a large sack in his hands. She could only assume it was the gold from their earnings. He had gone around the city exchanging everything for gold that could be easily separated among them. They had a room at an inn—three rooms. One for her and two split between the rest. Kilon had made noises about her getting preferential treatment, but if he thought she was going to share with any of them he was out of his mind.

The men had partied hard the night before. So hard she was almost surprised to see them walking straight. Doisy had disappeared with a young barmaid from the inn about halfway through the night and he looked as though he were much better rested than the others who were filtering in from different directions. Soon the entire group was standing together. All except Maxum. They waited. Kilon took to throwing stones at the feet of passersby, chuckling whenever he caught someone on the ankle and earned a dirty look for his trouble. Doisy was stretched out on a grassy patch of the square and Kyno was seated beside him plucking out blades of grass one at a time. Dru was keeping even with her as she paced back and forth.

"Don't worry, he'll be here," he reassured her.

"I'll believe it when I see it," she said.

"Me too," Kilon said. "Come on, we all know the fool's dead and drowned out there in the ocean. I say we each take twenty percent and then go on our way."

"You're a real cold bastard you know that?" she spat at him.

"Come to think of it," he sneered at her, "why divide it five ways? I say we cut the whore out altogether. It's not like she was doing anything for us to earn it."

"Hey, without her we'd have never gotten past that lock," Doisy said.

"We would have found a way," Kilon said with an indolent shrug. "Anyone could have forced that lock. I could have."

"And you would have gotten a body full of spikes for your trouble," she hissed.

"So *you* say."

"If not for her I never would have thought to do what I did," Dru defended her quickly.

"We would have figured it out. I could have fought that dragon. A few arrows in the brainpan will kill just about anything."

"Kilon, we're not cutting her out," Doisy said. "I've got the gold and I say it gets split the way it's supposed to get split."

"Seems like I could take that gold right off you," Kilon said threateningly as he swung his crossbow off his back and into his hands. "An arrow in *your* brainpan would definitely do the trick, cleric."

Doisy shouldered the sack and pulled his staff from its place across his back.

"You can try."

"I can succeed. A staff won't even get near me. I'll just sit back here at a distance and fill your handsome face with arrows. Staff won't do you much good, even if you could move around with the weight of all that gold on you."

"How about I relieve myself of the weight of all this gold by dumping it out in the middle of the square? Let's see how much gold you end up with then."

"You wouldn't dare," Kilon said, taking aim at Doisy's head.

Doisy pulled the cord on the bag and hefted it as though he were going to dump it. "Wouldn't I?"

"Enough."

The command was hard and succinct. With a gasp Airi spun around. She could hardly believe she was seeing him. He was in a new set of clothes, his hair slicked back into a tail held by a leather thong. He needed a shave but other than that he looked freshly bathed and in perfect health.

Airi pulled back her fist and punched him in the face. The blow landed squarely, but it looked like she hurt her fist far more than she hurt his face. She shook out her hand as he turned his head slowly back to her and smiled.

"I missed you too, my little firebrand."

"Don't call me that. I'm not your little anything. What I am is furious that you would leave me here thinking . . . thinking . . . thinking the worst had happened to you!"

"I told you I would be here."

"You jumped into the ocean miles away from shore!"

"It was a nice swim that's for sure."

"Oh!" she ejected furiously, clenching her fist and struggling not to punch him again. It was clear she couldn't hurt him, so why bother? Still, it was hard to curb the impulse.

"Come on. Take me to where we are staying and we'll count out our shares," he said.

They turned to go and Airi marched along with them

in sullen silence. Until she said, "They would have cheated me out of my share."

"They would have tried. Some of them anyway." He looked at Kilon.

"Why do you even have him here? He can't be trusted."

"Making changes in the group even though you've only been a member of it for a few days?" he asked archly.

"I'm just saying he's a very hostile influence."

"And he thinks you're a whore with no right to be following us. We all have our opinions." He shrugged. "He's a deadeye. I've never met anyone who can shoot like he does as fast as he does."

She frowned. "There have to be better choices out there."

"And when I meet one I'll replace him. He knows that. Yet he still doesn't try to blend with the group. Doesn't try to make friends. Doesn't try to play nice." Maxum shrugged. "I find him to be the most honest person I know. You always know what he's thinking at least."

"An honest person wouldn't try to cheat someone of their proper earnings."

"He thinks you have to fight for what you want. I can respect that."

"You're out of your mind."

"Like I said. He thinks the same thing about you."

"Only in his case it's true." She sighed. "Well, at least you're willing to give me a fair chance. That's something I guess."

He laughed hard. "I'll say that's something. You're lucky to be here."

"Tell me about it," she grumbled. "We all are. That dragon would have had us for lunch."

"We could have beaten him."

"Great. You're delusional on top of everything else."

"What else?" he asked, reaching out to run a finger

down the back of her nape, left bare by her tightly bound braids on either side of her head. He would have to see her hair down one day, he thought.

"Stop that!" she scolded, swatting him away. But not before she shivered. "And you know what else. Everything else!"

"You're just upset because you're wildly attracted to me and you were worried you'd missed your chance to be with me."

"Gah! That isn't even remotely true!"

"That's all right, you can protest and save face all you want. I know the truth anyway."

"That's it, I'm not walking with you." She marched up to walk beside Doisy, the sound of his laughter echoing in the air.

When they got to the inn they went to the room the men had rented and Doisy dumped the bag of gold on the bed with a sigh of relief. Gold was heavy . . . and that much gold was even heavier.

"Oh my goodness," Airi breathed with awe.

"And then there's the coin we took off the dragon." He went for a smaller sack Kyno had tied to his waist. The orc gave it to him and Doisy dumped it on the bed as well.

"How am I supposed to carry that much gold?" she whispered, still in awe.

"You don't, ya twit. You bank it or hide it. I prefer to hide it. Don't trust banks and a banknote can be taken off you," Kilon said.

"I prefer to do both. The rest I carry. Come on, let's get this separated and put aside so that we can go on to the next phase of our adventure," Maxum urged.

"And what phase is that?"

"Follow me and you'll find out," he said with a twinkle in his eye.

They sorted out the gold, Maxum's fifty percent take

enormous. But he took enough coin for expenses and more and tucked it into his saddlebags, which the boys had brought to the inn for him the night before. She was surprised Kilon hadn't gone through them and picked over them like a carrion bird. Maybe he had thought about it, and probably he would have if Maxum had missed their noontide meeting.

Airi shuddered, trying not to think of it. If she thought of it then she had to think of him swimming all of that way for hours on end. What a cold and lonely business that must have been. There was nothing that said his talisman protected him from the cold. He must have been freezing in the cold deadfall waters. And winter was hot on deadfall's heels. Soon camping out in the open would be unbearable. She was lucky her fortunes had turned.

And what a turn they had made! She had enough gold to retire in modest comfort—if she watched her coin closely. She could leave right then and never look back. Calandria was too big a city to suit her—she would prefer something more rustic—but she could leave from there and go anywhere on the Black Continent.

However, if she stayed she could perhaps find more fortune . . . enough to maybe take her all the way to the Green Continent, where she had always longed to go ever since she was a child. And now that she knew what it was like to travel on a boat—however brief it had been—she knew she could potentially make the voyage. But it was an expensive undertaking and required many modes of travel.

Still, the idea of it held an extraordinary amount of appeal. It was worth putting up with Kilon's nastiness and Maxum's arrogance and recklessness to achieve a dream like that.

They left the inn together, she and Maxum, each hoisting a hefty bag of gold. The first place they went to was the bank. Maxum traded a portion of his gold for a key to a lockbox. Then he followed a very burly man into the vault in order to retrieve the box from the wall of many steel boxes, each with its own number. He used the key in the box and dumped the entire sack of gold in the box under the watchful eye of the vault manager.

"Do not forget your number," the man said in a nasally voice, "and do not lose your key. The amount you paid rents the vault lockbox for exactly one full turning. Today is the fourth day of letting. On the fourth day of letting an annum from now your box will be emptied and the contents confiscated unless you pay to rent it another full turning."

"A full turning is more than enough time," Maxum said. And it was. For who would let their money lie for more than a full turning of all the seasons unless they were settled in the area?

Airi got a box for herself, although hers was a smaller box and she left only three quarters of her gold there. The rest she had surreptitiously tucked into her saddlebag in a hidden pocket and some in her thieves' belt as well back when they were at the inn.

Before they left the vault, Maxum turned to the vault manager.

"Tell me . . . as a banker you must know many people in this city, yes?"

"Of course," the man said, looking incredibly bored with them.

"Do you know someone who knows the Songs of the Gods? Someone very old who has heard many songs?"

The man's expression was blank and Maxum was about to repeat the query when he suddenly drew a breath and said, "Yes."

"Well can you tell me where I might find him?"

"*She* is a mem at the temple of Kitari in the old quarter of the city."

"A mem?" Maxum frowned. "Is there anyone else?"

"There are others I'm sure, but none that I know of. And mem Gia is the oldest woman alive in this city I'm sure and she knows all of the songs you could ever want to hear."

Now that was strange, Airi thought. Hadn't Dru told her that Maxum had had a fierce emotional reaction to hearing the Songs of the Gods in the past? Why would he be seeking them out now? And why was he so clearly set against anything to do with the gods one moment, but then wanting to hear about them the next?

"Very well. I guess she'll do. Thank you for your trouble." Maxum gave the man a great deal of silver and left.

"You really don't care how much money you spend, do you?" she asked him, still incredulous over his wild spending habits.

"Not particularly."

"Why? You aren't going to be young forever you know. You aren't going to be able to adventure once you've worn out your body. You spend money as if you have no future to worry about."

"Why worry about the future when you can live in comfort now? Tomorrow I might be dead."

"Not with that talisman you won't."

He looked at her from the corners of his eyes. "So you've figured out what it does?"

"For the most part. How does it work?"

"As far as I can tell, it keeps me from suffering any physical damage. But that doesn't prevent a man from being struck with an ailment of the heart of some kind. Or any number of other ailments."

"No, I don't suppose it would. So what is your plan exactly? To move through the world impervious to outside harm and spending money frivolously?"

"Sounds good to me," he said.

She growled with frustration at him. "Doesn't anything matter to you?"

"Why does it surprise you so much? A thief is inherently selfish, it's just inbred into you. Do you see me picking apart your nature?"

That stung. She didn't know why, because in fact it was the truth, but it bothered her to have him thinking she was selfish. She needed to be selfish. She needed to take care of herself. No one else was going to do it so it was up to her. She had learned a long time ago, from a very, very young age, not to depend on others.

She was selfish because everyone else had proven they were selfish first.

"I'm just saying you should look to your future."

"Maybe I don't think I'm going to have a future," he said, his tone coming across low and a little dark.

"Now why would you think that?" she asked.

"Never mind. Here's the old quarter," he said. "Let's find Kitari's temple."

Airi wanted to pursue the topic, but it was clear he was shutting her down. She had to respect that. If their positions were reversed she didn't know if she would want to talk about all her deepest darkest corners. It was probably best left alone.

They found the temple and she went to walk inside, but Maxum visibly hesitated on the step leading under the archway entrance. If she hadn't known he was the sort of man who'd face down a dragon, she might have thought that was fear in his eyes. But she shook her head, thinking she was mistaken, and by the time she looked back at him the expression was gone and all that was there was steely determination. He crossed the threshold and then walked into the forechapel.

Airi stopped the first mem she saw and said, "We're looking for mem Gia."

The mem took her measure a moment, peering down

at her from her significant height and down the blade of a long, strong nose.

"What do you wish of Gia?"

"We—"

"We were told she is the most pious of mems and we wish to pay tribute to Kitari through her," Maxum talked over her. She found it curious that he didn't just tell the mem the truth. But as she watched the mem's hard stare she realized what he did—she wasn't letting anyone close to Gia without some inducement. And right on cue Maxum said, "We are here to make a donation to Kitari . . . through mem Gia, of course." Maxum untied his purse from his belt, hefting the coins with a jingle, then pulled open the drawstring and tipped the bag so the mem could see the gold inside. The mem's eyes widened considerably. Since the mems lived solely through donations of food, cloth, and coin, such a contribution would be more than welcome and Maxum knew it.

But his whole purse? There had to be thirty gold coins in there! If the man was so bent on giving his money away he should just give it all to her and she'd be off to the Green Continent quick as a whip. As it stood that would leave him with only the coins in his saddlebags at the inn to pay their way for the rest of their trip . . . and who knew how long that would be or where it would take them? Sure, there was quite a bit there, but the way he spent money . . .

"Why yes . . ." The mem licked her lips. "You understand Gia is old and we usually don't allow her to be bothered by penitents."

"But we're not your usual penitents," Maxum said.

"No. No of course not." The mem shook herself to attention. "Follow me."

They did and the mem led them through the main chapel and into the dormitory wings. Mems dressed in the long flowing violet robes worthy only of the priestesses of the queen of the gods hurried to and fro around them. The robes they wore were of fine cloth, thick and with a soft sheen to them, and each mem wore a circlet of gold around her head, in reflection of their patron goddess's stature among the gods. They also wore golden slippers. Clearly Kitari's mems were well-off compared to some other mems in the temples of the other gods.

Each temple dressed their mems in a different way, according to their god, and each had different rules of conduct. But a lot of people had fallen away from worshipping the gods—and often he would see mems on the verge of being destitute and starving. These days if the temple wasn't self-sustaining it did not survive for long. This temple seemed to self-sustain and then some.

They were led through a maze of corridors until they were brought to a door at the end of a long hallway. The mem lightly rapped on the door.

"Well, what is it?" a voice barked from inside.

"Some penitents for mem Gia."

"Tell them to pray with someone else. Gia isn't well today."

"Um . . ." The mem cleared her throat and gave them an apologetic smile. "These are very special penitents, mem Collona."

"Is it the king?" she asked, still through the door.

"Er . . . no . . ."

"Then tell them to go away!"

"Now see here, mem Collona," she said, though with very little strength. Clearly she was intimidated by mem Collona. It made Airi wonder what she looked like if she could make this formidable woman quail in fear. "These are very *special* penitents." As if stressing the word "special" this time would make the difference.

"Go away!"

"Enough of this," Maxum barked. He grabbed for the

door handle and shoved the heavy door open. He walked into the room boldly.

It was only a very quick set of reflexes that kept him from getting cracked in the skull by a heavy wooden staff. As it was he got hit on the shoulder. The staff came around for a second blow and this time Maxum caught it and yanked it out of the gnarled hands of the mem swinging it. The mem stumbled with the force of the removal.

She righted herself by some small miracle before she spilled into a pile at Maxum's feet like an old bag of bones.

And that was what she was. Old, stooped over at the shoulders, and as gnarled and bony as could be.

"Mem Collona I take it?" Maxum asked mildly.

"Who are you?" the mem barked. "Who do you think you are pushing into an old mem's room like this?"

"My name is Maxum and I'm here to see mem Gia."

"Gia isn't seeing anyone ever," the mem snapped.

"She'll see me," Maxum said.

"Oh yeah? And why's that?"

Maxum hefty his bag of coins, giving them a jingle.

The mem snorted out a phlegmy laugh. "Is that supposed to impress me? I've had too much gold thrown at my feet in my time to be impressed by a heavy purse."

Maxum eyed the mem dubiously. "You don't say."

"I do say. I see what you're thinking, young man. You're thinking I was always this old and ugly. Well, I'll tell you this, I was once as beautiful as Kitari herself!"

"Mem Collona!" the other mem gasped.

"Well, it's true. I was young and I was beautiful. Sexy as all too. I was known to tease a cock in my day."

"Gia!" the other mem cried, completely horrified.

Understanding dawned in Maxum's eyes.

"Mem Gia?" he asked.

"Gia Collona. Who're you?" she wanted to know, peering hard at them.

"My name is Maxum. This is Airianne. We heard you know all of the Songs of the Gods. Even those that were forgotten."

"Is that what you heard?" She reached out and snatched her staff back from Maxum's hands. Then, contrary to that quick and strong movement, she used the staff to hobble over to a chair. She lowered herself into it with a creaking of her bones. "Well! Don't just stand there gaping! Pull up a chair. I don't sing like those fancy bards do. I tell stories. If you're looking for a show go to the local inn."

"I don't need a show. Just some accurate songs."

She peered at Maxum as he pulled up a chair. The old mem suddenly turned an icy glare on the other mem in the room. "What're you standing there gawking for? I'm going to need some honey water for my throat. Seems like these two will keep me talking for a while." The mem hesitated until Gia barked, "Move, girl!"

The mem exited hastily, closing the door behind her. Airi pulled up to a little table next to Maxum. Gia Collona had seated herself in a chair with rockers on it close to the fireplace.

"So what songs were you looking for?"

"Actually . . . local songs. Songs indigenous to this area. To the Black Continent in general as well. Songs about objects. Special objects imbued with special powers. Forged by the gods."

Gia let out a raspy, gurgling cross between a laugh and a cough. "So that's it! Treasure hunters! You think you're going to find some kind of magical item to make you rich and powerful. Those are just tales, boy. No such real thing." But as she said this she was giving him a sly sort of look.

"Not treasure hunters. Not really. But power, yes. And I know for a fact that those objects can be real."

"How do you know this?" Again that sly look.

"I've found them."

With that Maxum reached into a pouch at his belt and withdrew the dragon's ring. He held it up and it glinted in the sunlight. "Asharim's Ring."

Gia scoffed with a snort. But she was eyeing the ring carefully. "Says who?"

"What do the songs say Asharim's Ring does?"

"Let's see . . ." She made as if she were accessing an old memory, but it was clear to Airi she already knew. "Something about making Asharim invisible to his enemies' eyes."

"To all eyes," Maxum corrected. Then he slipped the ring on and disappeared from sight.

If Gia was shocked she didn't betray the emotion. Instead she poked at him with her cane, as if testing if he was still there, then waited for him to remove the ring again. Maxum did so and immediately came back into sight.

"So. You found the ring. One ring doesn't mean there's other treasures to be found."

"That's my worry. I just want you to tell me some of the songs you know. Someone like you may know some songs from back when I was a boy. Unfortunately I no longer remember the details, I never did pay attention. A fact I regret."

"When you were a boy? That wasn't that long ago. Do you know how old I am? I'm 103 full turnings old. And still got most of my teeth." She snapped her teeth together in demonstration. Airi could easily imagine the old woman taking a bite out of some hapless person. "What about you, girl? You a treasure hunter too?"

"Right now I'm just following him."

"Eh. Fucking him are you?"

"I am not fucking him!" Airi gasped with shock and affront.

"Yeah but you will be. You look good together. It's probably only a matter of time."

"I won't be fucking him," Airi said firmly—more for her benefit than for the old woman's.

"We'll see," Maxum said, chuckling when she punched him in the arm. Hard. He didn't even flinch. Damn that talisman. She was going to steal the thing from around his neck and then punch him right in the eye!

"That's the way of it, eh? Well give in, girl! Give him the goods! You only live once, I say. Wish I'd done more fucking. Not much to fuck in a temple full of women. Anyway we're meant to be chaste here in Kitari's temple. But I wasn't always at a temple in the middle of a big city. Yes, do your fucking while you still can, girl."

"I really don't want to talk about this anymore," Airi said sullenly. Maxum chuckled and she punched him again. It didn't hurt him, but it still felt good.

"Eh, the young are so stupid. Idiots. I was an idiot when I was young. Don't take it too hard. So . . . songs. I got dozens of them."

"Do you know the one about the four brothers and the fountain of immortality?"

"Ah yes!"

"Any one but that one. And I don't need ones about Asharim's Ring obviously. Or Filo's Talisman. Other than that, I'm open to any that have a magical item in them."

"Hmm . . . interesting," she said narrowing her eyes on him. Then she sat back, rocked a little, and cleared her throat. "You want local? How about the 'Tale of Isa'?"

"Isa? I haven't heard of Isa before."

"Ah, then sit back. This is a good one."

CHAPTER
TEN

THE TALE OF ISA

Many ages ago there was a young maiden named Isa. She was just coming into her first blush, about her thirteenth full turning. She was the daughter of a miller and was made to walk the mule to turn the grindstone all day. She would walk when the rain made the ground slick and muddy. She would walk when the sun beat down on her. She had to walk through the mule's droppings and often smelled of horse dung.

Because of this the other young people of the village would make fun of Isa, making up chants about how she smelled bad. So Isa would go to the stream every day and wash the smell from her body and her clothes, but to no avail. The young people still teased her.

Isa despaired over this because she was of age now to begin to think of finding a husband. But who would want a girl who smells of mule droppings as a wife? The only way was to tell her father she would no longer walk the mule. But when she dared to tell her father this he beat her until she was black and blue all over.

"Until you can make me a rich man, you will walk that mule until you drop from exhaustion!" he said.

Then he sent her out to walk the mule around the grindstone.

That night, in the cover of darkness, Isa thought to escape her father's house. She was terrified he might catch her if she ran away. He would never stop looking for her since she was free labor and because she was passably pretty she might marry into a wealthier family than theirs was and keep him in comfort in his old years. Isa's father, you see, was not very bright. He was a selfish man who only thought of himself.

But Isa didn't see how she had much of a choice, so she left her father's mill that night with nothing but a few slices of bread, two silver coins she had saved up, and the clothes on her back.

Isa ran through the woods, avoiding all of the roads, knowing her father would be looking for her there the minute he realized she was gone. She followed the stream so she wouldn't get lost or turned in circles.

After a time Isa stopped to rest and eat one of her slices of bread. As she sat to do so an old woman came out of the trees and sat beside her on the grass.

"Well, child," the old woman said. "Have you a slice of bread for an old woman?"

Isa didn't know what to do. She only had two slices of bread and two silver and she would need that bread to eat later on when she got hungry. But as she looked at the poor old woman she could tell that she was very hungry so she gave up her slice of bread to the old woman.

"Thank you, child! That was the best bread I've ever had!" the old woman said when she was done. "But the best foods are those we eat when we are most hungry."

Then the old woman got up and walked away.

"I must get going," said Isa and she stood up and ran along the stream for a long while. The day ended, but Isa did not stop, wanting to put many miles between her and her father. She didn't know what she would do, but she knew she couldn't go back unless she had enough money to make her father rich enough to let her live her life free of the drudgery of milling. And, despite all his bad character, he was still her father and she loved him and was loyal to him.

"I must make my own way in the world and one day return to him and take proper care of him."

As she traveled on she began to grow hungry and should have regretted giving away her other slice of bread, but it had made the old woman so happy that she could not feel too badly about it. Instead, when it grew light enough to see, she found some berry bushes and used her small purse to hold as many berries as it could then sat down beside the river to enjoy them. Just as she was about to eat a young child appeared. The child was a thin little waif with dirty clothes and a smudge on his cheek.

"May I have some of your berries?" he asked in his most polite tone.

Isa could tell the boy was very hungry, so she beckoned him over and shared her small pouchful of berries with the boy. There was barely enough to appease her hunger, but it was sufficient.

"Thank you!" said the boy and he waved to her as he ran off.

With a sigh Isa began to walk along again. Before long she came to a road. There in the middle of the road was a man with a cart with a broken wheel. He looked so sad as he sat there looking at his broken wheel.

"I have broken my wheel," the man said. "There is a town ahead, but it will cost two silver to get it fixed and I only have one. Now my family will starve if I don't make my deliveries. Could you go into the town and ask the wheel maker to fix my wheel for one silver? Maybe he will change his price for a pretty girl."

Isa agreed and took the broken wheel. It was heavy

and dirty and smelled of horse dung and Isa thought,
Here I am back where I started! Smelling of manure!

She found the town and the wheel maker, but when
she asked if he would lower his price he laughed in her
face.

"Bah! If I lower it for you then everyone will want the
same deal!"

So Isa thought of the man and his starving family and
put one of her silvers in with the one the man had given
her. The wheel maker was satisfied and fixed the wheel.
Isa then rolled it all the way back to the man in the road.
The man thanked her profusely and offered her a piece
of bread from his lunch.

Well, at least I'm not hungry anymore, Isa thought.
Then Isa went back to the town and bought some mea-
ger supplies with what money she had left. It was about
enough to last her a week . . . and only if she didn't give
any of it away!

Isa walked on, once again leaving the road, afraid her
father was looking for her. Now she had to figure out
how to make her fortune when she was dirty and smelling like a horse! She went back to the stream and washed
up as best she could. When she came out of the stream
to get her clothing she found a handsome young man
there, dressed in expensive garb, with laughing eyes.

Naked and embarrassed, Isa went to fetch her clothes,
but he snatched them away from her.

"Give those back!" Isa cried.

"These dirty, smelly old things? You are better off
without them!" Then he got up on his horse and rode
away, taking her clothes and all her supplies with him.

Isa sat down in the grass and wept. She should never
have come away from her father's place. Here it was
barely two days and she was naked, penniless, and alone
in the woods.

With no other choice, Isa stood up and began to walk. Maybe she could find someone to help her somewhere.

As it happened, Isa came out of the main body of the woods and into a glade. There in the center of the glade was a temple to the goddess Meru, the goddess of the hearth, of home, and of harvests. Goddess of women and wives.

Isa stumbled inside, hoping to find a generous mem who could help her, if only to clothe her, but the temple was empty. So she did the only thing she could think of to do. She knelt before the altar of the goddess and began to pray for guidance and support of some kind. Perhaps if she prayed she would clear her mind and be able to think on what next to do.

As she prayed a woman entered the temple. Isa had been praying so intently she had not seen where the woman had come from. But she was the most beautiful woman Isa had ever seen and she had a kind smile. She sat beside Isa and gently took her head in her lap and began to stroke her cheek.

"There now, child. It will be all right."

The woman was so kind and reassuring that Isa immediately felt better. She sat up and regarded the beautiful woman.

"Are you a mem here?" Isa asked the woman.

"Do I look like a mem?" she asked with a laugh.

It was true that she had the full bodied curves of a mem of Meru, but she was not wearing the wheat skirts the mems of Meru wore. The woman wore a fine gown of jilu silk and a garland of wildflowers within her long, tresses.

That was when Isa realized who the woman was. She glanced up at the statue of Meru that she had been praying at and saw her depicted there with a garland of wildflowers in her hair.

"Yes, child, I am Meru," the goddess informed her,

her green eyes shining as richly as the greenest grass, her hair the color of ripe wheat. "And I was the old woman by the river. And the hungry child. And the man with the broken wheel. Again and again I tested you and again and again you impressed me with your generosity of spirit."

"Were you the man who took my clothes away?"

"No. I would never do anything to humiliate you. But that young man will be made to pay for his actions."

"Oh! Do not be cruel to him! It was only a joke. I am sure he meant to return the clothes."

Meru's eyes lit with pride. "Again you show generosity, even toward those who wrong you. Some may call that weak, but I say it is a true test of strength. It is easy to be kind to those who are kind to us. It is much more difficult to be kind to those who are cruel to us. That young man was very cruel and he must be made to pay for his actions.

"Isa, I will reward you for your kindnesses to me."

Meru then touched her shoulder and a gown of the finest jilu silk flowed against her skin, warming her with its soft thickness.

"Oh, thank you! This is a most generous reward!"

Meru laughed. "This is not your reward, child! I simply didn't want you to catch your death of cold. Here is your reward." She rubbed her hands together with a flourish and suddenly a dagger appeared in her palms. It was encrusted with flawless rubies and made of gold. It was easily worth a fortune.

"This is the Dagger of Truths. Whoever wields it cannot be lied to and cannot be cheated. From now on all of your transactions in life will be honest ones. This is a very powerful weapon. If used to break the skin of another person all the weight of his or her lies will be brought to bear against them like a harvest. And believe me when I tell you that such a harvest comes with a crippling amount of pain."

"But . . . whatever will I do with this? It is too much power for one woman to hold."

"It is the right amount of power for a woman with a good soul to bear. And when you die this dagger will return to this temple and await the next worthy person to wield it. Now go, go forth in the world and deal honestly with others. But before you go . . . that boy who stole your clothes. Go to him and demand he repay you in some way for your pain and humiliation. He has great wealth and the dagger will see to it he deals honestly with you."

"Where will I find him?"

Meru stood up and guided her to the entrance of the temple. There stood a white stag, its great rack of horns beautiful and tremendous.

"The stag will lead you."

With that, Meru gave her a gentle touch on the cheek and disappeared. Isa didn't have time to absorb all she had experienced for the stag was already walking away from her. Picking up the train of her gown, she hastened after it. The stag led her to a road which led her to a great house just outside of a town. The stag stood on the doorstep briefly then bounded away into the woods. Isa knocked on the door and sure enough, the young man who had wronged her stood in the doorway. At first he did not recognize her, but then she said, "Do you remember me? By the river we met."

The young man's eyes widened and he took in her beautiful gown which easily cost the same as his own clothing had.

"My lady! I am sorry . . . I mistook you for a serf's daughter! I would never have—"

"So if I were a serf's daughter it would make it all right, what you have done to me?"

The young man blushed and had to answer honestly, for she held the Dagger of Truths.

"No, my lady. It would not have been right."

"You will make it up to me. You will pay me in gold for my trouble." Isa did not know where this confidence was coming from, but she was glad of it.

"I will. Perhaps two . . . no twenty . . . no one hundred gold coins?" the young man said, struggling for the lowest price but unable to do anything but deal fairly with her. Apparently the dagger had a good idea as to what would be fair on her behalf.

"That will suit me well."

The young man had to find his father in order to pay the exorbitant sum. The father balked, but the dagger made him pay. Instead of one hundred gold coins, she took ninety-eight gold coins, a horse, and some supplies to get her back home.

Then Isa rode home to her father.

"Father, here is some coin to keep you comfortable. I am no longer going to walk your mule. You may hire someone to do it." And of course, her father had no choice but to deal with her honestly and fairly.

Isa then found a small cottage of her own and settled into it for the rest of her days, and everyone who dealt with her had to deal with her honestly and fairly.

CHAPTER
ELEVEN

~~~

Gia sat back and stretched out her gnarled limbs. The other mem had brought her honey water during her telling of the song and now she took a sip.

"That's it? A dagger that makes people tell the truth?" Maxum asked. "What use is that?"

"What use is that?" Airi asked incredulously. "No one could ever cheat you again! Everyone would have to deal fairly with you. No one could lie to you. Don't you think that's a powerful weapon to have?"

"I suppose . . . but I was looking for something with more power. Something useful in a battle."

"Don't sell the dagger short, boy," the old mem said. "The weight of a person's lies can crush them if felt all at once. All you need do is nick the skin and the person would be brought low."

"Hmm. I suppose that's something." The more he thought about it, the more he saw the benefit of it. "Where do you think the dagger is now?"

"In Meru's temple I imagine . . . waiting for a worthy wielder."

"Where is the temple?"

"Well, if I knew that wouldn't I go and get it for myself? But the story tells you something of it. It is along a stream, in a wooded glade. About two days' walk from Isa's village."

"What village was that?" Maxum asked.

"Well . . . let's see . . . if I remember the song right she came from the village of Corm. Corm is but three days' ride from here on a fast horse. But I warn you, not just anyone can walk in there and claim the dagger. They would no doubt be dealing with Meru directly. If she is even offering it still. Then again it may already have a wielder. It may not be there at all."

"I'll take my chances. Any other more useful songs you can think of?" Maxum asked.

"I have dozens of them. Maybe you should be more specific about what you want."

"I want something that will make me undefeatable in battle. Even against a god."

"Against a god! Ha! No one can fight against a god," the old mem said. "That's madness."

"But if I were . . . what kind of weapon would I use to defeat a god?" Maxum asked.

The mem clacked her teeth together a few times, thinking.

"Have you ever heard the Song of Faya?"

"Faya? Wasn't that the one about a great warrior woman who fought a great beast that even the gods could not destroy?" Airi asked.

"Yes. And the gods gave her Faya's Wrath, a god-made blade that hit true to the heart of every creature it was wielded against. It never missed the heart when stabbed into the body."

"Yes! Faya's Wrath! That is exactly what I need!" Maxum exclaimed.

"Good luck finding that one. The song says it was lost down an inky well somewhere in the Golan Desert."

"How was it lost?"

"The song says Faya fell in love with a man, and that

man, being what men are, betrayed her by bedding a serving girl from the desert village of Hartung. Faya, in a fit of rage, pierced her lover's heart with Faya's Wrath . . . and she was so devastated by the loss she cried black tears into a well and threw her sword into it where it was lost forever. Others have tried to find the sword and the well to no avail."

"Others were not me," Maxum said firmly.

The old woman threw back her head and chortled with a raspy laugh. "Others thought the same. Either weapon is a fool's errand. But if you ask me the dagger is the more powerful of the two."

"A sword that can pierce any heart? Maybe even the heart of a god? That is worth ten thousand Daggers of Truth. But since the dagger is closest we will look for it first. Then we will go to the Golan Desert and find that inky well."

"And dive in after it?" She chortled again. "I hope you can hold your breath a long time. It is said to be bottomless."

"Everything has a bottom. And as a matter of fact, I can hold my breath a very long time."

What he did not say was that thanks to a sea witch's spell he could breathe under water. Something that would come in very handy in this case . . . as it came in handy when he was caught out in the ocean as well. It was one reason he had not been afraid to jump into the water. Even so, if he had drowned he would have simply healed and drowned again. It would be painful but it would have allowed him to make his way to the surface. But perhaps the talisman would have helped in that regard, keeping him from being injured. He wouldn't know because the spell was in place so really it did not matter.

Maxum stood up and held a hand out to Airi. She

took it without thinking and let him help her to her feet. The old woman laughed.

"Give in, girl. It'll happen sooner or later."

Airi flushed and snatched her hand out of Maxum's. He chuckled. He had some time and he had an inn with a proper bed arranged. He had every intention of doing what the old woman said they should do. Now all he had to do was convince her it was a good idea. One worth exploring in slow, deep ways.

The idea made him hard in all of an instant. He shifted his belt around so a pouch hung in front of that evidence, and luckily Airi remained oblivious, but he was pretty sure Gia had noticed. She was cackling again.

"Don't forget my donation, boy!" Gia said, rapping her cane on the floor.

"Of course." He took off the pouch of gold and put it in Gia's lap.

"Well, well! Been in a dragon's den, eh?"

"How did you know—?" Airi exclaimed.

"I'm not a mem for nothing! Every mem has a special gift. Mine's knowing where things have been. This gold has been in a dragon's hoard."

"That doesn't mean we got it from there," Maxum said.

"No, but she just told me you did."

"Come on," Maxum said to a sheepish Airi. "Let's go before you tell her everything else."

"That's not fair! You've already told her what we're going to be looking for!"

"Good luck with all that," the mem said dismissively as she began to count out the gold she'd been given. "Come back anytime." She had clearly dismissed the bickering couple.

Maxum took Airi by the arm and led her back out of the temple of Kitari.

* * *

As they walked through town Airi couldn't help but think about the story of Isa. She would have liked to hear the story of Faya told from the beginning, but clearly Maxum didn't have the patience for that.

"So this is your big plan? Look for a temple in the middle of the woods somewhere around the village Isa came from? I don't see the prospect of earning much in the way of gold and treasure in that and that's what these guys are in this for."

"They've got enough gold to last them for a while. A good long while. They know we're not just in it for the gold."

"Well, I'm in it for the gold," she said with a frown.

"You don't have to come. But I promise you if you do you will find a reward worth having. There's always a dragon or treasure hunt to be had out there. But my main goal is to get those blades. Most especially Faya's. Once I have that . . ."

"What? What will you do with it?"

He shut down. "Nothing. It's not your concern."

"Why are you gathering all of this power? First the talisman to make you invulnerable. Then the ring to make you invisible. Now you want these blades. Just how much power do you need?"

"As much as is possible," he said darkly. "I don't expect you to understand and would prefer you stop trying."

"Why can't you just be straight with me and tell me?"

"Let's find the others."

She growled in frustration, but marched after him all the same. She had to be out of her mind, she thought. She was following a power-mongering man who had a tendency to disregard the safety of his men. All he wanted was whatever he set out to get . . . to the eight hells with everything and *everyone* else.

He was going to get her killed. No, actually, she was going to get herself killed. She was the idiot following him. But at least these next two items on his list seemed relatively harmless to pursue. No great dragons guarding them. But there was a goddess involved.

"You think Meru is just going to hand over that dagger to you?"

"I don't know. I guess I'll see when I get there. I have to find the temple first. One step at a time."

"And how will you find the temple?"

"The way Isa did. By following the river."

"That's extremely vague. Following it for how long? What direction?"

"Well, I'm going to go with downstream. It just seems like if I had a choice of direction along a river I wouldn't choose to go against the current."

"She was trying to avoid her father. Maybe she thought the same thing and chose to go upstream to throw him off."

"You're thinking like a thief, not a frightened girl of only thirteen full turnings."

"This is just hopeless."

"Then don't come!" he said with a sudden roar, swinging around to get face-to-face with her.

"Oh, I have to come, just to watch you fail miserably. Even if you do find the temple I couldn't think of anyone less worthy of that dagger than you."

"I can think of one person," he said meanly.

"Well at least I'm smart enough to admit it!"

She turned her back on him with a huff and resumed her march toward the inn. They moved through the city in sullen silence until they reached the inn. The inn common room was empty except for Doisy who was whispering into a buxom barmaid's ear, making her laugh and blush prettily. Airi shook her head with a smile. The man oozed charm and sex appeal like no one she'd ever known. She wouldn't admit it, but it did sting a little that he hadn't tried to get into her bed. True, there had hardly been any opportunity since Maxum had been occupying it most of the time. But he could have tried last night when Maxum was missing. She would have rebuffed him, but he could have at least tried. It made her feel a little rejected . . . a feeling she didn't like so she pushed it aside and focused on other things.

Like not kicking Maxum somewhere where it would hurt most. She was appeasing herself by reliving the memory of kneeing him betwixt the legs.

She stomped up the stairs to the inn rooms and went into hers. She checked her saddlebag for the gold she had placed there, not trusting it had been left alone. Oh, the men were there keeping an eye on their things, but the men were not to be trusted as far as she could throw them . . . well, maybe just Kilon. She didn't think the others would steal from her . . . but then again, she was a thief. She expected everyone to be stealing from everyone else. It was just the nature of the world to her mind. If you had something, there was invariably someone who wanted that something and would do whatever it took to relieve you of it.

That went for relationships as well as goods and gold. There was always someone out there looking to steal a friend or a man away from a woman. It was usually the trusting fool's closest friend. People simply were not to be trusted.

And right on cue, Maxum pushed into the room.

"Hey! This is my room!"

"Our room. My things are in here." He went to his saddlebags and nosed around inside of them for a moment.

"Well then take your things and go find another room," she said.

"Can't. There isn't one." He looked at her and gave her a wolfish grin. "We'll have to share again tonight."

"Right now I'd rather share with Kilon!"

"I could arrange that. But I'd sleep with one eye open. He's just waiting for the right opportunity to present itself that will allow him to get rid of you."

He didn't really think Kilon would kill her, did he? Cold-blooded murder just to get rid of an annoyance? She paled. Knowing what she did of the man, she couldn't put it past him.

"Then I'll sleep with Doisy," she said.

"Might be a little crowded. I'm fairly certain he's going to be sleeping with that barmaid tonight. Then again, it wouldn't be the first time Doisy's had two women at once."

"Then I'm going to another inn. I'm not sleeping with you."

He was up against her with a step, the room being as small as it was. He pressed his chest to her back his hands settling on her hips, his nose nuzzling her ear through her thick braid.

"You would sleep alone and unprotected somewhere else? Come on. Would it really be so bad?"

She shivered as his warm breath washed down the side of her neck.

"I've slept on my own for all of my life," she said, clenching her teeth as a warm, wanting sensation was born in her belly. No! She refused to be conned by his charming ploys! He was just doing this to gain dominance over her, to prove he was the one in charge of her destiny. Well, that wasn't going to happen. Only she was in charge of her life.

And then he pulled her hips back into his body, bending at his knees a little so that her bottom nestled snugly against his very obvious erection. She gasped in a breath as she felt the heat of him penetrating her pants, the hard length of him an unmistakable thing to be reckoned with. She went to pull away but he held her tight and fast.

"Always fighting," he murmured, his lips brushing down the side of her neck. "Wouldn't it be simpler just to relax and flow into the moment?"

Simpler? With him? Never. There was nothing simple about him.

"I'm not fucking you," she ground out between her teeth as she fought with the swirling, melting heat rushing all around her body.

"No. You're not," he agreed. "This would have so much more depth than simply fucking." He let one hand slide off her hip and come around to rest on her belly right above her pubic bone. He pressed his palm into her, his fingertips teasing where her curls would be had she been naked. She felt naked. She felt raw and exposed to him. She knew this was just a game to him, but it didn't seem to keep her from responding to him.

For just a moment she relaxed against him, simply allowed herself to feel everything he had the power to inspire within her. She just wanted to enjoy it for a moment. She would have to fight him off in just a second, but for this moment she wanted to stop fighting and simply feel. Feel what it would be like to allow herself to be a woman aroused by a man. She hadn't known that feeling in so long . . . too long. Not long enough. She tried to remind herself that there was a price that would be paid for giving in to cravings of the flesh. She could become pregnant. Though thanks to the dragon's hoard she could easily afford to raise a child now. *And what a child it would be,* she thought. As handsome as his father, fair haired and green eyed. As stubborn as his mother. As clever as them both. What an amazing child that would be.

She jolted at the thought. The last thing she wanted to do was raise a child alone in the world. If and when she had a child the father would be present, would be willing to face up to the responsibility. Would be able to take over if something should happen to her. It wouldn't be like it had been for her . . . a child raised by a woman alone, only to have her die and be left with nowhere to go at the young age of only eleven full turnings.

The cold hard reality of that doused whatever passion she had been feeling. Maxum would never be responsible as a father. There was no future between them. She could barely stand to be in the same room with him at times! No. Maxum would be off chasing power and glory and wouldn't think twice about his responsibilities to a child.

She broke away from him with a little cry, wrenching her body around to face him, her eyes burning with frustration and fury.

"No. It would be fucking," she spat, the word as cold and hard as it needed to be. "And it would potentially have ramifications. Are you willing to face up to them? Would you stop all your glory-hounding ways and settle into being a father and provider?"

His gaze turned hard and harsh.

"I am not seeking glory. Those days are done for me."

"Then what are you doing?" she asked, her tone suddenly imploring. "Just give me a little something to understand you better!"

His jaw clenched tight, a muscle ticking stubbornly. It was obvious he had no intention of letting her in the least little bit.

"And that is why I will never go to your bed, Maxum," she said bitterly.

She bent to grab up her saddlebags and then stormed

out of the room and down the stairs. She found Doisy and walked up to him.

"I'm going to another inn. I'll be back here an hour after dawn."

"Why aren't you staying?" he asked, glancing up to the balcony that ran along the guest rooms. Maxum had exited his room and was standing at the railing watching her with dark, brooding eyes.

"There's no room for me," she said.

"But I thought . . ." He glanced back up at Maxum meaningfully.

"You thought wrong."

"I see. Well, I'll tell them. I'll make sure they wait for you."

"If they do they do, if they don't they don't. I'll be fine either way," she said with a shrug.

Doisy looked at her hard for a moment. "All right. But you shouldn't let him chase you away if this is where you want to be. He may be our leader, but I'm fully aware of what kind of bastard he can be. Still you'll never want for anything as long as you're with him."

"Oh, I'll want for something. I'll want for peace of mind. See you tomorrow," she said, turning and leaving him behind.

Doisy watched her go, then watched Maxum come down the stairs and head for him.

"What did she say?"

"That she'd be back an hour after dawn tomorrow."

"We might be gone by then," Maxum said punitively.

"We might? We've never left town that close to dawn before."

"We will if I say we will," he said coldly.

"All right. It's up to you. But you're the one who said we need her. And she has come in handy."

Maxum looked at the door of the inn, as if looking might conjure her up somehow.

"She may be more trouble than she's worth."

"Kilon would agree. You'd make him so happy."

"Nothing makes Kilon happy."

"This is true." He looked at his leader thoughtfully a moment. "What would make you happy?"

"You mean besides wringing her little neck?"

"Besides that."

"I don't know. I . . . honestly do not know." Maxum glanced out a window. "I better get going."

"Right. Sunset."

Maxum eyed him a moment. Doisy didn't know why his leader left at sunset every day, but he wasn't so obtuse he hadn't noticed it. And it wasn't that he didn't care. Whatever it was that had him leaving and staying away until after juquil's hour . . . it was serious. Doisy could sense that. Serious enough to have him jumping overboard in stormy seas. It didn't get more serious than that.

But if Maxum was deluding himself into thinking his men hadn't noticed or didn't have concerns, then he was not the man Doisy thought he was. Maxum was far too smart for that.

"One day" was all he said before he turned and left.

One day.

One day he would tell them what was going on.

But clearly, today was not that day.

CHAPTER
TWELVE

Airi didn't know what to expect when she entered the inn common room the next morning. Half of her fully expected them to be gone . . . and that half wished that was exactly what would happen, taking all the decision making out of the equation for her. The other half . . . well . . . she wanted them to be there. She wanted to join them on this next adventure—if for no other reason than to see how it all worked out.

So in truth she was relieved when she saw Doisy and Dru and Kyno readying their belongings. Doisy hefted a bag onto his shoulder and came up to her with a grin.

"Ready for our next adventure?"

"Are you?" she countered. "Has he told you what he's planning next?"

Doisy shrugged. "No. But I'm betting it'll be interesting."

"Is that why you stick around? For the entertainment?"

"Sure. Why do you?"

Good question. "For the same reason, I guess. And gold. I want gold."

"Don't we all?"

"But I'm not sure how much of that we're going to see

this time out. He's not looking for a dragon's hoard this time."

"What is he looking for?" Doisy asked with mild interest.

"A weapon."

"Ah. Well, weapons have value. Especially enchanted weapons."

"How did you know it was enchanted?"

"Why else would he go out of his way looking for it?"

"Oh. True. Sorry." She was treating Doisy like he was an idiot. The man might be a bit shallow, but he wasn't stupid.

"Don't worry about it. Come on, let's pack up the horses."

She nodded and turned to follow him through the door when out of the corner of her eye she saw Maxum leaving his room and stepping out onto the balcony. He was a commanding sight, a man sure of himself and his purpose in the world. He wore skintight breeches in a buff color, a linen shirt dyed a dark indigo, and a tooled leather vest. The shirt gaped open at the neck and she could see the chain to the talisman. His boots were a strong hard dark leather. They were loud against the wooden floorboards of the inn.

He looked down in her direction and a brooding expression entered his eyes. Well fine, she thought. If he was going to pout she'd just let him. She was sure he wasn't used to not getting his own way, but he was just going to have to cope with it. Hopefully he would get over it before too long. Otherwise it was going to be a very uncomfortable journey.

Once again she entertained the idea of staying in Calandria. But she only did so for a brief moment. There was time before winter set in. She would see how things went until then. If things didn't work out right she could always come back with Hero later on.

They were on their way out of the city within the hour. They traveled on in relative silence for a good long time. Then Dru pulled up beside her and gave her a shy sort of smile.

"We missed you at dinner last night."

She laughed. "You're speaking for the group?" she asked.

He flushed. "Well . . . I missed you. Doisy was preoccupied as usual." He gave her a meaningful look, making her laugh. "And Kilon was his usual sour self. Kyno . . . he never says much of anything. But when Maxum got back, it was clear he wasn't happy you were gone."

"How was that clear?"

"Well. He kept grumbling something about 'stubborn, willful women.' I can only assume he meant you."

Good, Airi thought. Let him think long and hard about the way he treated her.

"I wonder where we are off to this time," Dru said.

"I'm going to hazard a guess and say the village of Corm."

"Why there?"

"I'll let Maxum tell you that."

Dru let it be and once again she found herself wondering how these men could so willingly follow Maxum wherever he wanted to go without question. It was a level of trust she wouldn't have associated with any of their personalities save maybe Dru. The young mage seemed very much the trusting sort.

It was well past noontide before they broke their trip to have something to eat. Her bags were packed with fresh supplies, so she was able to make quite a nice lunch for herself. As she sat down under a nearby tree, Maxum finally broke his wall of silence and rejection by coming over and sitting down beside her.

"We can't continue on like this," he said, surprising her. "If I offended you, I'm sorry."

She was shocked by his apology. He had never struck her as the sort to apologize for anything he did. She would have thought the eight hells would freeze over first. So, of course, she regarded it with suspicion.

"All right," she said carefully. "This trip will go much more smoothly if you promise to keep your hands to yourself."

He frowned a moment, then a slow, lazy sort of smile tilted over his lips. "I can't make promises I have no intention of keeping."

"Oh! You're impossible!" she cried, throwing a grape at his head. "Why do you have to act like this? Why can't you just be . . ." She floundered for a word. "Decent!" she said at last.

"What about me ever struck you as being decent?"

"Nothing. That's the point."

"There isn't any such thing as a decent person. As a thief I would think you would know that already."

"Not as a thief, but as a woman. But as hard as my life has been, there are some decent people out there. I've actually come across a few."

"And stolen from them?"

"No! I never steal from anyone who can't survive without whatever I take."

"You tried to steal my talisman."

"You could have easily survived without it."

"How do you know that? Now that I have the talisman nothing can harm me. If you had taken it someone or something might have killed me."

"That would have just been the natural order of things. It wouldn't have hurt you to lose it is the point."

"You're wrong. It would have hurt me very much. But you didn't take the time to find that out. Now who isn't decent?"

"All right then," she said, immediately challenging their small truce, "tell me why you need the talisman so much."

"Isn't it enough that I say it's important? Do you have to know all the details?"

"I'm a very detail oriented person," she said.

He fell silent, eating the cheese and bread he had brought over.

She sighed. "Why is it so hard for you to open up a little? I'm not asking you to bare your soul."

"That's exactly what you're doing, you just don't realize. Suffice it to say, I'm going to need every advantage I can get out of these magical objects."

She ate another grape, chewing thoughtfully as she regarded him. "You're going to tell me one day," she predicted.

"Well, that day is not—"

"Today," they said in unison.

She laughed at him and he smiled. He was so incredibly handsome when he smiled. It was bewitching.

Maxum was thinking the very same thing about her. Damn her, she was caught in his blood like a cold he couldn't seem to shake. And like a cold he felt as though he were burning up with fever whenever he was around her. Why? She wasn't anything special as far as women were concerned. She was too small for him. Too short, too slender. Too much like a boy . . . except for those surprising curves of hers that, thanks to him and that corset, were set off to quiet perfection. When he'd had his hands on her yesterday, when he had drawn her body into his, it had felt a little bit like coming home. Like finding a special place meant just for him.

And then she had torn it all away, rebuffing him hard for something that hadn't even happened. A child? What child? And there were ways of preventing a child. Didn't she know that? All she had to do was ask Doisy. The man had ways of keeping women from getting pregnant. He had to or else he'd have bastards all over the countryside.

He would have to see to it she and Doisy had a conversation about it. But it had to be done delicately or she'd get her back up again. He wanted her to know he wouldn't do that to her. He wouldn't just use her and leave her to deal with the consequences alone. He was a bastard, but not that much of one.

But he wasn't going to be anyone's father either. Or significant lover. He was cursed. And he was on a mission. He didn't have the right or the inclination to become close to anyone. That was why he liked his men. No one was looking for any great friendships or any kind of attachment. There was no responsibility to that. They could just as easily leave him as stay.

The same was true of her. She could take him or leave him. She was no more into attachments than he was. He was sure of it.

"Have you been on your own all your life?"

"Since I was eleven."

"That's young for a girl."

"My mother died. There wasn't much of a choice."

"But she was good to you. Your mother?"

"Yes. As good as any mother, I guess. She loved me, if that's what you mean. I never doubted it. But life was hard on her. She had to scrape by. We starved sometimes. She worked hard to make a life for me, but it shouldn't be that hard. You shouldn't have a child if it's going to be that hard."

Ah. Now he understood her fear of becoming pregnant. She had grown up the hard way. Not that it was easy for anyone in this world.

"My father was the condant of a small city. As the children of the ruler of the city we had . . . I guess you could say a comfortable life. But my father was hard on us. Cold even. He expected us to become great warriors and make our own way in the world. My eldest brother, Dethan, was meant to be condant upon my father's death and he was, but he was very rarely at the city. He was heading a massive army, acquiring cities as a child would acquire a collection of toys. He fought in the name of Weysa and for the glory of it all. He wanted to be immortalized, wanted to be remembered for all of the days of the future."

"And did he reach that goal?"

He grimaced. "He did. But it was not all that he thought it would be."

"It never is," she said.

Airi felt more comfortable right then. Relieved, in fact, that he had finally deigned to share something of himself with her.

"How did you survive on your own at eleven? It must have been very hard for a small young woman like you."

"It *was* hard. I learned to do what needed to be done to take care of myself."

"You learned to steal."

"Some. I worked for my food and board too, you know. I'm only a thief when I have to be. I stole from you because it was either that or go hungry."

"And now look where you are. Comfortably rich in a matter of days. Isn't it funny how fate turns us?"

"Believe me, I'm thanking Hella every day."

"The goddess of fate and fortune has very little to do with it. She doesn't care about what happens to you, you can bet on that."

"You say that, and yet you talk as though you believe in the gods."

"I believe the gods are there. And they are, trust me. But the gods don't have time for us the way people pray they do. They are selfish, cruel creatures."

"They sound no better than the rest of us mortal be-ings."

"They aren't. Come on. Let's go. We're still two days out from Corm if the innkeeper was telling me true. But it's right along this road."

"That will make for easy going. That's something I guess."

"We will find the temple," he said firmly. "And we will get that blade."

She didn't respond to that. There was nothing to say. They would or they wouldn't. Fate and fortune would guide the way. Of course, it didn't hurt to hedge bets.

Sunset approached and Maxum chose a campsite for them before heading off into the forest to be by himself.

One of these days, Airi was going to follow him. She had already made that agreement with herself. She would follow him in secret and get the answers she wanted. However, it would be hard to do that with four baby-sitters watching her every move. She would have to be clever and devise a plan. If there was one thing she was good at, it was getting what she wanted when she wanted it badly enough.

She set up her bedroll close to the fire they built and then very obligingly set up Maxim's bedroll for him—on the opposite side of the fire. She didn't want him to think their truce meant she was going to give him the opportunity to make good on his threats.

Kilon hunted for food, managing to skewer two rab-bits. They were plump and well fed, so there was plenty to go around. Airi made certain a portion was set aside for Maxum. Full, she leaned back against her saddle and closed her eyes. Doisy began to sing one of the Songs of the Gods very softly. She supposed that knowing Maxum would not be coming back until after juquil's hour he felt it was safe to do so. He sang one of the songs about Kerion, the mortal lover of the goddess Meru. She found that to be a coincidental choice considering they were looking for Meru's temple.

The tale said that Meru fell in love with Kerion when she happened upon him bathing in a stream. He was the most beautiful man she had ever seen. Even more beautiful than the gods. But she feared he would be vain and shallow and decided to test him. She appeared to him as a homely young woman. Kerion was with his companions that day and bragged that with his beauty he could seduce any woman, young or old. His friends saw Meru in her homely appearance and they challenged him to seduce her. Being beautiful Kerion was used to a certain amount of adulation from others and he expected he could seduce even the homeliest woman. But Meru resisted his attempts to seduce her at every turn, frustrating the arrogant young man. After a time the bet was considered lost and Kerion had to pay for his failure. But he did not mind that for finally he had found a woman worth winning. She cared nothing for his beauty and he cared nothing about her ugliness. Eventually he learned to like her for who she was and eventually he came to love her. Once she was certain he had learned his lesson and learned humility, she finally allowed him to seduce her in her homely disguise. And afterward still he loved her. So she stood up, discarded her disguise, and showed the blinding beauty of her countenance to him.

They were lovers from that point onward. Meru lifted him from his mortality, making him a demigod, allowing him to live by her side in the eight heavens with all of the gods.

This was only the happy story of Meru and Kerion. There was a second story where Kerion betrays Meru by sleeping with a mortal woman and falling in love with her. In a jealous rage, Meru turned the girl into a doe and then sent a hunter to hunt her. The hunter killed the doe, but Meru's rage was not satisfied. She stripped Kerion of his beauty, turning him into a hideous beast and banished him to a labyrinth in the middle of a vast desert where he would live out his immortality.

Yet another example of the ways in which the gods could be just as fallible as the mortals they were supposed to guide and protect. Was it any wonder that many had stopped worshipping the twelve gods? But still there were many who did. She was not a worshipper herself. As far as she was concerned there were far more mortal things to worry about than to worry about the existence of the gods.

"Doisy," she said when he was done, "what god do you worship?"

"I am a cleric for Mordu, of course, the god of love!"

Airi laughed. "I should have guessed!"

"Indeed you should have."

"And you are a healer."

"Among other things. I can cure many ills and prevent them from coming in the future. Not entirely of course, there is no healer who can do that. But to some extent I can help keep a body healthy."

"What could you do to keep me healthy?"

"You are quite healthy enough on your own," he said. "But now that you mention it, I can prevent you from getting with child."

That made her go still inside. "How can you do that?"

"There is a potion you can drink."

"Why would you tell me about this now?" she asked suspiciously.

"I will not try to hide it from you . . . our leader asked me to mention it to you if the opportunity arose."

Airi's face burned hot suddenly and so did her temper. "Oh, he did, did he? Well you can tell him that it won't make a difference! I still wouldn't fuck him if he were the very last man alive!"

"I think you can tell him that yourself," Doisy said

with a chuckle. "I think I should like to keep out of the middle of it. But should you need the potion you only need to ask. Perhaps you can use it in the future for some other . . . purpose."

As hot as her temper was, there was something tempting about Doisy's potion. She had kept out of men's beds for almost all of her life for fear of getting with child. Doisy's potion meant that could change if she wanted it to.

"Could you show me how to make this potion? In case I need it in the future for *someone else*."

"I most certainly can do that. It is actually quite simple and you can obtain the ingredients in any town apothecary."

"How long does it last?"

"From one woman's blush to the next. It is expelled with your blush and then must be renewed."

"I see. And it never fails?"

"Never. I give it to every woman I bed before I bed her. It has never failed me."

She gave him a slow smile. "Show me how."

When Maxum returned to the campsite it seemed the truce he'd established with Airi had been obliterated somehow. She made no secret of her temper with him and he wondered what he had done since leaving the campsite earlier.

The mystery of it was solved when Doisy enlightened him. The cleric informed him that she had not taken kindly to being steered and manipulated. But, the cleric also informed him that she had learned how to make the potion and had ingested it to try its flavor.

Or so she said. Maxum saw it as if she had waved a battle flag, commencing an attack. Now there was nothing stopping him from seducing her if he wished to. All he had to do was get past all her prickles and temper. If only she would stop fighting him. He knew she desired him. Whether her mind had wanted it to or not, her body had responded to his.

He could use that. If he waited for her to come around to the idea in her mind he would be waiting a very long time he suspected. That meant a full-on seduction was called for, and he was a man of many talents when it came to that.

He found it intriguing how fired up he was over her. His focus had been so pure before she had come to the group. He had a goal: to gain as much power as possible and then fight and kill a god. Only then could he be free of this damned curse. Sabo's cruelty knew no bounds. He would never lift the curse of his own accord. No. Death was the only way.

But then she had come and now he found his focus split. Now he found himself wanting to conquer two goals. One far more pleasant than the other. And why shouldn't he? When he attacked Sabo at last there was a good chance that the god could strike him down in spite of all these magically imbued items he was collecting. After all, it was the gods who had made the weapons in the first place, wasn't it? Could they not just as easily destroy them?

He didn't know, but he was gambling that they couldn't. Just as he was gambling on his ability to win over a very stubborn thief. He would win her and enjoy her—one last human delight before he threw his life to the wind.

Yes. The more he thought about it . . . the more he knew he would make it happen. He would conquer both goals. He would win.

He would win.

CHAPTER
THIRTEEN

The next day went pretty much the same as the first. Maxum tried to call another truce with Airi, but this time she wasn't biting. She turned up her pert little nose and turned her back on him. She spent the day riding with either Doisy or Dru. She even chose Kyno's company for a little while rather than ride beside him.

But that was okay. The challenge of it lightened his spirit so much he began to whistle as he rode.

She remained untouchable all the way to the village of Corm. Once they entered the village Maxum stopped by the first house he saw that was occupied and asked after some refreshment. The man invited them in and traded some bread and stew for gold. He also was forthcoming about the story of Isa.

"It's made us famous that story. The village is three times bigger than it used to be. And people come by all the time in search of that temple. You got the look of you. You won't find it, you know. No one ever has."

"So no one knows what direction it might be in?"

"North or south, people have looked both ways for centuries. You won't find it, I tell you."

"Thank you for your time and your stew," Maxum said politely and they took their leave of the man. "Let's

find the river and go from there. We'll search south for a
few days then come north and search that way. We'll
find it."

"So we're looking for Meru's temple?" Doisy asked.
He whistled long and low. "Not much treasure to be
found in a temple."

"The treasure will come," Maxum promised. "We
just have to do this first."

Airi looked at him dubiously. She knew full well that
after this he planned to search for Faya's Wrath. There
wasn't likely to be much reward in that search either. All
they knew was that it was in an inky well in the middle
of the Golan Desert. Desert travel was tough going, especially when searching blindly for something that likely
didn't exist at all. She wondered how long his party of
men would put up with such a search. Not very long she
wagered.

They were leaving the old man's cottage when Airi
saw a small half-naked child in the middle of the muddy
street. It had been raining a soft drizzle for most of the
day and now the ground was soft. The child looked very
thin and its eyes were too big for its head, its head too
big for its frail body. The child was so dirty she couldn't
even tell if it was a girl or a boy. Her heart turned over
in her chest. She walked away from Hero and approached
the child.

"Where are you from?" she asked.

"My mum's house."

"Where is your mum?" she asked with a smile.

"Over there." The child pointed to a ramshackle cottage on the edge of the muddy street. There was no door
on the sagging framework, the thatching on the roof had
gone threadbare in places. Airi walked over to the door
and peered inside. There, lying in a wooden pallet, was
a sickly woman.

"How do you fare, my lady?" she asked gingerly from the door. "I've come across your child."

"He's not being a bother to you, is he? He's usually such a good boy," she said, the congestion in her chest making her cough mid-sentence.

Airi looked around. She saw wet spots on the dirt floor where the rain had come through those threadbare portions of roofing.

"Your boy is fine. But I worry for you, my lady."

She laughed at Airi's address. It was probable no one had ever called her "my lady" in her life. The laugh led to horrendous racking coughs.

"Have you no one to look out for you?" she asked the woman.

"It's just me and Lorre," she said as she struggled to sit up and get to her feet. Airi hastened to stop her.

"No need to get up, little mother. I am no one special."

Airi sat her back onto the bed then knelt beside her so she wouldn't have to look up to see her face.

"Please," Airi said softly, "let me help you."

She went into her thieves' belt and withdrew two gold coins, enough money to feed a family of two for two months. Then she thought better of it and came up with four coins. She pressed them into the woman's cold, frail hand.

"Enough to feed you and the child while you are ailing."

"I cannot! It is too much! I have always taken care of us by myself."

"Get well and then you may support him on your own. There is nothing wrong with accepting help when it comes."

The woman bit her pale lip. Her eyes filled with tears. "I cannot say no. We are starving. My boy is starving. I thank you, my lady," she said fervently.

"Get well. Care for the child. That is thanks enough."

Airi rose to her feet and walked out of the cottage. Standing in the doorway was Maxum, and he had a most curious expression on his face.

"What?" she demanded of him.

"Nothing," he said, holding up his hands.

He was quiet as he followed her, but she could feel his amusement. It danced in his eyes. She ignored him and went to the blacksmith's shop.

"Sor, do you have a thatcher in town?"

"I'm the thatcher round here." He eyed her. "You got a roof that needs thatching?"

"Yes. See that house right there?" She pointed to the woman's house.

"Farra's place?"

"Yes. I want you to thatch her roof and do it as soon as possible. Here's one gold for the job."

It was an exorbitant price to pay, far more than was required, but she didn't really care.

"All right. Will do it!" The man took her money. Airi turned around to leave and nearly ran into Maxum's chest.

"Don't you have somewhere else to be?" she demanded of him.

"Not when this is such an interesting a place to be."

"What's so interesting about it?" she asked him, her tone hard and warning.

"I find it interesting that the woman who has been harping on me for giving my money away since I met her is suddenly throwing hers away left and right."

"I'm not throwing it away. I am doing it to help somebody. There's a big difference between doing it to help someone and doing it just because you want to get your way."

"If you say so," he said.

"I do," she said with a stubborn lift of her chin. "Now shut up about it."

"You know what I think?"

"That isn't shutting up," she pointed out in a surly tone.

"I think you see some of yourself in that child. He reminds you of what it was like to grow up all alone with your mother."

"You're thinking too hard," she said shortly.

"You're all soft at heart, admit it!" He laughed.

"I'll admit you're an ass, how about that?" she said, unable to keep her cheeks from going hot.

"Don't be like that. It's a good thing, Airi. You're a good person."

"Good people get shit on. You know that," she said bitterly.

"And yet you did it all the same. I'm proud of my little thief."

"I'm not your anything. Now go away!"

"All right. Let's get this journey started."

With that they mounted their horses and rode out of the village, heading for the river.

"We have to figure out how far she went."

"She followed the river until she encountered a road. That should help."

"A road?" he asked.

"Yes. She encountered the man with the broken wheel on a road."

"That's right! So we just ride until we meet with a road."

"There may be more than one," she retorted.

"More than one with a village close by? Remember she took the wheel to a nearby village."

"True. If the village is still there. This story is centuries old."

"Corm was still there," Maxum pointed out.

"True again. I guess we'll see."

"We have to judge how far it would take a young girl

to walk in a day and a half. If the story is accurate, that's how long it was before she hit that road."

"Just how much treasure is there going to be in this temple?" Kilon asked gruffly.

Maxum was silent for a beat. "I am thinking none but what we're looking for. But don't worry. The treasure will come later."

"It better. I'm not in this just so you can make off with the goods."

"You don't have to worry. I've never let you down before, have I?"

"No, just nearly gotten us killed a few times," Doisy chirruped.

"That's the price you pay," Kyno said in his low, gruff voice. "Gotta pay to get the goods."

Airi felt anxiety twisting in her stomach. What would these guys say or do when they realized there was no treasure to be had? It made her wonder why Maxum was traveling with them in the first place. Did he even need them any longer? Why hadn't he gone his own way? The next stages of this journey would be best done alone, wouldn't they? He was searching for a specific piece of straw in a pile of straw. It would take a miracle for him to find either weapon.

But she held her tongue. The men seemed to know what they had let themselves in for by following Maxum on his wild schemes and so far it had paid out for them. Who was she to argue with his apparent success?

Maybe Maxum just needed them so he wouldn't be alone. He was a leader, and a leader needed followers to be complete, didn't they? So for now she would be a follower. She would see where the journey took them.

They traveled down along the river at a steady pace, looking ahead for any signs of a road. It was a long shot that they would ever come across the right road and there was no telling how accurate the song had been.

Sunset approached and they made camp, Maxum going off into the woods as he always did, Airi's eyes on him the entire time.

"Don't do it."

She looked at Doisy. "Do what?"

"Don't follow him. It's been tried. I tried. I followed him through the woods once and lost sight of him for a few moments and then he was gone, as if the ground had swallowed him whole. Besides, if he caught you at it there'd be the eight hells on your back."

"I'm not afraid of him."

"You should be. I know I am. You haven't seen it yet . . . the way he fights. It's like he becomes this madman. As if a demon has possessed him. He would have fought that dragon . . . and he would have won. I believe that with all of my soul."

Airi looked back to the trees where he had disappeared. "I'd like to try following him all the same. I'm a thief. I know how to move quietly and without detection. He wouldn't even know I was there."

Doisy shrugged carelessly. "It's your life. Do with it what you will. But I say you're better off not knowing."

She would be better off if the man would simply open up a little and tell her what it was he did every night.

"Hello, what's this?" Kilon said suddenly, getting to his feet in a slow, crouching way, drawing his crossbow off his back. Airi looked in the direction Kilon was looking in and saw a magnificent white stag, its rack speaking of its great age and strength. It was standing at the edge of the clearing they had chosen for their campsite and was watching them without fear. It had probably never seen people before and didn't realize it should be afraid. Very afraid.

Kilon drew his sights on the stag and Airi screamed out, "No! Ha! Run!" She crossed into Kilon's sights, blocking his shot recklessly. The stag started and then leapt away in bounding leaps that crashed through the underbrush.

Kilon roared with fury and pointed the crossbow directly at her chest. "What'd you do that for, you stupid little twat!"

"There's no need to kill it! Do you have any idea how rare those are?"

"I don't give a fuck! That was our dinner!"

"We don't need an entire stag for dinner. It would be a waste of meat because we'd have to leave behind what we don't eat."

"Why the fuck should I care about that? We eat or we starve . . . I don't care if it's the last stag in the world! We hunt it and we eat it. That's the natural order of things. Now we'll go hungry tonight because of you!"

"We won't starve. We have plenty of supplies. And you can just as easily go hunt rabbits and other small animals just like you've done every other night we've been out here," she snapped at him. "It's done and I'm glad it's done. So stop aiming that thing at me or you'll find yourself with a dagger in your balls."

"I have half a mind to pull this trigger. Then that'll be done and I'll be glad it's done. You've been nothing but trouble since you came here. I've had just about more than I can take. You're a problem. A problem that needs fixing. And I say I fix you right now!"

"Kilon, knock it off," Doisy ground out. "Put the bow down. If you so much as scratch her, you'll have to answer to Maxum for it."

"I ain't scared of Maxum. What'll he do to me? Fight me? I can take him any day of the week."

Doisy barked out a laugh. "No, you couldn't. If you think otherwise you're a bigger fool than I took you for. Drop the bow and go hunt something else for dinner."

Kilon growled, but he dropped the bow. Airi didn't realize she'd been holding her breath until it left her in a gush of relief. She was no fool. She knew Kilon could have easily have pulled that trigger and thought nothing of it. She was less than nothing to him and he could not care less if she lived or died. Apparently he preferred her dead. She was really going to have to be careful around him. As it was it had been reckless of her to step in the way of his shot. She had no idea what had come over her. Kilon was right to a point. They were hungry and the stag was meat. It was the natural order of things that he be hunted. It was a matter of survival at times.

But they could survive without killing the magnificent beast and she wasn't regretting what she had done. The idea of someone like Kilon ending its life was just too bitter to swallow.

As she had predicted, Kilon was able to kill a few pheasants for their dinner and she prepared them in silence. She had been cooking out in the open for quite some time and had learned how to make halfway decent meals over a campfire. The birds were big so it took some time before they were done. Once food was on his plate Doisy began to chat with everyone, trying to break the hard tension that had fallen over the group.

Dru and Kyno engaged him, but Kilon was his usual surly self and Airi didn't feel much like chatting. Doisy tried to find out more things about her, but she avoided his queries, not wanting to share any part of herself in front of a man who'd rather she were dead.

"I'm glad you did it," Kyno said under his breath some time into their meal. He had come to sit closer to her. His remark took her by surprise.

"Did what?"

"Stopped him from killing the stag. It was beautiful."

Airi gaped at him. Then she smiled. The big lumbering orc was a softy at heart. She hadn't gotten to know him very well and this was a surprising insight into him.

"I'm glad too," she said. "Although I've definitely given Kilon more reason to hate me."

"Did he need a reason?" Kyno asked grimly. "But don't you worry. I won't let him touch you, my lady."

Again he surprised her. She hadn't realized Kyno was such a gentleman. Or perhaps he was just being that way with her. It made her feel special and definitely warmed her heart to him. Damn it. Despite her efforts to remain unattached to these men, they were starting to get under her skin. Doisy with his irreverent ways, Dru with his shy ones . . . and now Kyno whose heart appeared to be as big as the rest of him.

And then there was Maxum . . .

She shook her head and decided it was best not to delve into that hornet's nest of emotion. Never had anyone frustrated and annoyed her as much as he did . . . and yet there was something so compelling about him . . .

"Where are you from, Kyno? The orclands?"

"On the border. That's how my mum . . . well, she didn't much like the way I came about. But she loved me in the end. I'm doing this for her, so she can live the way she deserves to live. It's a hard life on the border of the orclands. So I moved her to a big city and I send her gold to keep her fed and content."

"It sounds to me like you're a good son."

He shrugged one large shoulder. "My mum never asked for me, did nothing to deserve me other than to be too pretty and catch an orclord's eye. She said when he took her against her will he took a little part of her with him . . . and when I was born it filled the hole that was left. So I loves her back best way I know how."

"And is there any special woman in your life, Kyno? Other than your mum, I mean," she said with a wink. He chuckled. It was a deep, rumbly sound and she liked it very much.

"No. Not as yet. I figure I'll meet someone someday.

Maybe if I goes to the orclands there be a nice big orc girl waiting for me. But I'm a halfbreed so . . ." He shrugged. He didn't have to say anything else. The orcs were snobs in a way. Oh, it was fine for the men to get children on the women of the other races like Kyno's father had, but when it came to marrying their daughters only purebreeds would do.

"What about a girl from the other races?"

"Don't you think they're too small?" He frowned as he thought on it. "I might break one."

"Don't you . . . I mean . . . surely you've . . . I saw you in the inn. You were . . . indulging in women."

"I likes to touch and play with them in public like, but no, I don't touch in private."

He couldn't mean . . . was Kyno still a virgin then? No, surely not. There had to have been someone. There were orc girls or even giantesses who roamed the world. He had to have met up with one.

"Kyno . . . have you ever . . . been with a woman?"

The giant man flushed. He scrubbed a hand through his hair and dipped his head in embarrassment. "Don't tell the others," he said.

"Oh, I won't. Your secret is very safe with me," she reassured him quickly. She put her arms around him, only reaching halfway around his back, and gave him the best hug she could manage.

"Thank you, my lady."

"And what's with the 'my lady'?" she said teasingly. "I'm hardly anyone's idea of a lady."

"You're mine," he said with finality. "Best lady I knows."

"Only lady you know," she said laughingly.

"I know some others. But not many." He paused a beat. "If you wasn't so small . . ." He trailed off meaningfully.

This time it was her turn to blush.

"Besides . . . Maxum wants you."

She frowned. "Well, Maxum isn't going to get what he wants."

"Maybe," he said, giving her a knowing wink. It was the first time she realized how long his lashes were. And that he had very pretty blue eyes. No orc purebreed would have blue eyes. Theirs were either red or black.

They chatted like that until well after juquil's hour. Maxum returned in silence and sat down on his bedroll which she had assiduously located across the way from her once again, the fire in between them. The amusement in his eyes told him the stubbornness of the act was not lost upon him. Still, she knew that if he put his mind to it one little campfire wouldn't stand in his way.

Airi was tired, so she went to bed shortly after, snuggling down under her blanket against the chill night. It wasn't lost on her that another warm body would have been a nice thing to have right then.

But it wasn't worth the trouble.

Chapter
Fourteen

~⸻⸻~

It was mid afternoon of the next day when they finally came to a road. A stone bridge crossed the river and a dirt road crossed their paths. Airi and Maxum exchanged a look. Now all they had to see was if there was a village within walking distance.

"Over the bridge or the other way?" she asked him.

He thought about it a moment. "We'll try over the bridge first. If we don't come to it in an hour we'll double back."

She figured it was as sound a plan as any. They were on horseback. A girl pushing a broken wheel couldn't have gotten all that far all that fast.

After an hour and a half of riding, they realized they had gone the wrong way and doubled back.

The village, when they came to it, was no longer a village. It was an abandoned collection of run-down and rotted cottages. There was an old smithy in the center of the town and Maxum's eyes lit with hope.

"This is it!" he said triumphantly.

"This *may* be it," she corrected him. "There could just as easily be a village with a smith down a road in the other direction."

"This is it. I can feel it," he said stubbornly.

She didn't argue with him further. She was feeling the sense of excitement as well. Could they really be close to finding the temple? Somehow she knew it would not be so easy.

"Do we camp here?" she asked.

"No. We can go a little farther," he said, clearly wanting to push on.

"Do we follow the road or the river?"

"The river. The story said she bathed. That means she was near water."

"All right then, the river it is." She kneed Hero's sides and trotted off back down the road they had come on. When she reached the bridge she turned to Maxum. "Which side?"

"The same side I'm thinking."

There was a lot of ifs and maybes to be had all around, but she was game for the experience, wherever it might lead them. They went on until just before sunset when, as usual, they stopped to make camp so Maxum could do his disappearance.

After they had built their fire and cooked their dinner, the group sat in silence for the most part. That was why they heard the twigs snapping as someone made their way to them through the trees. Kilon leapt up and pulled his crossbow first thing. Airi was on her feet a half second later holding out a placating hand to a man not prone to being placated.

"Let's see who it is first before you start shooting," she said to him through tight teeth.

They knew it wasn't Maxum—it was too early yet. There was always the possibility he had come back early, but since he never had before there was little doubt that these were strangers approaching.

A young woman came out of the trees and into the clearing where they'd made their fire. She saw Kilon's aggressive stance and immediately backpedaled toward the woods.

"Wait!" Airi cried out. "We won't hurt you."

"Won't we?" Kilon growled.

"We won't," Airi said harshly.

"I-I-I saw the fire. I-I-I thought you might . . . h-have some food."

"No, Now get lost, kid."

"Of course we do," Airi said, ignoring Kilon. The girl was obviously hungry enough to do the same. She stepped forward.

"I don't eat much," she insisted. "I smelled food and I thought . . . maybe . . ." She trailed off and shrugged.

"Sure. Come closer to the fire. You look cold."

"Trusting bitch," Kilon muttered under his breath.

"Ignore him. That's what I do."

"O-okay," she said, sounding very unsure. But Airi's bravery and the girl's empty belly compelled her to believe her, it seemed.

"What's your name?"

"Sarda."

"Here, Sarda," Airi said, handing her the leg and thigh of the rabbit Kilon had hunted earlier. The girl fell on it like a ravening wolf, stuffing as much of it into her mouth as she could get in one bite, as though she were afraid Airi would snatch it back away from her.

"There's plenty. Take your time," Airi assured her, handing a plate of wild potatoes to the girl. The girl popped a whole one in her mouth and said something through a garbling mouthful that sounded like "thank you." The girl's eyes rolled back in her head with pleasure every time she took a bite.

"That's Maxum's dinner you're feeding her," Kilon said. "He's not going to take kindly to an empty belly."

"There's plenty here for everyone," Airi said, nibbling

on a potato herself so the girl didn't feel like she was eating alone.

Sarda swallowed. "You don't know how much this means to me," she said before taking another bite.

"I think I have an idea. There've been days I've gone hungry. Once I didn't eat for a whole week."

"It's been three days for me."

"Where's your coin? Where're your people? You may be eating now but you'll be starving again tomorrow," Kilon barked. "Best to get it over with."

"Get it over with?" she echoed.

"The business of starving to death," he said before he kicked back and relaxed against the tree he'd laid his bedroll near. Airi wished there was a nice gnarled root right underneath it when he slept tonight.

"Best to take it one day at a time," Airi said to Sarda, offering her some wine from her leather flask. She'd been saving it for some sort of special occasion, but the girl needed more than water to fortify her. The wine would help build up her strength . . . provided she didn't drink too much.

"How'd you come to be out here in the woods in the middle of nowhere?"

"Same as you, I reckon. Just traveling."

"It's getting cold soon and you're going hungry. Don't you think its best you found a place to hole up for the winter? Make a little coin."

"I'm going to . . . as soon as I find a place big enough where people are looking for hired help. I was told there was a village down the road a ways back, but it was abandoned. Someone's idea of a joke to send me all this way for nothing."

Airi grimaced. It was a cruel thing to do. Poor kid. She needed a break.

"Well . . . you could travel with us to the next—"

"It ain't your place to say who travels with us!" Kilon

belched out in sudden anger. He made as if he were going to get to his feet and smack Airi for her insolence. Sarda cringed and scurried back away from him. Airi stood up and went toe to toe with the bastard.

"I realize that," she hissed. "If you'd let me finish my sentence I was going to say we just have to ask our leader if it is all right. Now sit down and shut up!"

Kilon backhanded her. Hard. She went flying back and slammed into a tree. Kyno was on his feet in an instant, his body blocking Kilon from following up on the strike. He grabbed Kilon by the front of his shirt and gave him a rattling shake.

"Don't you touch her again! You'll answer to me, Kilon! I'll pop your head like an overripe grape!"

There was really no way any sane man would argue with that terrible voice and that overwhelming, gigantic presence, but Kilon, apparently, was not a sane man. As Airi picked herself up from where she had fallen, wiping a hand across her bloodied mouth, she heard him say, "Then you teach that fucking cunt not to mouth off to me or I'll smack her again and I don't care what you think you can do to me!"

Fury blinded Airi. She lunged forward, reaching to claw out the bastard's eyes. She was jerked back just before she reached him, slamming backward into a thick, hard trunk of a body. Strong hands held her around her upper arms.

"All right, what the hell is going on here?" Maxum demanded. "I leave for a few hours and suddenly everyone's at each other's throats?"

"Suddenly?" Airi spat. "That man is an evil little serpent spitting poison into this group every moment of every day. Are you really so blind you can't see it?"

"All I see is my group acting like a bunch of unruly children and it is going to stop *now*!" His voice was just as terrible as Kyno's had been. Kyno dropped Kilon and he got his feet under him. He turned hate-filled eyes onto Airi.

"You just keep that little whore away from me. It's your group, you say you want her—although we all know it's your cock that wants her—so what you say goes. But I'm warning you, she mouths off to me again and I'll rip her tongue out!"

"If you touch her I'll—" Maxum began.

"I'll plunge a dagger in that black heart of yours so fast you'll be dead before you touch me! You get one free shot and that was just it. It'll never happen again," she spat back at Kilon.

"One free shot?" Maxum asked. He quickly turned her around in his hands and got an eyeful of the blood running out of her nose and from between her lips. She'd been hit so hard it was a wonder she hadn't lost any teeth. As it was her teeth had cut the inside of her lip and it was beginning to swell painfully. "He *hit* you?"

"Well he didn't sing me a lullaby," she said churlishly.

Maxum suddenly let go of her, pushed past her, and with two steps and a powerful drawback of his fist, punched Kilon in the face. Kilon went down and the other men quickly jumped in to keep Maxum from doing further damage. But apparently Maxum was done because he stepped back from the man.

"That's what'll happen if anyone raises a fist to anyone in this group! They'll get it mirrored back on them from me!"

Kilon was just about unconscious so he didn't have a reply. Maxum turned back to her, taking her arm almost gently into his hand, then he called Doisy over.

"Can you heal her for me?" he asked.

"Of course."

Maxum grimaced. "When you're done you can do Kilon too."

Doisy nodded. He didn't express any kind of resentment or partiality to the situation and Airi realized she felt a little hurt by that. She would have thought she'd at least earned a little friendship with Doisy. A little loyalty. But she should know better than to depend on anyone but herself.

"Now, does anyone want to tell me what started this?"

"I-I did," Sarda stammered.

"No, you didn't," Airi said firmly. "This was my fault. He got under my skin and I provoked him."

"Provoked him how?"

"Does it matter?" she asked, her tone surly.

"It does. It'll tell me whether or not I should fine you for your behavior."

"Fine me? Fine *me*? He's the one who hit me! He's the one who is always being so nasty it makes everyone's stomachs go sour!"

"I'm not arguing with you about whether or not he'll win any personality contests. I want to know what you did to start him up. And then I want you to tell me who in the eight hells she is," he said, nodding to Sarda.

Sulkily, Airi told him word for word what had happened and how Sarda had happened upon them.

"This is *my* group. I will decide who stays *or* who goes for that matter. I'm going to get tired of you trying to manipulate things to your liking if you aren't careful."

"Manipulate?" She stared at him aghast. "I wasn't trying to manipulate anything! I just wanted to suggest—"

"Just like you keep suggesting I get rid of him?" He jerked his head to Kilon.

Suddenly she could see it from his perspective. But damn it all, she hadn't meant to be manipulative. When she bit her battered lip, he softened toward her. "To be fair I don't think you are doing it with great machinations in mind. Just . . . be careful, all right?"

She nodded. "All right." But after only a beat she said. "So can Sarda stay?"

He laughed incredulously. "You are unbelievable!"

"Just until we reach another town. Just to keep her safe until then. Please?"

Maxum sighed, shaking his head and a smile twitching at the corners of his mouth. "Only to the next town. And I swear, if anything goes wrong I'm going to take it out of your hide."

"All right. But it won't!"

"It better not."

Airi smiled happily and let Doisy tend to her nose and mouth.

CHAPTER
FIFTEEN

A iri woke the next morning to the sound of the river flowing nearby. Everyone else was still asleep and dawn had barely broken. She went to her saddle and grabbed her bag off it. She carried it down to the stream and looked for a secluded spot. She found a small copse of trees circling the edge of the water, creating a concealing inlet where the current was not running so fast. She stripped out of her clothes and, grabbing a bar of scented soap from her bag, she slipped into the icy cold water. Her teeth were clattering at first until she grew used to it. Then she began to briskly scrub at herself with the soap. It was a woman's fragrance, this soap one of the few things she spoiled herself with when she could afford to. She had bought a new bar in Calandria and she smelled deeply of it quite a few times as she took her bath. Then she unplaited her braids and scrubbed it through her hair.

"You're elven!"

Airi gasped at the deep voiced words of surprise and out of habit she covered her ears before she thought to cover her naked body. She dropped down in the water so it was up to her neck.

"No sense hiding it now," Maxum drawled as he came to the water's edge.

He was right. She dropped her hands from her gracefully pointed ears and lifted her chin.

"Are you going to tell the others?" she asked.

"It's none of their business if you don't want it to be."

"I don't."

"Why are you hiding it?"

"I would think that would be obvious."

"Well, I know elves have a bad reputation for being elitists and cold natured, and they are considered to be cruel to those not of their race. Their prejudice runs deep and therefore the other races do not trust them, but that doesn't mean you are like that."

"We already know I'm untrustworthy," she said.

"But you're not a snob. An elf wouldn't be caught dead with a band of misfits like mine."

"Well, I'm not all elf."

"A halfbreed? That explains why you're so short. But halfbreeds are as rare as genten diamonds. Elves simply do not breed outside of their race. Was it like our orcish friend? Were you the product of—"

"No. Not as my mother told it. She said she loved him . . . and that he loved her. But he died when I was two. I don't remember him at all. It was hard for my mother, raising an elven child. I've been hiding my ears since my hair was long enough to cover it. I don't know why I still do it. I just . . . I have enough against me to start with. It's easier if people don't know."

"All right. I can respect that," he said, and she could see by his expression that he did understand. And that he didn't care if she was elven, orcish, or kataanese. It gave her a sense of relief . . . and a strange sense of belonging.

She shook the feeling away. She didn't belong anywhere. She had based her entire life on that concept. She didn't belong and she didn't want to belong. Belonging meant trusting others with parts of yourself, making yourself vulnerable in emotional ways. She was not the sort to do that and she wasn't going to start now. Especially not with someone as untrustworthy as Maxum . . . or his men.

That was unfair, she realized. There was nothing inherently untrustworthy about Doisy and Dru or even Kyno. They had done nothing to earn her mistrust except they were people. People were undependable. Life had taught her that hard lesson and she shouldn't forget it. Maxum's men may not have betrayed her yet but life had taught her that it was only a matter of time.

Everyone always let her down.

Always.

"All right, now that we have that out of the way, would you mind leaving so I can get out? The water is very cold."

"Get out? I was just thinking about getting in." He sat down on the bank and removed his boots. Then he stripped off his vest and then his shirt.

"Don't you dare!" she squeaked as he stood up, all gloriously bare-chested and began to untie the fastenings of his pants. Despite her distress, she couldn't help but stare at the golden play of muscle beneath skin as he moved. The light dusting of hair on his chest faded as it went down and then darkened below his navel in an arrowing line that led straight to where his hands were loosening his pants. Suddenly she badly wanted to see what he was threatening to show her . . . so she didn't put up much of a fight as his pants were skimmed down his legs, leaving him magnificently naked before her. Something in the core of her went warm, battling the cold of the river, making her shiver at the contrast.

He walked boldly forward and into the water, giving her an all too brief look at all he had to offer . . . but brief was more than enough. He had been fully aroused, hard as can be and jutting proudly forth from his body. He gasped when he hit the water and she smiled. That ought to cool his ardor some, she thought. But then she realized he was coming toward her. And that he was naked and so was she!

She suddenly began to swim away, trying to force her cold body to work, but in the end she was trapped because outside of their little cove the water ran fast and white and it was too dangerous for her to swim out into it. He caught her easily, dragging her body up against his, his warmth so penetrating and so inviting as it came close . . . connected . . . contacted. She had been wrong about the cold of the water affecting his arousal. He was still fully, dangerously erect. He drew her up to him, her breasts flattening to his chest, his erection nestling against her belly. Heat bloomed across her face and her body. She went stiff in his hold.

"Let go of me!"

"No. Is it true what they say about elves? That beneath that cold exterior they run incredibly hot?"

"I wouldn't know. I'm only half elf and I was never raised around elves. In fact, my mother seemed to think that if an elf saw me he would feel honor bound to eradicate me, since I'm an impurity to the species. It's another reason why I hide. Just in case it's true."

"Any elf that tried to eradicate you would find himself in the fight of his life."

"So will you if you don't let me go!"

Only, the warmth of his body was so inviting in the cold water and she found herself snuggling up into him. He noticed with a grin.

"I don't think that's what you really want. In fact, I'm thinking you are way out of touch with what you really want."

"You have no idea what I want," she said. "You only know what you want. It's always about what you want."

"I'm not going to lie and say I don't want you because I've made that abundantly clear." He reached to take her hand, brought it below the water and between their bodies where he slowly curled her fingers around his erection. "Clear, yes?"

"Yes," she whispered as she willed herself not to stroke him, or hold him or shape him. To feel every inch of him.

Clearly her willpower needed a lot of work because before she knew it she was doing exactly all of those things. He sucked in a breath as she molded him to her palm and drew her touch from the base of his staff all the way to the tip. He was so hard and so hot . . . even in the cold of the river. And as she touched him . . . as she learned him . . . she felt an answering heat blooming between her thighs.

Her opposite hand still held her soap and in spite of herself and her internal berating, she touched the soap to his chest and drew a soft circle with it. Before long she had worked up a lather and was dipping the soap beneath the water, washing his taut abdominal muscles. He took a sniff and grimaced.

"Sweetflower. I'm going to smell of sweetflower."

"I could always stop," she offered, hoping he didn't accept. She had plans for her soap.

"Not on your life. Having Airianne the elf give me a bath? I wouldn't trade that for anything in this world."

"Shut up before you ruin it," she said with a frown. Then she opened the hand she still held around him and the soap skimmed down the long length of him. She worked the soap into an earnest lather against him, slicking her touch as she stroked and stroked and stroked him. He groaned deeply and she could see a muscle ticking in his jaw.

She suddenly felt a great sense of power in that moment. It was a feeling quite unlike anything she'd ever experienced before. She had the power to give him pleasure . . . and it was *working*. He was aroused . . . because of her. He was moaning with pleasure . . . because of her. He could be brought to climax just like this . . . *because of her.* The potency of that kind of power was heady and being who she was, she wanted to test the bounds of it. The hand with the soap in it went down to slowly wash around his sac, her hand toying with the malleable flesh, and all the while her opposite hand stroked and stroked and stroked until he swore softly and reached to tangle a hand in her wet hair. Gripping it tightly he made sure her eyes met his.

"Do not make me come," he demanded of her.

"Why not?" she asked, her voice rough with unused passion.

"Because I want to be inside of you when I do."

"That isn't going to happen," she said, her soft tone anything but convincing. He laughed, groaned deeply and laughed again. It was as though he was having a hard time controlling what emotions he wished to show. His eyes were on fire, burning like a cadium tree burned, with a wild green fire. Something in the wood made it burn green, just as something in her touch made him burn for her.

"I don't believe you," he said almost tauntingly. "I think you want me just as much as I want you."

Then, to prove his point, he slid his fingers boldly between her legs, immediately feeling the viscous difference between the wet of the river and the wet of her welcoming body. He gave her a sly smile.

"There now see, let there be truth between us."

"All right," she said breathily, "so it's true I want you. I am a woman and you are a man. You aren't all that hard to look at and it's been a while since I've lain with a man." *About ten full turnings,* she added to herself. "It makes sense that I might want something . . . just something."

"You want to fuck. Fornicate. Have sex. Lay with. Tumble. With *me*. No other man will do. Admit it."

"I'll admit no such thing. You're merely a convenience." She lifted her chin stubbornly. "Plenty of other men would do."

"Dru?" he asked. "Kyno? They're right within reach. What about Doisy? He's always up for a turn with the ladies." But even as he said it, a vicious stab of jealousy tore through Maxum. He didn't want her to say just any man would do. He wanted her to say only he would do.

He slowly, steadily worked his finger inside the tight sheath of her body, seating his palm against her clitoris where he began to rub her insistently.

At her stubborn silence he said. "Tell me who you want. Tell me I'm not just a warm body." He withdrew from inside her body and she cried out softly in instant regret. She grabbed his arm. He drew his finger lazily around her clit, warming her up, making her moan. "Yes? What is it?" he asked her.

"Please!"

He worked quicker, in tighter circles and she began to tremble in his arms. Her mouth dropped open slightly, her breath came in soft pants and her eyes slid closed. She was falling into the sensations he was creating.

And then he stopped and drew his hand away, leaving her with only the icy cold water against her flesh.

"Wait! Stop please!" she begged him, grabbing hold of him when he went to move away from her.

He turned back to her hard, grabbing her face between his hands and dragging her up to his mouth. He kissed her fiercely, as if his soul was on fire, as if he would set hers ablaze as well. Heat fought to survive against the chill water as it bloomed down her body. His tongue danced with slow drugging need one moment and with fierce ferocity the next. She was breathless, and all she could do was hang on tight, hold her body as close to his as she could manage.

He ripped his mouth away, leaving their hard breaths filling the air.

"Tell me what I want to hear," he demanded of her.

She shook her head.

Damn her she was so stubborn! But he wasn't going to let her get away with pretending he didn't matter. He didn't understand why, didn't bother to examine the impulse too closely in the moment, but he was determined to have all of her or none at all.

He turned to swim away from her, but realized belatedly that she still had her hands wrapped around him. How could he have forgotten? She'd been driving him mad since the very first touch.

"Let go of me," he murmured when his movement did not break her hold. She silently shook her head, not meeting his eyes, staring at his chest.

"Do you have something to say to me?" he asked.

She mutely shook her head again.

"Then let go. Face up to what you're doing. You're making the conscious choice to let me go. So make the choice." He reached down to cover her hands beneath the water where they held him and her grip tightened, though not yet painfully. Still, she literally had him by the balls and it would almost be amusing if it weren't so serious.

"Fine," she whispered.

There was a pause, a long breath where he waited to see what she would do next. Waited and wanted.

"It's you," she whispered. "Not anyone else. I want you."

Then she let him go and swam away, leaving him shocked and surprised. Shocked she had admitted it, surprised she had then left him. It took him a moment to wake up and swim after her. By the time he caught up with her she was hauling herself up onto the riverbank. She hurried to where she had left her clothes and he was hot on her heels.

"Why are you leaving if you just said—?"

"Where are my clothes?" she asked him accusingly.

"Wherever you left them I imagine," he said impatiently. "But you're not getting dressed. You're going to stay with me and we're going to—"

"No, we're not," she said definitively.

"But you just said—"

"Yes. And that's the reason why it's not going to happen. The fact that no one else will do tells me that I am foolishly getting too attached to you. It tells me that I need to protect myself, not open myself up to further attachment."

"But why? I don't understand what is so bad about a little attachment."

She looked at him as if he had sprouted five heads. "This coming from you?" she asked incredulously.

She had a point. Why wasn't he running away like she was? He should be terrified of the idea of anyone getting too attached to him. His was a cursed existence. He had no right to get close to anyone. And he had a goal that would very likely be the death of him. He should be encouraging her to leave—to leave the group entirely— rather than risk her getting too much attached. But . . .

"Do not assume to know what I want. All you need to know is that I want you, Airi. Whatever comes tomorrow will come tomorrow and we will deal with it when it does, but for right now . . . I want you in my bed."

She bit her lip and seemed to hesitate. But then, "No, Maxum, you'll only hurt me."

"Yes," he said quickly. "I probably will. People always hurt one another and I will not lie and make promises otherwise. But when you find a little joy, a little pleasure with someone, you have to take advantage of it. You have to have something to make life worth living, something to create a little balance in your life."

She couldn't help herself, she smiled. Give him a few minutes more and he might start quoting poetry. She tried to remind herself that he was just saying these things to get his way, to get her body under his. And the truth was that she was on the verge of letting him have her. And that was why she wanted her clothes so she could run back to camp and be around other people; hoping that would deter him for at least another day.

"Where in the eight hells are my clothes?!" she cried out in frustration as she looked for them. Then she noticed something else. "Where in the eight hells are *your* clothes?"

Maxum looked around on the ground where he had left his clothes and boots.

Nothing. They were gone. Except for . . . a piece of paper. He picked it up and read what was written aloud.

"Please forgive me, I had no choice. Sarda."

"Sarda took our clothes? Why in the eight hells would she do that?"

"Because it wasn't just our clothes. Didn't you have a saddlebag with you?"

"Oh my god! She stole all my things! My *gold*!"

"This is what happens when you start trusting strangers, Airianne!" he barked out at her.

"You're the one who said she could stay!"

"Only because you were making those puppy eyes at me and saying 'Oh please, Maxum! I am using your attraction toward me to get my way, so please let her stay!' And then you batted your lashes at me or some such shit."

"I never batted anything! And I wasn't taking advantage of your attraction to me!"

"Ha! Examine yourself more closely, Airi. You'll find the truth. Just as I know the truth is I gave in to you because of that attraction even though my gut said otherwise. My gut told me another woman, especially a weak one, would be nothing but trouble. I should have listened to myself instead of letting my dick do the thinking for me."

"Oh! You are such a . . . a . . . a bastard!" she said at last, unable to come up with anything stronger because she felt too much truth in his words. But she'd be damned if she was going to admit it while she was standing cold and naked in the middle of the forest.

She wrapped her arms around herself and began to shiver violently. Maxum saw her and immediately stepped in to her to pull her close and she tried swatting him away.

"Come on! Let me warm you up!" he said forcefully. "Stop fighting for once and do something that's good for you for a change."

She quieted when she realized he had a point. She was fighting just for the sake of fighting him . . . of not giving in. The truth was she needed his warmth badly and she had to accept it or risk freezing to death.

"Let's go back to camp," Maxum suggested. "I have clothes there we can use."

"Wait."

CHAPTER
SIXTEEN

~~~~~~~~~~~~~~~~~~

She had gone still in his arms, her shivering dropping to a low shuddering, and she placed a hand on his chest and nodded to the east. There, standing at the edge of the trees, stood a white stag. It was the largest stag she'd ever seen, even larger than the one she'd saved from Kilon's arrows.

Suddenly everything clicked in her mind. She pushed out of Maxum's hold and walked toward the stag. The moment she moved toward it the stag began to slowly walk into the woods and away from camp. It didn't bound away in fright, it simply walked. Airi followed it, taking a moment to grasp Maxum's hand and pull him along with her.

"What are you—"

"Shh! Don't you see?" she asked him in a low, excited whisper. "Don't you see the parallel to the story of Isa? The boy stole her clothes while she was in the waters bathing and then she came upon the temple of Meru. Maybe she didn't just happen upon it . . . maybe something led her there. Just as the stag led her to the young man's house."

"So we're going to walk naked through the woods because of a white stag?" He was questioning, but he also saw the brilliance of her conclusion. She was right! This could be the way they had been looking for.

"Do you have any better ideas?"

"None at all," he said with a chuckle. "But I hope it's not far. If I step on one more twig . . ."

"Hush. The last thing we need is for you to break the enchantment by complaining. We are dealing with a very delicate balance of circumstances here."

He nodded and said nothing further. The stag led them quite a distance, but soon they emerged into a beautiful glade and there, in the center, was a small marble temple, a marble statue of the goddess Meru standing inside the atrium. Airi led Maxum up the steps and into the atrium. There, standing off to the right, stood a beautiful woman in the crimson robes of a Meru mem. She was taller than most women, her figure strong and sturdy, her curves round and lush. She had hair the color of honeyed wheat that was plaited in one long braid that swept the floor. Her eyes were a vivid forest green.

"Meru," Maxum said.

It wasn't a guess, she realized, or even a supposition based on the story. He spoke it as if he had met Meru before and now recognized her.

Airi immediately dropped to her knee and bowed her head. She tugged on Maxum's hand to get him to do the same, but it took a long minute before he knelt as well. He did not, however, bow his head. He never once looked away from the goddess's face.

"Airianne the elf," Meru said, "you have come searching for me?"

"I have. I am searching for . . . for the Dagger of Truths." She figured honesty would be best here.

"And you feel you are worthy of it?"

"I . . . I don't know about worthy . . . but I believe I could put it to some use in my life."

"And are you a truthful person?"

"No," she said honestly. "Life has made it necessary for me to lie."

"I can see that it has. But if you wield the Dagger of Truths or even carry it on your person you will not be able to lie. Are you prepared to give up your need for falsehoods?"

Airi hesitated. Significantly. She was a thief. Lying was an essential part of her life.

"Will I be compelled to blurt out the truth even when not asked for it?" she said.

"No."

She could work with that.

"Then yes. I am prepared for that."

"Good." She lifted a hand and suddenly in a flash of light a dagger, in a gleaming ebonite sheath, appeared in her extended hand. The blade handle had no gems or jewels encrusting it, just simple silver metal worked into delicate scrolls on the hilt and a grip wrapped in simple red leather. "Here is the Dagger of Truths. You have passed the tests and proved yourself to have a pure heart and so I take comfort in handing it over to you. It has been a long time since it has been wielded, no others save Isa proving to be of honest enough heart to wield it."

"Tests?" Maxum asked.

"The child in the village. The stag in the woods. The helpless girl you know as Sarda. These were all tests I have sent to you."

Meru waved her hand and their clothes appeared on their bodies. They felt warm, as if they had been dried over a fire.

Then Meru turned to Maxum. "You have not passed the tests, so you may not wield the blade. I know this was your intent but the blade may only be wielded by the chosen one—and only by a woman. This is the way of things."

Maxum felt a wash of disappointment run over him, but he would not allow this opportunity to pass him by.

"Meru, I have come to beg your assistance," he said.

He felt Airi's surprise, but to her credit she said nothing.

Meru methodically walked forward and laid the Dagger of Truths into Airi's hands. She took it, bowing her head in thanks.

"What is it a god may do for a mortal?" Then she tipped her head. "But then again, you are not mortal, are you?"

Again Airi twitched with surprise. Again she made no comment.

"I am going to kill Sabo, but I need the help of Weysa's faction to do it."

Meru laughed, a light but rich sound. Everything about her had that feeling of richness to it. A feeling that there was so much more than what they saw on the surface.

"You think you can kill a god?"

"Can't I?"

Meru looked at him and tilted her head. She narrowed those grass green eyes on him. "It is possible. Perhaps. But there is much risk in killing a god. There is much in the way of consequences when such a thing happens. Are you prepared to accept those consequences?"

"I have no choice."

Her eyes turned hard. "That is not an answer. Certainly not one worthy of my help."

"I only meant to say . . . I will do anything to see Sabo destroyed. It is the only way I can be free of my curse."

"Are you sure it is not revenge you seek? Vengeance for the many years you suffered at his hands? Suffer still?"

"No. Not vengeance. I deserved my punishment. But now I believe I deserve to be free of it. The only way that will happen is if Sabo reverses the curse . . . or is killed. We both know Sabo will never willingly release someone from pain and suffering. He is the god of pain and suffering. He thrives on it."

"Yes. He is cruel and has taken his powers to a cruel place. All of the gods have known this for some time. But none of us can touch Sabo. Only a human being can unseat a god. If all of his followers were to suddenly renounce him he would be destroyed."

"That isn't likely to happen," Airi said, looking from Meru back to Maxum. She couldn't believe what she was hearing. She had so many questions and they were multiplying with every second.

"No. It is not."

"There must be another way," Maxum said. "I can do battle with him."

"Yes," Meru said thoughtfully. "That is possible. But you will only get one shot at it. If you fail it will be up to the gods to punish you for your hubris once again. It will not be hubris if you prove yourself worthy by winning, but if you fail to back up your claims of greatness . . . well . . ."

"All I need is for you and Weysa's faction to keep the rest of Xaxis's faction away from me as I battle Sabo."

"It is true, Xaxis will not want to lose a member of his faction and will not honor the code of challenge. Very well, when you are ready you will call to me. Go to any temple of mine and pray to me. I will bring you to Sabo and Weysa's faction will surround you. You will do battle with him and whatever will be will be."

"How will I know if I am ready?" Maxum asked, sounding suddenly unsure.

Meru regarded him thoughtfully. "You are almost ready now. You have invisibility, which will help you catch him off guard. You have invulnerability, which will protect you from harm. And you have Weysa's

Champion—the god-made sword Weysa intended for your brother, her champion, to wield. But you will need two further items before you will be ready."

"What items?" he asked, with an eagerness to his tone Airi had never heard before. It was clear how badly he wanted this. That it meant life and death to him. "Faya's Wrath?"

"No. You have a sword much more powerful than Faya's Wrath already. Weysa's Champion was forged by six gods. It was meant to slay even the strongest of Weysa's opponents. I would safely say that includes a god. In the right hands at least. Will your hands be the right hands?"

"They will," he said strongly.

"Again, is it hubris? Did you learn nothing from your time in the earth? Or are you a true champion meant to rid the world of man of a cruel and vengeful god?"

"I've learned that immortality comes at a price but that price has been paid. Several times over. My brothers are free from their curses, so should I be."

"Your brothers have found the way to true freedom from curses and everything else. Women. Their wives are their salvation. Their truth. Is this woman yours?" Meru asked, looking to Airi.

"I—"

But Maxum cut her off. "She is a woman without equal; you have seen that for yourself otherwise you would not have given her the Dagger of Truths. And she is mine."

"You are in the presence of the blade of truths and so you cannot lie to her," Meru pointed out, leaving Airi shocked into silence. "Very well. It is clear. Here is what you will do. You need two more items of magic if you think to defeat the god Sabo. One is the Ring of Strength. Only with this ring will you have the strength to fight a god and land a killing blow. But be warned, the ring is in a labyrinth deep in the Killing Forest and is guarded by a great and terrible beast. A beast birthed by the gods themselves.

"Next you will need the Cuff of Cadence. It can change the speed at which you move, and can alter the speed of others. Only in this way will you be able to slow the speed of a god and to quicken yourself to battle him. But this cuff is worn around the arm of a demigod named Xzonxzu who lives in the city of Gorgun. A wealthy and well-protected man. It will not be easy separating it from him since he can use its power any time so long as he is wearing it.

"Find these things and bring them to the temple with the sword, the ring of invisibility, and the talisman of invulnerability. Together they will be enough to defeat a god . . . provided you are warrior enough to complete the tasks before you."

"I will prove myself worthy of your trust," he said solemnly.

"I do not trust you, champion. I honestly do not see you succeeding but if you were to succeed it would deal a deadly blow to Xaxis's faction. We have been planning for some time to find the opportunity to free Kitari from Xaxis's guard. She has been forced to fight on his side, but we have been sent signs from her that tell us she is only a hostage and she wishes to be free. In fact, your brother gave up his immortality to provide one of those signs.

"We will use your battle with Sabo as an opportunity to free Kitari. It will keep the other gods from interfering in your battle and whether you win or lose we will still have freed Kitari. This is the only reason I am supporting your cause. No man should have the power to destroy a god . . . and yet you will. But I do not believe you will succeed . . . unless this woman is by your side. Only with our true mates can we be whole enough to accomplish the impossible."

"You are the goddess of women, your wisdom is keen. I will heed your advice in all things." This time Maxum did bow his head.

Confused and overwhelmed by all she was hearing, Airi had been struck mute. She was staring at a goddess—a goddess!—and had listened to a plot to kill a god! She couldn't even begin to know how to deal with something like that.

Meru came up to her, lifted her chin with two fingers and peered down into her eyes . . . into her soul it seemed.

"Just remember, my little chosen one, the dagger cannot lie. Sometimes there are truths too painful to bear, and sometimes there are truths we are not yet ready to hear. Be careful what questions you ask. Be certain you want the truth that will be spoken. And the dagger will make people deal fairly with you, but make sure you deal fairly with them in return. The dagger is yours for as long as you live, but it can be taken away if your heart becomes impure or unjust."

With that she turned and simply faded away, the temple dissolving with her, leaving them kneeling in the grasses of the glade.

Maxum was the first to get to his feet but she quickly followed. He began walking back toward camp and she was hot on his heels.

"You want to kill a *god*?" she spat. "Are you out of your fucking mind?"

"Keep your voice down," he hissed back at her.

"Oh why? So some other god doesn't overhear me? They are omniscient, Maxum! They know everything, see and hear everything!"

"No, they do not," he said, stopping suddenly and turning to her. Her momentum sent her crashing into his chest and he closed his hands around her upper arms to help her regain her balance. "Look, I know a lot more about the gods than most people do. I've listened to every song from every storyteller on two continents now. The one thing true in almost every song is that the gods are almost as human as we are! They play, they fight, they make friends and make enemies. They fornicate and have children. They feel everything we feel . . . sometimes to an even stronger degree. Certainly to a more dangerous one if you happen to get caught in the middle. But the one thing I learned was that no god anywhere could possibly pay attention to every being at every time. In the Song of Delleran, Xaxis was 'taken by surprise.' In the Song of Holybore, Hella was caught bathing naked in the woods, unaware of the watcher. In the Song of Jukessa, Mordu was unaware of his wife's affair. Mordu, the god of love caught unaware of a human loving his wife. So you see, they cannot hear and know everything at all times."

He released her and turned to go but she grabbed hold of him and spun him back around.

"All right then, answer me this . . . why do you want to kill a god? What curse is . . ." She stopped and understanding dawned. "From dusk to juquil's hour. That is when the curse happens isn't it? What happens to you during those hours?"

He looked for a moment like he wasn't going to answer, but eventually he said, "I am dragged into the depths of the soil and rock of the ground and there I am crushed and suffocated."

Airi's mouth dropped open in horror. "For all those hours?"

"Every minute of them."

"But . . . why? What could you possibly have done?"

"Have you ever heard the Song of Four Brothers?"

"Well, yes. The four brothers climbed Mount Airidare

and stole drinks from the fountain of immortality and as punishment—" She broke off her eyes going wide. "You are one of the brothers, aren't you? This is why you want to kill Sabo. To get vengeance on him for—"

"No! This is not about vengeance. It is about freedom. All I want is to be free of this curse. The only way for me to be free is if Sabo willingly releases me from it . . . or if he is destroyed. Sabo thrives on pain and suffering, he would never release such a delightful source of it. I have no other recourse."

"But to fight a god? That is the act of a madman! You may be immortal, but you are not invincible. You can be killed somehow!"

"If a god-made sword separates my head from my shoulders then I will die, no doubt going straight to the eight hells to continue my torturous existence." He plucked at the talisman around his neck. "But thanks to this my head cannot be removed from my neck. I *am* invincible."

"As long as you are wearing it! What will keep him from snatching it from around your neck?"

"I will. He would have to get past me and Weysa's Champion."

"This is madness," she whispered.

"I agree. But what other choice do I have?"

She could see no other alternatives open to him. Songs of Sabo's creative brutality to men were sung far and wide and in gory detail. The god of pain and suffering was the god men prayed to when they wanted their enemies to suffer and die. When men wanted vengeance they prayed to Sabo. In a pantheon of emotionally flawed gods, he was the cruelest.

When she had no response he turned and walked away from her. She hastened after him once again.

"All right then . . . you're going to fight a god. But

what is this 'she is mine' crap? You lied to a goddess you wanted help from."

"I lied?" he asked.

"Well, yes. I'm not yours. I'm—"

"You're wielding the Dagger of Truths, Airi," he said softly, giving her a speaking glance. "I couldn't have lied even if I wanted to."

Airi stopped dead in her tracks and gaped at him. When he didn't stop she was forced to hurry and catch up with him once more.

"I am not yours! I don't belong to anyone but me!"

"You are mine. You are one of my men. One of those whom I am responsible for. A responsibility I take very seriously."

"Ha! Do you? You weren't acting so responsible when you brought us into the dragon's den."

"I do take it very seriously. And I didn't bring you anywhere, you followed me—of your own accord I might add."

Well damn it, he had a point there. But she wasn't going to let him off the hook that easily.

"But even so you know that wasn't what she meant when she was talking about women and finding a destined mate to make you whole or some crap like that. You don't believe in that any more than I do and you certainly don't feel that way about me."

"Are you stating facts or are you asking me a question?" he asked her. "Do you want to hear the truth? Ask me and let the dagger do its job."

She opened her mouth to do exactly that, but then a sudden fear filled her. What if he said . . . ? No. No, he wouldn't. Couldn't. *Didn't* feel that way about her. He just wanted to bed her. That was all. There was no emotion attached to any of it.

Then why was it so hard to ask the question? It was a

simple question with a simple answer. An answer she thought she wanted to hear.

Or did she?

Confused, she shook her head and decided it was best not to ask right then and to deal with it later, when she'd had more time to think about it.

"So what now?"

"We go to the Killing Forest and find the labyrinth. The Killing Forest is only a week's travel from here. Then we go to Gorgun and find the demigod and the Cuff of Cadence."

"Gorgun is a month's journey at least!"

"Do you have somewhere else to be?"

"Winter is coming!"

"So I expect we will be cold." He shot her a sidelong glance. "We can keep each other warm."

The words sent a wave of heat flushing across her cheeks and then down through her body. The invitation was clear and direct. The response was not so simple.

"Your men aren't going to follow you on these crazy quests without having something to show for it."

"A labyrinth is usually lousy with treasure, especially one being guarded by a great beast. You think that ring is going to be the only thing it's guarding?"

"You can't know that for sure."

"No . . . and the men know that each venture has two possible outcomes. Either we make money or we don't. This is a job. We have to work at it. Treasure doesn't just fall into our laps. There's a long journey between here and the cuff. I am sure there are many treasures to be plundered along the way. And if not . . . we're going to the house of a rich demigod. There's certain to be some payoff there."

She fell silent as they walked back toward camp. Then she asked, "Why do you keep them with you? As you said, you are invincible now. You don't need them to fight for you. To protect you. Why do you have them with you?"

"Because I owe it to them," he said. Then he stopped suddenly and glared at her. "Damn that dagger," he ground out.

Suddenly Airi had a new sense of power. He had to answer any question she asked as long as she had the dagger in hand and he had to do it honestly.

"Why do you think you owe them?"

"It was a long road to find the talisman. With very little payout. Sure, the dragon's den made up for a lot of that, but they had my back as we battled our way through the catacombs where the talisman was buried. We saw things there—dead things come to life again— that you would never want to see in your life. If not for them I would have died in the process of getting this talisman and it is going to be key in my battle with Sabo. I could never have succeeded without it."

"Fair enough," she said. "But you don't owe them anything. As you said, they followed you willingly."

"It's how I feel," he said quietly. "That's all that matters."

He had a point. She looked upon him with new eyes. Here was a man of great honor, for all he liked to portray himself as a greedy fortune hunter. A very brave man, to think of battling with a god. It was an impossible task, one that very well might mean his death or worse . . . more torment. Worse torment. If he failed there would be no escape from his torture.

She thought of that as they approached the campsite. Thought about how terrible the torture was that he suffered. What would the men think if they knew? She suspected she knew. They would not want to be around a man who was cursed by the gods. They would think of themselves before they would think of Maxum. Just as she would have done. Might still do. She had to seriously think about whether or not she wanted to be a part of this insane journey. Winter was coming, she told herself. She never traveled during winter if it could at all be avoided. She had enough money to keep her comfortably for a long time, certainly through the winter. And with the dagger there was potential for an endless source of income. She could go into some sort of trade, the dagger would force everyone to deal with her fairly. She could easily make money without having to worry about anyone taking advantage. The downside was that she would always have to speak the truth herself whenever she carried the dagger. She hadn't yet decided on how to deal with that. A thief needed to lie. It was just the nature of the game.

But with some proper thought she wouldn't need to be a thief any longer. For her thievery had been a means to an end—not something she relished and took great joy in. She could con and lie with the best of them and took pride in her abilities, but she could just as easily live without all of the danger, the lies, and the manipulations. In fact she would prefer it.

They came up on the camp and found the men were already up and ready to leave. They were simply waiting for them to make an appearance.

"About time," Kilon barked. "Just because you two feel like screwing in the weeds doesn't mean you get to make the rest of us wait. We should have been on the road already."

"We weren't—" Airi began indignantly.

"We leave when I say we leave," Maxum said, stepping up to get face-to-face with Kilon. "And what I do with my time is my business. I'm getting tired of your attitude. If you want to stay a part of this group you better find some congeniality somewhere inside of you."

Kilon's jaw worked, but he didn't say anything in return. Maxum, clearly deciding the matter was handled, went to saddle his horse. When she went to her saddle she was reminded that Sarda had made off with her saddlebag. Inside had been her gold, a change of clothes and about a dozen other little things she used throughout the days. Now she would have to replace everything, including the bag itself.

She sighed and glanced over at Maxum. Now she would have to depend on him for everything once more until she got to Calandria and the bank. Luckily she had been wise enough to keep the vault key in a small hidden pocket on her saddle itself. Otherwise she would have been right back where she started.

The idea of being stolen from . . . it just irked her. If it had just been a test, why hadn't her things been returned to her?

She fondled the dagger for a moment. *Had it been worth it?* she asked herself. It was hard to tell so early in the game but she thought the loss of a little gold and a few articles of clothing would pale in comparison to the worth of the thing.

She pulled the blade out of its shining black sheath and had to marvel over the fine workmanship of it. Well of course, it would be fine. It was a god-made weapon. There could never be anything finer than god-made weapons. It would never rust and, if rumor was true, it would never dull. She had never come close to seeing a god-made weapon in her life. If she had, she probably would have stolen it.

But god-made weapons were rare. She wondered if Meru had forged this weapon herself or if Hondor, the demigod who was blacksmith to the gods, had forged it.

It didn't matter, she realized. What mattered was the power of the thing. The men had no idea what it was she held in her hands and it was probably best that they didn't. But they would begin to suspect quickly if they found themselves telling truths they would not normally share. So for the time being she tucked the dagger away into her remaining saddlebag and then cinched the girth to the saddle tightly around Hero's belly.

She mounted shortly after and rode up abreast of Maxum. She didn't know why; she should have held back like she always did and avoided him. She could tell by the fleeting look of surprise on his features that he had expected her to do just that. But she was tired of running and hiding from him like a child. She knew him better now, better than any of the others, and that meant something to her. It might not mean much to him in the end, but it meant something to her.

She almost wished she hadn't found out all these truths about him. Knowing all the details of his tortured life was going to make it harder for her to deny him anything . . . including access to her body.

Oh, who was she kidding? She was not denying him access to her body because she didn't want to deny him. Not any longer. He had proven just how much passion there could be between them. How much pleasure. And it was a pleasure she found she craved almost above anything else. She had never freely indulged in a dalliance with a man. Oh, she had been hot and furtive with a boy back when she had been in her teen turnings, but that was the sum of her experience.

But Doisy's potion meant a certain freedom she had never experienced before and Maxum's passion for her, mature and hot and wild as it was, promised to be something far beyond the fumblings of her youth. True, she was young yet, but she was far older and wiser and she suspected she would appreciate a liaison with a man far and away above what she had experienced before.

And what a man he was. Complex and powerful, potent and sexual, tempestuous and tortured. There would never be anything like him to cross her path in her life again, she thought, so why shouldn't she take advantage of him while he was around? She could simply use him for the pleasure he could provide and then walk away when the time came. And the time would come. It always did. Whether it would be her leaving him or him leaving her, it would come. Even if she followed him through to the end of these quests she would watch him pit himself against a god . . . and that would be the end of it. She didn't care how many talismans or totems he managed to acquire. A god was a god and there was no way he could fight a god and survive.

But in the end that meant he had very little time left in this world. At the end of it he would either be dead or consigned to some kind of hell for the rest of his days. If these were his last days, shouldn't she provide some companionship and some pleasure he could take memories of with him wherever he ended up going? Shouldn't she try and give him enough pleasure to hopefully outweigh a small portion of the terrible torment that awaited him?

She was suddenly angry with him . . . angry he would throw away his life. But the anger quickly faded when she realized he was only living half a life to begin with. The other half was lived buried deep in the ground. She shuddered as she thought of it, thought of what it must be like to be dragged beneath the surface and suffocated by the heavy soil. What must it feel like to have the weight of all that rock and dirt pressing in on him, crushing him from all sides at once?

Unable to help herself, she reached out and touched a hand to his thigh.

Maxum looked down at her hand with no little amount of surprise. It was an intimate gesture, one that he never would have thought she would instigate. He had fought with her for every intimacy thus far. This one was finally being freely given.

He didn't know how to feel about that. He was afraid

she was doing so out of pity for him, now that she knew his situation. He did not want pity. Especially from her. He would rather she continue to fight him tooth and nail. Besides, the fighting was half of the fun. He wondered if he would grow bored with her when she finally gave in to him. If it was the game that kept him so interested.

Well, there was only one way to find out. He covered her hand on his thigh, squeezed her fingers, then picked up her hand and leaned over to touch her finger to his mouth, which he then promptly and baldly sucked into his mouth. He felt her hand tense, saw her eyes widen, then she flushed and jerked her hand away. She glanced back at the men behind them, clearly afraid they had been seen.

What should it matter to her if they were seen? The men already thought he was fucking her. Little intimacies like that would merely remove all doubt. And he would be fucking her. Tonight, if he had any say in the matter. There had been enough games, enough fighting. If she felt sorry for him he would use that to his advantage to get what he wanted. It would be just another tactic, he told himself. A weapon to be used against her. Then he would purge her from his system and be done with her.

And he *would* be done with her. Whether it be now or a month from now when they achieved the retrieval of the cuff. As soon as he had the cuff he would challenge Sabo and either he would die or ... well, he hadn't thought much about what would happen if he should succeed. He didn't want to look beyond the moment he was presently living in. He couldn't afford to crave things he did not yet have. It would make him sloppy, would weaken him to think of everything he could be losing if he failed. He would not take half measures. He would not live his life if it meant he would suffer for half of it every damned day. He would be free or he would be nothing. There were no other options.

He would not change his way of thinking for anyone.

Not for anyone at all.

CHAPTER
SEVENTEEN

I t began to rain.

It was a miserable, heavy rain that drenched them all thoroughly, and any good spirits they might have had became quickly sodden. Camping that night in the rain meant cold provisions for dinner. Airi had dried meat and crackers in her remaining saddlebag, so she was not required to ask for anything from Maxum. She had been confused for most of their travel that day, not understanding herself. Did she want him or didn't she? Was she being a child or was she going to act like a mature woman and make up her mind? She had thought she had her mind made up, but then he had put her finger in his mouth and the ferocious heat it had inspired in her had shocked her to her core. Somehow that one action had just as much power over her as he'd had when he'd put his hand between her legs in the river.

That was the key phrase. Power over her. Would she be giving him power over her? Would she be giving something of herself away?

And what of the rest of the men? It was one thing to have them suspecting she was lying with Maxum, quite another to remove all doubt. What would Doisy, Kyno, and Dru think of her then? Did she care?

She realized she did and that was a whole new level of disturbance. When had she begun to care about them enough to be concerned what their opinions of her were? When had she ever cared about what anyone thought of her? She hadn't cared about anyone's regard since her mother had died and she'd been forced to learn what a hard world it was, a world where it wasn't worth trying to please everyone.

She kept to her own bedroll that night, dodging Maxum's halfhearted attempt to draw her close, huddling deep beneath wet blankets. When she awoke the rain was even worse, lashing hard and rolling with thunder.

"Where are we headed now that we've given up on finding the temple?" Doisy asked. Maxum had told the men he thought finding the temple was a waste of time and that he had been mistaken to search for it. Then he had whetted the men's appetites with promises of a dangerous labyrinth with a treasure guarded by a great beast. The men only needed to hear the word "treasure" and they were on board.

Airi didn't know why Maxum had chosen not to tell them about the temple, but when she thought of it she agreed it was best. The only thing that had come of it was the dagger and the men would have wanted their equal share of it. There was no way to share a weapon that had been entrusted to the bearer by a goddess, so it was best to save them all the trouble of the squabbling.

The rain continued and grew colder over the next few days, making all thoughts of seduction fly far away, as they made their way into the Killing Forest. There was a reason why the forest had been so named. It was dark and full of dangerous creatures. Being blinded and slowed by rain made it unwise to journey within, but Maxum kept pushing them farther. Airi knew why. His goal was so close now he could probably taste it. Whether it ended in victory or loss, the confrontation was almost at hand. He wanted it badly. And she didn't blame him. But pushing them like this was likely to get one of them killed.

They were riding single file when the rain finally began to ease. A sudden sound caught Airi's attention to the right. She heard a shout and began to turn, but then was tackled off her horse by a powerful force of nature. She hit the ground hard, her breath knocked out of her. She barely registered a mouth full of fangs snarling over her, the thick claws digging into her breasts, the heavy weight of the beast as it roared into her face.

Then suddenly the creature stopped roaring and fell face-first into her chest. Headfirst. Its head had been severed from its shoulders with one sharp swing of Weysa's Champion and now the head lay on her chest while the body was bleeding buckets of blood onto her. Gagging she shoved the head of the thing off her and scrambled to get out from under the body. Maxum's hand was there a second later and with one strong tug he yanked her to her feet and pulled her up against his body, hugging her tightly.

"It's all right," he soothed her. "It's over."

She pushed away from him hard. "What do you think you're doing?" she shouted at him.

"Saving your ass!" he shouted back, a look of surprise coming over his features. "I would think you would be grateful!"

"Fine! Thank you for killing the . . . whatever it was."

"Razorbeast," Doisy supplied.

"Thank you!" she snapped. "But I'm not some delicate flower in need of comforting! Get that out of your head right now!"

The belligerence bled right out of Maxum and he chuckled. "Oh. I see. It's not the rescue that upset you, just the comforting afterward."

"Damn right!"

"Forgive me, my lady," he said with a flourishing bow. "I forgot who I was dealing with. I should have let you kill the beast yourself."

"Yes, you should have! I can take care of myself."

"Of course you can," he said with a smug smile. "Next time I'll know better."

"Well . . . as long as we have it clear . . . I . . . I mean you can help if I'm in trouble and you happen to be there," she said awkwardly.

"All right then. No comforting and help only when necessary. It's all clear now."

"Good," she said. Then she looked down at her blood-soaked clothing. "Ugh! This is my only set of clothes!"

"I heard a stream to the left. We'll go there and you can wash up. You should be used to wearing wet clothes by now. Wash them out and wear them."

"I'm not getting naked in front of you guys."

"Don't worry. We'll find you a nice private spot."

"I'm not getting naked in a place called the *Killing Forest*," she said with a huff.

"Then bathe with your fucking clothes on! Can we get on with it already?" Kilon exploded.

Airi mounted Hero and they made their way to the stream. She quickly took off her corset and waded into the stream in just her breeches and the shirt she wore under the corset. The water was fast-running and blood clouded into it as she washed it off herself and the corset. When she was done she hung the corset from her saddle to dry and mounted Hero in just her wet clothes.

Maxum wished she'd put the corset on. The wet material of her shirt was clinging to her unfettered breasts and he could see how hard her nipples were from the cold. It immediately made him hard and craving, a position he didn't want to be in when riding through a dangerous area.

He noticed she had taken the Dagger of Truths and

tucked it into her boot as a backup to the ones she already had in her sheaths. She was leaving nothing to chance.

They were more on their guard as they went. They were following a small worn path, and shortly they came to a cottage nestled into a clearing. She wondered who would be brave enough to settle in the middle of the Killing Forest. Maxum dismounted and, holding his horse's reins, he walked up to the cottage door and knocked.

The door was split in two and slowly the top half opened to reveal a man no taller than Airi was but with a strong and stocky build.

"Well met, my friend," the man said. "So look at you all." He sounded nervous. Who wouldn't be when outnumbered by a rank of men and women? At least she thought he was outnumbered. The cottage was so small it couldn't house that many people. "What can I do for you this day?"

"Well . . . we are in need of a hot meal and all of our supplies and the land around us are wet. My friend"—he indicated Kilon—"can do the hunting and bring fresh game if you but provide the fire and a few hours of your company."

"You would hunt in the Killing Forest?" the man asked with surprise. "You must be brave."

"A beast's a beast. They all fall," Kilon said shortly.

"Well then, with an offer that does little to inconvenience me and brings fresh game to my table I say welcome!"

The man opened the bottom half of the door in welcome.

They tied up the horses then made their way inside the cottage. It was a small cozy space, one room in all with a plank bed tucked up into the far right corner and a small table and two chairs in the near right corner. The left side of the cottage was taken up entirely by a huge fireplace. The blaze in it was healthy and hot, warming the room considerably. Everything felt dry and comfortable and Airi, shivering from the wet, went to sit by the fire in hopes of drying her clothes on her body. It seemed the warmer the room around her was the more she suddenly felt the cold.

Maxum introduced everyone and Kilon left to go hunt some dinner. Everyone made themselves comfortable on the floor in front of the fire and the man sat down in his rocking chair by the hearth. He picked up something he had been mending and began to rock.

"So where are you all from and what brings you here to the Killing Forest?" the man, who was named Ty, asked.

"We're from all about," Maxum said, speaking comfortably for the group. "And we are in search of an adventure."

"Well you've come to the right place . . . though you'll find more death and danger in the Killing Forest than you will adventure."

"But that's the kind of adventure we like." Maxum paused a beat. "We've heard there is a great labyrinth full of treasure in the forest."

The man paled and dropped his mending, looking at them, one at a time.

"You want no part of that place," the man said. "Any rumors you've heard of treasure are lies. The labyrinth is a place of death, plain and simple. As dark and dangerous as the forest is, the labyrinth puts it to shame."

"How do you know they are lies?" Doisy asked.

"You aren't the first men to come through here looking for the labyrinth. The men come, but they never leave. They go in but never come out. If there is treasure there it stays there. So do yourself a favor and stay away."

"Well, we'll think on what you have said for certain. In which direction lies the labyrinth?"

"I will not tell you," the man said stubbornly. "I will not be responsible for more deaths."

"But then we will have to search blindly for it in the forest. Is that not more dangerous?"

"Better to search blindly for your death than to go to it directly."

Maxum coaxed the man some more, but he would not be moved. Kilon came back with a black stag, more than enough for them to feast on and the man seemed grateful for the meat that would be remaining.

"My friend will hunt you down enough meat to get you through the winter if you'll tell us where the labyrinth is," Maxum said.

The man hesitated. "Enough for the whole of the winter?" he said. "Are you that determined to get there?"

"We are," Maxum said.

But then the man shook his head. "No. I will not tell you. It will be hard to hunt on my own through the winter, but better that than to have your deaths on my head."

"You are so certain we will die?" Maxum asked.

"I am."

Maxum stood up, glancing out at the waning light of day. He had to go or he would be caught in the middle of the cottage. The curse would not care if there was a building in its way. It would come up through the floorboards, destroying the man's house.

"Enjoy your meat. I will return shortly."

"You are going out by yourself? To what purpose? We already have our meat."

"I must think on things awhile," Maxum said as he approached the door. "Save me some dinner. I will return in a few hours."

He left. The man shook his head, his balding pate

gleaming in the firelight. "He is mad to walk about for no reason."

Ty fell silent and went about preparing their dinner. Soon the cottage was redolent with the smells of cooking venison. The group had not had a hot meal in nearly a week and they were salivating at the promise of roasted meat.

Dinner came at last and they ate with relish. Airi's clothes finally dried and she was finally beginning to feel warm. She became drowsy and was dozing sitting up over her plate, which was resting in the nest of her crossed legs. She caught herself from falling over twice before Ty chuckled and said, "I cannot share my bed, but you are all welcome to sleep out of the wet before my fire. The Killing Forest is no place to be camping in the open."

"And yet you live here?" Airi said.

"It was a young man's game originally. I came here full of vim and vigor and determined to live where no man would ever live. Now I am too set in my ways to go. I am still young enough and strong enough to survive here. It has been a hard life and has made me a hard man. I am resigned that one day this forest will get the best of me; I will die here as I have lived here. But that day is not today and I am determined it will not be tomorrow."

The group brought in their bedrolls and opened them to dry by the fire. The smell of must filled the air and soon the blankets were dry.

By the time Maxum returned half of the men had gone to sleep in their now-dried bedrolls. Only Airi and Kilon remained awake . . . in spite of Airi being so tired she could barely keep her eyes open. She had made it a point to never go to sleep before Kilon did. She simply did not trust the man. But once Maxum returned she felt safer, a feeling that perplexed her, and she finally snuggled down under her blankets and fell asleep.

She was awakened some time later to a crash of sound and she opened her eyes to see two figures, one in the bed struggling with one hovering over him with a knife.

"Tell me where it is!" Kilon barked, shoving his blade to the man's neck.

Airi leapt up with a cry, rushing across the room to tackle Kilon. But Kilon was still about fifty rocks heavier than she was and would not be easily moved. He shoved her to the floor and went back to struggling with the man.

"Tell me or I'll slit your throat!"

"To the east! The east! Take the path to the well and then go east into the woods—you can't miss it for it stretches for miles!"

"Kilon, let him go!" Maxum barked.

Kilon released the man and backed away from him. He tucked his knife into his belt.

"There see? Easy. None of this coaxing crap. A straightforward way to a straightforward answer," Kilon said.

"Get out! Out of my house!" the man cried.

"We'll get out when we're good and ready to go," Kilon snapped at him.

"Kilon!" Maxum turned to the man. "Of course we'll leave. And I'm sorry for my friend's behavior." Maxum reached down a hand to help Airi up to her feet. The group went to their bedrolls and began to pack them up.

"Why're we leaving?" Kilon drawled. "There's nothing he can do to make us go."

"We're leaving because this is his house," Maxum snapped. "And you disrespected his hospitality."

"Sure. Fine. But I got us our answer. Labyrinth's to the east. Now let's get going. Rain's stopped. It's almost light."

"I could've used some more sleep," Doisy grumbled. "You're an ass, Kilon."

"Let's go," Maxum said.

* * *

They reached the labyrinth by sunset. It was a wall of trees and bramble that went on in either direction for as far as the eye could see. Maxum had to leave so they had no opportunity to search for an entrance. They made camp and built a fire. Kilon disappeared into the trees just as Maxum had. He returned a short while later with another black stag.

"This is more than we need," Airi complained.

"So take the leftovers back to the old man at the cottage," he sneered. "You're too soft. You'd never survive on your own."

"I've been on my own all my life!"

"Where? In cities? Thieving in a city is an easy life compared to being out here in the open. Thieving will do you no good out here."

"I do more than steal for a living. I can fight."

"Sure you can. You'd poke at something with that pretty little dagger you got there in your boot and it'd take your head off for your trouble."

"You know, I'm getting sick of your attitude," she snapped.

"And I'm sick of the smell of your cunt. But Maxum says we've got to deal with each other so until I'm running this group, I'll deal."

She felt herself go a little pale. What did that mean exactly? Was Kilon planning on taking over the group? They all knew what that talisman could do. It wasn't like Kilon could kill Maxum in his sleep.

But he could steal that talisman off him just as easily as Airi had stolen it, put it on himself and make himself invincible. The idea of a man like Kilon being invincible put a cold weight on Airi's heart. Because of that, she unrolled her bedroll right next to Maxum's. She would do what she could to protect him in the night. She had no doubt that Maxum could take care of himself, but it would be nothing to cut that charm off while he slept. Airi would hear anyone come near them even in her sleep. She had been sleeping with one eye open for a very long time. She would use that to Maxum's benefit.

Maxum lifted a brow at the sight of their bedrolls lying in close proximity to one another as opposed to the fire being set between them, but he made no comment about it. He ate his dinner in silence, staring at the wall of the labyrinth in front of him. The wall had to be twelve feet tall and everything about it was alive and growing. From the trees that anchored it to the bramble that grew thickly from one tree to the next to the ivy that climbed the wall of brambles. Moss grew on the trees as well. So the wall of the labyrinth was a brown and green living thing.

The first thing Maxum tried was to find an entrance. They rode to the north down the right side of the wall for a mile until it stopped in a corner and began to go in an eastern direction. They followed this for two miles until the next corner and began to follow the wall to the south. Eventually they made it all the way around the wall and there was no entrance that they could find whatsoever.

"All right then, this is our first challenge," Maxum said as he drew his sword and dismounted. Using Weysa's Champion he began to slice through the bramble between the trees. The sword cut through the bramble easily, but within a minute the severed ends of the bramble began to grow and thicken and become part of the wall again.

"You'll have to do it hard enough and fast enough to create a gap we can all pass through quickly before the bramble grows back in together. It's an impossible task," Airi said. "There must be a way in—we just haven't found it yet."

"Where do you suggest we look, since you're so full of bright and shiny ideas all the time?" Kilon asked.

Airi bit her lip and thought about it, as she walked Hero back and forth in front of the wall. "Well," she said looking up the wall, "we haven't tried climbing over it."

"That would mean leaving the horses and all of our gear behind," Doisy said hesitantly. "In this forest the horses would be dead in a day without someone to watch over them."

"Then someone has to stay behind. Someone who can protect them on his own," Maxum said. "Dru."

"Me? Alone here? How do you figure I'm the best one to protect them?"

"You could make them invisible to the eyes of prey. In a fight you could make someone see multiples and not know which one to attack . . . enough to help you get away maybe. You can blur an attacker's sight, making it nearly impossible for them to find a target. All of these things can protect you while you wait for us here."

"No," he whispered. "I can't do it."

"You can," Maxum said firmly. "And you will. If we aren't back in say . . . four days, you can consider us lost, take our horses and go."

"He can leave my horse behind. And my gold. I'll be making it out of here just fine," Kilon barked.

"All right, Dru?" Maxum asked.

"I guess so," the mage said reluctantly.

"Good. Come on, let's gear up and get up over this thing."

They prepped themselves, taking with them the essentials for survival. Airi turned her saddlebag into a pack, strapping their food supplies to her back. There was no telling if there'd be anything worth hunting in the labyrinth. No telling anything at all about it. They were going into this blind.

Being the lightest and the fastest, she was the first to try the wall. It was actually easy to grab on to the vines and branches that made up the wall and she climbed steadily to the top. When she reached the top she threw one leg over to the other side and took a moment to look out over the top of the labyrinth.

The maze was staggering. It was contained within a couple of square miles, but the intricacies of it were boggling. The first thing she noticed was that while the outer walls were made of living branches and such, the inner walls were all stone and mortar with ivy growing in some places. They wouldn't be able to climb the sheer walls to look out over the top of the maze unless there was some sturdy ivy growing, and it didn't look as though there would be much of that the deeper into the labyrinth they went.

As she had sat there looking, Maxum had climbed up beside her. Together they looked out over the maze.

"I guess we're heading for the center," he said, clearly as overwhelmed by the convolutions of the maze as she was. "It's impossible for us to map it from here. We can't even see it."

"I guess we'll have to find it the hard way," she said.

"Not so hard. You just have to mark your way so you don't double back. I happen to have some chalk. We'll make it to the center and back by following the marks."

"You make it sound so damn easy," she said with a sigh. "But it won't be."

"I know it won't be," he told her, meeting her eyes. "None of this will be easy." He called down to the others. "Come on!" Then he began to climb down the other side. She followed him, the nearest part of the map already plotted out in her head. She was blessed with a good memory, so hopefully it would serve them for some of the way at least.

When they were all on the ground on the other side,

Airi said, "Let me lead this first part. I saw enough to start guiding us to the center. Hopefully there will be ways for me to climb up and map out the next sections as we go."

Maxum knelt down on the stone slate that was beneath their feet and drew a large circle with an X through it.

"We find this we find Dru. Now let's go."

CHAPTER
EIGHTEEN

They plodded along through the first part of the maze with nothing of note happening. The labyrinth appeared to be abandoned of all life, save a few birds that flew over the top of it. Whenever he saw one, Kilon would shoot it and retrieve the body and his arrow. He tied the game to his belt for later.

As they went, Airi began to question something in her head. She looked at Maxum and quickened her step, hoping he would as well, putting some distance between them and the others. It worked and soon she was able to whisper, "What will happen at sunset?"

"I imagine the same thing that always does. The ground will swallow me whole and then spit me back up later on. I'm usually returned to the same spot I was taken from."

"And if you're not? You'll be separated from the rest of us."

"We'll have to hope that doesn't happen."

"And it's not as though you can simply walk off like you usually do. Go too far and you'll get lost. Stay too near and . . ."

"And you can all be sucked down with me. I have my

marking chalk. I won't get lost unless I'm brought back somewhere else."

"There's going to be a lot left to chance. There's a chance you'll be exposed. When the ground takes you it will destroy parts of the labyrinth."

"If it can be destroyed. It might repair itself just like the vines did. This labyrinth is magical. Anything is possible. I'm definitely worried that come sunset things will get bad for us."

"I don't want you to get lost or separated from us." She lowered her voice further. "I don't want to be left with Kilon to manage on my own."

"You'll have Kyno and Doisy. You won't be on your own."

"Kyno and Doisy are followers. They will follow the strongest personality, the one they think can get them through or get them wealthy. As strong as I am, I'm not strong enough to go head to head with Kilon. He's bigger than I am, meaner than I am, and he hates me with a gods-given passion. I don't know why, but he does. Has from the moment he set eyes on me."

"Don't take it personal, he's like that with every woman. That's part of the reason why we haven't had one in the group until now."

"Gee. Thanks. I feel so special. You should have warned me about him. Maybe I would have gone my own way."

"You were destitute. You didn't have many choices."

"I could have figured something out." She relented. "But I'm glad I joined you overall. I'm a much wealthier woman and now I have this lovely dagger." She patted her boot near the side of her calf.

"Sounds like a winning situation so far." He leaned a little closer, his arm brushing hers. "And just think how many more benefits you could have if you'd only let me in your bed."

It had been such a long time since he had made any attempts to get there that she was taken aback by the suggestion.

"We're in the middle of a deadly labyrinth and you're trying to get me in your bed?" she asked incredulously.

"What better time? We could die tomorrow. Why put it off?"

"You're . . . you're . . ."

"Incorrigible? Undeniable? Charming beyond your wildest dreams?"

"An ass! I was going to say you're an ass!"

"And here I thought you couldn't lie with that dagger strapped to your leg."

"I'm not lying. It's the truth."

"In your eyes maybe. But admit it, you find me undeniably attractive."

She dodged the question so she wouldn't have to tell him the truth. He was arrogant enough as it was.

"The only thing I'll admit is that you're an ass."

"That was a dodge," he said with uncanny instinct. "So you can't lie, but you can dodge the question."

"That wasn't a question," she pointed out.

"Hmm. Interesting. Let's try this then. Do you find me undeniably attractive?"

"Yes," she said, even though every part of her wanted to scream a protective "no!"

"Aha! So things must be formed in a question. All right then . . . do you want to—"

"Stop it!"

". . . sleep with me?"

"No!" Sleeping had very little to do with what she wanted, she admitted to herself. But it allowed her to tell him a truth. That meant she could interpret certain questions the way she wanted to if she thought carefully about them.

"Hmm. Very interesting" was all he said. But he didn't

look at all disappointed. Or deterred. He looked like he was thinking about it. Thinking about a way to change her mind.

They went a little farther along the labyrinth when she reached the end of what she had mapped out in her mind. She searched around for the next few turns until she saw a wall with a growth of ivy climbing up it. She grabbed hold and scaled the wall, grateful for her light weight that allowed her to scrabble up without the entrenched ivy breaking and sending her spilling back down to the stone floor. She struggled up until she was on top of the wall and could map out the next part of the maze. To her disappointment there was still a great distance to go and she still couldn't see the center of the labyrinth. The path they had to take was so intricate that even though they had walked for what seemed like ages, they hadn't made much progress. They wouldn't be reaching the center by sunset, that was for certain. And, as she looked, she noticed something else. In a little while the walls would no longer be flat on top. There were what looked like razor sharp spikes clustered along the tops. It would prevent her from looking over the top of the labyrinth in the future. So she forced herself to remember every bit of what she could, grateful she had always had the ability to recall a picture of something in her mind once she had looked at it.

She dropped down to the ground and grimly told them what she had seen. Maxum did not visibly portray any anxiety, and she didn't know for certain, but she could imagine he felt anxious about being caught in the labyrinth with no way to map their progress.

"We'll worry about it when the time comes," he said instead, and indicated she should lead the way. He fell into step beside her silently, occasionally stopping to mark their path so they would have a much quicker exit than they would an entrance. It was hard to tell what would happen once they reached the center, and a hasty escape might be necessary.

They were still walking a couple of hours before sunset when they turned a corner and suddenly, there on the ground was one of Maxum's chalk markings.

"We've gone in a circle!" Kilon said angrily.

"That's impossible! I have the map in my head!" Airi said, completely perplexed as to how it had happened. She'd led them through all the right turns. She knew it.

"What are we following her for anyway? She's an idiot," Kilon said.

"Hey! Say that again and I'll knock your teeth in!" Airi snapped.

"I'd like to see you try cun—"

"And call me that again and I'll cut your balls off!" she threatened, pulling her dagger from her boot. She was so tempted to break his skin with it, to see what power the dagger really had. To see what the power of all of his lies come back to haunt him would really be like.

"Let's see how far back we've traveled," Maxum said before the altercation could get any worse. It cut off Kilon's broiling reply to her. Good. She didn't want to hear any more from him. She'd be happy if someone would cut out his tongue. Preferably herself.

They followed Maxum's markings a short distance before they realized they were back at the marking again.

"That's impossible," Maxum said. "We haven't traveled far enough to come full circle. Something odd is going on." He walked ahead of them and went around the bend, all the while studying the wall. Airi found some ivy and scrambled up the wall, grateful there were no spikes yet. She watched Maxum's progress and suddenly he disappeared and reappeared at a point distant from where he had been and close to where they now were.

"It's some kind of portal! A . . . a door of sorts that's jumping us from one part of the maze back to where we have been already," she said as Maxum came around the bend. "We have to go another way."

"That's so odd. It's utterly seamless to me as I'm walking. Do you know where the portal is so we can avoid it? Is there another way around?" Maxum asked.

"I know where it is and there's another way around but it's going to take longer. And we better hope there's no more of those portals because I don't see another way to go after this change."

Airi glanced toward the setting sun then shot a look at Maxum. "Maybe we should stop for the night? We can use some of these dried vines to make a small fire."

"Not much of a fire," Doisy said. "Just enough to cook with. Not enough to last the night. It's going to get cold."

"We'll all sleep close together to conserve warmth. We'll put Airi in the middle since she's smallest, me and Doisy on either side of her then Kyno and Kilon on the ends."

Kilon grumbled something about "special treatment," but he shrugged out of his pack and threw down his bedroll. Maxum used Weysa's Champion to shear off vines from the walls in several places and Doisy built a fire using his flint and stone.

Maxum sheathed his sword and pulled Airi aside.

"How many turns to the portal?"

"A right, a left, then another right. Don't go past the end of the wall."

"All right. I'll see you in a few hours."

She nodded. "Don't get lost."

"And miss sleeping tucked up against you? Not a chance."

She laughed and punched him playfully in the arm. Damn him anyway, he really was a charming ass. When he wanted to be. And somehow that was far more appealing to her than Doisy's endless amounts of charm and good nature. She liked the differences in him. The fire and unpredictability.

Maxum had carried her bedroll for her and now, as she watched him go, she rolled his and hers out side by side. Then she took off her pack and sighed with relief. It had grown heavy these past hours.

They propped the game birds over the fire using metal rods to skewer them and after a while they were ready for consumption. Airi made certain to save some aside for Maxum. She had expected to feel something, some kind of rumbling to indicate Maxum's having been drawn beneath the surface of the soil, the destruction of the labyrinth happening in the wake of it. But there was nothing.

When juquil's hour came and went, she began to grow anxious. Would he be able to find them again? It was dark now. He hadn't been able to take any kind of flame with him. It wouldn't have done him any good. It was turning into the second hour after juquil's hour and none of them had gone to bed save Kilon. The rest of them sat anxiously waiting for Maxum.

He arrived several minutes later. Airi was so relieved to see him she threw herself against him, into his arms. He hugged her to himself with a chuckle.

"It's all right. I got turned around a little, but I did your trick of climbing the wall and saw the light from the fire."

"We kept it burning as long as we could just for that reason. It's almost cold now. We're lucky you made it back at all."

"Lucky indeed," Doisy said grimly. "It would be nice to know why you find it necessary to leave every night . . . including under these circumstances. You can't tell me it's to go off and meditate. I used to think that was what it was. Now I'm pretty sure it's not."

"You'd be right about that," Maxum said grimly. For a moment it looked as though he might share the reasons why with the others, but in the end he didn't. He went to the waning fire and to his food. He ate in silence and finally the others went to bed, doing their best to sleep close to each other to conserve body heat.

"Go on," Maxum said to her. "Go to bed."

"Not without you."

"See. You do want to sleep with me," he joked. Then understanding dawned on him and Airi saw it happen. Her belly clenched as he said, "I asked the question wrong, didn't I? I asked if you wanted to sleep with me but what I should have asked was—"

"The answer is yes, all right?" she said quietly, looking away from him and grateful for the darkness the dying fire left. "But that doesn't make a difference here and now. This isn't the time or the place."

"No. It isn't. But the time will come," he vowed. "And it will come soon. Make certain you are ready for it."

"I already am," she confessed softly.

The admission surprised Maxum. As had his fear when he'd found himself unable to figure out which way to go when he'd been returned to the labyrinth. As he had suspected, the labyrinth had repaired itself . . . but it had not repaired itself in the same way as before. He had arrived at a totally different landscape. If not for seeking out the fire, he would have lost them entirely. It had been a close call.

Now he got up and crossed to her, holding out a hand. She took it and he helped her to her feet and, for a moment, he drew her up against his body. The feel of all of her soft curves coming against him was grounding. They had to make it to the center of the labyrinth tomorrow.

They couldn't afford another close call like this. He couldn't afford it.

Because he knew one thing and one thing clearly. He would not die without having known her. His quest could wait. He would put it aside for a short time just to have the time to be with her. Then he would continue onward to his destined battle.

With this in his mind, he took her mouth. He kissed her slowly and deeply. Heat blossomed between them and hunger reared its head. Of its own volition his hand reached out and cupped her breast. His thumb brushed the top of it where it swelled above her corset. Frustrated by the item of clothing he reached for her laces and untied them. She let him. Let him loosen the ties and draw the corset up over her head, leaving her in the black linen shirt. He dropped the corset to the ground, the puff of air it released blowing out the last of the fire. In the utter darkness he reached to cup her breast again and this time his thumb stroked over the turgid peak of her nipple. She sighed softly and leaned her weight against him.

He wanted to draw her shirt down, exposing her breasts to the cold night air. He wanted to take her nipple in his mouth and feel it against his tongue . . . between his teeth. He wanted to suckle her until she moaned. And, as if he had done all of those things . . . as if he had his mouth on her, she did moan. As if she read his thoughts and knew what he was thinking.

"Not here. Not tonight," he said hoarsely.

She nodded, he could feel it. He then led her over to their bedrolls and lifting the blankets he tucked her in tightly against him, his chest to her back, her bottom nestled against the evidence of how much he wanted her.

Like that, they fell asleep.

CHAPTER
NINETEEN

When they woke the next morning the sun was shining brightly, warming their cold bones. The stone had leeched the warmth from their bodies in spite of their close sleeping arrangements.

There was no way to start a fire and no way to cook, so they broke their fast with crackers and hard cheese. And a little bit of cured meat. They were stingy with it, not knowing when they'd next be able to build a fire. Airi found a place to climb up and reorient herself to where they would next be going and she led them around the tricky portal. Then she brought them into a section of the labyrinth where things completely changed. The spikes were set on the tops of the walls, the stone became red brick. The ground became wavy and uneven, making the walls equally so. When they reached the end of what she had plotted out for them, she rubbed her hands together and turned to them.

"Okay. This is it. This is where I've lost the map. We're doing this blind from here on out."

"We'll do a right left right left pattern. That should take us in deeper. Let's try and stay oriented. Keep the sun to the west as it sets," Maxum said.

"We have to get there soon," Kyno said.

"We do. This place isn't as big as all that . . . just tricky," Maxum said.

No sooner had he finished speaking than an unholy screech filled the air. Instantly on guard everyone drew a weapon and they all put their backs to a center point against one another, as though they had practiced the move a hundred times. Suddenly from over the wall came a creature like nothing Airi had ever even heard of, never mind seen. It was shaped like an eye that had been plucked from someone's skull, only a thousand times bigger. It had to be at least three feet in diameter. It had a large iris in its center, a black pupil in the middle of that. The iris was a sickly shade of yellow and the orb itself was pale yellow like a jaundiced eye and shot through with bloody veins. Beneath the iris was what looked like a mouth full of jagged teeth.

It floated toward them, screaming again, and Kilon let loose an arrow, catching it below its mouth. He drew again, but it took time and by the time his arrow was nocked the thing was on them. It scattered them, fear and necessity driving them apart. It focused on Kyno and the giant orc swung out with his sword. A second scream rent the air and suddenly there were two of the things. The second focused on Airi, but Maxum was there, swinging Weysa's Champion in a deadly slice that severed the thing in half. The two sides of it fell to the ground with a squishy plop, the mouth seeking out one last garbled scream. The second one was filled with arrows now and Kyno lifted his sword with several mighty thrusts. The thing, whatever it was, went limping off with high-pitched whines.

Breathing hard, the quintet took stock of one another, finding everyone to be unscathed.

"We're getting close," Maxum said. "The labyrinth is starting to get nervous."

"You say that as if it is a living thing," Airi said.

"I think it is. It heals itself. It changes itself. It protects itself. In a way it feeds itself on the bodies of those who came before us. What would you call it?"

"When you put it that way, I'd have to agree. We best stay on our guard from here on out. The next ones might not be so noisy."

They began to move again and it wasn't such a short time before they came into an open area with a fountain at its center.

"Is this it? Is this the center?" Kyno asked.

"It can't be. All of that to protect a fountain?"

"Fountains can be dangerous things," Maxum said ominously. Airi gave him a sheepish look. She had forgotten. But he never would.

They approached the fountain cautiously. Kyno reached out and touched the water before Maxum could say, "No don't!"

"It's just water," Kyno said. He sucked a drop off his fingers. "Tastes like water."

"Kyno that was very foolish!" Airi scolded. "What if it's poisoned?"

"Didn't taste poisoned. Besides, I'm thirsty."

"Kyno, don't!" Maxum commanded, grabbing the giant's hand before he could scoop water and drink. "It may not be poisoned but many fountains are the gods work and can come with a price."

"Or a reward," Kilon said. "Look."

He pointed and they all looked. The bottom of the fountain was encrusted with gems. Without another word, Kilon waded into the fountain and using a dagger he knelt and pried up one of the gems. He held it up. It was the size of a small fist.

"Look at that!" he cried.

Doisy and Kyno exchanged a look and then they too were in the water, prying up fabulous stones and stuffing them into their pouches.

"This can't be it," Maxum said uneasily in a whisper. "Where's the beast? Where's the ring?"

"I don't know," Airi whispered back.

Right then, Kyno reached out and leaned against a cherub decorating the fountain center. Suddenly there was a rumble and the sound of grinding stone. Abruptly all of the water went rushing out of the fountain as a piece of the fountain fell away and opened into a flight of stairs. The stairs were covered in the stones that the men had been gorging themselves on.

"Come on. It's getting late and we still have work to do," Maxum said.

"But we've found it! We've found the treasure!" Kilon said.

"Then what are the stairs for?" Maxum argued.

"I don't know and I don't care. It's dark down there and I'm not going down. I'll get my fill of these stones, thank you, and then I'm heading out."

"You do that, but you head out alone. I'm going down there."

"Me too," Airi said. "Just imagine, if this is what's at the *entrance* what will it be like when we reach the real treasure?"

"I'm with Maxum," Kyno said, hurrying over to his side.

"Guess I am too," Doisy said breezily as he moved to Maxum's side.

"Fuck the lot of you," Kilon said grouchily. "Fine. But if we find nothing, I get what I take as my full share. None of this sharing out to those who don't deserve it!" He glared pointedly at Airi.

"If it weren't for her and her memory, you wouldn't have even gotten here," Maxum drawled. "She gets equal share just like everyone else. Now are you coming or not?"

Kilon stood there like a surly bear for a moment, then he sheathed his dagger and moved to the stairs.

"There's torches down here," he said uneasily. "And they're lit."

They all exchanged looks. That told them that some living thing was keeping those torches fresh and lit. Maybe the labyrinth was alive or maybe something else was, but they'd be on their guard either way.

The torches illuminated a long corridor and they slowly went toward the end, where there was an opening.

They heard a screech and stopped dead in their tracks. It was a soft sound, more like a creak that went on for a long while. Then there was a hissing and popping sound. That screech . . . hissing . . . popping . . . it repeated itself, sometimes rising in cadence, sometimes deepening in tone. Whatever it was, it was a living thing making those sounds. They all drew their weapons, Airi filling both her hands with daggers, making sure the god-made one was in her right. She was strong with both hands, but the right was her strongest.

They edged up to the room and came around the door.

And there, sitting in the center of the room, was a hydra—a gigantic beast with many heads on many long necks. Airi's quick count brought up ten. Each head was of a different size and a different type of ugliness. There seemed to be a central head and the others were more like satellites around it. All of the heads had mouths full of teeth and all of them had very large eyes.

And all those eyes spied them and swung around to face them. The thing screeched angrily and charged at them.

"Airi, the chest!"

Airi was readying for battle, so she ignored Maxum's cry at first. There were ten heads and five in their group—

that meant each of them had to take out two heads and she planned to do her part.

Maxum went for the central head, somehow hoping that if he cut it off the thing would die. But one slice with his sword was not going to do the trick he realized when his sword stuck into the tough hide of its neck. But at least he had made it a third of the way through and the beast was bleeding profusely. He yanked back the sword, releasing a plume of blood that drenched him down the front of his body. He hacked at the neck again this time cutting it nearly through. One more hack and the central head went flying.

Three of the other heads suddenly targeted him and he found himself in the center of gnashing, violent teeth and fetid, moist breath. He couldn't be harmed, but that didn't keep the mouths from clamping down on him and trying to rend him in two. One bit down into his shoulder, another bit into his legs and then they pulled in opposing directions. Roaring with fury, Maxum began to hack at the head clamped on his shoulder.

Meanwhile, Kyno's sword was not god-made, so it was taking a great deal more work for him to make any impact on the head that was focusing on him. A second head came down on him from the other side and just as it was about to clamp onto his head an arrow thunked into the middle of its forehead, making it jerk back and scream in pain and rage. The arrowed head turned to glare at Kilon, who was reloading. Kyno had told Airi that Kilon used several kinds of arrows, some more deadly than others. Some tipped in fast-acting poisons. Airi could only pray that that was exactly what he was using. Maybe they could poison the thing to death. But somehow she knew it would not be so easy. And, unlike Maxum, they were going to get hurt.

Airi dodged one head, then another, teeth snapping at her heels. She bounced herself off a wall and leapt on the back of the neck of one of the heads and with all of her strength she plunged both daggers into the thing's skull. It screamed and flung her off, sending her slamming into a wall with a bone-jarring, head-ringing strike. She fell to the ground in a dazed heap, watching as the head she'd attacked suddenly went limp, seemingly lifeless. Ears humming, she struggled to get her feet back under herself. As she did this she saw Kilon send another head dropping with a series of arrows shot straight into its brainpan.

Doisy fought with a staff, so he had very little effect on the heads that were attacking them. Still he tried to do his part. When he saw Airi was down he hurried over to her, grabbed her hand, and closed his eyes. The healing he provided washed over her immediately and her brain finally righted itself.

"Thanks!" she said, getting up and leaping back into the fray.

By the time she got back in the fight there were five heads down, Maxum having taken another out and Kyno having done his in. Airi leapt onto the back of another head and did the same as before, only this time she entered its brain via daggers in its eyes. She stuck her daggers in and swirled them around, scrambling the soft tissue. The head dropped down dead. That was half the monster's heads down and something was happening to it. It seemed to be staggering around. That was when Airi noticed what Maxum had been trying to point out before. A huge chest, about six feet in length and in height was nestled between its legs, of which it had six.

She knew then that Maxum had wanted her to go after the chest . . . to look for the ring while they distracted the beast. But if she did that it would leave only Maxum, Kyno, and Kilon to do any damage because Doisy was only useful in battle to a point. He proved his value though as he dodged heads in order to heal a wound Kilon had taken on his bowing arm. After he was healed, Kilon took the opportunity to fall back against a wall just beneath a torch. He pulled a heavy tipped arrow and stuck it in the fire. The tip of the arrow blazed hungrily to life and he sent it soaring into the nearest head. The arrow extinguished the minute it hit the creature's slick skin. Airi sighed with disappointment and hesitated as she tried to think of what would be the best thing to do. She decided to ignore the chest and focus on defeating the beast. Once they killed the beast they would have time to find the ring.

That was when two heads suddenly focused on Kyno. They shot forward and grabbed him, just as they had done to Maxum, grabbing his upper body in the mouth of one head and his legs in the mouth of the other. With one great tortious move, it ripped Kyno in two.

Airi screamed in horror as the heads twisted to and fro, flinging the two halves of Kyno's body around like flags in the wind. Horrified and enraged, Airi recklessly charged one of the two heads. But it was a planned attack for all it was a furious one. She switched daggers into their opposite hands and with a huge snap of her arm sent her dagger flinging end over end until it sunk into the eye of one of the heads with a thunk. The head drooped lifelessly on the neck in almost the same instant as it was struck. She filled her free hand with her third and final dagger and switched the daggers back to their proper hands again ... putting the god-made weapon back in her right hand.

It turned out to be unnecessary. The great beast staggered and fell as Maxum took off its eighth head, leaving only two. The ninth head shot forward dizzily, lashing out at whatever was closest, catching Airi's arm with its jagged teeth. She cried out as her flesh was ripped away, and Maxum roared out in fury, stabbing Weysa's Champion into the thing's head and killing it.

Kilon shot one last arrow into the tenth head and the thing fell down dead, its huge body exhaling a final time in a huge huff of breath.

Airi dropped down onto the ground as well, gasping for breath through pain and physical and mental exhaustion. Maxum hurried over to her, shouting for Doisy.

"It might be poisoned! Help her! Quickly, man!"

"I'm all right," she assured him softly, reaching out to filter fingers into his thick hair. "But Kyno . . ." She wanted to be tough. She really did. And she didn't know why it mattered so much to her, but it made her so sad to think he'd gone his entire life without the comfort of a woman because of the prejudices in the world. Now there was no time left for him to find that comfort. It was over. He was over. And it brought her to tears to think of it like some kind of . . . some kind of *woman*.

She scrubbed bloody hands across her face, swiping at the tears.

"Oh great. Now she's crying! This just gets better and better!" Kilon spat. "Listen sister, he's dead and that's the end of it. It happens. Price we pay for the work we do. You gotta get over it if you think you're going to make a living like this."

After that bit of unfriendly advice, Kilon walked over to the creature and began yanking arrows out of its body, cursing every time one of his shafts broke.

"Hey," Maxum said softly to her. "Don't worry about it. I'm just as pissed as you are."

She looked at him in surprise. How had he known? That her tears were those of anger, not just some weak womanly fretting.

"He was just getting started," she said, sniffling.

"Yeah, he was. But he'll be in any one of the eight heavens now, he gets his pick. He'll be happy there."

"I hope so."

"We've seen the face of the gods," he whispered to her. "We know the heavens are as real as the hells."

She nodded to him and felt comfort and gratitude. She looked at his face and saw pain there. Guilt. She wouldn't let him do that to himself.

"You said it every time. We made our choices. We followed you of our own accord. You didn't force any of us."

"Still . . ."

"No," she said firmly. "He died exactly the way he wanted to. Fighting for a better life."

"He could have had that better life if he'd just stayed behind."

"He was taking care of others as well," she told him.

He looked at her in surprise. "I didn't know that."

"He told me. His mother."

"I'll see to it she gets his share," he said.

"What? No! That money goes to us now!" Kilon ejected.

"Kyno died for his share and he's going to get it!" Maxum barked at the greedy man. "And his mum will get half my share as well. Enough to keep her in comfort the rest of her life and then some."

"Provided what's in there is worth having! Worth Kyno dying for."

"Oh, you could give a snergle's ass what Kyno died for!" Airi spat at him. She looked at the chest. It was trapped beneath half of the creature's body. It would take a monumental effort on their part to free it. Especially without Kyno . . .

Airi looked down at her right arm when the wound began to knit together. She pulled her arm out of Doisy's grasp and said, "Thanks."

"But I'm not finish—"

"Later," she said grimly. "We have work to do . . . and a friend to bury."

CHAPTER
TWENTY

They removed the creature from on top of the trunk with a great deal of effort. When the body finally rolled free, Maxum held Kilon back from opening it. He did the honors himself a moment later. Inside the enormous crate was a small box, a sword, and a crown.

"That's it? That's what we almost got killed for?"

"It must be a very special sword and crown," Maxum surmised. He opened the box and saw the ring inside of it. He took a breath and exhaled it slowly.

"Another ring? Is that what we're here for? What's this one do?" Kilon went to snatch it from the box but Maxum was quicker. He palmed the ring then slid it on his finger where it would be safest. "This is my share," he said. "The rest is for the party."

Kilon's eyes narrowed. "You'll give us all the rest of it . . . just for that ring?"

"Yes."

"Well then, I call ownership of the crown."

"I'd take the sword if I could wield it," Doisy said, "but I can't so it seems to me we'll do what we've always done. We pool it all, Kilon. Sell what we can and divvy up the gold."

"But I want the crown," Kilon said stubbornly.

"If your share can cover the cost of it you can have it. But we share out first!" Doisy was adamant.

"Doisy has it right. If you can afford the crown with your share you can have it. Otherwise it gets split. Now, let's take these and go bury our friend. It's almost sunset and I want to start getting out of this maze as soon as possible."

"It should be faster going on the way out, now that we have markings to follow. Let's just hope there aren't any more surprises," Doisy said.

Stepping out of the fountain a short while later, Doisy and Kilon stopped to pry as many stones out of the floor of the fountain as they could carry, and by that time the sun was setting.

"We'll camp here. Go get some of those torches from below and we'll have a fire," Maxum said.

"You know something . . . that makes me wonder . . . a ten-headed monster can't light and tend torches. How did they get lit and stay lit?" Airi asked.

"Only the gods might know. They set that thing here to guard a treasure," Maxum said.

"Yes but . . . who fed that thing? Who—"

"Will you shut up about it? Who cares? As long as we don't run into whoever or whatever it is, I don't care *who*," Kilon said.

"Leave it to you to look on the short side of things," Airi said.

"Leave it to you to be a smart-mouthed bit—"

"Enough! I'm tired of you two bickering!" Maxum snapped.

"Bickering! That's what you call the way he treats me?" she said, completely aghast that Maxum didn't see the truth of the matter.

"I am just trying to keep the peace," Maxum said through his teeth at her.

"Fine! Go off and do your thing," she said, shooing him away. "I'll keep watch over things here."

"And I'll help," Doisy said quickly before Kilon could react to that.

Maxum stalled a moment, looking unsure of the situation. But he had no choice but to go so he chose an exit out of the center of the maze and walked a safe distance away from the group.

Back at the campsite they had built a small fire. There had been no birds flying overhead this deep into the maze, another thing that gave her the creeps, so they had no fresh meat for dinner. They made do with their dried staples. Doisy laid out their bedrolls, putting as much distance between Kilon and Airi as was possible.

"Someone should keep watch all night tonight. Who knows what else this place has in store for us," Airi said.

"I think the worst of it is over," Kilon drawled as he sat back against the fountain. He had filled his bags with precious stones and was content to wait for daybreak and their eventual escape from the maze.

Airi had yet to pry a single stone from the fountain. She should. She should carry her weight. She should earn enough to help Kyno's mother live a secure life and to secure her own future. But somehow it was the furthest thing from her mind. They had left Kyno down in that oubliette, in a shallow grave dug in the earthen floor by swords and daggers. In a way it was a warrior's burial. She didn't know how she would find Kyno's mother, but she would find her. He had said he had moved her to a big city. Maybe one of the others knew which. She would find her and tell her what a fine warrior and man her son was. She would hear of her son's death from a stranger and a friend.

She was keeping watch when Maxum returned, the cold seeping into her bones. She had been leaning toward the fire, but now that he had returned, she leaned toward

Maxum. She sat up with him, tucked up under his arm like they were sweethearts. She should have protested the sentimentality of the thought, but she was simply too tired. She fell asleep under the protective wing of his arm.

They made their way out of the maze in record time. They practically ran the whole way out, racing from marking to marking until they found themselves faced with the wall of bramble trees and ivy. They began to climb and she was so elated she began to call out, "Dru! We've made it! Dru!"

They topped the wall and looked over. There, sitting in a makeshift camp, sat Dru. He was stunned and elated to see them, hurrying up to meet them.

"I feared the worst! Oh, thank the gods!"

"We made it. Now let's get out of this forest!" Airi said.

"It's almost sunset," Maxum said quietly.

"Oh. Well . . . we'll make camp with Dru then. Maybe Kilon can get some game. I'm starving."

"Maybe Kilon can't," Kilon said contrarily. "I don't answer to you."

"No, but you answer to me," Maxum said. "Go. Hunt. Maybe it'll improve your mood. Airi, you cook what he gets, right?"

"Right," she said, not minding "women's work" in the least if it meant hot food.

Maxum then took his mount and rode off into the dense woods. He had yet to test the ring and its power and he was eager to do so, but not where others would see. He didn't mind Airi knowing, couldn't avoid it actually, but the rest . . . he didn't want anyone knowing just what kind of treasure he had acquired. He didn't want them knowing anything about where all of this was headed.

When he left his horse and walked a safe distance away, he let the ground have him, let it suck him under. When it spit him back out hours later he moved to the nearest tree, laid his hands upon it, and pushed.

The massive fwey tree creaked, then moved, then fell over as he ripped the roots right out of the ground. He lifted the tree as if he were lifting a large branch, though there was some effort involved. It wasn't as if he could do it with a push of a finger. He did break a sweat after holding on to it for several minutes. But the fact was his strength had been multiplied by several times. The ring was doing its job and it would be what he needed in his fight against Sabo. Now there was only one thing left to get and that was located a month away from where they presently were. It would be hard travel on horseback. And winter was coming.

On the plus side . . . Airi had finally stopped fighting him. He knew it was only a matter of time now and he looked upon it with relish. He would have her . . . and soon.

He wondered at himself, wondered at the power of the pleasure that the idea of having her gave him. He thought he should be worried—that any attachments might serve him ill in the coming future. A man with nothing to lose was what was needed to defeat a god.

He had to be a man with nothing to lose.

Or perhaps a man with everything to lose. With a reason to fight that god other than for his own selfish respite from a curse. He had learned to live with this curse . . . but he would not be worth having if he came burdened with it and so could not give of himself. Not until . . . not until it was all over.

He returned to the campsite and, as usual, she had waited up for him, keeping watch over everything as the others slept. It was wise. They could not relax their guard as long as they were in the Killing Forest. There were too many savage beasts both humanoid and not roaming the woods. It was a miracle Dru was still there, unscathed.

He went and sat beside her. She quietly set his plate before him and then watched him eat. If something was on her mind she wasn't sharing it with him just then.

"Come here," he said when he had finished and put aside his plate.

She came without argument and tucked herself up against him under his arm. He touched her face then, tracing the shape of it, the delicate curves that belied the strength within her. She had fought as hard and as bravely as any man would have. More than most would have. She had not cowered.

He touched the place on her arm where her shirt was torn from the beast's bite. Doisy had healed her almost to perfection. There was a thin scar as a reminder of what she had done. A battle wound. One she could point to and tell stories about when she was at an inn trading glory stories with the old and hardened men who wouldn't believe her for a second. Who could believe something so small could help defeat something so big?

"I'll have to mend it," she said, speaking of the shirt.

"You're lucky you still have your arm."

"We're all lucky." She frowned as she no doubt thought of the one who had not been so lucky.

"Most of us," he said needlessly.

"Most of us," she agreed.

"Tomorrow we leave this forest behind, find a good inn, take a bit of respite before we make our way to find that cuff."

"It's a long journey."

"It is," he said, suddenly unsure. Did she mean she wasn't willing to go? Suddenly the idea of it left him cold. No. He had to convince her to come. But before he could open his mouth she said, "Don't worry. I'm in this until the bitter end."

He marveled at her, that she now knew him well enough to predict his thoughts and, perhaps, his emotions. It was a warming sensation. A comforting one, to know that someone knew him. Cared enough to know him. Even if it was a little thief who never wanted to care about anyone but herself. It was easier that way, he realized. When she cared she got hurt. She had cared about Kyno. Now she hurt.

He pressed a kiss to her forehead. "Sleep," he said. "Tomorrow will come soon enough."

"What about you?"

"I'll keep watch. Go on. Go to sleep."

"I'll sleep here," she said, snuggling down deeper against him.

He didn't argue with her. It felt too good having her there to argue.

They made it out of the Killing Forest in one piece and found the nearest road away from it. They traveled every day until sunset and made their way south toward the city of Gorgun. But there were many cities in between and they needed to find one to lighten their load of precious gems.

The first city they came to was a thriving port city called Corcouhn. Doisy collected the loot from their adventure and went about his job of converting it to gold—all except the crown, which Kilon was bent on keeping for himself. Airi accompanied him as a guard against thieves. It took one to spot one, she said, and he would be traveling with a great deal of gold and gems and needed something to protect him other than a staff.

Plus, with her dagger, everyone had to deal with them fairly.

Once he had finished his trade the amount of gold he had achieved was staggering. This would get her anywhere in the world she wanted to go ten times over and have a rich living besides. There was no longer any reason for her to play the role of a thief. There was no longer any reason to follow Maxum and his men. She no longer had to subject herself to Kilon's acrid presence.

So why was she so bent on staying? Why didn't she leave while the leaving was good? She asked herself this question over and over again. As she locked away her portion of gold in the bank, adding the key to the place where her Calandria bank key lay hidden, she had no good answer. The only answer she had was . . . Maxum. She had promised to see him through to his goal, whatever insanity it might be, however much she disagreed with it. Perhaps she could convince him not to throw his life away. Yes, he was cursed but at least the rest of the time he could lead a normal life. That was something wasn't it? Something worth having?

They stayed at an inn and Airi said nothing when Maxum put her saddlebags in his room and did not get her a room of her own. She supposed she could have gotten one for herself, but they both knew that wasn't going to happen. When juquil's hour came that night, things were going to change. Forever. For better or for worse.

She didn't know which . . . and she didn't care.

CHAPTER
TWENTY-ONE

~~~~~~

When Maxum returned to the inn he found Airi in their room waiting for him. He immediately noticed that she had spent some of her gold on a sleeping gown made of the sheerest and shiniest silk he had ever seen. She lay on her side in the bed, her head propped up on one hand, her platinum blond hair spilling free about her shoulders. He could see every soft curve of her body, every swell and every hollow. Her nipples were dark and pointed, as if the room had a chill which, thanks to the fireplace within it, it did not. He could see the shadows beneath her breasts, the tuck of her waist where it led to her hip and the triangle of darker blond curls leading down to her closed thighs.

He had never seen a more provocative image in his life and he thanked Hella briefly for the fate and fortunes that had led him to that moment. It was not likely to be anything he forgot any time soon. This, he thought, might just be something worth fighting for.

"You've bathed," she said, taking in his wet hair.

"Always," he said. "Well, whenever I can. I take off my clothes whenever possible to keep the dirt out of them, but that doesn't protect my skin and hair. I—" He broke off, realizing how inane the conversation was. She didn't really care why he did it. Not right then. And she could figure it out for herself anyway. "You look very clean yourself." He groaned inwardly. What an asinine thing to say! There she was, laid out like a sensual banquet and all he could say was she looked *clean*? "I mean, you look amazing. Beautiful. Delicious," he added for good measure.

That last got to her and she blushed. The reaction must have made her uncomfortable because she sat up and drew her legs into her chest.

"Don't," he said. "Please. Please don't cover up."

She slowly dropped her knees and smiled, that confident smile he was more used to. The ballsy one that had gotten her this far in life. She then came up on her knees and shuffled to the edge of the bed closest to him. The hem of her gown got caught under her knees so the gown pulled taut against her breasts and belly as she reached out to him. He took her hand and let her draw him in close. The fronts of their bodies touched and she looked up at him with her bottomless jade green eyes that were, ironically, so much like his own. With their fair looks and matching eyes they would make a sickly adorable couple, if they weren't who they were. No one could look at them and find them adorable.

He reached up and touched the sun-browned skin of her cheek. She was no pale, sheltered miss. She lived out of doors and took the sun into herself. It made her warm, and smooth, and vibrant. She had freckled a little, but it was mostly a uniform tan. It made the pale pink of her lips stand out and they shone when she licked them nervously.

"So you like what you see." She made a statement of it, not a question, giving him no room for rejection or any power to damage what he suspected right then was a very fragile ego. Oh, she was strong, larger than herself, and had the confidence and personality to go with it, but right now she wasn't showing how strong she could be . . . she was showing how soft she could be, and she wasn't used to it.

"Yes," he answered her anyway. "Can't you tell? I can barely move from wanting you."

That made her smile and he could see her confidence trebling.

"Is that why you still have all your clothes on? Because a girl might think other things if she was laid out in a gown like this and a guy just stood there without—"

He was out of his vest in a flash, whipping off his shirt a second later, making her chuckle. He sat down on the bed beside her to pull off his boots and she got up to help him. When she bent forward the gown gaped at the neck and gave him a full display of breasts left pale and untouched by the sun, their fullness a thing of beauty. To think she had once been confounded by them, strapping them down and hiding them from the world. He was glad she had taken to the corset. On so many levels.

Unable to resist, he reached out and took her right breast in his left hand, squeezing to test the fullness of it, loving the way she filled his palm. She drew in a soft breath of surprise, but did not otherwise stop what he was doing. She let him fondle her as she pulled off first one boot, then the other. When she stood straight, his other hand joined the first, taking her free breast in hand and molding her slowly and firmly. Her nipples were so hard. He took them between his fingers and tugged at them, being as gentle as he knew how. He'd figured out a while ago that she wasn't as experienced as she would like him to think she was. An experienced woman would have found out about potions like the one Doisy had given her a long time ago. Experienced women didn't blush every time a man touched them intimately like she was doing now.

But she battled herself because of that lacking experience. She would rather die than confess to him or herself that she didn't know exactly what she was doing. So he was left to wonder exactly what the sum of her experience was. She wasn't a virgin . . . or . . . oh gods, he hoped he was reading that right. He was the last person in the world who should be allowed to handle a virgin. He didn't think he'd have the patience to treat her right. Not the way he was feeling right then.

"I'm going to do so many things to you tonight," he promised, "that you've never even dreamed of."

"I have quite an imagination," she warned him with a smile.

"I'm wrong. I can't do it all in one night. I'll start off slow . . . and work my way up."

"You're assuming there's going to be more than one night," she said with amusement.

"Oh, there will be. We have a long journey ahead of us and you are going to be in my bed every single night of that journey. Let's get that much straight right now."

She could have argued with his high-handedness, but she didn't and it pleased him.

"Very well," she said. "I needed someone to keep me warm anyway." She punctuated the remark with a careless shrug.

"I'll do that and more," he promised, grabbing handfuls of the gown and in one swift movement shucking it up and off over her head.

She laughed at him, but he could tell she was trying to keep her courage up as she stood gloriously naked in front of him.

"Gods you're beautiful," he said as his hungry eyes roamed over her bare, delicious skin. She preened under the compliment, courage no longer necessary. Good. She should feel confident. She should always know how powerful and stunning she was in all things . . . but in this above all.

He reached out to bracket her hips in his hands and drew her in close between his knees until the soft swell of her breast was beneath his nose and pressed against his lips. It only took a turn of his head to brush his mouth over one of those distended nipples. He parted his lips and tongued her, the taste of her melting like sugar on his tongue. She tasted sweet and sexy, as if she had flavored herself just for him, just to entice him. He drew on her until he heard her breath catch and then he released her with a slow lick of his tongue. Then he switched to the opposite breast and did the same.

She released a little moan as he swirled his tongue around the fat juiciness of her nipple and it made him harden. He was already hard with wanting her from the moment he had laid eyes on the delights displayed before him, but that little moan made him realize she was capable of turning him on in so many more profound ways.

His hands were roaming her skin slowly and sweetly, caressing every curve, stroking into every hollow. He had never felt skin so soft, smelled anything so delicious and inherently feminine. And all the while he tasted her. His mouth drifting over her skin, his tongue catching her in luxurious, lazy licks.

He built her up like that slowly, savoring every moment. He then surprised her by twisting her hips in his hands, turning her fully around so that her back was facing him. Then his tongue was sliding down the channel of her spine, bumping over the vertebrae until his mouth was stroking into the curve of the small of her back, then tracing out into the splay of her backside. He licked her buttocks, nipping at them sensuously, and he felt her tense ever so slightly with every contact, as if she was waiting for something she wasn't comfortable with to happen . . . and yet found surprising pleasure instead. Her little sigh told him the latter.

He slid his hands over her exquisite curving ass and stroked down to her thighs. He shaped her lovingly, worshipping her as she deserved to be worshipped. Then he trailed light fingers down her thighs before bringing his hands back to her hips and turning her to face him once more. He leaned forward and pressed an open-mouthed kiss to the space between her lower ribs, his tongue flicking gently against her skin. Then he trailed down to her navel and dipped his tongue in there. He sealed his mouth to her skin right above her blond curls and sucked at her gently.

He straightened and pulled her forward until she was straddling his legs.

"This is hardly fair. You've stopped removing your clothes," she said breathlessly.

"You could always remove them for me," he said silkily.

"I could," she agreed, reaching down to toy with the ties to his breeches. She untied them slowly, thoughtfully, loosening the waistband until they barely clung to his hips. Then she boldly slid her hand down the front of his pants and found him, wrapping strong fingers around his jutting length. He groaned at the blissful sensation. His pulse pounded in his ears and in his cock. It rose to her touch as if it had a mind of its own.

She stroked him from root to tip, the way she had done in the river. Only this was much better. There was no icy water to defray the heat of her warm fingers around him. His balls tightened with excitement. He wanted to be inside of her more than he had even dared to think. He had never wanted a woman so badly. Probably because she had been so hard to win. But this victory was a sweet one. As sweet as they came.

He pushed her back for a moment and stood up, shucking off his pants with her hand around him the entire time. She liked touching him. Which was just fine because he liked her touch. Liked it too well, in fact. The tip of his cock was oozing in anticipation of her.

When he was on his feet he towered over her, so he sat back down on the bed and pulled her close again. She parted her legs, one thigh on either side of his, and he could feel her moist heat against his thigh. He reached to engage her mouth with his and they kissed as deeply as two people could. As he kissed her he slid his fingers along her thigh, palm up, until he connected with her sweet damp flesh. She was wet for him. Wanting him. He found her entrance and slipped a finger inside her. She contracted around him, his intrusion both alien and wanted. She moaned softly into his mouth and he devoured the sound and her.

From that moment on a sense of urgency enveloped them. They'd been engaged in foreplay for days . . . longer even, and now they were so close they just wanted to crawl inside one another. He reluctantly withdrew his hand from all that glorious tightness, but he knew he wanted that tightness around him in other ways. Even better ways. And in order for that to happen he had to make way for himself.

He pulled her up his thighs until she came to straddle his hips on the bed, bringing her heat against him in fantastic ways. She still had hold of him and she stroked him even as she pressed him to her wetness. She guided him to her entrance, easing him inside and then moving her hand away so she could grip his shoulders and take him all the way inside her with a hot undulation of her hips.

Maxum groaned with the pleasure of it, the feel of her tightening around him, welcoming him with a flood of juicy warmth. He gripped her hip with one hand and embraced her breast with the other. He broke from their kissing to take the rosy tip of her breast into his mouth and reveled in the reaction of her tightening around him that was his reward. He cursed, hardly ready for the intensity of it, but far from ready to let it end. She began to ride him in slow, aching waves, the strong muscles of her thighs and belly used to clinging onto horseback now gripping him.

He laved first one breast then the other, sucking at her harder the more she rode him. He took his free hand from her hip and searched at the apex of her thighs for the sensitive nub that would give her her greatest pleasure. And he wanted to give her her greatest pleasure. He wanted her to come apart in his hands. To scream out *his* name. To know that *he* owned her now. In every way a man could own an independent, fiery woman, he would own her.

His fingers swirled against her and she gasped. She let her head fall back and her eyes close and he immediately stopped. Her head snapped up and her eyes narrowed on him.

"That's right. Look at me. Look right into my eyes and make damn sure it's me you see. Me you feel," he ground out to her. He started to pleasure her with his fingers again and she kept eye contact with him this time. It trebled the intensity of what they were feeling, to be so connected like that. And he wanted that intensity. Wanted it more than anything. Maybe even more than freedom from a curse he no longer deserved.

The thought shook him to his core. It was something he normally would not want to acknowledge, but it was impossible to escape in that instant. And it gave him more pleasure than he thought could be possible. The urge to climax struck him hard and it was all he could do to prevent it. It shocked him how powerful it felt and why it felt that powerful. He knew when he reached that apex it was going to strip him bare and raw . . . but he would not reach it alone. He would make her feel it too.

He began to thrust up to meet her, one hand coming

to grip her hip and buttocks the other buried in the nest of curls toying with her. She began to moan, guttural erotic sounds that built in intensity until she began riding him harder. Her eyes never left his but he could tell she wanted to . . . wanted to shut her eyes and shut herself away from acknowledging the depth of what she was feeling. But neither was she a coward. Never a coward. So she was gazing deep in his eyes when she came for him for the first time. She shattered like glass, splintered and sharp and clear. It was so incredible to see and feel that he came hard and fast. He shouted out, a primitive sound that came from the bottom of his soul.

And all the while they looked hard into each other's eyes.

As they came down from the high of it, breathing hard and damp with perspiration, he felt her pulling back. Felt her closing herself off and away to somewhere safe. She looked away from him.

"Wow," she said breathily, lightness in her tone. "Let's do that again real soon."

"Just give me a few minutes and I'll be happy to oblige. But in the meantime . . ." He looked at her with a devilish glint in his eyes. Fine. She wanted to play? Wanted to keep it light as if the intensity of the past few minutes hadn't happened? He was game for that. He was no more eager to search his soul than she was.

"In the meantime?"

He stood up, lifting her as if she weighed no more than air . . . which to him she did . . . and turned to lay her out on the bed. Seeing her stretched out, naked and waiting, was everything he needed.

For the moment anyway.

He turned her over onto her stomach, though she resisted the whole time, looking over her shoulder at him.

"What are you doing?"

"I told myself when I got you naked I would kiss every inch of your body."

"Oh?" she said breathlessly.

"Yes. And I'm starting with the back."

She sighed, long and deep.

"Be careful," she said. "I could get used to this."

"That is entirely my plan."

CHAPTER
TWENTY-TWO

In the weeks that followed, as they traveled to Gorgun, Maxum made good on his promise to keep her in his bed every night. The only exception came when she had her woman's blood. But even then he slept with her and touched her, soothing her when she became uncomfortable, massaging her to release the knotted tension of the day in her shoulders and back. It was hard going, their journey, and it was incredibly cold. But they warmed each other every night and she'd even taken to sharing his saddle with him as they rode, conserving body heat between them.

Snow threatened to fly any day, but they hoped to make it to Gorgun before then. When possible they traveled from inn to inn, spending their hard-earned money on beds, none wishing to sleep on the cold ground.

There were other benefits to beds as well. But there were also drawbacks. It allowed for much more privacy, more intimacy, and Airi was feeling the danger all too keenly. She had felt it their first night together, when she had been trapped in his gaze the first time he had made her climax. She had known right then that she was in danger and she had fought with herself every second to keep from fleeing for her life, to keep her heart safe, intact, and untouched.

But then she had realized it was much too late for that. Maxum had wormed his way into her soul when she hadn't been looking and now she cared for him to a degree which she had never cared for anyone in her life. Not since her mother had died.

She lectured herself on her stupidity. The man had destined himself to battle a god and despite all of the trinkets he adorned himself with to help him with that, she knew the odds of him winning such a battle were very slim indeed. Sabo was a *god*. He commanded powers that mortals like them could barely comprehend. She was terrified she was losing her heart to a man who would simply throw it away, all in the name of his vengeance against a god.

Oh, he said it was about freedom from his curse, but she knew vengeance when she saw it. There was hatred inside this man and she didn't blame him for it for one second. She had never seen what his curse was like, but she didn't have to see it to imagine it. The crushing weight of all of that soil and rock, dirt filling your mouth and nose, suffocating . . .

She shuddered just to think of it.

She didn't know what to do. She should be putting distance between them, but instead they just became closer with every touch. And what amazed her was that he did not balk at the intimacy. She would have thought he would have hardened his heart against anything that might deter him from his goal, but he didn't appear to be doing that. Oh, he had made no great declarations of love and really, she wasn't expecting any. He was not a poet or a bard and would not be the sort to speak of love. He was a man of actions, so he showed her love. In every touch, in every coming together, he showed her love. And she showed him love in return. Damn her for being stupid, she showed it and felt it.

They arrived at Gorgun after a month of travel just as the first snow began to fly. They had ridden in the cold all day, hoping to make the city by sunset. They arrived mid-afternoon, with enough time to find an inn and begin to warm themselves from the cold that seemed to sink into their very bones.

They were in the common room but for some reason the inn was barely inhabited. There were two other patrons, the innkeeper who was a short, rotund sort of man, and an aging barmaid who wore a peasant blouse that showed off her shoulders and corseted cleavage as if she were a woman ten years younger. Still, Airi could see how she had once been an attractive woman, before the hard life of a barmaid had settled onto her.

Maxum wasted no time getting to the meat of their visit to Gorgun. He called the innkeeper over to their table.

"So what is this I hear of a demigod living in this city? Is it true that one touched by the gods lives among you?"

"It is true that there is one touched by the gods in this city," the innkeeper said. "But I would not say he lives among us. Above us is more like. He has great wealth and power and he is the ruler of this city. His name is Xzonxzu and you would be wise to steer clear of him."

"Where does this Xzonxzu live?"

"He lives in the heart of the city in the grand citadel there."

"How would one go about meeting this Xzonxzu?" Maxum pressed.

"You are a foolish man if you think to meet Xzonxzu. He has little patience for us mortals and becomes bored with us quite quickly. Also"—he looked to Airi—"you would be wise to keep your woman away from him.

Xzonxzu has a large appetite for women and devours them like a hungry child devours candies."

"We will keep that in mind," Maxum said, his arm tightening around Airi's waist. She had tried to sit beside him earlier, but he had possessively insisted she settle into his lap. She had become quite a favored ornament there in their travels this past month and she had learned not to argue with him when he desired her.

Maxum thanked the innkeeper for his information with a tip of gold. The innkeeper beamed at them and from that moment on hastened to make them as comfortable as possible. The barmaid, having seen they were of money, now became very attentive to them. She tried flirting with Doisy who, oddly enough, did not seem all that interested. It wasn't that she was too old . . . Doisy had proven himself to be unprejudiced to age, size, or anything else when it came to women, so Airi was left to wonder what the reason was. She put it down to fatigue. They had been traveling hard these past few days with no inns on the way. It would be nice to have a warm bed to sleep in.

Maxum placed a kiss on the side of her neck and she smiled and curled into him. Honestly, she amazed herself. She had never in her life gotten moon-eyed over a man before. Never under the blue sun had there been anyone likely to touch her. But now she was being touched by more than a man. A mythical man. He was larger than life and thus just the right size for her. Mainly because that was what it had taken to get her attention.

But now that he had her attention, what was he going to do with it? That was the question that had begun to haunt her. She didn't want to change him. She just wanted to change his mind. There had to be a better way to solve his curse. Given time maybe they could find it.

But time was almost at an end. Tomorrow or the next

day he would have the cuff. Then he would go to Meru's temple and challenge a god.

And she'd be damned if he thought he was leaving her behind with nerves and a breaking heart to sustain her. She was going to be there with him until the bitter end. She could promise him that much at least.

Sunset came and went and when he came back to her she was waiting just as she had waited for him every night for over a month now. Tonight was different though. They were on the cusp of the end of their journey. Tomorrow it could be all over for them.

This was immediately reflected in their lovemaking. She attacked him the moment he walked into the room, throwing her body against his, driving her fingers into his wet hair and pulling him down for her kiss. Her feet came up off the floor and her legs wrapped around him like a desperate vise. He gripped hold of her, letting her attack him and holding her to him for every second of it. She was wearing the sheer nightdress he so loved seeing on her, naked beneath, her body hot and soft and strong as it clung to his.

She made no bother with preliminaries. She went straight for the drawstring of his breeches and whipped it free of its tie. She created the gaping in the front that she needed to get her hand on him, to draw him out, to bring him to the cusp of her body. A single thrust and he was inside her, making them both grunt with satisfaction.

Maxum had barely gotten the door closed before she had attacked him, and now he turned toward it, shoving her back up against it and thrusting hard and deep now that he had sufficient counterforce. He hit into her hard and fast, his passion heating with every driven thrust. She felt heat bursting across her every nerve ending and in her passionate desperation she came almost instantly. She cried out as her body convulsed around his, but he never once broke his stride. He continued to thrust hard and fast until she exploded in a second, blinding orgasm. Her fingernails dug into his shoulders, her teeth bit into his lip. He chuckled and thrust, fondled her breast and thrust, devoured her mouth and thrust. The pace was blinding and hot and she needed it more than anything. Her need overwhelmed her, swallowing her whole as she leapt into her next orgasm, this time taking him with her. He roared out his pleasure, pounding into her the entire time until finally . . . finally he could continue no longer. His knees folded under them and they slid down along the door to the floor.

Trying to catch her breath, she also tried to hold her tongue. She didn't want to ruin the intensity of the moment by starting what would probably end up in an argument.

But she failed miserably.

"There must be another way," she said softly against his ear.

He tensed. She could feel it inside of her as they were still connected. But mostly she felt him go tight all around her as she sat nestled in his arms and lap.

"There is no other way and you know it," he said quietly. He met her eyes and brushed her hair back from her face with a gentle hand. He tucked the strands behind her delicately pointed ears. "Do you think this is easy for me? Before I met you I had nothing to lose. I thought that would make me the best kind of opponent. But now . . . now I'm not so sure."

"What do you mean?" she asked, fighting the urge to hold her breath.

"I mean . . . I feel things now I hadn't felt before. Not in this life and not in the life I had before the curse." He trailed gentle fingers over the crest of her cheek. "Do you know how beautiful you are?" he asked her. "I can never convince myself that you really do want to be with me.

Of all the men in the world, someone like you has chosen someone like me."

"I can say the same of you," she said with feeling. "I have never felt beautiful until you told me so. I've never wanted to feel that way. But now I find I am vain because I bask in your regard of me as though I were some fine lady with gently bred manners and social graces. And yet you never treat me like I am weak or docile or any of those other lady-mannered things. You relish my independence and my strength. You make me feel stronger than I am. Better than I am in all things."

"You should feel strong and beautiful and independent and all of those things that make you *you*. You may be small of stature but to me you are larger than life. There is more of you than I could ever hope to manage."

"Quite right," she said primly. "I am a handful and then some. I will always keep you on your toes. I refuse to be tamed or predictable."

"There is no danger of that," he assured her with a chuckle. Then he sobered. "But I am in danger, for in this battle I will have a weakness. One I didn't have before. And yet . . ." He toyed with another strand of her hair. "And yet I feel I have a strength a thousand times stronger than this ring could ever have provided."

The remark warmed her even as it troubled her. "I don't want to be a weakness for you. I want you to have every ounce of strength and power you can possibly have. We should travel the globe gathering more trinkets to assure that you are undefeatable and I . . ."

She stopped for he was shaking his head and she already knew it was too fanciful a notion. There was nothing more they could do.

"We will get the cuff tomorrow," he said quietly, "and then I will spend one last night in your arms before going to Meru's temple. There I will pray for the beginning of the end of my curse or the end of my existence. I hope to carry the strength you give me with me but I cannot do that if you deny me it."

"What do you want me to say? That I give you my blessing and support you with all of my heart?" She did not cry. She never cried. But tears edged into her voice and it quavered as she spoke. "I would never deny you anything. And you already have all of my heart."

It was the first time she had given her feelings voice, and she felt naked and vulnerable for doing so. She had put it all out there, shown him everything. What would he do with it? Would he laugh it off? Would he crush her with his next words? Would he . . . ?

"As you have mine," he whispered, touching his mouth to hers in an achingly sweet kiss. Tears filled her eyes even as her heart soared and tumbled in a turmoil of emotion. He loved her. He loved her and had said as much aloud for her ears to hear rather than just letting his actions be interpreted as such. She hadn't been sure, but now . . . oh, but how could he love her and still leave her?

No. That was selfish and unfair. She would not do that to him. As painful as it was, she had to support him in whatever decision he made.

"I am with you," she breathed. "Whatever you do, wherever you go, know I am with you. And because of that you will be a thousand times stronger than any cruel god."

He wrapped his arms around her and held her tightly to his chest.

"Is it possible to love you even more?" he asked with wonder.

"Certainly. I am a magnificent creature and only get better with time. You have said so yourself."

He laughed. "And now I have given you too high a regard of yourself. You will be impossible to live with."

"But you *will* live with me," she said, her tone suddenly serious. "You must promise me you will defeat Sabo and come back to me."

He looked into her eyes a long moment before saying, "With you as an incentive to return, I will be undefeatable."

"See to it that you are," she said, her chin lifting.

"Yes, my lady. As you command." Then he kissed her, stood up with her, and brought them over to the bed. He arranged her beneath the covers and undressed and joined her.

"What are your plans for getting to Xzonxzu?" she asked once he had curled around her and had settled them warmly together.

"I think I will go in the guise of a diplomat from another city. Perhaps Calandria. It is far enough away that there is little likelihood there is one already here. I will make it seem as though I wish to open trade with his city. When there is money involved, even demigods want to listen."

"It is hard to know that. He already has vast wealth. He may not even wish to be bothered."

"I will do my best to make him think it is worth his while. Tomorrow I will hire guards and servants so I will look wealthy and prosperous."

"You are wealthy, and in your way prosperous."

"But I don't keep appearances to that effect and so I must. Tomorrow we need to hire people. I plan to be in the demigod's citadel by nightfall."

"You know . . . I *am* a thief. You could always use me—"

"No." His tone was hard and sudden. "I will not risk you. There is no telling what the citadel's defenses are like. It could be like sneaking into a jailhouse."

"But those are the easiest places to sneak into," she argued. "Security that tight grows lazy and lax. There's always a place where—"

"I said no. We will not discuss it any further."

Irritation flooded through her. His high-handedness didn't sit well with her in the least. Well, he could be as stubborn as he liked; she was stubborn too. And already an idea was forming.

"Very well," she said easily. "I will not sneak into the citadel."

"Thank you. I will rest easier knowing that. Now go to sleep."

She closed her eyes and with a sly smile on her lips she went to sleep.

CHAPTER
TWENTY-THREE

The bulk of the day was spent finding retainers and outfitting them in livery. Maxum sent out a petition to see Xzonxzu.

It was three days before the petition was answered. By the time the reply came Maxum was fuming and chaffing. Airi did her best to calm him, to remind him they had waited this long, a few days more wouldn't matter. He had calmed considerably in the end and she had entertained him with her body and her light sense of humor. They left the other men to their own devices and did things together in the city, shopping and eating and going to the town fair. Apparently the first day the snow flew was the first day of the winter fair every year and it went on for several days. There was much to entertain them and she could almost forget why they were really there.

Until the messenger had come to the inn granting Maxum an audience with the demigod that afternoon. Maxum would have preferred morning, a time not so close to sunset, but he could not control the situation any more than he already had.

He was ready to go to the citadel and was waiting at

the bottom of the stairs in the inn's common room for Airi. She had dawdled behind and he was growing impatient, wondering if this was by design . . . a subconscious sabotage on her part. But then he shook the notion off. She knew how badly he wanted this, and she was willing to stick with him as long as it took. She had done nothing but support him all along, even though she thought this was madness. And for some time now he was beginning to agree with her. He should simply accept life for what it was, live with Airi . . . maybe make a family with her if she was amenable to the idea. He had never wanted children before—his life as a goldsword had prevented him from putting down any kind of roots.

But he had never felt as strongly as this before. He had never known a woman so incredibly compatible with himself. Her fight and vigor, independence and fearlessness—he'd never known a woman like that before.

He heard the door to their room open and he looked up. The other men, dressed in servants' livery, all fell into a shocked silence as they looked up along with him. For there stood a woman none of them recognized.

She was dressed in a beautiful winter gown of white, with a bodice embroidered in meld metal thread, a metal which was like gold, only it was emerald green in color. The metallic threading picked up the light and gleamed back at them. Her skirts were full and floor length, as was the fashion for the area, and they too were embroidered in meld metal. The fabric appeared to be jilu silk, a heavy silk appropriate for the cold weather but just as shimmery as the meld metal.

She was wearing a fashion corset. It was beneath the bodice of the dress and came up to the midpoint of her breasts. She was wearing it tight so that her breasts looked as though they were moments from spilling over the top and had the bodice been even a millimeter shorter, he would have been able to see a touch of her nipples.

The bodice left her shoulders completely bare, her sleeves not beginning until a good distance down her arm, but then covering her fully to her wrists. Around her arms was a heavy pink shawl of jilu silk with a violet fringe. Looped over her wrist was a silk drawstring purse.

Airi paused at the head of the stairs and looked down at the men, judging their reactions to seeing her in this traditional feminine garb. Doisy's eyes were lit up with appreciation and they scanned over her multiple times. Dru's mouth was hanging open in shock and awe. Kilon . . . well, Kilon looked even more disgusted with her than usual, if such a thing were possible. But none of that mattered, all that mattered was Maxum.

Maxum's reaction was one of confused hunger. This was not the Airi he wanted with a passionate hunger—this was a stranger. And yet his craving for her only intensified. Seeing her dressed in so many clothes immediately filled his mind with the desire to take them all off her, piece by piece. She had her hair dressed up in an elegant coiffure, one that shockingly left her ears uncovered. That, perhaps more than anything, disturbed him. There would be many people who would take exception to her as an elf. She had hidden her ears all of her life, why would she bare them now?

She came down the stairs in a walk that put far more slink and sexuality in her spine than elegance and breeding. She came to face him and raised a fair blond brow.

"What do you think? Am I passable?"

"I . . . I . . ." Maxum was at a loss for words for a moment. Then, "What the hells are you doing in that outfit?"

"I'm coming with you."

"Not dressed like that you're not!"

"Maxum, there's nothing wrong with the way I'm dressed," she said in a lightly scolding tone. "I am dressed just like any other lady of his court would be."

"You're not just any other lady!" he erupted. "Why are you doing this?"

"Maxum, you're a wealthy dignitary. You must have a wife or a mistress or even a sister. Take your pick. I'll play whatever role you choose. Although with these"— she touched her ears and for the first time he realized she was wearing earrings in them . . . and a matching necklace and bracelets—"I would stick to mistress or wife. But you must choose one. And you must take me. The one thing that is very clear from what we've been told is that Xzonxzu has a hunger for women. I figure the rarer the better to get his attention. And what would be more rare than a cold-blooded elf? I imagine he would find it to be quite a conquest to get close to me. Certainly close enough that I can gain access to the cuff."

"No! I told you I didn't want you stealing the cuff!"

"You said you didn't want me to sneak in. I will be walking in the front door by your side."

"Maxum," Doisy said, "she's got a point. Regular people bore the hell out of Xzonxzu. Look how long it took him to respond to your petition. He couldn't care less about you. But with a temptation like Airi, he will be more likely to keep you close in order to gain access to her. That will allow us to remain in a position where we can freely move about the citadel. She can keep Xzonxzu busy while we go about the business of stealing the cuff."

"Busy how?" Maxum demanded. "By selling him her body? Absolutely not!"

"I will not sell him my body!" she exclaimed utterly aghast. The reaction filled him with a sense of relief. At least she hadn't been suggesting that much. He wanted the cuff badly but not that badly. "But he doesn't need to know that. It will be a very powerful flirtation, but nothing more I assure you."

"Well, at least you have that much sense," he said tightly.

"Maxum, come on," Dru chimed in, "you have to see the benefit in this. She will be the perfect distraction."

"Provided he even finds her interesting," Maxum said with a frown.

Airi had to look shocked. "What are you saying? That I'm not woman enough to get his attention?"

"No. Not at all. You are more than woman enough. But he is a demigod who has no doubt made his way through thousands of women, a different one in his bed every night. You may not be novel enough to garner his attention."

"Oh, I'll be novel enough. You just leave that part up to me."

"She's fresh pussy," Kilon said crudely. "Exotic too. He'll like her every bit as much as you do."

"See, even Kilon agrees . . . in his way," Airi said with a roll of her eyes.

"That doesn't comfort me," Maxum said, his frown intensifying. But he tilted his head and then gave a reluctant nod. "All right. I can see how it could work. But the moment you feel you're in over your head you do whatever it takes to get out of there. And I don't want you trying to steal the cuff—that's our job. You just keep him busy while we look for it."

"Agreed!" She clapped her hands and rubbed them together eagerly. "Come on. This guy doesn't have a chance!"

"Wait a minute," Maxum said, narrowing a look on her. "Are you armed at least?"

Airi gave him a look that said, "Do I look stupid to you?" before she lifted up her skirt and showed him the Dagger of Truths strapped to her inner thigh. She had strapped it on upside down so she could pull it faster if she needed to, even with the skirts in the way. Somewhat mollified by the sight, Maxum nodded and held out his arm like a proper gentleman. It made her snicker, but at a quelling look she primly took his arm and began to act everything the genteel and wealthy woman should be. She didn't have much experience at it, but she'd seen more than enough of it to do a fair imitation. She acted like just the sort of vapid creature she would have stolen from in the past. Only, she added an air of mystery and sensuality to it. She had to attract him at all costs. And no matter what Maxum said, if the opportunity to grab the cuff presented itself, she was going to take full advantage of it.

They approached the citadel and were allowed entrance into the main entryway. There they were met by a man, tall and reedy and pale in complexion, who then led them into an antechamber. They were announced loudly as Sor Maxum and Lady Airianne of Calandria and the doors were opened to admit them to a massive room done in fair colored marble with veins of gold running through it and soaring domed ceilings with tremendous frescos painted all around the curve of them, depicting stories featuring a strong, central male figure. Airi assumed this was a pictorial tale of the demigod's triumphs and battles. She would have a chance later to study them, but for now she focused on the man they were approaching.

"Honored guests, you will kneel before the god, Xzonxzu," the reedy man commanded as soon as they had approached the man sitting in a golden throne. Both Maxum and Airi went stiff at the idea of bowing before anyone, but playing their roles to perfection they bowed to the "god" Xzonxzu. Briefly Ari wondered if the gods knew of these blasphemous claims to godhood. Perhaps this was part of the reason why Meru had sent them to Xzonxzu's door. To take the demigod down a peg.

Airi began to wonder which god had elevated Xzonxzu to his demigod status. In order to become a demigod a god had to bless the mortal with immortality, strength, and wealth—or so the stories went. But if that were the case then Maxum would qualify as a demigod now. Perhaps he was one. Meru had gifted him with the means to become the strong man he needed to be. And wouldn't it take a demigod to battle a god and even hope to come out alive?

The man in the throne was not as large as Airi had expected, but he was clearly as youthful and strong as one would expect of a demigod. He sat indolently on the throne, a gold and bejeweled crown on his head. He wore a toga of white embroidered in metal—gold, most likely—and wore rings on almost all of his fingers, a bracelet on either wrist, an armband of gold and silver on his left biceps and a sparkling diamond earring in both ears. If she had to surmise, it would be that every one of the stones on his body was the most valuable stone of its kind in cut and clarity. Each one refracted the late afternoon sunlight that was pouring in through the mullioned windows all around the throne room.

"So," Xzonxzu barked. "Calandria wishes to open trade with Gorgun? Why have you not come sooner than this?"

"The path from one city to the next was much too long and took far too much time to be wise," Maxum answered quickly and truthfully. "It was not possible to come sooner." Again, it was the truth. But then Maxum did some creative truth telling. "But now that we have thought to use ships for the better part of the journey to Okun and then do overland travel, the route has been shortened considerably."

Maxum and the group had not made use of this

method of travel themselves because of Maxum's limitations, but it was entirely plausible for a trade route. Airi was impressed by his quick thinking. A blossom of pride unfurled in her breast.

But what was most important about the exchange was that Xzonxzu had never once taken his eyes off Airi. She met his gaze and smiled, nodding her head in acknowledgment of his regard.

"And who is this bedazzling creature you have brought before me?" Xzonxzu asked, getting to his feet and stepping down from the dais to come and take her hands in his. He spread her arms wide as he eyed her critically from top to bottom and back again. Then his eyes fixated on her ears. She blushed, but not from feeling complimented. She was still self-conscious about her ears and it felt strange to have them so openly regarded. But her coquettish blush charmed Xzonxzu and he smiled at her. "Are you not used to being complimented, my lady?"

"On the contrary," she said. "My master does so regularly. But I have never been told so by a god."

"So you are his mistress? Well, he is a very lucky man. But tell me," he said then in a conspiratorial whisper, "why should I open trade between our two cities?"

"Why, to make money of course," she said.

He laughed. "An honest woman. Very refreshing. But I have more than enough money. I do not need more," he said, sounding bored with the whole idea.

"There is no such thing as too much money," Airi said. She winked. "Just as there is no such thing as too much love."

The demigod threw back his head and laughed. "This is quite a woman you have here, Maxum," he said in a boisterous tone. "You must stay for eventide meal. You will be my guests."

"When is your eventide meal?" Airi asked.

"And hour before sunset, why do you ask?"

"Only to know when we should return."

"Return? You will not be leaving! I must hear all about Calandria for I have not been there myself. You will tell me all about what you wish to trade."

"Of course," Airi said with a smile.

They spent the next pair of hours lying through their teeth but telling nothing but truths the entire time. Maxum and Airi played off one another beautifully and anyone who saw them would believe they were exactly who they said they were. Maxum paid very little attention to Airi, allowing her to sit next to Xzonxzu and flirt with him outrageously. He had to pretend it didn't bother him in the slightest when in fact, it did bother him a great deal. But they were a team, working together toward a common goal.

The rest of the group, acting the part of servants, stood close under the guise of serving their master when, in fact, they were on high alert in case something should go wrong. Doisy was serving Maxum his wine and punctuating the service with the occasional, "Will there be anything else my lord desires?"

"I must say, you have very well-trained servants and clearly they are very loyal to you. What does that one there do?" Xzonxzu asked, pointing to Kilon.

"He is my bodyguard and protector."

"Ah. He has that look about him. The look of a killer. You would not convince me he is anything else."

"Kilon has done his share of killing on my behalf and on the part of others."

"As I said . . . you are very fortunate." Xzonxzu looked at Airi, lifted her hand to his lips and kissed her palm in a very traditional show of respect to a lady. "Very lucky indeed."

"And now, my lord, I must take my leave of you for a few hours," Maxum said.

"Absolutely not. I forbid you to go. I am enjoying your company too much."

"I am sorry but I have an appointment that must be kept."

"No business will happen between you and any citizen of my city unless I allow it to happen! You will stay!"

"My great and wondrous lord," Airi spoke up softly, soothingly, her hand coming to stroke down the demigod's bulging biceps. "Perhaps if I stayed and represented my master in his absence we can all be satisfied."

The demigod's eyes lit with appreciation and avarice. After all, she suspected she was the reason why he wanted Maxum to stay so much. "My master will return an hour past juquil's hour and we will spend the night here as your guests. Then, on the morrow you can show me your fine city as only you can do, being its great lord and master."

"My dear—" Maxum began to protest.

"Yes! That will be a fine arrangement," Xzonxzu said. "Go and do your business and rest assured I will take very fine care of your lady in your absence."

Maxum was not happy. He wanted to flat out refuse to let this happen, but he knew he could not do so and still maintain their charade. Airi shot him a look that said "Trust me," so he decided he would have to do just that.

"I will have to leave my attendants behind, to ensure she is well taken care of," he said, indicating Doisy and Kilon.

"That one may stay," he said pointing to Doisy. "But it is better you take your man with you into the city for your protection. Overall it is a good city, safe from many dangers because the citizens fear my reprisals should they break any of my laws, but there is still a bad element that would see your fine clothes and single you out to make a victim of theft of you."

Again, Maxum wanted to argue, but he could think of

no plausible reason to push the matter that would not end up causing friction. So he nodded and got up to leave with Kilon and Dru.

"My master, will you leave Dru for me?" She turned to explain to the demigod. "You see, he is my personal attendant. I should like to look my best if I am to represent all of Calandria."

Xzonxzu nodded with a magnanimous smile and gesture of his hand. So both Dru and Doisy stayed behind as Maxum left with Kilon. The very instant he was gone, she leaned in closer to the demigod.

"So why don't you show me around this grand citadel of yours," she said with a winning smile.

CHAPTER
TWENTY-FOUR

❧

"But of course," Xzonxzu said, getting up from the table and holding out his arm to her. She took it and wrapped her hand warmly around his arm beneath the bracelet ringing his biceps.

"This is fine workmanship," she said, admiring it openly. "I have never seen its equal."

"Nor will you ever. This was a gift from a god."

"Really?" she looked appropriately excited which wasn't too hard for her to act under the circumstances. *Could it be? Could it be the cuff, worn so openly?* "Which god?"

"My patron god, the one who rose me up to my godly status. Jikaro."

"The god of anger and deception?" She gave a light shudder. "I should be afraid to meet him in person."

"He is a massive fellow, about three times my size. He is strong of body and of temper."

"And what did you do to deserve this gift and the gift of your godhood?" she asked.

"Do you not know the stories?"

"I am afraid I am ignorant. Please forgive me. My master may have mentioned something, but I do admit to not always paying attention to him when he is droning on about certain things."

"You are a very naughty mistress," he said teasingly.

"I confess that I am," she said. "But you will not hold that against me I hope," she said.

"I will not, I can promise you that. I rather like naughty mistresses. They are the very best kind."

"Then why do you not have one of your own?" she asked him.

"I had one once but she was not worthy enough once I became a god so I discarded her."

Airi let that roll off her. "So tell me the story of how you came to be so blessed by the gods."

"I will simplify it by telling you there was a woman Jikaro wanted—more than he had ever wanted a woman before. He needed a warrior to woo and win her and then hand her over to the god when the time came. But it was not easy to win her. Her father was a tyrant and demanded her suitors go through many rigorous tests before he found them worthy of her. The tests were so deadly that no suitor had ever survived."

"But you survived."

"I did. It was no easy task, I will admit. The tests nearly killed me."

"I wonder that Jikaro did not simply take the girl."

"I wondered at that myself, but far be it from me to question the motives of a god. He wanted her to be wooed and so I courted and won her. And on the night of our wedding I handed her over to Jikaro."

"Was she not shocked and displeased to be so misled?"

"I do not know. Why would she be though? She was to be loved by a god. That is an honor to any woman."

"Indeed you are right. Any woman would be a fool not to accept the attentions of a god," Airi said, openly baiting him.

"You are a very clever woman that you understand this." He looked quite pleased.

"So tell me about this item," she said, stroking the armlet.

And of course, thanks to the dagger, he was compelled to tell the truth. But she suspected he would have told her regardless, for he seemed the boastful sort. "This is a very old and powerful artifact, from times long past and forgotten. It is called the Cuff of Cadence and it can do many wonderful things."

"Such as?"

He stopped their progress and turned to face her. "I will show you."

Then, suddenly, there were flowers in his hand. She had seen a blur of movement and he was no longer standing exactly where he had been an instant ago, but he stood before her with the dusk roses in his hand. Dusk roses bloomed only at dusk, so the blooms were ripe and full. She gasped and clapped.

"How did you do that?" she asked as she took the small bouquet in her hands.

"Easily. The cuff allows me to move faster than what appears to be the blink of an eye to you from one place to the next. Or I can slow the movements of others. Watch." He waved a hand at a passing servant and suddenly her movement seemed to slow until she was barely moving, and yet there was still momentum in her body. She was moving, but at an infinitesimal pace.

"Amazing," Airi said.

"As long as I wear it no one can move faster than me. I could slow the working of the entire city if I wished!"

"Really? That is quite powerful then!"

"The man who owns this is more than a man. He is a god."

"He is indeed," she said with appropriate admiration.

So. She had found the cuff. But the only way to get it off him without his knowledge . . . well, it wasn't possible. Not even her best sleight of hand could unlatch the cuff and remove it from his body without him knowing.

There was only one possible solution.

She would have to kill him and remove it after he was dead. But if he could slow down the actions of others at a mere thought, she would have to catch him completely off guard.

"Now later I will have something to show you," she said.

She should bide her time. It would be best to wait until as close to juquil's hour as she could before acting so that they could flee the city together as soon as possible. But that meant dodging Xzonxzu's attention for the next few hours.

"What is it?"

"A gift from a god," she said honestly.

"What is it? I insist you show me now for I do not believe you are telling the truth!" He seemed heavily offended and she realized she had made a miscalculation. Instead of being intrigued, he felt threatened. Knowing that someone else had a gift from a god made him feel diminished and he was not happy about it.

"Very well, I was hoping to do this later when my master returned . . ."

"Show me!"

Airi bent down and lifted her skirts, glancing up between her lashes as she did so. She exposed her bare leg and immediately his anger dissipated and avarice once again entered his eyes. The avarice of a man wanting and coveting another man's woman.

She withdrew the dagger from its sheath in a blinding flash of movement, acting before he had a chance to react with the powers of the cuff. All she needed to do was break his skin and that was exactly what she did, nicking him across his cheekbone. Then the next thing she knew he had backhanded her hard and the dagger went flying out of her hand as she hit the wall on the opposite side of the corridor and slid to the floor.

"Foolish woman!" he roared. "I am a god! You cannot hurt a god!"

Airi spit blood as Dru leapt in to protect her, casting his blurring magery so the demigod could not focus on any of them enough to harm them. Then he cast his multiply spell which cast multiples of each of them so that the guards coming up on them could not tell which was the real target.

Airi shook off her dizziness and lunged for her dagger, but the demigod was there before her and picking it up. She felt as though she were moving through molasses, her speed inconsequential in the face of the cuff.

Why wasn't the Dagger of Truths working? If she so much as cut the skin of a victim the power of all his lies should come to bear. But Meru had not told her how long that would take or in what manner it would come. She had been foolish. Foolish to act so rashly. Now they would all die because of her.

And just as she thought it Xzonxzu dropped the dagger to the ground as if it had burned him, and indeed the imprint of the dagger was suddenly burned into his palm. That was when she realized that no one but she was able to hold the dagger.

As he roared in outrage the cry suddenly choked off. Xzonxzu seized violently, doubled over, and fell to his knees on the floor. The nick on his face where she had cut him began to grow, his skin splitting and tearing and spilling blood until half his face was engulfed in the wound. Black ichor began to ooze out of the wound and all over his body Xzonxzu's skin was bubbling and expanding as though he were being filled with air from the inside. Other rents appeared in his skin and they too began to leak blood and blackness until he was striped with tears in his flesh and his skin was slick with black and blood. Then Xzonxzu exploded from the inside out, dousing everyone in blood and ichor.

Airi wiped blood out of her eyes and saw Xzonxzu's skeleton lying in a heap on the ground, bits of flesh still clinging to it. And there, wrapped around the fleshy bits of his arm, was the cuff.

Airi leapt for it. Aware that there were guards bearing down on them she stripped the bangle from the flesh left behind and closing her eyes she tried to focus on slowing everything down, on freezing it in place.

When she opened her eyes the entire world had frozen still. Dru, Doisy, the guards . . . everyone was barely moving. The cuff, meant to be worn around a man's biceps, was too big for her to wear, so she gripped it with everything she was worth. Then she dove for her dagger. She hurried to the nearest guard and cut him with it. She did the same for the three others she saw then hurried back to Dru and Doisy. She reached out and touched them, grabbing a wrist in each hand, and suddenly they came to her speed.

"What the hells?" Doisy said.

"It's the cuff. We have to go before anyone finds us, and we have to get word to Maxum that he's not to return to the city."

"How are we going to do that? We don't even know which direction he's gone in and there are three gates leading out of the city."

"Then we'll each have to take a gate."

"The guards will lock the city down! They'll be searching for us!" Dru said.

"Why? Their lord and master is dead. There's no one to dispense justice now. And from what I've heard they'll be glad to be rid of him. I know I would be. What a pompous, overinflated jackass."

"But how do you know he's dead? He . . . he's a god."

"Demigod. But you have a point. However, I doubt even a demigod could survive . . ."

"What did you do to him?" Dru asked. "What was all that about a gift from a god?"

So they had overheard that part. "I'll explain later. After we leave this city." She stopped then, suddenly remembering something the demigod had said. "Wait. He said he could slow the entire city. What if I freeze the city, leaving us with the time to find Maxum and make our escape . . . as best we can in any case."

"Wait a minute," Doisy said. "You have to take something else."

"Something else?"

"Something valuable. We traveled all this way . . . I'm assuming for that," he said nodding toward the cuff, "But Kilon is going to want his share. The minute he sees how that thing works he's going to want it. The only way to mollify him will be with cold gold."

"Fine. Apparently we have all the time in the world now. Let's find the coffers and be done with it. If this man is really a favorite of Jikaro, we could be looking at a very angry god of anger and deception. Although, one might think he would appreciate such a great deception." No easy trick considering the truths they'd had to tell.

Finding the coffers took more time than she would have liked. By the time they had emptied them to what Doisy felt would be Kilon's satisfaction, Airi was feeling exhausted. That was when she realized it took great mental effort on her part to maintain the frozen aspect of the world around her. She wondered just how far she was reaching out with this power when they exited the citadel and found the entire city was also frozen still.

She wondered if she could tighten up the area of affectedness, limiting it only to the city walls. Perhaps then it wouldn't take so much energy to maintain. For all she knew, the entire world was moving at an infinitesimal speed. Or maybe they were the ones moving at a super fast speed. She couldn't really tell. They made it back to the inn and, exhausted, Airi released the hold she had over everything. The world revved up around her, coming back up to speed. She figured they had very little time before the alarm was raised, if indeed it was raised, so they found Kilon and packed their bags with all due haste.

Kilon's eyes went large with greed when he saw the bags of gold they had acquired, but that was only until he saw the cuff and realized what it could do. When he did, there was going to be trouble. She just knew it. To Dru's and Doisy's credit, they said nothing about it.

"Come on, we have to figure out where Maxum went and stop him before he goes to the citadel," Airi said.

"He left via the west gate so I imagine he'll come in the same way. He said he'd stop by here first. We could just wait—"

"We've just stolen half the city's treasury," Airi snapped, irritable because of her weariness. "Do you really want to wait where everyone knows we were staying?"

"Listen you, you watch your mouth when you're talking to me or I'll—"

"Enough!" she shouted into his face even though she was shorter than he was by half a head or more. "This is no time for your petty threats! We are in danger. Maxum is in danger! Let's get out of this godsforsaken city before all the hells catch up with us!"

Kilon's jaw worked a minute, as if he were gearing up to lambaste her. In the end all he did was hiss, "Your time is coming, little girl. You mark my words. He'll get tired of you one day—one day soon—and then you'll be getting what you deserve from yours truly."

He grabbed up his saddlebags and left her presence.

Gods help her the day that man lost all restraint and

came after her. She wasn't fool enough not to know how dangerous he was.

Just as they stepped outside of the inn a loud horn and bells began to ring out over the city. It didn't take a genius to figure out it was the city alarm.

Airi dug the cuff out of her bag and said, "We better hurry before they close the city gates!"

She closed her eyes a moment and focused. When she opened them the city was once more frozen. She took Doisy's and Dru's hands in hers and nodded to Dru to touch Kilon.

When Kilon realized what was happening and how and why, his dark eyes narrowed on her and the cuff but he remained surprisingly silent. Airi knew full well he would be asking for his share of the fortune and he would exact a high price in exchange for his share of the cuff.

Together, linked, they made their way to the west gate. As they stepped through the gate they realized that Airi's ability to freeze was more a matter of them moving faster than everyone else. At least this time it seemed to be. It seemed to take less effort for them to move at a hastened pace than it did to lock everyone in place. So she concentrated on doing just that and they headed off the road to a place where they could keep an eye on the gate yet remain hidden from view. If Maxum entered via this gate, they would be able to see him.

Juquil's hour came and went, the city and Airi's group now moving at normal speed. The gates to the city had been shut and locked and the guards at all the gates had been running around madly for the better part of a few hours. The city was clearly on guard and she imagined they were searching high and low for Airi and their group.

So much for them not caring what happened to their master. Or maybe it was because they had robbed the city vault. Whatever the reason, they had to keep an eye out for Maxum.

CHAPTER
TWENTY-FIVE

When he showed up on the road leading to the gate, Airi sighed in relief. She ran out of their hiding place and up to his horse. She had taken the time to change out of her women's finery, and was back in her light, serviccable clothing with only a cloak to keep her warm. Maxum saw her coming and reined in. He flung himself from the horse's back and Airi threw herself into his arms the minute they were on equal footing.

"What did you do?" he demanded of her.

"I had no choice! All it took was one small mistake and . . . here!"

She held the cuff out to him and he took it in stunned fingers. "You got it?"

"Yes," she breathed.

"Airi, that was damned stupid of you!" he roared in her face.

She smiled in reply. "Yeah. I know. But there's no sense fighting about it now. It's done and done for the best."

Maxum was surprised. He would have expected her to get her back up and fight to defend her actions, but instead she simply admitted he was right and went to move on. The fact that she didn't act defensively threw him and diffused his anger tremendously.

How could he be angry with her? She'd gotten the cuff.

She'd gotten the cuff.

Even though he knew she didn't want him to fight Sabo, she had gotten it for him anyway. She was fighting for him when she could have fought against him. She could have sabotaged him at any point just to get her way and keep him with her. And yet . . .

Maxum threw his arms around Airi, scooped her up off the ground and spun about with her in his arms. He kissed her soundly, taking her breath away so that she came up for air with a gasp. She laughed at his joy and shared in it with him, even though her heart was breaking into millions of frightened pieces. She had made this possible. She had made it possible for him to do the thing that would destroy everything they had.

"Come on," he said against her cheek, "let's put distance between us and the city. There is another city about two days' ride to the east. We'll go there and find the temple of Meru."

Two nights. That meant all she had of him was two nights and both of those nights would be spent camping in the cold and snow. She wanted her last night with him to be more memorable than that. So she turned his face toward hers, met his eyes and said, "You will give me my night first."

Maxum brushed at the strand of hair that had escaped her mussed coiffure, pushing it back behind her small pointed ear.

"Yes, love," he said softly, tenderly, "you will have your night."

The words calmed the fire of fear inside her a great deal. She had resigned herself to his doing what he was going to do, now all she could do was support him and be with him until the bitter end. And he might not realize it, but she had every intention of watching this battle as it unfolded. She would make a special request of Meru and she believed Meru would grant it to her. She didn't know why she believed that, but she did. She had to. The alternative was to wait in obscurity, never knowing what had become of him.

Now that they were clear on that, they separated after one quick kiss and mounted their horses. They began to ride for the city of Badu, leaving the open road and traveling through the woods in case search parties from Gorgun came down the roads.

They didn't make camp until sunset the next day. They were all tired, but grateful they had escaped the city unscathed. Once Maxum had left the group to deal with his curse, Kilon said, "I want my share of that cuff."

"You'll get your share in gold, just as always," Doisy said.

"There's not enough gold in those sacks to even come close to what the power of that cuff can do!" Kilon said. "With that cuff we can walk into any bank, any vault, any city at any time! I want my share of that cuff and I'm going to have it."

"You'll take gold for it or you'll get nothing, because you're not touching that cuff. It belongs to Maxum," Airi said coldly.

"It belongs to all of us. That's the rules of the group," Kilon spat. "He's already got that talisman and that ring. Don't think I don't know there's something special about them. I may not know what it is, but I'm not stupid. A man doesn't risk his life against a ten-headed hydra for a simple gold ring unless it does something."

"You got your share of compensation for those items. You got that crown you wanted so badly," Doisy said.

"What's a crown? It's just gold and gems. I thought it

was special somehow, to be guarded by that creature. But it doesn't do a damn thing worth having it for. But that cuff . . . that's worth having."

"Put it out of your mind, Kilon," Airi said hotly. "You'll get that cuff over my cold corpse and then Maxum's as well."

"I've been wanting the first for a long while now," he hissed in her face. "I'm itching to put an arrow right through your pretty green eye, bitch, and don't think I'm afraid to do it. I'll get that cuff if it's the last thing I do. Now, you can hunt your own fucking supper. I'm not feeding you anymore. I'd rather like to watch you starve."

"You'd do that? Make yourself go hungry just to spite me?"

"In a heartbeat," he sneered. "And I ain't going hungry. I'm hunting my own and cooking my own. I'll even feed the men besides. But you . . . not a single morsel."

Kilon then hoisted his crossbow and walked out into the dark woods.

True to his word he hunted for himself, cooked for himself, and even offered to feed the others, but both Dru and Doisy declined and Airi felt her heart swell at the show of loyalty and solidarity. Still she felt guilty that they should suffer even in the slightest and tried to get them to take Kilon's offered food, but they refused.

Airi had hunted her own food before, but never in the dark. So she sat near the fire on her and Maxum's bedrolls and waited for juquil's hour. She knew she was not safe without Maxum around to keep Kilon in check. Something needed to be done about him, and it needed to be done tonight.

Doisy and Dru waited up with her, the message clear. None of them trusted Kilon enough to sleep with him there any longer. It had been a long time coming, but it had finally reached a tipping point between Kilon and the group.

Kilon waited as well, whittling at an arrow he was making and whistling as if he hadn't a care in the world. When there was the snap of a twig in the woods and Maxum suddenly appeared . . .

Everything happened so fast. Kilon lifted his crossbow and fired. The bolt hit Airi just inches away from her heart, imbedding itself into her shoulder. Kilon was on his feet in a flash, reloading and coming to stand over Airi, the crossbow aimed directly at her heart.

"Give me the cuff or she's dead," he said to Maxum. "I know I can't hurt you because of that talisman, but I can hurt her. And don't think of using the cuff. I can fire a lot faster than you can figure out how to use that thing."

Maxum wanted to hurry to Airi's side, but he was frozen in place because of the threat to her life. He hadn't learned how the cuff worked. He had intended to practice with it that night. Now he regretted not doing so earlier.

"Quickly! Give it to me! My finger's twitching!" Kilon hissed.

Maxum reached for the cuff on his biceps.

"No don't!" Airi cried. She was clutching the bloody shaft sticking out of her shoulder.

"Shut up, cunt, or I'll kill you anyway!"

The words infuriated Maxum. Right then he knew that giving up the cuff would not save Airi's life. Nor any of them. Kilon had murder in his eyes and he wouldn't be happy until someone or all of them were dead. Maxum could not be harmed, but Doisy . . . Dru . . . Airi . . .

Using all his mental will, he tried to freeze the tableau before him the way Airi had said she had done it.

To his shock and relief it worked. Everyone froze in

place, their movements slowed to an infinitesimal rate of speed. He didn't waste any time launching across the fire and tackling Kilon.

The moment he did, time returned to normal and Kilon's crossbow shot wildly. But Maxum ripped the weapon out of his hands and then used it to clock him upside the head. Then, once he started, he couldn't seem to stop. The strength given to him via the ring made it short work to beat Kilon to death with his own crossbow. The minute he was satisfied the man was dead, Maxum hurried over to Airi, gathering her up into his arms, his eyes imploring Doisy.

Doisy, who had been frozen in shock, suddenly came to life and hurried to Airi's side.

"I can't heal her until the arrow's out."

Maxum grabbed the arrow at the point where it had entered her body. "This is going to hurt," he warned her grimly.

"It already does!" she gasped.

Then, without another thought, he snapped the fletching off the tail of the arrow and with a hard shove pushed the arrow the remainder of the way through her shoulder. Airi screamed out into the cold, dark night, her body convulsing in his arms with the agonizing pain. Blood came gushing out of the wound and Doisy's hands immediately pressed against the rent in her flesh. Airi was cursing up a storm, her feet kicking out blindly.

"I'm going to fucking kill that bastard!" she screeched.

"He's already dead, love. I'm so sorry," he said, kissing her on her damp forehead. "I should have gotten rid of him ages ago. I just thought we would need him to get the cuff."

"I know. It's all right," she said through teeth gritted against the pain of Doisy's fingers pressing into her flesh.

"It's not all right! Look at how close he came to your heart!"

"He missed on purpose. He would have had no leverage if I'd been dead."

"Is that supposed to make me feel better?" he asked tightly.

"A little," she said with a wan laugh. The pain was beginning to subside as Doisy's healing magic did its job. Soon the bleeding stopped and then, after about a half an hour, her flesh knitted together, leaving nothing but an ugly bruise and an angry looking scar behind. Doisy sat back with an exhausted sigh. Airi's blood was all over his hands, they were both a mess, but she was healed.

"That's all I can do for now. After I get some sleep I can finish the rest of the way. I'm just so tired . . ."

"It's all right," Airi said to him reaching out and grasping his hand. "I'm fine. Go to sleep."

Doisy nodded and stood up and he made his way to the edge of their campsite and used snow to wash his hands. He then fell into his bedroll and lay back with an exhausted sigh. He was asleep within minutes.

Maxum took care of Airi. He cleaned her up, got her a fresh shirt from her belongings, and gently helped her out of the corset. Kilon had planned his attack on her carefully. He had known the corset would have potentially deflected any arrow he shot at her, so he had chosen the place where she was most vulnerable. Thinking of it made Maxum's hands tighten on her. She seemed to know what he was thinking because she reached to squeeze his hand and said, "It's over now."

He nodded and dressed her, using Doisy's trick to wash away the blood left on her body. Dru remained politely turned away as he did this, but when he had her dressed and had carried her to her bedroll, Maxum addressed the other man.

"Watch her while I clean up the campsite," he said.

Dru nodded and they watched him haul Kilon's body

up off the ground. He carried it into the dark woods and, when he returned empty-handed, he set Kilon's horse free with a smack on its rump.

Then Maxum settled down beside Airi, gathering her up close to his body, and giving her as much warmth as he could.

"I'm sorry," he whispered against her ear.

"Do not feel guilty," she told him. "You thought we needed him. You didn't know it would come to this."

"I did know. The way he treated you . . . a man with no respect for someone can easily discard that someone from their lives without a second thought. I should have seen this coming, but I was so focused on what I wanted . . . so let me feel guilty, as I should."

"It will serve no good purpose if you do. You have other things you need to focus on. In two days' time you will be facing the god of pain and suffering in a deadly battle. All of your focus must be on that if you intend to win. Practice using the cuff. That is what is most important. I will not have you unprepared."

Maxum shook his head and held her tighter. "Not tonight."

"Yes, tonight. Because tomorrow night will be ours and I will not have your focus split. You will make love to me with no distractions. For those hours I will be your only focus. Then, when you leave me, you can put me aside in your mind and focus on the battle to come."

"Put you aside?" He laughed a hollow sounding laugh. "I do not see how that is possible. In so short a time, in such an absolute way, you have become part of my mind . . . and my heart and my soul. I fear there is no separating you out any longer."

Airi's throat went tight and her heart soared to hear those words. It meant everything to her that she meant so much to him. It made facing the future somehow easier.

"Well then, hold me closer. Draw on the strength I can give you. Use the love you feel for me as your ultimate weapon in your fight against Sabo. Because he will not have that advantage. When he fights you, he will not have the knowledge that he is loved beyond all reason by someone. That will make all the difference."

Maxum hoped it was true and, hearing her speak of her love for him made him feel it was true. He felt the strength of it in every fiber of his being.

"Now," she said with soft encouragement, "practice using the cuff."

He nodded his head and did so.

CHAPTER
TWENTY-SIX

~~~~~~~~~

A iri had waited for him with anxiety crawling through her stomach and tension knotting up her shoulders. They had made it to the city unscathed and, as far as they knew, unhunted. After a trip to the bank they had found out which was the very best inn in the city and gone to stay there. Airi had carried her bags up to what would be her and Maxum's room with a heavy heart. She had bathed while she waited, and even primped a little in the looking glass. She had looked down at the filmy nightgown Maxum so loved on her and in a moment of sheer panic thought she should have gone to buy something new ... something exciting and fresh ... something special for what could be their last night together.

She had started to dress to go out and look for something, knowing there would still be vendors open in a city like this and that she still had some time before Maxum returned, but in the end she decided it didn't matter what she wore. The night was already tainted. She almost wished she hadn't asked for it. Almost wished he would go to Meru's temple and get it over with. The not knowing was killing her. But then in the very next thought she had felt tears threatening because she knew this one night would never be enough.

At juquil's hour she called the tavern's servants to her and had them change the bath for one with fresh hot water. He would be there soon and she knew he would be soiled. The lake they had passed on the way into town was frozen over, making it impossible for him to bathe the remnants of his curse away. So she would do it for him.

She knew he would not dally, that he would come straight to her the very instant the ground coughed him up. And she was right. She was tipping the maid who'd dumped the last bucket of hot water in the tub when he arrived. She shooed the maid off and closed the door behind her. She stood facing the door for a long moment, her back to him. She closed her eyes, took a deep breath, and then schooled her expression into one of ease and contentment. She felt neither, but she would not waste her time with him making him feel guilty for her pain.

She turned to face him, a small smile on her lips . . . hardly the effort she'd meant to make. She lifted her chin and smiled wider. There. That was better.

"You came back quickly," she noted as she crossed over to him. She could feel the cold on him, emanating from him like dead ice. His lips were blue in spite of his warming up on horseback as he traveled to get to her. She shivered as the cold crept beneath her robe and the thin gown beneath it.

Still, she reached out and took his hands in hers, the iciness of his fingers penetrating her.

"Come," she said, "let's get you into this bath."

"A man has never laid eyes on a more inviting image than this," he said, his eyes roaming over the room with its large poster bed, blazing fireplace, and copper bathtub with steam rising from its waters. Then his gaze fell to her and he looked at her from head to toe, taking in her freshly washed, loose platinum hair and her white satin wrapper. It gaped at the neckline and he could see she was wearing the gown he favored on her. Of course she would do that, he realized. She had proven herself to be thoughtful and, now that she was wealthy enough to buy a good-sized town or a small city, she proved herself to be just as generous to a fault as he was. This was why Meru had chosen her to bear the Dagger of Truths. As selfish a creature as she purported herself to be, he had seen her softer side. Airi had the uncanny ability to put herself in the shoes of another and figure out what it was they needed or wanted.

Just that morning she had divined that Maxum needed to finally explain to his men what was going on. They deserved the truth, had proved their loyalty to Maxum and to Airi time and again. It was far past time. But Maxum had realized that the one remaining obstacle keeping him from doing so was Kilon. He had not wanted to bare his soul in front of a man unworthy of trust. Airi had recognized where his thoughts lay and how difficult it was for him to let someone in. The only reason she'd gotten in was because Meru had exposed him to her. If she hadn't done that . . . who knew where they would be right now? With his stubborn, guarded nature . . . who knew?

So she had supported him when he'd called a halt to their progress, and had finally told them everything. The men had seemed only mildly surprised by any of it. Doisy had said, "Well, I rather thought there was a bigger reason for all of this treasure hunting, but not quite that big!"

And that had pretty much been the size of it. The men heard, accepted, and then moved on as if nothing had changed. They had not deserted him or gone their separate ways, although they had both the means and right to do so. They had not complained or exhibited fear over being so close to someone so cursed. They made it seem like it was nothing to them.

So Airi had proven herself wise and empathic. She was the perfect bearer of the dagger, and the perfect bearer of his heart. He didn't know when he had fallen in love with her exactly. It could even be possible it had been that moment when he had realized she'd had the balls to pick his pocket, leaving him hard and wanting. But it was more likely to be the day he had seen her leap onto the head of the hydra, fearlessness and outrage in her eyes. She had never been more beautiful.

Except perhaps now, when she was trying to be so strong and brave in the face of devastation. Yes, by all the gods, he loved her. And by the end of the night tonight she would know it with every ounce of her being.

Airi looked up into his eyes and the feeling she saw there was bald and easy to read. Her heart fluttered in her breast in response to his naked emotion.

"Come, let's get you cleaned up. You're covered in dirt and ice cold besides," she said. She pulled the tie to his heavy winter cloak and it sheeted down to the floor around his boots. Her fingers then went to the ties of his shirt until the neckline was gaping wide, showing the peppering of dark blond curls there. He stripped his shirt off over his head, leaving him bare chested. The only thing he wore on his body now was the cuff, the talisman, his rings, and a fine layer of dirt.

She urged him to sit on the bed then knelt at his feet in a graceful movement. She then worked off first one boot then the next. He stripped the woolen socks from his feet. She rose up higher on her knees and, settling her breasts into his lap, she began to untie his breeches. Once they were loosened she stroked a slow hand down over the ridges of his abdomen until she reach the thickening line of curls left exposed by his loosened pants.

He caught her hand and lifted it away from his body, then he grasped her beneath both arms as he hauled them both up to their feet.

"Bath first. Then I'm going to explore every inch of you."

"You like doing that," she noted. "Perhaps I should draw you a map so you don't have to keep rediscovering me."

"I would burn such a map to ashes. I would much rather be forced to refamiliarize myself every chance I get."

"Come to the bath, your hands are like ice," she said, shivering a little.

He let go of her and dropped his pants to the floor. Kicking them away he went to the large copper tub that stood before the roaring fire. He tested the water with a finger, but realized it was a useless gesture because his cold hands would register the water being hotter than it was. He decided to just risk it and stepped into the wide tub and lowered himself into the hot water. It was the perfect temperature to his mind and his body began to warm in leaps and bounds.

Airi meanwhile had knelt beside the tub. She grabbed a sea sponge from a small dish on the floor that held a pearly looking blue soap. She placed the sponge on his chest and began to wash him, but his hand stayed her instantly. "That isn't going to make me smell like dusk roses now is it? I have a battle tomorrow and I don't want to go into it smelling pretty."

It was an attempt at levity, but it fell flat. Only because he had spoken aloud of the elephant in the room. He let go of her hand as she washed him again, playing the game. "It's jimsof leaf soap. A very manly fragrance. You will smell positively unbeatable."

He gave her a small chuckle. "If I'd known that I wouldn't have put us through all the trouble of getting this . . . and these." He pointed to the cuff on his arm and then the rings

"Or this." She stroked a finger against the talisman hanging around his neck. "You never did tell me the story of how you got this."

"Ah. Nothing too exciting. I had to trick a mage into giving it to me using just my charm and my wits."

"How did you do that?"

"Almost the same way you got the cuff."

"But I used flirtation and a woman's wiles . . ." She trailed off and understanding lit her features. "You didn't!"

"Of course not," he said with a chuckle. "He had a predilection for brawny, warrior types and I pretended to have one for magi. A little flirtation, a little trickery and pickpocketing and the talisman was mine."

"Pickpocketing! You stole the talisman and then I stole it from you?" She laughed uproariously. "One would think you would have seen me coming, having used the same ploy yourself to get it!"

"Do not think I wasn't wholly embarrassed by that. You should have heard me. Doisy will tell you. I called you every name in the book. But even so, I had to admire you. Damn you."

She chuckled. "Well, it is done with now and all to the better. It was the most valuable thing I've ever stolen in my life," she said, her tone softening with her emotion as she looked into his eyes.

"Yes, it was, wasn't it?" he said softly, reaching to stroke warm fingers down the side of her face. "Catching you outside that jewelers was sheer dumb luck . . . and my luck has been spot-on ever since then. Let's just hope it continues."

There was that elephant, trumpeting into the room again. It felt as if the beast was standing on her chest.

She went back to her task of bathing him, covering his

chest and shoulders and back with swirls of soap, every so often going back to dip the sponge in fresh soap. She washed away all the soil and grime left behind. She traveled the length of his legs, scrubbed between his toes. She worked her way back up his legs and his inner thigh until she found him beneath the water hard and wanting her. Their eyes met and held as she washed him in a variety of strokes. Maxum broke eye contact with a groan as his eyes rolled back in pleasure.

Gods how he wanted her.

He opened his eyes and reached out to stroke two fingers into the neck of her wrap and gown.

"Take this off," he said, pulling at the wrap.

"But then I'd have to stop touching you," she said with a frown.

"I'll touch myself in your absence," he said, making her eyes widen. She licked her lips and looked down at the clouded water that would keep her from seeing him do that. She frowned again. "Do it," he said, his hand going beneath the water to take her hand away from his body. She kept her hand next to his just long enough for her to encourage him to wrap his fingers around himself and together they stroked him several times. Once she was satisfied he had taken over, once her entire being seemed to be humming with sexual arousal, she pulled back her arm and stood up at the side of the tub. She undid the tie to her wrapper and let the heavy silk slide down her arms and off her body. It settled into a silky pile at her feet. Then, without him bidding her to do so, she stripped off the gown as well, leaving her standing there womanly and naked and all his.

His. She was his . . . as much as so independent a creature can belong to anyone. His woman. His lover. His soul mate. And he believed that . . . that they had been destined for one another. And it was the one and only thing he had to thank his curse for. If not for his immortality he would have been dead bones two hundred full turnings ago. If not for him being driven to end this curse he would never have stolen that talisman, never have stopped at that inn and never would have met her.

She stepped into the tepid water of the bath and lowered herself along his body, their chests pressed together, their legs tangling in the confined space. Water sloshed over the sides of the tub with her every movement until she was settled at last. Then she took his hand from around his shaft and resumed her strokes. She worked him from root to tip, over and over again, first slowly, then quickly, then slowly again. The varying paces were maddening . . . and wonderful. But if she thought their first coupling of the evening was going to consist of just her hand on his body, she had another think coming.

He took the opportunity to stroke over her skin under the water, touching her fading tan along her shoulders and the tops of her buoyant breasts. He skipped touching her nipples, although he could see they were hard and eager for it, and stroked his touch around to her back. He caressed her over every last bump and ridge of her spine, then curved a hand around her backside. He tried to pull her into a better, more accessible position, but was thwarted by the tub.

"Damned thing," he growled as he suddenly came to his feet, pulling her to him as well. He reached for the rinsing bucket and poured the warm water over them both. Then he scooped her up into his arms and stepped out of the tub. He was tossing her down onto the bed seconds later.

His haste was amusing, but she did not laugh. She was too drawn in by the intensity in his eyes. He spread her out wide on the coverlet, arms perpendicular to her sides, legs parted, hair streaming back in a platinum waterfall.

"Do not move. Don't even touch me," he warned her.

"But—"

"Not one touch. You touch me and I stop touching you. Not until I say it's okay, understood?"

She eventually nodded, but he could tell she didn't like the idea. This was like asking her to give up control, not something she did lightly . . . not even for him. But tonight was different. Tonight there was no room for egos to get in the way.

He stroked his fingers over her throat and felt her swallow. His touch drifted to her collarbone, shaping and outlining the prominent bone. He moved on to her breastbone and then embraced one full breast with his hand.

Airi felt the touch all the way to her toes. Something had heightened all of her senses it seemed. Maybe it was the desperation that was shadowing them, maybe it was just because he wasn't allowing her the freedom to touch him back. She couldn't tell. She had to clutch at the bedspread with both fists to keep herself from driving her fingers into his hair, especially when he bent his blond head and touched his tongue to her nipple. He danced it against her in light flickers, then laved her hard and sucked her into his mouth.

Airi moaned low and deep, her body going tight with tension and wet with arousal. Her legs shifted restlessly. She wanted to wrap her legs around him, but she was pretty sure that would constitute touching. It was so hard for her to obey his directive, especially when he started kissing and licking his way down her flat belly to her dark blond curls. She lifted her hips into him as his mouth brushed through those curls. His hands appeared on her thighs and he parted them, spreading her wide open, exposing her to the heat of his breath against her most intimate flesh. Then he went straight to the source of her pleasure. He burrowed for the little bud of nerves with a hard, pointed tongue. She moaned and gripped the bedding tighter. There was something about not touching him that made the act so much more erotic. It had such incredible power and it was humbling how it made her want him more than anything. More than independence, more than wealth, more than life. She would give it all just to have him safe with her when this was all said and done.

Tears filled her eyes as his mouth worked powerful magic against her. She cried out as a blinding orgasm ripped through her. She gripped his hair in her fingers, holding his head to her body, refusing to let him move. It was only as she was coming down from her peak that she realized she had grabbed hold of him when she wasn't supposed to have. But he did not seem angry about that. In fact he had a well-satisfied smile on his lips, as if he had been the one to climax.

"Let's try that again, shall we?" he said, taking her hand out of his hair, pressing it down into the bed. He did the same with the other. The message was clear . . . she wasn't to touch him. Again.

"No, please . . . I need to touch you. More than I need breath, I need to touch you," she begged him.

The expression that washed over his features was not one of ego or arrogance, not one of a self-satisfied man who could make a woman beg, it was the face of a lover loving to hear how much he is wanted. How much he is loved.

"Then you shall touch me all you like, my pretty elf. Touch me anywhere and everywhere. All that I am is yours to experience. But I expect the same in return. Free access to you anywhere and everywhere."

"All that I am is yours to experience," she echoed breathlessly.

The response satisfied him and he surged up the length of her body until his sex was nestled tightly up against hers. He undulated his hips, rubbing his hot, engorged flesh along the valley she provided.

"Good," he said on a whisper. "Because I've been wanting to try something for this past month . . ."

"What?" she asked, excited and full of trepidation at the same time.

"This." He lifted her hair, pulled it aside and exposed her pointed ear. "Is it true what they say about elves? That the tip of the ear is like a clitoris?" His tongue shot out to touch the point of her ear and she gasped. "That, if an elven woman tucks her hair behind her ear it is considered a blatant invitation to sex? That it's akin to masturbating in public?"

"Maxum!" she gasped, suddenly breathless and unable to draw enough oxygen as he toyed with the second most sensitive erogenous zone on her body.

"I love the sound of my name on your lips," he said, his lips and breath hot against her sensitive ear. "I'd love to hear you scream it tonight. The sound will carry into my dreams . . . into my memory. It will be a sound I will never forget, no matter what comes."

"Please . . . don't speak of it." Not while she was this open and exposed. She would fall apart and never be able to put herself back together again.

He seemed to understand and hushed her soothingly and then licked the tip of her ear. He used his tongue to draw it into his mouth and she went weak and wet as he sucked on her gently and provocatively.

He attended to her slowly, his mouth on the point of her ear, his fingers seeking between her thighs. It wasn't long before she shattered like stained glass, colorful and beautiful and sharp.

She was rolling in repletion when he kissed her mouth. She smiled beneath his lips. And the moment she thought she had never been so happy was the moment she felt her saddest. Try as she might she couldn't forget what was coming.

But he didn't give her time to fall apart. He moved his leg between hers, drew her thigh up to his hip and ran his hard length along the center of her body, wetting himself in her juices. Then he looked down into her eyes, connecting with her so that she knew his soul was touching hers, and thrust hard inside her.

She gasped in a loud breath, her heart pounding in her chest in a mixture of pain and pleasure. Pain for what was to come, pleasure for what was. He made love to her as he had the first time, looking into her eyes the entire time, stripping himself just as bare as she was. When she came this time her cries mingled with his, only after it was done hers turned to soft sobs almost immediately.

"Shh," he hushed her softly. "Have some faith," he said. "Have faith I will win the day tomorrow. Do you believe in me?"

"I believe in fact. He is a god, you are a mortal."

"I am immortal. I am strong. I am protected." He touched the talisman.

"He is a god," she repeated.

"What does that mean?" he asked her. "Do we even know what it means to be a god? Do we even know what limitations they have? What true strengths? Do we know anything about them? I know they cannot hear all of us at all times. I know they could not take my immortality away from me when I stole it for myself. They have limitations. I will find out his weaknesses and I will win. I have to win," he said softly, kissing her cheek. "I have every reason in the world to win."

She gave him a wan smile and nodded. "You are right. There is a good chance you will be victorious. Meru would not have sent you for the cuff and the ring if she didn't believe that. But she is using you to help sway the war between the gods into the favor of Weysa's faction. She doesn't care if you live or die."

"I think she does. Anyway, we will see. But that is to-morrow . . . and your night is only beginning."

She lifted her chin, setting her jaw stubbornly. "You are right," she said then, more strongly. "You are strong enough to beat him. I believe in you. And I will not waste the time we have together crying like a woman."

She pushed him off her, hearing him chuckle as she rolled him to his back. She slung her leg over him so she was straddling his thighs and he saw a devilish gleam in her eyes.

"Now I believe it is time to make *you* cry." She took his hands and spread them out to his sides. "Don't touch," she warned him.

He chuckled. "Turning the tables on me?"

"Yes." Her gaze held a world of passionate promise. Maxum closed his eyes for a moment to try and gird himself against the prospect of Airi on a mission to se-duce him. He was already seduced, didn't she know that? Everything else was just a bonus.

He opened his eyes and watched her do her worst.

CHAPTER
TWENTY-SEVEN

~~~~~~

Maxum walked into the temple of Meru with a heavy heart. Airi was standing by his side, supporting him to the last, and doing it without any tears. Those tears the night before had been her last, and he knew she wasn't even fighting to hide them. She believed in him. She would believe in him to the end. She feared for him, but she believed.

Maxum went to the temple's offering stone, whereupon a variety of objects was laid, given as offerings to the goddess from those supplicants that were trying to win her assistance in their lives. Most often it was women who longed to bear children for their husbands, or pregnant women who wanted a specific sex for the child or for the child to come out healthy. She was the goddess of all things fertile, so even farmers came and made offerings to her in hopes that their fields would grow ripe and healthy that season. Those took shape as sacks of grain or freshly butchered animals. At the end of the day Meru's mems would take the offering and use them to feed themselves or clothe themselves, so that nothing went to waste. By supplying the well-being of Meru's mems, the supplicants were doing Meru a great favor. In this way their prayers could be answered.

Or so it was believed. Maxum didn't really know how often such requests were answered. He imagined that if Meru had to answer every single prayer that went up to her every single day all over the world, she would quite exhaust herself. But it was a known fact that many prayers went unanswered. When they went unanswered the supplicant could only assume it was against a god's wishes. Or perhaps they had not prayed hard enough. Or that they had in some way done something to displease the gods. There was a lot left open to interpretation. A lot an average mortal did not have an answer for. All they could do was guess and listen to the Songs of the Gods as guidance to what the gods truly wanted from them all.

But as he stood before the altar Maxum was forced to wonder if it was more than a matter of a god's wishes or temperament. That perhaps it wasn't in their power at all to do the things the supplicants asked of them. He hoped this was the case because it meant there was weakness to be found. That they were not all-knowing and all-seeing. They were not all-powerful. He had already proved the all-seeing part to himself . . . and the all-knowing. Now he wanted to prove they were not all-powerful.

He looked to the left and right, checking to see if the room was cleared, then he lowered himself to a knee and began to pray.

"Meru, I have come to do what I promised to do. Come to me and we will begin and end this thing. I beg you to hear me and to adhere to your part of this bargain."

There was no response, so he tried again.

For the better part of an hour he prayed to a goddess who had apparently turned a deaf ear to him. But he had come too far to give up now, so he persisted. A mem entered the altar room and came to ask them if there was some guidance she could offer. Airi politely declined the invitation. The mem looked perplexed, but she left them to their prayers and went about her business.

It was just turning into the noon hour when Meru suddenly appeared, her rich wheat-colored hair arranged wildly about her shoulders, her body dressed in a dress of flowing white fabric.

"I have heard your prayers," she said, moving quickly to him, "and we have coordinated our attack. Weysa's faction will keep the other gods from interfering in your battle, but the rest is up to you."

"I am ready," Maxum said.

"Are you?" she asked. "I do not think you fully understand the ramifications of what you are going to be doing. The responsibility to the world should you win."

"I know the world would be better off without pain and suffering."

"There you are wrong. For we must have pain and suffering in order to appreciate what goodness is. In order to appreciate what pleasure is. A world cannot function without pain and suffering." Meru turned to Airi. "You should know that most of all. For I think you will feel great pain and suffer great loss if he leaves you."

"I will," she said, but her voice was strong. "But he will not leave me . . . and I will not leave him. I wish to watch the battle."

"A war between gods is no place for a mortal. You would most certainly be killed."

"Airi, no!" Maxum cried at the same time.

"I will not be able to sit here never knowing what has become of him! I must see this for myself. I beg of you, please!"

"Perhaps," Meru said after a brief moment, "there is a way. I will turn you into a tree on the edge of the field and you will witness the entire battle, but no one will know you are there. But be warned, if I should fall or die or be taken captive, I will not be able to turn you back again. And also, as a tree you will be vulnerable as any tree might be to being bent or crushed. If the battle should be taken near you you could be severely harmed or damaged . . . or even killed. But otherwise, you will have full view of the entire field and the entire battle."

"Yes!"

"No! Airi, no! I cannot battle knowing you are that close by!" Maxum said, his upset clear in his tone. His anger a tangible thing. "I won't have it!"

He knew it was the wrong thing to say even as the words were leaving his mouth. Airi's entire being bristled with anger and stubbornness.

"I will not just sit by waiting like some warrior's wife who has sent her husband off to the wars and might wait months to learn what has become of him. I am not made that way! I will be by your side through this thing."

"But as a tree that cannot move or defend itself? Think, Airi!" he implored her.

When he put it like that she bit her lip anxiously. "Then what do you suggest? For I will not allow you to go off without me!"

"There is another way," Meru said. "The ring of invisibility. You can give it to her so she may watch and remain out of sight, yet be able to move quickly and defend herself if necessary. However, you will be giving up an advantage by giving it to her rather than wearing it for yourself."

"No! Maxum, you need the ring for yourself!"

"Airi . . . it is the only way I will allow you to be there," Maxum said grimly.

Airi was torn. Was it so important that she be there that she would be willing to take away this crucial advantage?

"If it helps you to choose," Meru said, "the ring will only be good enough to use once against Sabo. The moment you betray yourself he will be able to strip away your invisibility."

"That once could mean the difference between winning and losing," Airi said.

"No. The fight will last much longer than a single blow. It will be a very small advantage," Meru said.

"Then it is settled. You will wear the ring, Airi." Maxum reached to pull her close to his body and pressed a fierce kiss to her lips. "You are right. You should be there. I will take great strength from knowing you are there with me. But only if you are invisible to detection, otherwise Sabo could use you against me. You must promise me that you will not betray your location for any reason. You will remain silent no matter what happens."

"Maxum . . . I will not allow myself to become a weapon to be used against you. I will be your strength. I will be there for you, should you need me."

"It is done then. Give her the ring. The other gods of Weysa's faction have gathered and we are to meet on the field of battle with the other gods immediately."

Maxum handed her the ring and she slid it onto her thumb and instantly disappeared from sight. She reached out and took his arm so that he would know where she was. He bent to kiss her lips blindly, and she met his mouth with desperate hunger. Then, in the blink of an eye, the temple melted from around them and they appeared in a golden field full of wildflowers and lined with large oak trees. Here it was not winter, but instead felt as though it were a warm, sunny day.

Maxum gave her a little shove toward the edge of the field and she quickly followed his suggestion. She hid between two of the massive oaks, using them as protection against what was about to come.

There, in the field before her, stood six magnificent beings. Beautiful people who seemed larger than life.

These were the gods of Weysa's faction, she realized. The warrioress dressed in full armor must be the goddess of conflict, Weysa. The rest of the gods were also dressed in armor, including Meru whose armor appeared magically before Airi's eyes.

She could guess at the identities of the other gods. Hella, the goddess of fate and fortune, was deemed to be a little on the mad side, something about being able to see all those pasts and presents at once having made her a little unbalanced. She appeared to be talking to herself, even though she was holding the hand of another male god. She assumed this was the god Mordu, her husband. For what went better with fate and fortune than love? The god of love held his wife's hand and patted it gently in comfort. Airi swallowed. What good would a madwoman do in a war of the gods?

That left Lothas, the god of day and night, and Framun, the god of peace and tranquility unidentified. But it was almost too easy to identify Lothas because his hair was half the gold of daylight sun and half the black of night. One of the males was decidedly taller than the other, although both were extraordinarily tall. Framun, it appeared, was the taller of the two.

That was when the opposite side of the field began to fill with gods, each winking into existence in the blink of an eye. She recognized Xaxis, the god of the eight hells, right off as their leader. He was a stocky god, with black hair and eyes the color of burning embers. By his side, her hand held tightly in his, was a statuesque blond goddess who reeked of power and strength. She immediately assumed this was the goddess Kitari, the queen of all of the gods. Maxum had told her that it was believed that Kitari was, in fact, a prisoner of Xaxis's . . . that she fought against Weysa's faction against her will. And yet he had brought her to be by his side in this battle. He must at least have some confidence in her.

The only other god she could identify was Diathus, the goddess of lands and oceans, because other than Kitari she was the only female on Xaxis's side. She thought the god with the hard, angry eyes might be Jikaro, the god of anger and deception, but she couldn't be certain. That left Grimu, the god of the eight heavens, and Sabo.

"So, Weysa," Xaxis boomed across the field, "at last you have decided to stop cowering from us and finish this battle once and for all!"

So this was why it had been easy for them to arrange this battle. Xaxis had thrown down the gauntlet himself some time ago. As far as he knew she was merely taking him up on the offer.

"This battle will end," Weysa said, "and when we are victorious you and yours will come to heel and behave yourselves from now on!"

"What is this little man doing here?" Diathus cried pointing to Maxum. "We had a deal, little man! You were not to raise your sword in Weysa's name!"

"And so I am not," Maxum said. Oh gods, he looked so small compared to all these stately creatures! "I want no part of your war. I want Sabo."

The god she assumed was Sabo released a little chuckle, almost as though he were shocked the mortal had dared single him out. As if it might just be a fine joke. Then he leaned forward to peer at him.

"You!" he cried out, a sudden rage singing through him. "Who let you out?"

Diathus cringed a little. "I'm afraid that was me. I didn't know he was going to be such a bother."

So Maxum was right. They were not all-knowing. Otherwise Sabo would have known he was free all this time.

"I will put you back under the ground where you belong!" Sabo growled. Then he was launching himself across the field at Maxum. With battle cries, the other gods surged forward across the field and clashed in the resounding sound of god-made weapons. Airi ignored all of the others and fixated solely on Maxum.

Sabo plowed into Maxum at full bore, and Maxum hit the ground. They skidded to a stop, churning up a furrow of dirt in the tall grasses. Sabo stepped back away from Maxum, seemingly surprised that he had not been injured by the attack.

Sabo swung his sword high and with a crushing blow struck at Maxum. Maxum parried with Weysa's Champion, but it wasn't enough to keep Sabo's sword from striking him at his neck. When Sabo pulled the sword back and saw Maxum was not injured he said, "What's this? You are immortal, not invulnerable!"

"It would appear you are wrong about that!" Maxum ground out as he launched himself at Sabo, swinging Weysa's Champion hard. Sabo went to parry him but was clearly shocked when he didn't have strength enough to block it completely. Maxum's sword struck him in the collar and drew first blood.

So. A god could bleed, Airi thought with wonder and more than a little relief. If a god could be wounded, then maybe he could be weakened. Maybe Maxum could win after all!

Maxum was thinking the very same thing. Renewed hope surged through him as he attacked Sabo in earnest. As he struck several brutal blows with Weysa's Champion, Sabo lunged forward and caught hold of him, grappling with him, each with a blade a hairsbreadth from the other's neck. Then, suddenly, Sabo released him, jerked back away from him and laughed.

"Missing something?"

Sabo held up the cuff. He had snatched it from Maxum's arm. Maxum had been tricked into letting him too close. How had he known what the cuff could do? Why hadn't Maxum used it from the start?

Damning himself, he knew it was over. As long as Sabo had that cuff his head was as good as gone from his neck. It would be nothing for Sabo to slow down time and then divest Maxum of all of his protective talismans.

"Oh, don't worry, little man," Sabo said wickedly. "I have no intention of using this until I'm good and ready. First, I will fight you as you men do, to prove to you the might of a god has no need for such trickery. Yes . . . I think I will toy with you for a little while. That will please me."

Maxum was grateful for the god's hubris which had him tossing the cuff carelessly to the ground at his feet. He had no intention of putting it on and using it himself! But then, as Sabo bore down on him, Maxum realized he didn't need the cuff. His strength was beyond anything he had ever known. His prowess with the blade he wielded was a thing of beauty. Something that Maxum could respect even as he faced it down.

For the better part of an hour the two traded blows in equal measure, neither wounding the other, neither making way. Then Maxum struck again, drawing blood a second time in Sabo's thigh.

Roaring with pain and outrage the god stood back and growled out, "You may be invulnerable to a blade, but you are not impervious to pain!"

He reached out and gripped the air as if he were gripping Maxum around his throat. Maxum cried out as a look of sheer agony crossed his features. He sank to his knees and screamed out again.

"That's right, little foolish man, I am the god of pain and suffering! I will show you pain you have never known! You think you have suffered thus far? It has been nothing compared to what I am going to do to you now!"

Maxum had never known such agony. He had thought

the pain of being crushed and pulverized for endless hours of endless years had been a pain beyond all others, but Sabo was proving to him that it had been a drop in the bucket compared to what could be. What *would* be, if he lost. If he lost this battle he would be taken from Airi's side and made to suffer in ways he could not imagine. And through that Airi would suffer too.

No. He had promised her he would succeed, that he would come out of this alive and well. That they would have a future together. He would not break that promise to her.

Meanwhile, on the sidelines . . .

No! Airi cried silently, knowing she could not shout out. She had promised Maxum and right now it was crucial she did not split his focus. But . . .

She looked to where the cuff lay forgotten on the ground. It was right in the middle of the battlefield. She knew that if Maxum were to have any chance at winning, he would need that cuff.

Her mind made up, she ran out onto the field. Her heart was pounding in her chest, her legs pumping madly as she dodged fighting godly opponents. She skirted around Maxum and Sabo, refusing to watch Maxum writhe and suffer, staying focused on her task.

She reached the cuff and threw herself down onto it. The minute she got it in her hands she focused and the field slowed to an infinitesimal crawl. Panting hard for breath she raced over to where Maxum lay struggling on the ground. She touched him and his body collapsed out of time with the freeze. He was gasping. Panting hard, shaking his head and trying to right himself. She touched his face and he jerked.

"Airi?" he asked.

"Yes!" She took off the ring and he could see her.

"Airi, what are you doing over here?" he demanded with a roar. "Get out of here!"

"Maxum, I got the cuff."

She held it out to him and suddenly he looked up and saw the frozen battlefield. Saw Sabo locked in place like a fly in amber.

Suddenly Maxum reached out and jerked her into his arms, kissing her soundly.

"My good little thief!" he cried in delight. "I can't believe you did this!"

"Are you not mad now?"

"You've just saved my life. You've just given me exactly what I need. How could I ever be mad? Now . . . give me the cuff. Let's get you off this field. Put your ring back on."

She did, making sure they kept in contact so she didn't let him become part of the frozen field once more. He hurried her off the field dodging petrified opponents. Then he took the cuff from her and put it on his arm.

"Stay safe. Don't come back out. I'm ending this now," he said.

With that, he took over the use of the cuff, focusing on keeping everything locked in place as he hurried back to his position before Sabo.

Maxum let his fury come screaming forth, roaring in rage as he lunged for Sabo.

With a battle cry he raised his sword high and sliced it down at Sabo's neck. The god's head went flying from his shoulders.

Maxum and the battle roared into normal time. Sabo's body crumpled to the ground and then suddenly burst into flame and ash. The fire dissipated after a second and Maxum sucked in his breath hard.

And that was when the true pain began.

Maxum screamed at an earsplitting pitch as fire burned through his blood. The talisman around his neck burned up and disappeared, the cuff seared to his arm and then it too seemed to melt away. The ring of strength on his finger did likewise. Maxum curled up into an agonized ball of pain and cried out again.

That was when he felt cool, shaking hands on his face, felt gentle, soothing lips against his.

"Shh," she soothed him. "It's over. It's over and you are free."

But he didn't feel free. He felt as though his very soul was being burned out of his body. But the coolness of Airi's touch made it better. He wanted to tell her to flee the field of battle, but she felt too good and he was being far too selfish.

After a while the pain became bearable, the throbbing in his head manageable. It seemed as though it took forever, but eventually the roaring in his ears died down. When he opened his eyes he appeared to be alone, but the feel of Airi's hands in his hair told him otherwise, the gentle humming of her soothing voice gave her away.

"You have won, my love," she whispered over and over again. "And see there? Weysa's faction has also won. There is Xaxis, kneeling before her in surrender. Kitari switched sides mid battle, and with Sabo gone . . . they were outnumbered. They had no choice but to surrender. Diathus was the first to realize the futility of the battle and she threw down her weapons first, even as Xaxis screamed at her to pick them up again. Now she is putting Xaxis and the other warring gods in chains and Kitari is standing over them as queen."

"Xaxis," he heard Kitari sing out. "You have held me hostage these many full turnings, and I will not forget that. Let this field of battle show you that you will never rule the gods. You will never have dominion over all the aspects of godhood as you had hoped. You see," she said to Weysa, "his goal was to kill each of you in turn and assume the mantle of your power."

Weysa nodded. "No one god should ever have that

much power. In the time before time our power was separated for the good of all and so it shall remain."

Weysa then turned toward Maxum. She approached him and he felt Airi tense protectively around him.

"So you have killed the god called Sabo. Well, it has been a long time coming."

Airi suddenly became visible as she removed the ring of invisibility and Weysa took in a light breath of surprise.

"Are you then ready to accept your role?" Weysa said.

"Role?" Airi echoed.

Meru came up to them. "Yes. I warned you there would be consequences to your actions, Maxum."

"Is this pain the consequence? Will he feel this forever?" Airi asked in distress.

"No. It will soon pass. It is the pain of becoming a god that he feels. His remaining mortal self is being burned away leaving him to become a god in full stead of the god Sabo."

"God? I do not wish to be a god!" Maxum protested.

"Someone must take on the mantle of god of pain and suffering, and as it has been decreed long before the gods were what we are now, he who kills a god must take his place," Weysa said.

"I will never be so cruel a god!" Maxim declared.

"Nor do you have to be," Meru said gently. "Sabo chose to take his power to a dark place. He chose to inflict pain and suffering on all and sundry. You may choose to take it to a different place. You may choose to relieve the pain and suffering of others, to become a benevolent god."

Maxum slowly sat up, Airi's hands there to help him. "Have I no choice in the matter?"

"None," Weysa said definitively.

"But what of Airi?"

Weysa laughed. "We have all had more than our share

of mortal lovers! What's more, you now have the power to make a demigod of her. So she may be with you from now into the oblivious future."

Maxum looked to Airi in question. Tears jumped into her eyes and she nodded. He laughed shortly and drew her into his arms.

"You will begin training at once," Weysa declared. "Meru, since you were so kind as to bring him here . . . and since she is your champion . . . perhaps you would be willing to train him?"

"I would be very happy to," Meru said. "Anything to be rid of Sabo! I have hated that god for eons! He has hurt many of the women I have sworn to protect over the years and there was little I could do to stop him. Now if only Jikaro . . ."

"No more meddling, Meru. If all humans get it in their heads that anyone may become a god there will be nothing but trouble."

"Maxum, the powers of the cuff, the ring of strength, and the talisman of invulnerability are now a part of you. You no longer need to wear them to have the benefit of them and they cannot be removed. As such you are now one of the most powerful gods among us. Sabo, luckily for you, was one of the weakest. Many of us are invulnerable as you are, but he was not. He was more demigod than god. But you . . . you will take this power to an exalted place. I can feel that," Meru said.

"Yes. He will. He is a man of great strength and honor. He would never wish to cause anyone pain who did not deserve it," Airi said confidently.

"And so it shall be," Weysa said. Then she raised her voice for the field to hear. "Let it be sung in all the Songs of the Gods that this day Sabo was defeated by the man Maxum, who then became god in his stead. Let it be said that Maxum will be a benevolent god, that he will ease that which Sabo wrought."

Then she turned to Maxum. "We will write down your journey to this state of being and hand it down through the temples. We will let it be told that all statues of Sabo are to be destroyed and that the temples shall raise images of you in their stead."

"I do not need that," Maxum said with a frown.

"No, but the people need it. They need to know they can pray to you to relieve their suffering. How else will you know what to do for them? We are best connected to people through our temples. We hear people the loudest when they pray there. You will learn this."

"But how will I ease all of the suffering in the world? How can I be everywhere at once?"

"Alas, you cannot. Nor can you rid the world of all suffering. Man creates enough suffering, they do not need a god to help them. But Sabo took delight in it all the same," Weysa said. "You must select your actions wisely. You must appreciate that relieving the suffering of one might cause suffering to another. You must think and weigh very carefully before you act. Again, you will learn this. Meru will teach you. Now, we must tend to our prisoners."

"Prisoners? How can you imprison a god?" Airi asked.

"You cannot. Not for very long or the world begins to suffer. But we can curb them for a little while at least. Then we will let them free to do as they have always done, but at least now the balance of power will remain in place. Our queen will remain our queen and you will be on the side of the good."

"I will," Maxum said with a nod.

"Very well. Until we meet again in the house of the gods," she said, nodding back to him.

The gods all vanished from the field save Meru and the new god of pain and suffering. And, of course, one little demigod to be.

"You must show me how to make a demigod of Airi," Maxum said immediately.

"There are criteria to be met to become a demigod that even we gods must adhere to."

"Such as?" Maxum asked.

"She must be a proven warrior. She must have had grand adventures and done great things. She must have acted in the name of a god."

"She has done all of that," Maxum said.

"So she has," Meru said with a chuckle. "Damn. That means I must find a new wielder for the Dagger of Truths. The dagger can only be wielded by a mortal woman. And it is so rare that I find a worthy female," Meru tsked.

"I am sorry for that. Perhaps I can help you look?" Airi said.

"No. I have my own methods, as you have learned. I will find someone one day." She held out her hand for the dagger and Airi handed it to her. "Now come. I will take you to the house of the gods and there your training will begin."

"Can Airi come?"

"Not until you make a demigod of her. And in order to do that, you must learn."

Airi swallowed hard and looked at him. "It's all right. Go with her. I will be waiting when you are ready."

Maxum was indecisive. He didn't want to leave her. Not for a second.

"How long will this take?" he asked Meru.

"Oh . . . years I'm afraid. But I will teach you how to make her a demigod first thing so she can be there for you as you learn."

"And how long will that take?"

"That depends on you. Don't worry, you can visit her as often as you like once you learn how. Now come. Let's get this started. You will enjoy the house of the gods, most especially the food of the gods. There is nothing like it in the whole of your experience."

Maxum stood up on shaky legs, his body still hurting from his transformation into godhood. Airi came with him, supporting him. He looked down into her treasured face and smiled.

"I will be back for you," he said solemnly.

"I know you will."

He kissed her hard and then reached out for the hand Meru offered him. He leaned into the goddess and kept Airi's eyes until the very instant he disappeared.

Airi blinked and then found herself back in the temple.

She swallowed back the pang of pain that came with being separated from him and reminded herself that the outcome could have been much worse. Sabo could have destroyed him.

What was a few days apart compared to that?

EPILOGUE

ONE FULL TURNING LATER

A iri was doing the laundry.

Oh, she had more than enough money to afford a laundress, but since she had come to Calandria she had taken to doing it herself. There was something soothing about the rhythm of it. Wet. Wring. Wet. Wring. Scrub. Wet. Wring. Wet. Wring.

She pushed a straggling bit of hair back off her forehead and leaned into the bucket for another piece of clothing.

She felt a tickling sensation against her ear and she brushed at it. She'd worn her hair down and loose today, which she supposed hadn't been wise considering the work she was doing, so her hair tended to drift over her sensitive ear at the oddest times. Whenever it did it reminded her of the last time someone had stimulated her ear and her body would go warm and tingle all over.

And then she would miss him.

She didn't know how long it took to learn the basics of being a god, but he had promised he would come for her . . . and he hadn't so far. But in spite of Doisy's insistence that she had been forgotten, she refused to believe it. Even after a full turning of the seasons, even as the snow settled around her again, she believed he would come for her.

Something tickled her ear again and, frustrated, she swiped at it.

She connected with something.

Gasping she whirled around and saw him standing there, his fingers teasing at her ear through her hair, a smile on his face.

She hauled off and hit him. Slapped him right across the face and shouted, "Where have you been?"

He chuckled and caught her hand before she could hit him again.

"I'm invulnerable, love. You can't hurt me."

"Well it makes me feel better!" She blinked back the sudden pricking of tears in her eyes. He had come. *He had come.*

"What are you doing here? Women's work?" He sounded aghast.

"It . . . helps," she said.

"Helps what?"

"Helps keep me from missing you, you big idiot! Where have you been?"

"I've been in the house of the gods. But you knew that. I told you I'd be back."

"A full turning later!"

"A full—it has not been a full turning!" he exclaimed.

"Yes, it has!"

"Well . . . I . . . time must move very differently in the house of the gods. It felt like only a few weeks to me."

"Well, it felt a hell of a lot longer for me."

He gathered her up in his arms against himself. "I'm sorry. I'm so sorry, love. I never meant to do that to you."

Slightly mollified, she allowed him to hug her tightly.

She heard him breathe in her scent. He exhaled a contented sigh.

"I missed your smell. I missed the feel of you."

"I missed you too," she confessed on a hot, strangled whisper.

"I can do it now," he said. "I know how to make you a demigod."

"I don't care about that. I just care that you're here."

He pulled back, found her mouth, and kissed her as deeply as she had wanted to be kissed for all these seasons past. She sighed happily as he pulled back and looked down into her face.

"If you're amenable to it, I think I should like to lick your ear for a little while."

She blushed hot in a dozen places at once.

"I might be . . ."

"Might?"

"Well . . . I suppose I am."

"You're not sure?" he asked with a chuckle.

"I'm not sure you deserve it."

"Oh, come now . . . surely you can forgive me a little slight."

"Little!"

"All right, a big slight. But surely you can forgive me."

She sighed. "Of course I can. If you kiss me like that again."

He did . . . and she forgave him instantly.

It was weeks later when Maxum took Airi to meet his brothers. Using his powers as a god, he gathered the four brothers and their families into the fortress of Dethan's political seat in the city of Hexis. Children ran about them noisily, playing and squealing as their parents sat before the fire in a group and got to know one another.

"I had always wondered what it would take to get

Maxum to settle down," Dethan said with a chuckle. "Who knew that all that was needed was for him to become a god."

"Is that all?" Garreth said mildly. "Sounds easy. I think I should try it myself."

"You will *not*," Sarielle, his wife, said. She moved to stir the fire, but Garreth snatched her off her feet and into his lap. Such was the case for all of the brothers. Each sat with their woman nestled firmly and protectively in their laps. Even Jaykun, whose wife, Jileana, was once again heavily pregnant with his child. Jaykun rubbed his large hand around and over her belly again and again, the movement soothing and rhythmic.

"No. I will not. I am done with tempting the gods," Garreth said.

"As are we all. But just in case, it is good to know we have someone there who is on our side," Jaykun said.

Airianne smiled lazily as she dropped her head to her lover's shoulder and watched the children play. Most of them were under the age of four, so it was more about watching them totter about and grasp at things that caught their fancy. Sarielle's young twin sisters, beginning to grow into the first blush of womanhood, played with the children and kept them entertained.

"Will you be wed?" Dethan's wife, Selinda, asked Airi and Maxum.

Airi colored. They had never talked about such a thing. Afraid it would make Maxum uncomfortable and put him on the spot, she laughed it off.

"Surely there are more important things to worry about."

"More important than pledging myself to you heart and soul?" he asked. "Name one."

She pinked up with pleasure and pulled his head close for her kiss. "All right, you have me there."

"Unless you don't want to—"

"No, I want to!" she hurried to assure him.

He smiled with pleasure, his eyes turning wicked and hot as they looked her over. "I've never slept with someone's wife before."

That surprised her. "You were never married . . . before?"

"No. I never was. You are the only one who has ever, and will ever, win my heart. The only one I would ever want to make such a commitment to."

"I never thought to see the day," Jaykun said.

"I never thought any of us would fall to love. Marriage was always a means to an end in our former lives," Dethan said. "Now it is something far deeper and more meaningful." He looked with pride from his wife to his three children. "I would not trade a single day of the torment I suffered, for it led me to you, little juquil." He brushed an affectionate finger down Selinda's nose.

"Agreed," Jaykun said, giving his wife a kiss.

Airi smiled but then gasped when Maxum nosed his way through her hair and lightly tongued the tip of her ear. Blushing furiously as her whole body went weak she buried her face against his neck and pinched him on his arm.

"Stop that!" she whispered heatedly.

"Make me," he countered in a whisper that brushed his lips over her ear again.

She stood up out of his lap suddenly, her hand grasping one of his as she affected a loud yawn and a stretch. "Wow, I'm beat," she said.

"Does a demigod get tired?" Garreth asked with a knowing twinkle in his eye.

"Yes as a matter of fact they do," she said primly. "And so do gods if they know what's good for them."

"I think that's my cue," Maxum said, getting to his feet.

"But it's not late. The children aren't even in bed yet," Sarielle said, being purposely obtuse.

"It takes a lot of godly energy to bring us all together like this. Godly power is not infinite."

"You learn something new every day," Dethan marveled.

"It was lovely to meet all of you. And your families. We'll see you in the morning," Airi said, waving her fingers in a waggle of goodbye before she yanked Maxum down the hall with her.

"We don't even know what room we're staying in," he said with a chuckle.

"We'll find one. As long as it has a bed that's all we'll need."

"True. My, my, you're in such a rush. I wonder why?"

"Shut up," she said, opening a door and peeking inside the room. "Nope. No bed there."

"We could always go back and ask—"

"Nope. We'll do just fine on our—aha! A bed. And it looks unoccupied." She yanked him into the room and slammed the door shut at his back.

She grabbed him and kissed him madly. It wasn't long before true heat burned away all of his amusement, passion bursting forth to overwhelm them both.

"I like your brothers," she whispered as he began to kiss her down the side of her neck. "But don't go climbing any mountains with them ever again."

"My mountain climbing days are over. So are theirs. Not a one of us is out to seek adventure any longer. And now that the war with the gods is won . . . we can all settle down with our women and make happy homes and healthy babies."

She went still and drew her head back to regard him curiously.

"Do you want to make babies?"

He returned her regard measure for measure. "I

wouldn't presume to tell you what to do with your body. If you don't want to make babies then we won't make babies."

"It's not that! I would love to make babies! I just . . . I didn't know that you wanted to."

"Airi, you and I would make the most beautiful babies in the world and the eight heavens besides, why wouldn't I want that?"

Airi's eyes teared up and she sniffled. "But I'm going to make a lousy mother!"

"Nonsense. With a heart as golden as yours? Better to worry about what kind of father I'll make."

"Nonsense. With your loyalty and devotion . . . your determination and force of will? You can do anything you set your mind to."

"Very well. I accept," he gave her a sound kiss. "Marriage and babies. We'll have little demigods running around in no time. Let's start making them right now!"

He scooped her up and threw her onto the bed.

She landed with a bounce and giggled exuberantly. "If you insist!"

"I do. And I'm a god. We tend to get our way."

"I've heard that somewhere I think." She squeaked when he ran his hands up her legs beneath her skirts. He found her bare bottom and he groaned. "You're so warm and soft. Although," he cocked a raised brow at her, "must you wear this?"

He jerked her dagger out of the sheath she'd strapped to her inner thigh and held it up before her nose.

"Old habits die hard," she said with a shrug.

He tossed the dagger aside and worked to untie the sheath. It came free and he tossed it aside wherever the dagger had gone. That left a bare expanse of inner thigh to be explored. He did so eagerly.

She gasped and then sighed.

"I love you," she said on an intense whisper.

He lifted a brow. "Do you now?"

"Indeed I do. Now you're supposed to say you love me back."

"I'm a man of actions, not words." He went about untying the laces to his breeches.

"I always liked that about you," she noted with a grin.

It was when he had finally thrust inside of her that he said, "I love you more than life. Everything I do is for you. Nothing would matter if not for you."

She sighed and wrapped her legs around his waist.

"Words and actions. I'm a very lucky demigod."

"And don't you forget it."

Dethan stroked Selinda's hair, his affection for her radiating from the action. He looked around at his brothers and was satisfied. He had led them on folly all those decades ago, seeking for something that, in the end, had never been the prize worth winning. Each brother now knew something that meant far more than immortality or riches or glory.

It seemed an age since those things had mattered to him. For a long time since, his life had been filled with Selinda. The war with the gods was over, but he would keep his agreement with Weysa and battle in her name until he was no longer able to. Until age and infirmity ruled him. Until he was ready to spend his golden years surrounded by his wife and his many children.

It sounded like one of the eight heavens. The one he would choose.

"I love you," he whispered in her ear. She pinked up, looking as pleased as a mouse with cheese.

She did not reply. She did not need to. He knew her feelings. Just as she knew his without him having to say the words. But he said them all the same. And as he watched his brothers each lean in to whisper in their wives' ears, he knew they were saying the same thing.

Finally he was truly proud of them. Proud of them and the lives they had made.

He sat back in his chair and took pleasure in that.

A great deal of pleasure.